DESPERATE MEASURES

VOLUME 1

DESPERATE MEASURES

VOLUME 1

SAMUEL VOYLES

Emmons House Publishing
Since 2001

Published in the United States of America.

Emmons House Publishing LLC

Corydon, Indiana 47112

emmonshousepublishing@gmail.com

Cover designed by Pixelstudio

In loving memory of

Mrs. Allison Faith

PART 1

CHAPTER 1

THE KLIMMINGS FAMILY

Oceans of blue covered the sky as the bright sun rose on April 5. Birds chirped and tweeted, creating morning music that filled the air. They continued until their music was interrupted by the obnoxious sound of an alarm clock.

BEEP! BEEP! BEEP!

Miranda Klimmings, a woman in her mid-to-late twenties, rose from her bed and quickly shut off the alarm clock, causing the displeasing noise to cease. The only sounds remaining were the sounds of the birds from outside.

Miranda brushed her long light brown hair out from in front of her face. She got out of bed and slipped on her slippers, making her way out of her bedroom. She went down the stairs, rounded the bottom, and made her way across the entry hall and into the dining room, where she saw her father, Peter, sitting at the head of the table.

Peter, who had blond hair with gray scattered about it, sat reading the morning news on his tablet, as he did each morning. Across the table from him sat his wife, Vicki Klimmings, who also had blond hair. She was sipping her coffee when Miranda entered the dining room.

"Good morning," Vicki cheerfully said. "It's a gorgeous day outside." Peter glanced up to see who had entered the dining room, but soon after, went back to his reading.

"I could hear the birds chirping outside," Miranda said as she poured herself a cup of coffee. "It's sounding more and more like spring out there." She turned around and sat down in her seat, which was to the left of Peter. Three empty chairs sat between her and Vicki.

"So," Peter spoke as he read from his tablet. "Do you have any plans for today?"

"I think I am going to spend most of today at Jason's," Miranda said before taking a sip of her coffee. "Why do you ask?"

"I was hoping the family would come to the White House tonight," said Peter. "We're having a state dinner for the United Kingdom's prime minister and his wife."

"You don't seem very enthused about this," Vicki said.

"State dinners are one of the things that I hate most about being president," Peter proclaimed. "That, and having to deal with the Secret Service."

"Yes," Vicki said. "Remember how much of a pain they were when you wanted to continue living in our house and not at the White House?"

"Oh, I remember," Peter said. "They are still trying to convince me to move into the White House. I don't think they like it that they can't come in here unless it is an emergency."

Peter took a drink of his coffee and then noticed the time on his watch. "It's time for me to go," he said as he set down the newspaper and stood up from the table. "My motorcade will be arriving at any time now."

Vicki also got up from her seat at the table. "I best be going too," she said. "I need to head into the office soon. Today isn't going to be a perfect one for many people."

"Is the company still not doing so well?" Peter asked.

"The company is doing fine," Vicki explained. "It's just with the recent recession; many Americans can't afford to switch to the newer forms of renewable energy. So, unfortunately, this leaves us no choice but to lay off some employees."

Peter stepped toward Vicki, embracing her in his arms. "Can't you just have Ben do the laying off?"

"No," Vicki responded. "Benjamin is under so much stress these days. I can't have him do this too."

She looked Peter in the eyes and added, "Besides, these people are more corporate-level employees who work in our main headquarters downtown."

"Mind I ask how many employees are losing their jobs?" Peter asked.

Vicki took a deep breath and sighed, "About fifty."

"Dammit," Peter sighed. "And how do you think this will look to the stockholders?"

"That's why I'm the major stockholder at Klimmings Incorporated," Miranda chimed in. "Remember, you gave me fifty-one percent of the stocks, so if I'm not selling any stocks, then most of the other stockholders aren't either. They trust me."

"And so do I," Peter said as he placed his hand on Miranda's back, reassuring her that he trusts her. "I couldn't have left the company in better hands when I decided to run for president. I think you all have done better at handling this recession than what I would have."

* * *

Ben Klimmings sat in his office at Klimmings Incorporated, housed inside Klimmings Tower, located in the downtown D.C. metropolitan. Ben flipped through the monthly report on the financial statistics for the company. He took a big sigh and then closed the piece. He then rubbed his eyes before pressing a button on the telephone on his desk.

"Yes?" said a woman through the telephone speaker.

"Doris," Ben replied. "You can go ahead and send them in now."

"Yes, sir," Doris said. Soon after, Ben's office door opened, and three businessmen came in. Their ages ranged from their late forties to their mid-sixties.

"We hope that you got a chance to look at the report," the oldest of the three men said.

"I did," Ben said. "It's no secret that Klimmings Incorporated has had a bit of a setback with the current state of the economy lately, but I see no major problems in our future."

"As members of the board, we would like to say different," the youngest man said. "The board thinks that this is a serious problem, and it needs to be dealt with if this company is to survive."

"Guys," Ben said as he stood up and tightened his navy blue tie. "I want to reassure you that as the chief financial officer, there is no major problem. Yes, Americans don't want to switch over to renewable energy right now, but that's not something that we really need to be worrying about. We are still doing very well with business in China. In fact, I've heard that the Chinese government wants us to open a plant in Hong Kong."

"That's true," said the older man. "But our biggest concern is what is happening here in the United States."

"We don't need to worry about it," Ben repeated himself. He was beginning to become irritated with the three men. "In a year, two tops, the recession will be over. There's nothing to worry about. My family has run this company for thirty-eight years now, and they've dealt with worse."

"Yes," said the oldest man. "But your father is the president now, and that seems not to be helping the situation out."

"What do you mean by that?" Ben asked, slightly squinting his left eye.

"Well," the oldest man began. "Your father hasn't done anything to help the situation out. Unemployment numbers are up, and more businesses keep losing money, yet he sits there in that mansion of his."

The man continued, and as he did, Ben clenched onto the back of his chair. His irritation with the three men had reached its boiling point. Their recent comments had enraged him, and without thinking about it, Ben very quietly said to the men, "Get out."

The oldest man cupped his hand over his ear and said, "What was that?"

"Get out!" Ben yelled. "Get the hell out of my office!" Ben shoved his chair out from behind his desk, causing it to roll across the room. He moved to the front of the desk and pointed a finger at the three men. "How *dare* you insult my father in front of me!"

"We're sorry, Mr. Klimmings," said the youngest man in an attempt to calm down Ben.

"Just leave," Ben demanded. "I don't want to talk to you all. Get out!" The three men gave each other a look and then hurried out of Ben's office. After the door shut behind them, Ben moved his chair behind his desk and then plopped down in it, releasing an audible sigh. He ran his hands across his face and then pressed the button on the telephone, buzzing Doris.

"Yes, Mr. Klimmings," Doris answered.

"Don't let any more members of the board into my office," Ben said. "I don't want to be disturbed by those bastards."

"Yes, sir," replied Doris. "Also, your mother is here, and she would like to see you."

"Well, send her in," Ben said. He recollected himself and straightened up his tie just as the door to his office opened, and in came Vicki.

"Well," Vicki said as Ben stood up from behind his desk. "Those bastards are the people who own our company. Each of them holds a big chunk of stock."

"Yes," Ben said. "But just because they own a larger piece of stock doesn't mean that they can choose what to do with the company." He threw his arms up and shrugged. "None of them are even close to owning a majority. They each own about three percent apiece."

"You're right," Vicki said, and she put her hands on Ben's shoulders. "But you also have to remember that Miranda owns fifty-one percent of the stock, and she decided not to be on the board."

"That's only because Dad enthroned her the stocks," Ben complained. "All I got stuck with is this." He turned around and gestured at the office.

"Benjamin," Vicki explained. "You may not be happy with what your father gave you all before taking the presidency, but at least it was something. You make thirty million dollars a year. He could've sold the company, but he didn't."

"Mom," Ben said. "I love my job, but I think the board is out to get me."

"Of course they are!" Vicki exclaimed, throwing her hands up into the air. "They want more power. Trust me. I have to deal with them every day!"

A short silence fell in the office. "Well, I guess this is a little better than what he gave you," Ben stated.

"Being the chief executive officer and chair of the board is not so bad," explained Vicki. "Yes, you have to deal with the board members every day, but in the end, you always get to be reminded that you run the company and your decisions are what matters.

Vicki grabbed ahold of Ben's hand and looked him in the eye. "Benjamin, there is nothing to worry about. As long as I am in charge of this company, I will never *ever* do anything that removes you from your role here.

* * *

In her small townhouse located on Elm Street, Delilah Klimmings rolled out of bed. Next to her was a man fast asleep. He laid there shirtless with the bedsheets covering the lower half of his body. Delilah stared at his built biceps, defined jawline, and back muscles as he slept. She admired the man and let out a short, satisfied sigh before realizing that she was standing there naked.

Quietly, trying not to make a sound, she crept over to her undergarments and slowly slipped them on. She quietly left the bedroom, passed through the living room, and then into the kitchen. She opened one of the walnut cabinets and pulled out a box of pancake mix. She assembled the ingredients to make pancakes when the man entered the kitchen. Delilah turned to him just as he had finished pulling his boxer shorts back on. "I see you're making pancakes again today," he said as he kissed her.

"I can never seem to sneak away and have breakfast ready for you, Clark," Delilah said as a grin appeared on her face.

"Honey," Clark said, grabbing her by the waist. "We've already had breakfast."

"Clark!" Delilah exclaimed.

He giggled. "And it was *so* good," Clark said, smiling back at Delilah. "You're the best thing to have ever happened to me."

"You too," Delilah said as she continued to cook. "I just wish that we could do this more often."

"We can," Clark responded before kissing Delilah again. "We can spend all the time in the world together." He then proceeded to kiss her on the neck. "I'm yours, baby."

Delilah pulled away from him. "Clark," she said. "You know I can't do that."

"Divorce him," Clark said. "I can provide so much for you."

"But you can't provide the stuff that he can provide for me," Delilah said, turning back to the pancakes and flipping them over.

"Delilah," Clark said as he put his hands on her shoulders. "Your family owns Applegate Technology. It's one of the ten largest companies in the world . . . even larger than Klimmings Incorporated."

"Yes," Delilah said, turning back toward Clark. "But I don't own any part in their company."

"I'm sure that they will give you some part of the company," Clark said. "Your dad owns it. It's not public."

Delilah looked at Clark and kissed him. As they continued to kiss, Delilah turned off the stove.

* * *

Next door to the Klimmings Mansion sat the Applegate Homestead. Inside, Jeremy Applegate sat in a chair scrolling through the morning news on his tablet. His wife, Cathie Applegate, was cleaning up the dishes left over from breakfast in the kitchen.

"Dammit!" Jeremy exclaimed as he tossed the tablet onto the floor.

"What's the matter, honey?" Cathie asked from the kitchen. "Did you stub your toe on the end table again? I've been telling you that we've needed to get rid of that."

"That's not it," Jeremy hollered from the living room. "It's that damn Peter Klimmings."

"What'd he do this time?" Cathie said from the kitchen.

"He's meeting with the prime minister of the U.K. today," Jeremy said as he stood up from the chair and began walking toward the kitchen. "I've had so much trouble trying to get my products to sell in the U.K."

"Are they still making you pay that outrageous import tax?" Cathie asked as she sat a bowl off to dry.

"Yes," Jeremy said, now in the kitchen. "Thirty percent and President Klimmings just welcomes him here with a dinner party and everything. I'm pretty sure that he is behind this tax too!"

"Jeremy," Cathie said as she set the dishrag on the counter and turned toward Jeremy. "I don't think he is behind it."

"Why? His son took our daughter. Maybe now he wants our money?"

"He didn't take our daughter. She wanted to marry Ben, and she's her own person and can choose whomever she wants to marry. And also, I seem to remember you giving Ben your blessing."

"That's because I *had* to," Jeremy grunted through his teeth.

"Yes," Cathie said. "Because they wanted to get married, and you and I were not going to interfere with their relationship. If it's meant to be, it'll work out. If not, they'll get a divorce like half of the country. It's not a big deal."

Cathie turned back to working on the dishes that sat in the sink while Jeremy stood there for a minute, not knowing what to say. Then, finally, he attempted to redirect the conversation back to where it was earlier.

"But they do want our money," he said. "Applegate Technology is worth so much more than their pitiful little company."

"Honey," Cathie said. "I know that you don't like them, but have you ever considered the fact that maybe they aren't out to bankrupt us?"

"Cathie, I'm sure of it."

* * *

Peter exited his motorcade outside the front entrance to the West Wing of the White House. He walked down a few hallways and entered the Oval Office. He called in his secretary as he sat down at the *Resolute* desk.

"Martha, I need to speak with my chief of staff," Peter said to his secretary.

Martha left, and after a moment, the phone rang. Peter picked it up and answered it. "Hello, Mr. Gates. I'd like for you to come over here so that we can discuss our little deal with the U.K."

* * *

Miranda knocked on a door to Apartment Suite 162. She waited for a few seconds before the door opened and was met by a man with short brown hair. "Hello, Miranda," he said. "Come on in."

"Thank you," she said as she entered the apartment, which wasn't very clean. Clothes lay scattered across the floor, with piles of clean clothes sitting on the couch and other chairs in the living room. "Jason, when are you ever going to clean this place up?"

"Sometime," Jason replied. He shrugged his shoulders and grinned. "It's on my to-do list."

Miranda chuckled. She moved some clean clothes over before taking a seat on Jason's rustic brown couch. "Have I ever told you how much I love your apartment?"

"You do all the time," Jason said as he walked into the kitchen to get two glasses of tea. "And then you tell me how it would be perfect if I cleaned it up some."

"It would," Miranda said as Jason brought in the glasses of tea and handed her one. "Thank you!"

"You're welcome," Jason said as he pushed the clean clothes off the couch and onto the floor.

"Why not just take them in your room?" Miranda asked.

"Eh," Jason shrugged. "I just don't feel like it."

"Well, I can take them in there for you," said Miranda as she sat her glass on the coffee table.

"No," Jason said, quickly jumping up from the couch. "I can take them in there."

He picked up the clothes and quickly scurried off to his bedroom. Miranda stood in the living room, trying to peek down the hall to see what he was doing, but before she got a good look, Jason came out of the bedroom, closed the door, and walked back into the living room.

"There we go," Jason said. "Now, what do you want to do?"

Miranda thought for just a second. "Hmm, I guess we could go to some shops. Would you like that?"

"Sweetheart," Jason said. "I'll do whatever you like."

* * *

Peter stood up from his desk in the Oval Office. He put on his suit jacket and began to walk out when an old-looking man came into the room. "Mr. Gates," Peter said. "Have you gotten those numbers ready?"

Peter had known Henry Gates since as far back as he could remember. Henry was a good friend to Peter's father, and after his untimely death, Henry remained a father figure in Peter's life. So when he was elected president, it only felt natural for Peter to ask Henry to come on as his chief of staff. After all, Henry Gates' opinion was one of the few Peter ever took into consideration when contemplating a big decision.

"Mr. President," said Henry. "We have a situation."

"What is it?" Peter asked.

"Sir," Henry explained. "About two hours ago, we received word from two Navy pilots that a Chinese jet was flying close to them. At first, we figured that it was accidental. But then, about five minutes ago, we received word that a second jet was flying near the Navy pilots. As this is a matter dealing with another country, I need to know what you want the pilots to do. Fly away or continue their exercise?"

Peter stood there for a second, considering all the things he had to deal with right now. "I don't think I want to risk creating any issues with the Chinese," Peter said. "Tell them to fly away and get back to their carrier."

"Thank you, Mr. President," said Henry as he turned to exit the office.

"By the way," Peter said, stopping Henry. "Let me know what happens to the pilots. I'm getting ready to head over for a state dinner with the prime minister of the United Kingdom. So if you find out what happens, no matter what I'm doing, let me know."

"Yes, sir," Henry said before leaving the office.

Peter stood silent for a moment, thinking. *I can't risk any type of conflict with the Chinese people. My company is doing so well over there.* Then, finally, he turned back and approached the phone that sat on the desk. He picked it up and called for Martha.

"Martha," he said when she answered the phone. "I need you to get ahold of my wife."

"Mr. President," she said. "Your wife is here."

Peter paused for a second. "Damn. I forgot. Thank you, Martha."

Peter put the phone on the receiver and began to head out of the office. Two Secret Service agents greeted him and led him down the hallways and into the State Dining Room. When he entered the State Dining Room, he saw Vicki standing with their youngest daughter, Gabby. Gabby had long blond hair and looked to be around seventeen years old.

"Thank you for coming," Peter said as he hugged the two. "I'm going to be pissed if they don't have us sitting together."

"Dad," Gabby said. "Remember the time I had to sit with the Russian advisors?"

"I remember that very much. And I don't want it to happen again!"

"Mr. President," said one of the butlers, interrupting the family's conversation. "They are ready for you."

"Thanks," Peter said to the butler. "Let's get this show on the road!"

Peter, Vicki, and Gabby were seated together. Vicki sat on one side of him, and the British prime minister sat opposite.

"Before the food is brought out," Peter said, standing up. "I would like to welcome the British prime minister to the United States. I hope your stay here is excellent."

Peter raised his glass and toasted the prime minister. When he sat down, the butlers started carrying out the food. The door opened to the room, and in came Henry. He crept over to Peter.

"How are they?" Peter asked him.

"Mr. President," Henry whispered. "We lost contact with the pilots. So we sent out a squadron of other pilots, and one of them found four crashed jets."

"What's this mean then?" Peter asked as he dabbed his mouth with a napkin.

"Mr. President," Henry said. "Right now, we can only suggest that the Chinese jets and ours collided with one another, causing all four of them to crash in the Pacific."

CHAPTER 2

RESPONSE

The door to the Oval Office opened, and Peter came out. By the way he stepped out of the office, Vicki could tell that he was furious. She stood up from the chair she was sitting in and hugged Peter.

"How'd it go?" Vicki asked, looking deep into his eyes. She could see the stress in them.

"I'm going to have to go to China," Peter sighed before rubbing his forehead. "But first, I want to visit with the family members of these pilots personally."

"Are you sure that that is a good idea?"

"Honey, I am responsible for these two pilots' deaths. I want to give their family members my condolences." Peter turned and looked at a picture that hung on the hallway wall. The photo was him and Vicki leaving Marine One and walking across the White House lawn. As he looked at the picture, he thought of how simpler times were before he had decided to run for president. He sighed again and turned around to face Vicki. "That, and I am the president of the United States," he said.

"I have a duty to serve and protect the people of this country, and by God, that is what I am going to do!"

"Dad," Gabby said, standing up. "How long are you going to be in China?"

"Until I can straighten this all out. Why do you ask?"

"I've got the prom coming up in May. I want you to be here so that you see me all prettied up."

"Honey," Peter said as he put his arm around her shoulder. "I've got to go over there and show them that they cannot mess with our country."

"But, Dad," Gabby whined. "I really want you to see me. It means a lot to me."

"I know," he said, hugging her. "I know."

* * *

Ben closed the door behind him. He was in his living room, and Delilah was sitting on the couch. "Hello, Delilah," he said.

"I've missed you today," Delilah said. "You were at work longer today. It's already dark out."

"Yeah, I had to deal with members of the board today. I think they want me out of the company."

"Why?" Delilah asked, standing up from the couch. "You're so good at your job."

"All I've had to deliver to the board for the past few months was crappy news about our finances," Ben said. "No, the company itself isn't doing bad, but we've been losing money."

"They should be understanding. It is a recession after all."

"But they're not!" Ben shouted, turning away from Delilah. He took a deep sigh before saying, "I don't think that they want me to be in the company!"

"Why not?"

"Because my dad is the president," Ben exclaimed. "I don't know, Delilah! Why must you keep asking me all of these damn questions?"

She stood still while Ben rubbed his face with his right hand.

"Honey," Delilah said. "What has happened to us? We used to not be like this."

"It was just a moment of frustration, Delilah," Ben said, turning to her. "Every person has them."

"Yes, but these moments of frustration have been happening a lot lately," Delilah said, stepping closer to Ben and holding onto his hands. "I don't know what's going on to cause them, and if you don't open up to me about everything that is going on, then I can't help you."

Delilah let go of Ben's hand and sat down on the couch, resting her elbows on her knees and looking to the floor. "I seriously think that there is something wrong with our marriage."

"And what do you suppose we do about that? Enter into marriage counseling?"

"No. I just think that maybe we need to sit and talk about this."

Ben picked up his keys. "I can't do this tonight," he said, opening the door. Delilah jumped up from the couch as he stepped out the door. "I'm getting a hotel room."

* * *

Miranda sat in the sitting room in the Klimmings Mansion. She was reading a book when headlights shined through the windows, illuminating the blue curtains. Miranda closed the book that she was reading and stood up from the sofa. She set the book down on an end table that sat to her right and walked out to the side hallway, making her way into the entry hall to the front door. The door opened, and Peter stormed in, followed by Vicki and Gabby.

"I can't believe this," Peter said in anger. "This pisses me off so much!"

"What happened?" Miranda asked Vicki after Peter passed by.

"Your father has to take care of China," Vicki said. "Two of their fighter jets crashed into and killed two United States Navy pilots."

"I'll tell you what I'll do," Peter yelled from another room. "I'll nuke the bastards. Let's unload our whole damn nuclear arsenal on them!"

"Honey, I don't think that is such a great idea," Vicki responded. "Klimmings Incorporated does business in China. They are a major source of profit for our company."

"I don't care," Peter said, returning to the entry hall with a glass of Kentucky bourbon. "I just can't believe that they did this." He took a sip from his glass.

"Peter, just go to bed and talk to the Chinese tomorrow."

"Can I not finish my drink first?" he asked before taking another sip.

"Take it with you," Vicki said and then pointed to the stairs. Peter took another sip and proceeded to head toward the stairs.

"Well, Mother," Miranda said. "I'm guessing that the dinner went well."

"Fine for me. The food came out, and your father left the room to deal with this crisis."

"What about you, Gabby?" Miranda asked, turning to Gabby. "How was your night?"

"Fine, I guess," Gabby said, shrugging her shoulders. "The food was okay, but there weren't any cute boys there. I think that I'm gonna go to bed too. Goodnight."

As Gabby left the entry hall, Miranda and Vicki both said, "Goodnight."

When Gabby walked up the stairs, Miranda turned to Vicki and said, "By the way, I didn't ask you how your day went in the office."

"It was okay," Vicki said. "I had to delay laying off the fifty employees until tomorrow, maybe even the next day. But, really, the only one who had a bad day today was your brother."

"How's that?"

"Well, the members of the board were harassing him about the ongoing recession. They say that it has made profits go down and what-not."

"He can't help that. Sometimes, I wish that I was involved in the board meetings. These members forget that I own fifty-one percent of the stock."

"I think that maybe you need to consider joining the board," Vicki said. "I really think that Benjamin needs you there."

"Why's that?"

"I know all of you so well," Vicki explained. "I can always tell when one of you all are hiding something, and I think that Benjamin is hiding something from us."

* * *

The night passed, and the following day came with rain. Cathie poured herself a cup of coffee as she looked out the window, observing the dreary, cloudy sky. Then, she walked into the living room, where her son, Ryan, sat shirtless watching TV. The morning news was on, and the events from the previous night dominated all the headlines.

"President Klimmings is set to meet with Chinese officials later today. This follows an accident over the Pacific Ocean which resulted in two Navy pilots' deaths," said the news reporter on the TV. "We expect that President Klimmings will make a statement to the press later tonight after he meets with President Wu."

"Looks like the Klimmingses will be having a rough day today," Ryan said as he looked up at Cathie, who was taking a sip of her coffee.

"Only Peter," she responded. "The rest will be on their own."

"I think that I need to give Delilah a call. I need to talk some sense into her."

"Don't you dare," Cathie said, setting her coffee on the end table that sat beside her. "Delilah is a grown woman. She needs to make her own decisions. I know that you are trying to be a protecting older brother, but she needs to have the freedom to make mistakes."

"Like marrying Ben?" Ryan said. "I don't care about her making her own decisions, but I do not want to be related in any way to that family!"

"And you think that I am fine with having Ben Klimmings as my son-in-law? The only member of that family that I think is somewhat decent is Vicki . . . maybe Miranda too."

Cathie looked back at the TV. She watched the news for a couple of minutes and then said, "I got better things to do than watch this."

She stood up and left the room, heading down the hallway. Ryan waited until she was out of hearing range before taking out his cell phone and calling Delilah. It rang a couple of times before Delilah answered.

"Delilah," Ryan said. "It's Ryan. Are you doing anything today?"

"I don't know. Why?"

"I just wanted to meet up somewhere and talk about some things."

"I guess that we could meet for lunch. How's about we go eat lunch at the President's Bar and Grill down on Pennsylvania?"

"That would be fine. I'll see you there at about one."

"One is great. I've got to go now. It isn't the best time right now."

"Okay. See ya there!"

"Bye!" Delilah hung up the phone and set it on the bedside table. She rolled over in her bed and saw Clark.

"Who was that?" Clark asked.

"It was just my brother," Delilah answered. "I'm going to have to go to lunch with him today."

"Darn! I was going to skip out on my lunch to come spend some time with you." Clark leaned down to kiss Delilah.

"Clark," Delilah said, pulling away. "We can't keep meeting here."

The smile fell away from Clark's face. "Why's that?"

"I want to leave Ben, but I don't want him to know that I have been cheating on him this entire time. That would destroy him."

Clark laid there for a moment. "You do have a point. We don't want him to do anything crazy."

Delilah leaned over and kissed Clark on the lips. "Thanks for understanding," she said. "I love you."

* * *

Miranda knocked on the door to Jason's apartment. She waited for a moment and then tapped again. Immediately the door flung open. "Miranda," said Jason, who stood on the other side of the doorway. "What are you doing here?"

"I thought that we were going to see a movie this morning,"

Miranda said. "I'm guessing that you forgot."

"Yes, I did," Jason said as he looked down at himself and the pajamas he was wearing. "I can go get changed, though, and then we can go."

"Nah," Miranda said. "I have a better idea." She leaned in and kissed Jason on the lips. He pulled away and looked her in the eyes. She looked back into his. Jason smiled and started kissing her again. He ran his hands down her back.

As they continued to kiss, they stumbled back and fell onto the couch. Miranda tore off Jason's shirt and ran her hands through Jason's chest hair. "Why don't we go to the bedroom?" asked Miranda.

"I have a better idea," Jason said while unbuttoning Miranda's blouse. "Why don't we do it on the kitchen counter."

"That's too hard on my back. I want something nice and comfortable to lay on. We've never had sex in your bedroom. It's always on the couch, or the floor, or the table."

"We are not having sex in my bedroom," Jason said.

Miranda rolled off the couch and stood up. "Why not?"

"My room is a mess. And also, I just wanted to make it a little more interesting."

Miranda took a deep sigh. "I'm not feeling too well." She buttoned her blouse back. "I think that I'm going to go home."

"Miranda," Jason said as he stood from the couch. "Please don't go. Not like this."

"I'll text you," Miranda said as she opened the door. She left the apartment, closing the door behind her and leaving Jason standing all alone. He grunted loudly and kicked over the coffee table in front of the couch. Then, out of anger, Jason grabbed the lamp off the end table and prepared to throw it across the room but stopped just before throwing it. Instead, he looked at it, took a deep sigh, and then set it back on the table.

* * *

Peter sat in his office aboard Air Force One. He contemplated what he would say to the Chinese officials when they held their meeting in Beijing.

"Mr. President," Henry said while standing in the doorway to his office. "The pilot wanted me to let you know that we are starting our descent down to the runway."

"Thank you, Mr. Gates," Peter said.

Henry turned and walked away. Peter waited until he was gone and then stood up from his chair and walked over to the tiny window in his office. He looked outside and saw the tainted sky Beijing was known for. Because of the thick smog, he could barely make out the skyline. However, Peter could make out the Applegate Technology Tower in Beijing. "Of course," he said. "I wouldn't put it past the Applegates to have some kind of part in this."

Peter turned around and stepped away from the window. He stepped over to the bookcase and saw some of his biographies and books that covered the history of Klimmings Incorporated.

"Mr. President," Henry said, now back in the doorway. "We've landed."

"Well," Peter said, stepping away from the bookshelves. "I guess that it is time to show these sons of bitches what the United States can do."

* * *

Vicki sat in her office, looking over the light lavender walls covered with pictures of her family. She thought about how this company had provided for her and her family for so many years. She also thought about how the lives of the forty-nine people that she had just laid off would be changed forever. She only had one more employee to lay off, and he just walked in the door. "James," Vicki said. "How are you doing today?"

"Fine," said James as he ran his hands through his brown hair. "Is there a problem, Mrs. Klimmings?"

James was a younger man, clean-shaven, probably in his thirties, and wearing a brown suit jacket. *He probably has a family—a couple of kids, and I am going to ruin his life.* Vicki thought as he came into the room.

"Not exactly," Vicki said before taking a deep sigh. "Please, take a seat." He sat down in one of the chairs in front of her desk. "James, do you know why I called you in here?"

"No. Have I done something wrong?"

"No. You've done nothing wrong."

"Well, why did you call me here then?"

Vicki stopped and took a deep breath. "The recession has hit everyone hard. It's something that hasn't been seen since the pandemic. Now, I'm not saying that Klimmings Incorporated is in serious trouble, but we have had to make cutbacks." She paused, allowing herself to take a deep breath. "Unfortunately, with these cutbacks, we have to lay off a few of our employees . . ."

"You can't do this," James interrupted. "You can't lay me off!"

"James," Vicki began. "You were one of the last fifty employees hired here in the offices."

"Yeah, but I have a family," James said, standing from the chair. "My wife and I just had our third daughter. We can't afford to go without a job."

"I'm sorry. If you want, I can give you some recommendations."

"No!" James yelled. "I don't need any recommendations! I need a job!"

"James," Vicki said, standing up from behind the desk. "You need to calm yourself down."

"You don't even care! You have all of that money and don't ever have to worry about paying the bills!"

"If you don't calm down, I will call in security!"

James stopped his ranting and looked Vicki in the eye. She looked back at him and added, "You'll get a month's severance pay, but after that, you're going to have to apply for unemployment. Now, I need you to turn around and leave this office!"

"Listen here," James muttered while leaning closer to Vicki. "You will regret this. You *all* will regret this!" He turned and stormed out of the office, almost hitting Ben with the door on his way out. He glanced over to watch James storm off down the hallway to the elevator.

Ben turned around and walked into Vicki's office to see her plop down in her chair. "I'm guessing that he didn't take that well?" Ben asked.

"Oh, Benjamin," Vicki gasped. She jumped up from her chair and thrust her arms around Ben, hugging him. "He was the last one. He was the only one who took it that badly."

"Mom," Ben said as Vicki released him. "It'll be fine. He'll come to an understanding about this whole thing eventually."

Vicki looked into Ben's eyes. "I don't know. It was pretty bad, and I feel so bad for doing it."

* * *

Delilah pulled into a parallel parking spot outside Presidents' Bar and Grill. She stepped out of her purple car, closed the door, and proceeded to walk up to the entrance. Once inside, Delilah saw her brother sitting across the dining room at a booth. So she walked over to his table and took a seat across from him.

"Delilah," Ryan said. "I'm glad you could make it."

"Yeah," Delilah said sarcastically. "What was it that you had wanted to talk to me about?"

"You're really in a hurry," Ryan laughed. "Why don't we order first?"

Ryan signaled for a waiter to come over with the menus. The waiter handed menus to Ryan and Delilah. "Our specials today are the 16oz sirloin that comes with jumbo shrimp and fries," the waiter said.

Before Ryan could say anything, Delilah said, "We will both have what President Klimmings would have. We are huge fans of his."

Ryan glared at Delilah as the waiter took the menus back up and walked away. "You really enjoy doing that."

"Yes," said Delilah before taking a sip of her water. "And you're too dumb enough to continue to fall for it. Besides, you may not like Peter, but he does order some good food here."

"Well, I guess that I can't argue with you there," Ryan said as

Delilah smirked and took another sip of her water. "Now as to why I asked you here."

"What is that?" Delilah asked, putting down her glass of water.

"It's about your marriage with Ben," Ryan said. "It's been causing a rift between Mom and Dad."

Delilah sighed. "Ryan, I am not going to leave my husband. He is the love of my life. We've been together for almost three years, and I'm not going to give up on that now."

"Why? He has done nothing for you. Tell me. How many nights has he been home before eight?"

Delilah paused for a moment. "He's been swamped. Ben has had to deal with a lot during this recession. I am not going to give him anything else to worry about. You're just going to have to suck it up and deal with it, Ryan, because he is not going to go anywhere!" Delilah reached forward and took a big gulp of her water. She set the glass back on the table and motioned for a waiter. "Someone get me a vodka tonic!"

"We haven't been here fifteen minutes, and you're already drinking?" Ryan said.

"I can't stand to be sober and have this conversation with you," Delilah said, becoming irritated. "Dammit, Ryan. I love you, but sometimes it is hard to deal with you."

"Same goes for you," Ryan said as a waiter set Delilah's vodka tonic on the table. "I don't know why you married Ben, but somehow that man captured your heart."

"He sure did," Delilah said, taking a drink of her vodka tonic. "And as of lately, I haven't treated him all so well."

* * *

Peter walked down the steps from Air Force One. At the bottom of the steps stood two Chinese officials. Peter shook their hands, and they began walking down a red carpet that led to a building door. Peter followed them, along with several members of the Secret Service and Henry. When he got to the door, two Secret Service agents darted in front of him and held open the doors. He proceeded to enter the building.

Peter walked down a hallway that led to a rather large room. The walls were red and decorated with Chinese flags and various dragons. In the center of the room was a table, and on one side of the table sat two Chinese men, and on the other side were two empty chairs. "President Klimmings," said one of the men who stood of from the table. "What a pleasure it is to meet you."

"President Wu," Peter said, shaking the man's hand. "What an honor it is to meet you again."

"If only it were under better circumstances," the Chinese president said. "Unfortunately, we have to have this meeting because of your country's act of aggression toward ours."

Peter sat down at the table, and Henry took a seat beside him. "Excuse me," Peter said in a confused tone. "I don't think that I understand what you are saying. My Navy pilots didn't do anything to yours. Your pilots crashed into mine."

"Ahhh," the Chinese president sighed. "But you see, my country believes that." President Wu leaned into Peter as he lowered his voice to a whisper. "It's one of the great things about having state-run media." President Wu let out a sinister chuckle.

Peter did his best to fake laugh as he glanced over to Henry. "President Wu," Henry said. "We are here to negotiate terms to set in place going forward. We don't want events like the one that happened over the Pacific to happen again. Our countries can't keep crashing our planes into each other."

"President Klimmings," President Wu said. "I think it would be better if we spoke alone."

"Yes," Peter said before turning to Henry. "Do you mind, Mr. Gates?"

"I don't," Henry said before leaving the table. Henry left the room, leaving Peter and President Wu alone.

"President Klimmings," the Chinese president began. "I want to discuss with you a . . . proposition."

"What would this proposition be?" Peter asked, leaning a bit into the center of the table out of curiosity and better hearing President Wu and his raspy voice.

"I want you to open a division of Klimmings Incorporated here in my country."

"Really?"

"Yes, but sadly, my people cannot afford all of the different green energy resources that your company offers. I know that this may be different for you and your company, but we want you to specialize in oil energy here in China."

"President Wu," Peter said. "I'm sorry, but I don't see why you want Klimmings Incorporated in here and why you think that I can help. I take no part in the business dealings at the company. My wife does all of that."

"Well," President Wu said. "If your woman is as smart as you are, maybe she will listen to us and open a division here."

"Excuse me. I also don't understand why you think Klimmings Incorporated can open oil power plants. We have never dealt with oil, only renewable, clean energy."

"My people can take care of that," President Wu said. "We want your company in our country. We think that this energy will sell well with the Chinese people. We just need an answer from you."

"Can I run this past my wife?" Peter asked. "I'm sure that we can give you an answer tomorrow."

"Certainly! Take all the time you need. We hope that this can be beneficial for both of us." He paused for a second. "And our countries."

Peter sat silent for a second before standing up and saying, "Well, I guess that I will see you tomorrow then." He shook President Wu's hand, turned around, and left the room.

After Peter left and the door closed behind him, President Wu turned around and left the room through a door on his side of the table. He took a few steps down the hallway before turning right and entering another room where a man with brown hair stood, his back facing the door.

"Well," President Wu began. "I gave them the proposition just like you had asked. You had better come through with your part of the deal, Jeremy."

The man turned around, allowing President Wu to see Jeremy

Applegate's face.

"Now, now," Jeremy said. "When have you ever known me to not come through with my part of the deal?"

CHAPTER 3

THE ANNIVERSARY DINNER

Miranda arrived home at the Klimmings Mansion. She took her hands off of her steering wheel and unbuckled her seatbelt, staying seated as her mind raced with questions. *What's the big deal with his bedroom? Why won't he let me in there?*

Miranda opened the door to her two-door blue car and slowly exited. She walked up the steps to the big oak front door of the Klimmings Mansion. Miranda turned to look at her vehicle, parked within the circular turnaround of the driveway. Hers was the only one parked out front. She turned back to the door, opened it, and proceeded to step inside the house, closing the door behind her.

Now standing in the entry hall, Miranda took a few slow deep breaths. Then she started right down the side hallway, passed the kitchen door, and took another right into the sitting room. Inside, she saw Gabby reading a book. Gabby glanced up to see Miranda standing in the doorway of the room. "Hey," she said.

"Hey, Gabby," Miranda responded. She took a seat in the chair adjacent to her. Gabby continued to look at her and noticed that something must be wrong.

"Are you okay," she asked.

"Yes, Gabby. I'm fine. I'm just . . ." She paused as she tried to collect her thoughts from the events of the day. "I'm just a little shaken up."

Gabby closed her book and set it on the end table next to the sofa. Then, she stood up and walked over toward Miranda. When she got to Miranda, she knelt beside her and put her hands on Miranda's upper arms. "Something is bothering you."

Miranda sat for a moment, trying to muster up some excuse. "I . . . uh . . ." she began. "Uh . . . I was almost in a traffic accident." She looked over to Gabby to see if she believed the lied she had just told.

"That must've been awful," Gabby said. "You must be shaken up then."

"Yes," Miranda continued. "It was a bit scary, but I think that I'll be fine."

* * *

Vicki looked up from her desk as three men entered her office. They were the same three board members who visited Ben earlier. "Gentlemen," Vicki began as she took off her reading glasses and set them on her desk. "What is it that you all needed to talk to me about?"

"Mrs. Klimmings," the oldest man said. "We have been very concerned with the way that your son, Ben, has been acting."

"Ma'am," the youngest man continued. "We haven't been making very much money, if any at all, and your son acts like it is no big deal."

"Gentlemen," Vicki said as she stood up from behind her desk. "We've been breaking even. So, as of right now, I see no reason to fret."

As Vicki finished her sentence, her phone rang. She glanced down at the phone and then back up to the men. "The country is in a state of recession, and I honestly believe that this will all be over soon." The phone continued ringing. She glanced back down at the phone and answered it. "Yes?" she replied.

"Mrs. Klimmings," her secretary said. "The president is on the line."

"Thank you, Pam," Vicki said before taking the phone away from her ear. She looked up at the men in her office. "That'll be all for our discussion today. You all can leave now."

The three men looked at each other, grumbling, and left Vicki's office. When the door shut, Vicki pressed a button on her phone. "Hello, honey," she said as a smile appeared on her face.

"Vicki," Peter said on the other line. "I have to ask you for a favor."

"Okay, what is it?"

"I have spoken with the Chinese president," Peter began. "He says that he is willing to look past the whole ordeal, but he wants Klimmings Incorporated to open up a division in China."

"Well, that should be easy to do. We were already going to be opening a plant up in Hong Kong, so it could be easy to just move it to wherever he wants it to be."

"That's not all. This division has to deal with oil."

"*Oil*? But we don't deal with oil. We deal with clean energy!"

"I know," Peter said. "But the bastard is dead set on it being an oil division."

"Our people don't know how to work with oil rigs and stuff," Vicki said. "How are we supposed to open an oil division there?"

"President Wu said that the Chinese will take care of it all."

"Okay," Vicki said reluctantly. "I guess that we can do that. Not sure what everyone else is going to think about us delving into fossil fuels when we've been focused on renewable energy, though."

"I know," Peter said. "And I have a reelection in about two years. How am I going to explain this to the American people when I vowed to try to reduce carbon emissions?"

Vicki paused for a moment. "When do I sign the papers?"

"I'm going to let President Wu know that you agreed to this, first. Then I'm guessing he'll send a representative over to the U.S. to hand you the papers."

"Okay. I've got to get off of here now. Try to make it home before tomorrow night. It's Benjamin's and Delilah's anniversary, and we are having a celebration dinner."

"I'll try to," Peter said. "I love you, honey."

"Love you too," Vicki responded before hanging up the phone and leaning back in her chair. She let out a deep sigh and ran her hand through her hair.

* * *

Delilah opened the bathroom door and slowly stepped out into the hallway. She looked over to her left and saw Clark standing at the beginning of the hallway. "Are you okay?" he asked.

She stood silent in the hallway, leaning her back against the wall. "Delilah," Clark asked again, proceeding to approach her and place his hands onto her shoulders. "Baby, are you okay?"

Delilah looked up to face Clark. She saw the look of worry in his eyes. He genuinely cared for her, which was the first time that Delilah had noticed. Clark wasn't in the relationship for the fame and fortune. He was in the relationship because he deeply cared about her.

"We've messed up," Delilah began. "I'm not sure how we're going to get out of this one."

"I'm not understanding," Clark said. He still looked apprehensive. Delilah held out her hand, showing him the pregnancy test. "Oh no. Are you?"

Delilah slowly nodded her head. "Yes, I am." She closed her fist, tightening her grip on the pregnancy test. "What are we going to do?"

"I'm not sure," Clark said. He paced briefly up the hallway before turning back toward Delilah. "I do have a slight idea, though."

"What is it?"

"I think it's time to leave Ben. We could get married and raise this baby as our own!"

"Clark," Delilah sighed. "You know I cannot do that."

"Well, why can't you?" Clark asked as he placed his hands back onto Delilah's shoulders, making eye contact with her. "We would be the best parents. I just know it, Delilah. Trust me."

The words rang in Delilah's head. She proceeded to make her way up the hallway and into the living room, where she placed herself on the couch. Clark followed and sat down in the armchair that sat beside her. "So whaddya say?"

"Clark," Delilah began after taking a deep sigh. "I have something that I need to share with you. It won't be easy for me to share, so please listen until I finish what I have to say." She looked up at Clark and noticed that the worried look had returned on his face. "It all happened about a month ago. You had those midterm exams to take for your classes, which I am so proud of you for doing so well on those, by the way." She looked up at Clark and smiled. His face showed a half-smile before resuming back to the worried expression.

"We've been together long enough that you ought to know by now that I get these urges," she continued. "I can't help them. One moment I'll be perfectly fine, and another moment, I want to sleep with the first guy I lock eyes onto." She paused for a moment and took another deep breath. "One night, I had one of those urges." She paused again. "And I guess so did Ben."

"No," Clark gasped. "You didn't, did you?"

"I did. Before I knew it, Ben and I were in bed and ready to go to sleep."

Shame consumed Delilah. She couldn't look Clark in the eyes. "I'm so sorry," she said as her eyes began to tear up. "But that baby could just as well be Ben's as it could be yours."

Clark took a deep breath and calmed himself. He looked Delilah in the eyes. "Delilah, I don't care if it's Ben's or not. If it's his, he doesn't have to know it. We could just as easily raise yours and Ben's baby as we could yours and mine."

Delilah sat silently on the couch for a moment. Her eyes had ceased producing tears, and her face slowly lost all redness in it. "Do you really mean that?"

"Yes," Clark said as he moved over onto the couch beside Delilah, taking her hands in his. "What matters most is that we are together."

Once again, Delilah had to take a moment to recollect herself before responding. "Clark, tomorrow is our anniversary. We always have a big family dinner at Finley's to celebrate. I can't leave Ben before that. It'll drive a rift between his family and myself, and I don't want to start crap with them. So if you're okay with it, how about I wait a few days before calling our marriage off?"

Clark thought the plan over in his mind. "Fine. Give it a few days, and then we'll get back with each other and make plans from there."

"Oh, thank you," Delilah said as she threw her arms around Clark. "I can't wait to be your wife."

* * *

Ben sat in his office ruffling through some papers. He glanced through them all before eventually tossing them down on his desk. Taking a deep breath and letting out a big sigh, Ben ran his fingers up the side of his head. He spun around in his swivel chair and faced the giant window behind his desk. His office had a clear view of the entire city of Washington. He sat in his chair, examining the city. In the distance sat the Capitol Building. Ben looked at the dome sitting atop the magnificent building, thinking about how many other Americans have dealt with similar scenarios that he was facing. His mind moved to consider how some had faced even more demanding challenges and handled it better than he was with this own. He knew he could never be as strong as they were.

"Knock, knock."

Ben turned to see Vicki standing at the doorway to his office. "May I come in?"

"Sure," Ben answered. "Go ahead and have a seat, too."

"Thank you." Vicki approached a chair in front of Ben's desk and sat down.

Ben moved his chair back up to the head of the desk and sat up. "I'm guessing that you are wondering why I am here right now," Vicki said to him.

"I would be lying if I said that I wasn't curious. So, what is it?"

"Well," Vicki began. "Your dad has struck a deal with the Chinese government that'll resolve the little ordeal over the Pacific."

"What's the deal?" Ben asked. "I'm sure that there has to be some sort of catch." He leaned forward. "Or else, why would they have shot down two of our military aircraft."

"They want us to open up a plant in China. And in the plant, they want us to invest in oil."

"Oil?! Why the hell do they want us to do that?"

"I'm not sure," Vicki said, shaking her head. "Somehow, it is imperative to the people over there and their government especially."

Ben shook his head for a second. "Okay. So sign off on it. You don't need my approval to go ahead with the project. You're the chief executive officer."

"Yes," Vicki said before leaning forward and lowering her voice. "And you're the chief financial officer, so that means that I need you to allocate about fifteen million dollars of company money into another account so that we can begin this project."

"Fifteen million dollars?!" Ben exclaimed, standing from his chair. "I'll be sure to get my ass ripped by the shareholders too!"

"Benjamin," Vicki responded calmly. "It's not that bad. You'll be fine. The shareholders don't have to know anything. It'll all be okay."

"No, I won't be fine! They've been on my ass about the income coming into this company. How's it going to look if I pull out fifteen million dollars at a time right now? That, and when you figure all the taxes and fees for the move, the total will be lower than that. So we'll be wasting our money."

The room sat silent for a few seconds. Vicki's eyes were locked on the floor. "That's the thing," she said as he looked up at Ben. "We won't be paying any taxes or fees."

"What?!"

"I have gone ahead and set up a dummy corporation on a Pacific Island that will allow us to maneuver around the taxes," Vicki continued. "And of course, the fifteen million is only going to be a start to what we need to allocate for this venture, but doing this will allow us to transfer the money safely." She paused for a moment. "No taxes, no fees, and no upset shareholders."

Ben sat in his chair and let out a sigh. "Nobody, except for you and I have to know about this," Vicki reassured Ben. "It'll be our little secret."

"So we are going to commit tax evasion?" Ben asked, throwing his hands up. "My father is the president of the United States, and we are going to commit tax evasion."

"Pretty much, but remember this, *he* appoints the Attorney General, and he owes a favor to him, so if anything does happen, then we'll be fine."

"No, we won't. That witch in the House will be sure to set up some investigative committee, and then that's all we'll hear about for the next few years."

"Benjamin Peter Klimmings, everything will be fine. Do you understand me?"

Ben looked at his mom for a second. Then, he shook his head and rolled his eyes. "Whatever you say."

"We aren't doing this because I want to," she continued. "We are doing this because we have to. The Chinese president gave your father no choice. Our company cannot afford to pay all those taxes and fees for opening a new plant in Beijing, so we have to do this to survive."

Ben spun back around and faced the window again. He looked back at the Capitol Building and thought of what this could do to his father's legacy. "I just want to do what is best for Dad," Ben confessed. "I don't want his legacy to be tarnished by any of this."

"Benjamin," Vicki began again. "This is what's best for your father's legacy. Peter has worked his tail off these last two years. He doesn't need a conflict with China going into the next election."

Vicki paused for a moment before making her way around Ben's desk. She approached the side of him and then knelt beside him. "Trust me. Nobody is ever going to find out about this."

* * *

Rain poured outside of President Wu's window. He looked out the window and watched as the rain and the blanket of thick smog mixed. Then, finally, he heard the door open to his office and turned his chair around to see Peter standing in the doorway.

"I was told to go on ahead and come on in," Peter explained.

"Yes," President Wu said. "I told my secretary to go ahead and have you come in."

"Anyway," Peter said as he took a seat in front of President Wu's giant desk. "I have spoken with my wife, and she has decided to agree on your deal."

"Good! Your woman has brains then, something that many women do not have, just ask my second wife." President Wu let out one of his sinister chuckles.

Peter forced himself to laugh. *I can't stand this man.*

"So when do you want to sign the papers?" President Wu asked. "I'm ready to begin construction."

"I can't sign the papers because I'm no longer a part of Klimmings Incorporated. Vicki is, so she'll have to sign the papers."

"Well, well," President Wu sighed. "I guess I am going to have to have one of my people make a trip over to the U.S. then. I want these papers signed as soon as possible." President Wu rose from his chair and walked around his desk. Peter stood from his chair and joined President Wu as he walked to the door.

"Let me get back in touch with you," President Wu said as he extended his right hand for Peter to shake. "We shall see what we can do from there."

"Sounds like a plan," Peter said as he shook President Wu's hand. He stepped out the door and turned to say something else when the door shut in his face.

* * *

Delilah sat on the couch in the living room of her home, watching TV. The six o'clock news was on, but she only paid half attention to what the reporters said.

"President Klimmings is expected to return to the United States tomorrow afternoon following his meeting with the Chinese president," a news reporter said. "The meeting followed an accident in the Pacific, which resulted in the deaths of two American pilots, as well as two Chinese pilots."

How am I going to tell Ben? What will his reaction be? Should I even tell him? Delilah's mind raced with questions. She couldn't stop the thoughts that ran through her head. The questions. The possibilities. The future. *What am I going to do? I'm going to be a mother. Everything is going to change.*

Delilah's mind continued to race when the front door to the living room opened, and Ben stepped in. He had just gotten home from work and looked very tired. Delilah remained silent as Ben shut the door behind himself.

"What are you staring at?" Ben asked after turning and noticing Delilah staring at the wall beside him.

She quickly snapped out of it and turned her gaze toward Ben. "Nothing. I thought I had seen something on the wall, but apparently, it was nothing. How was your day?"

"Strange." Ben put down his briefcase and sat in the reclining chair to Delilah's right. "It was very strange today."

"How so?"

"Well, I have to move fifteen million dollars to an account so that Klimmings Incorporated can finance a division to open up in China."

"That's wonderful! How is that strange?"

"I just have a bad feeling about it." Ben wasn't going to let Delilah know about the plan that Vicki had suggested to him. He needed to keep the details a secret should he decide to go through with it. After all, Delilah's dad was Peter's biggest rival in the business world. So, for now, Ben just thought about what he should do.

"Well," Delilah said as she stood up from the couch. "I think that I am going to start fixing some dinner."

Ben turned to face Delilah and said, "That'd be nice."

* * *

Clouds covered the sky the following morning as Vicki, Miranda, and Gabby sat at the dining room table. Miranda sat in her customary seat while Vicki sat in hers. Gabby was sitting in the chair on Vicki's left, leaving Miranda at the other end of the table by herself.

"Miranda," Vicki said. "If you want, you can move down here."

Miranda finished chewing her biscuit before saying, "I'm fine. I always sit here."

"Yeah, but you look so lonely down there."

"Come on, Miranda," Gabby chimed in. "Feel free to come on down here."

"I'm fine down here." Miranda took another bite of the biscuit that she was eating. "When is Dad going to be home?"

"Later this afternoon," Vicki answered. "He should be home before the big anniversary dinner tonight at Finley's."

"I'm so excited about it tonight," Gabby said. "I can't wait to gaze the night away by looking at Delilah's hot brother, Ryan."

"Gabriella!" Vicki exclaimed. "That is very inappropriate to mention. Now I'm going to be thinking about your fantasies tonight while we're supposed to be celebrating Delilah and Ben!"

Gabby glanced at Miranda with a smile creeping on her face. She then turned to Vicki. "Yeah," Gabby said. "I probably should be celebrating them. It's probably going to be their last anniversary anyways."

Miranda couldn't help but let out a laugh. She quickly grabbed her napkin, wadded it up, and held it to her mouth so that nobody could hear her laughing.

However, Vicki did not find Gabby's comment very funny. "You keep it up, and you won't be going tonight."

"Mom!" Gabby reacted, standing from her chair. "I was just joking!"

"Well, I did not find that joke very funny!" Vicki rose from her chair. She left the dining room, taking a left turn down the hall and leaving Miranda and Gabby alone. Gabby plunged back into her seat, and silence engulfed the dining room for what seemed like many minutes before a chime came from Miranda's phone. She pulled out her phone and noticed a text from Jason. Miranda opened the message to see a one-word message: *Hi.*

"Who was that?" Gabby finally asked.

Miranda locked her phone and set it on the table. "It was Jason."

"You don't seem very happy to have received a message from him.

39

Is there something wrong between the two of you?"

Miranda ran her hands through her long brown hair. "I'm not sure. I just don't know what to think right now."

* * *

Jeremy, Cathie, and Ryan were seated at a large round table in a restaurant. The table had ten total chairs around it. A few flowers sat in the middle, and menus were placed in front of each chair with a folded napkin and shiny silverware, adding more elegance to the setting. The Applegates were currently the only patrons in the restaurant. Every other table was empty, and the waiters and waitresses were standing along the outside walls of the room.

"This is ridiculous," Ryan said, breaking the silence in the restaurant. "When are they going to get here?"

"Settle down," Cathie stated. "We had to get here a bit early, remember?"

"Yes," Jeremy added. "Because of Peter, we had to be frisked and searched and groped just to eat dinner with our damn daughter!"

"Jeremy," Cathie angrily muttered. "Don't you dare ruin this dinner for our daughter! She and her husband have been married for three whole years! I don't want either of you to make any smart-aleck comments. Just be on your best behavior!"

"And just what exactly are you going to do if we aren't?" Jeremy asked arrogantly.

Cathie leaned over to Jeremy. "Remember that I cook all of your meals. You never know what I can do to them."

Jeremy sat for a second with a wide-eyed expression. Then, he turned to his son. "Ryan, we need to be on our best behavior tonight."

"I guess we can start now," Ryan whispered as he gestured toward the door. Jeremy turned to the restaurant's front door and saw Vicki, Gabby, and Miranda entering. The three approached the table and greeted the Applegates.

"How are you?" Vicki asked Cathie as she hugged her.

"I'm fine," Cathie replied. "Have a seat." Cathie offered the chair next to her for Vicki to sit, and Vicki accepted. Next, Gabby and Miranda sat down, leaving a seat open for Peter to sit in whenever he arrived.

"Is Peter not coming tonight?" Cathie asked after she sipped her water.

"He better be," Vicki responded as she watched Jeremy take a drink from his glass of water. "He left China this morning. For some reason, that president over there wants to be involved in a deal with the company. And in oil of all things!"

Jeremy coughed as he choked on his water. He beat his chest a few times, continuing to cough for a bit. "Really?" he asked once he stopped coughing long enough to get out the word.

"Yes," Vicki said. "It is very puzzling and peculiar to me."

"Excuse me," said a voice from behind Vicki. "Is there anything that you would like to drink?"

Vicki turned around to see a young man, in his mid-20s, standing behind her. He ran his hand through his thick brown hair before preparing to write down her response.

"Oh yes," Vicki said. "I'll have a glass of white wine."

After writing down Vicki's request, the waiter turned his attention to Gabby and Miranda.

"I'll have a glass of red wine," Miranda said.

"And I will have a soda," Gabby said. "But if you want to slip something stronger into it, I wouldn't be opposed to it. Tonight will be quite interesting!" Gabby chuckled slightly and glanced over to Vicki, who gave her a death glare across the empty seat between the two. The smile disappeared from Gabby's face. "Just the soda is fine."

The waiter informed them that he would be right back and went off to get their drinks. "Oh," Miranda said, pointing toward the door. "They're here."

The six at the table turned their gaze over to the doors and saw Delilah and Ben approaching the table. "We just ordered our drinks," Vicki said. "When the waiter comes back, you should be able to order yours."

Delilah took a seat next to Ryan while Ben sat on the other side of

Delilah and Miranda.

"I guess now all that we are waiting for is Peter," Vicki said. "He should be here in any minute."

"It's fitting, though," Jeremy added before he took another drink from his glass.

"Excuse me," Vicki said, irritated. "I think I misheard you."

"I just said that it was fitting," Jeremy said. "He's been in office for about two-and-a-half years and still hasn't come through on a fourth of his legislative promises."

"That's because he has the Republicans in Congress to thank for that," Ben chimed in. "They've been a pain in his ass since day one."

"Maybe he shouldn't be so demanding then. If he would listen to reason, then he would be able to pass many legislative documents that would benefit many Americans."

Ben glared at Jeremy. "Well, maybe if more people would work together . . ."

"Would you two just stop it?!" Delilah raised her voice. "God, you're like a couple of third graders."

"And what would you two like?"

Delilah recognized the voice from behind her. She turned around and quickly noticed who their waiter was for the night.

"*Clark?*"

"Excuse me," he said as he placed Vicki, Miranda, and Gabby's drinks onto the table. "What did you say?"

"Your name tag . . . It says 'Clark,'" Delilah responded, still shocked to see Clark at Finley's. "I would like a club soda. What do you want, honey?"

Ben stared at Delilah for a second. Then, he shook his head and returned to his menu. "I guess that I will have a glass of your Kentucky bourbon."

"I'll have them out quickly," Clark responded. "Then I will get your orders, unless if you all would like to wait for your other guest?"

Jeremy slowly shook his head, trying to signal Clark that he wanted to go ahead and order. But, unfortunately for him, Vicki was thinking otherwise. "Oh, we can all wait on him," she said. "We aren't going to

42

starve or anything, right, Ryan?" She turned her attention to him, and he looked up from his menu.

"Sure," he said unenthused. "Whatever."

Clark turned and left as everybody else continued to read through their menus. Delilah couldn't help but notice Clark back in the kitchen area. "Excuse me," she said, rising from the table. "I need to go to the ladies' room."

She made her way toward the bathroom when she saw Clark step out of the kitchen. He approached her, carrying the drinks, when she grabbed him by the arm and pulled him into the women's restroom. The glasses crashed to the floor.

"What are you doing?" Clark asked loudly. "I can get in trouble for that!"

"Shut up," Delilah interjected. "How's come you never bothered to tell me that you work here?"

"So now I matter?" Clark grabbed Delilah's hands. "I've snuck in and out of your house for the past few months, avoiding your husband. You said that you would divorce him, and now you're pregnant and are somehow sure that it is his."

"I told you," Delilah whined. "It may be yours, or it might be his. I just don't know. You seemed fine when we talked about it this morning."

"Well, you best be making a damn decision soon," Clark said. "I am not going to be waiting around forever for you. I see many young women every day, and some even slip me their numbers. If I have to continue waiting on you, then maybe I might just hook up with one of them."

"You wouldn't dare!" Delilah exclaimed. "What has gotten into you? I told you that I wasn't doing anything until after tonight."

"Delilah," Clark sighed. "I love you, but I am getting this feeling that you don't love me."

"It's just so complicated," Delilah whined as she ran her hand through her hair. "I can't leave Ben right now. I need to wait a couple of weeks."

"I'm beginning to think that it's not about Ben. Maybe it's about his money. That's all you care about."

He turned around to leave the women's restroom, but Delilah grabbed hold of his shirt before he left. Clark turned back and, in a brief moment, glared into Delilah's eyes. Then, he leaned in and gave her a long passionate kiss. Only when he felt Delilah kissing him back did he pull away, ending the kiss.

"If you and Ben aren't separated by the end of the week, you can kiss my ass goodbye," he said before turning and storming out of the restroom, leaving Delilah alone.

* * *

Jeremy remained seated at the table, ignoring the conversation between Vicki and his wife, Cathie. He looked around and noticed that other people had begun to shuffle into the restaurant. He had no idea who any of the people were.

He leaned over to Cathie, interrupting her conversation with Vicki, and asked, "Who are these people?"

"Jeremy," Cathie responded, clearly annoyed. "I don't know. I guess guests of Ben and Delilah."

Jeremy looked at the couple that had just entered the restaurant. He noticed that they hadn't been scanned by metal detectors or patted down by the Secret Service officers.

"What the hell?" he said just loud enough for the entire table to hear. Gabby let out a chuckle which prompted another glare by Vicki.

"What's wrong?" Vicki asked Jeremy.

"These people didn't have to be frisked like we were!" he said. "What the hell?"

"Maybe I just wanted to make sure that you didn't try to shoot me while you were here," said a voice coming from behind. The table turned their attention in the speaker's direction and saw Peter.

"Peter!" Vicki exclaimed, jumping from her seat to hug him.

"That," Peter said while Vicki hugged him. "And when you pay the people to come to the restaurant, they don't have to be patted down."

Jeremy's face showed his disgust for Peter because Cathie elbowed

44

Jeremy. Then, he turned to face her, and she mouthed, "Be nice."

"Daddy," Gabby asked from across the table. "When did you get in?"

"Just now." Peter took his seat next to Vicki and Gabby. Then he addressed the entire table. "I just returned from my critical trip to China."

"Question, Peter," Ryan interrupted from across the table. "Did you *actually* have a conversation with the Chinese president, or did you just bully him into obeying the U.S?"

The table sat quietly for a second. All that was heard were the sounds of the other people in the restaurant.

"Ryan," Cathie sighed. "Can't you all be civilized to each other? It's one night that all of us are together. We are here to celebrate Delilah and Ben's wedding anniversary! So let's all just calm down and enjoy the night."

"That might be easier said than done," Miranda responded.

"Why?"

"Because I just saw Delilah bolt out of the restaurant."

Once again, the table fell silent as everyone slowly turned toward Ben, who sat still in his seat. Then, after a moment passed, he picked up his glass of Kentucky bourbon, turned to face a waiter, and called out, "Waiter! I'm gonna need another!"

CHAPTER 4

AFTER THE ANNIVERSARY

The door opened to the Klimmings Mansion, and in came Peter, Vicki, Miranda, and Gabby. The four came in silent, and they turned to their left, entering the living room. Vicki took a seat in the first chair while Miranda and Gabby sat on the cream sofa. Peter walked over to the bar. "Anyone want one?" he asked as he started to put some ice in a glass.

"None for me," Vick responded. "But thank you anyway."

"I'll have one," Miranda spoke up. "I'd like to have a Scotch, please."

Peter poured a glass of Scotch for Miranda, paused for a minute to think over what he wanted, and then proceeded to pour himself a glass of Scotch. He turned and handed Miranda her drink before taking a seat opposite Vicki's chair.

"That was some anniversary party," he said, sipping his drink. "How do you think it is going at Ben and Delilah's house?" He laughed a soft laugh.

Vicki turned to face Peter. "It's not funny. I really fear for those two." She turned to Miranda. "The way you saw her storm out of the restaurant means that something was seriously bothering her."

"Yeah," Peter began. "She finally came to her senses." He took a swig of his Scotch.

"What's that supposed to mean?" Vicki asked.

"That the Applegates and Klimmingses should never be mixed. Their marriage was doomed from the get-go."

"Peter, I am tired of this constant feuding between you and the Applegates. She probably left tonight because she couldn't handle all of the bickering that went on before you showed up."

"I am going to have to agree with Mom on this one," Miranda chimed in. "I don't like to pick sides, but I can see why that would drive someone away. It was a little tense before you got there."

"What the hell?" Peter said before turning to Gabby. "What about you?"

Gabby turned to face Peter and smiled. "Daddy, I didn't pay attention to anyone tonight except for that hot brother that Delilah has. Ryan is so hot!"

"Well," Peter sighed. "I got no one on my side on this one." He took another sip from his drink.

"All we ask for is that you leave the feuding with the Applegates outside of our family," Vicki said. "It will make for a more peaceful time with the family, and it will make it a lot easier for Benjamin and Delilah to sort things out."

Peter took a sip of his drink and quickly realized something. He remembered an open seat for Miranda's boyfriend, Jason, at the restaurant.

"Miranda," Peter said. "What happened to Jason tonight? He wasn't at the dinner. Did something happen?"

Miranda took a deep sigh. "Not really. We are just taking a break from each other right now."

"How are you handling it?" Vicki asked.

"Fine," Miranda sighed. "I just don't know what to think about it all right now." She looked over at Vicki. "It's like you think you know someone, but then you don't."

Peter took another sip from his drink. "Well, what the hell does that mean? What did he do?"

Miranda stood up from the sofa and walked over to the bar. She looked up at the Klimmings family portrait that hung above the bar located in the living room. Her eyes scanned across the picture from left to right, pausing briefly on herself, Ben, and Delilah. "I don't know exactly," she said. "It just seems like he is hiding things from me."

"Well, that's never a good way to begin a relationship," Peter chimed in.

"Peter," Vicki added. "I wouldn't say that they just began the relationship. They've almost been together for a year."

"Well, she knows what I mean. This early on in a relationship is not a good time to hide things from your partner."

"When is it ever a good time to hide things from your partner?" Miranda asked after turning to Peter. She had tears pooling in her eyes.

The room sat in silence for a moment. The only sound heard was from the fire crackling in the fireplace to Peter's left and the ice rattling around in his glass. Then, finally, Gabby broke the silence. "What do you think Delilah is hiding from Ben?"

* * *

Her heels clattered against the sidewalk as she ran down the streets of downtown DC. Tears ran down her face as she continued running. People would turn around as she ran past, wondering if they should see if she needed any help. Yet, no one would go after her.

After a few blocks, Delilah Klimmings slowed down and took a seat on a nearby bench. The sidewalk was empty but illuminated with a lamppost nearby. She struggled to catch her breath.

She pulled out her cellphone and clicked on the contacts app. She noticed that Ben's contact was right above Clark's as she looked through the names. For a moment, Delilah sat there, staring at her phone. Confused and conflicted with what to do, she felt like she had the weight of her life upon her shoulders. Whatever decision she was about to make, it would go on to affect her for the rest of her life.

Finally, she made her decision. She clicked on Ben's contact, and just as she was about to press the phone icon to call him, a loud air horn wailed and jolted her, causing her phone to slip from her hands and bounce onto the cement. She turned to her left and saw a city bus pulling up. That's when she realized that she had been sitting at a bus stop.

The brakes squealed as the bus rolled to a slow stop, and the door flung open. In the driver's seat, Delilah noticed a man. He was a bit overweight, wearing a button-up shirt that was one size too small, and he had a hat on his head to cover up his greasy hair that peaked out the sides of his cap. He chomped on bubblegum and blew a giant bubble, popping almost instantly yet avoiding sticking to any of the stubble that lined his face. Finally, he looked over at Delilah and asked, "You needin' a lift?"

Delilah stood up from the bench and addressed him. "No, sir," she said nervously. "Just about ready to call a friend to come get me, that's all."

The man blew another bubble with his gum. "Well, it's not every night that a guy like me finds a pretty lady standing alone on the street. Are you sure you don't need a lift?"

"I am." Delilah took a small step back. "Thank you, though." She tried to flash a small smile on her face, but it ended up being some kind of warped mouth gesture.

"Eh, suit yourself," the man said before closing the door and hitting the accelerator. The bus roared on, emitting a black puff of exhaust out of the end.

As the bus moved on, Delilah let out a deep sigh. The conversation with the bus driver had deeply set off her nerves. She reached down, careful not to let her black dress touch the ground, and picked up her cell phone. Upon looking at the screen, she noticed a large crack. "Dammit," she said as she saw the break.

She looked at the screen some more and noticed that it still had Ben's contact information pulled up. She paused for a moment as some of the fights between herself and Ben played through in her head. Then, as the number of disputes built up, she couldn't help but hear the last thing Clark said to her tonight. *"If you and Ben aren't separated by the end of the week, you can kiss my ass goodbye."*

Delilah backed out of Ben's contact information and then chose Clark's. She stood there for a moment, wondering if she was doing the right thing, and then decided to call him.

* * *

"I can't believe she went barreling out of the restaurant like that," Cathie said. She was seated in the passenger seat of Jeremy's black Mercedes. Jeremy was sitting inside the driver's seat with her, and Ryan sat behind Jeremy. It was dark out as Jeremy drove down the highway outside the DC metropolitan.

"Why do you think she did it?" Cathie asked, turning to Jeremy.

"I don't know," Jeremy said, slightly shaking his head. "Maybe she came to her senses."

"Do you really think that? I know that their marriage has been a little rough lately, but I haven't seen them needing to be separated or anything."

"I don't know." Jeremy shrugged his shoulders.

For a moment, a silence fell over the Applegates. Then Cathie turned around in her seat and looked at Ryan. "Ryan, you had lunch with Delilah yesterday. Did she mention anything to you about this?"

Ryan thought for a moment, recalling his lunch with Delilah the day before. "No," he cocked his head a little. "In fact, our conversation was the opposite. I had wanted her to leave Ben, but she insisted that she wouldn't."

"Ryan Dean Applegate!" Cathie exclaimed from the front. "How could you?! You've done it! You've finally ruined their marriage!"

"Woah! Woah! Woah!" Jeremy interrupted. "I wouldn't say that Ryan ruined their marriage. Their marriage was doomed from the get-go." Jeremy looked in the rear-view mirror and smiled at Ryan. "She shouldn't have married into that family anyway."

"I don't understand why you hate all of them so much!" Cathie responded. "Vicki has always been nice to me. In fact, I might even consider her to be a friend."

"That may be the case, but you don't interact with that piece of crap she's married to. Ever since he became president, my business has lost profits, and other nations have imposed tariffs against me. He has to be involved in it somehow."

"Are you sure they aren't doing it because of you? You aren't the greatest with your choice of words sometimes."

"What the hell is that supposed to mean?" Jeremy spun around to look at Cathie. "I am great at choosing my words."

"No, Dad, you aren't," Ryan interrupted. "Sometimes you mean to say one thing, and then it comes out differently."

"Well, screw you both," Jeremy responded before returning his immediate attention to the road, sulking as he drove.

"Anyway, Mom," Ryan continued. "It wasn't because of me. Delilah had even expressed to me that she was feeling guilty over how she had been treating him lately." He paused. "It's like she really does love him."

* * *

"Wake up," a voice called out. "Wake up!" Ben moaned and groaned as he lifted his head from his hands. He struggled to open his eyes and focus. He felt dried drool on his hands.

"Do you want me to clean the room or not?" he heard again. Then, finally, he was able to focus on his surroundings. He was in his office at Klimmings Incorporated, sitting behind his desk. He noticed a lady in the room with a cart full of cleaning supplies. "You musta had one hell of a night by the looks of this place?" she asked and let out a small chuckle.

Ben looked around the room more and found two empty bottles of bourbon lying on the floor. He glanced back over to his desk and saw a glass with a small amount of leftover bourbon in it. He picked it up and swirled it around in the glass. "Did I drink all this?" he asked.

"I guess so," the cleaning lady began as she started to make her rounds on the room. "I came in here this morning and saw you passed out at your desk. Figured I'd wake you up before ya secretary came in."

Ben sighed, and it hit him. A massive headache made its way all around his head. He grunted. "What time is it anyway?"

"It's a little after five right now," the cleaning lady said. "People usually don't come into the building until about six-thirty or seven, though."

"Thank you," Ben said. He struggled to stand up from the chair and started to make his way to the door. After a couple of steps, he stopped, turned around, and snatched the glass up from his desk.

"Ummm . . . sir?" the cleaning lady mentioned.

"What?" Ben asked after stopping and turning to her.

"Don't you think you should probably go tidy up or something?" the cleaning lady suggested. "You know . . . before people get here."

"And why's that?" Ben grunted. "I got a little bit anyway." He heard the cleaning lady say something as he headed out of his office.

"Have you looked at yourself yet?"

Ben stopped at Doris' desk. He looked over at Pam's desk and then to Vicki's closed office door. He let out a deep sigh, sat the glass on Doris' desk, and then headed down the hallway to the elevator door.

* * *

Miranda, Vicki, and Gabby sat quietly at the breakfast table in the Klimmings Mansion dining room when Peter came into the room, already dressed for the day.

"Good morning to my lovely ladies!" he said as he took a seat beside Miranda at the long table. A servant came into the room with a plate consisting of bacon, toast, and scrambled eggs. "Thank you," he told the servant as she set the plate in front of him.

"Would you like some coffee or orange juice, sir?" she asked.

"Oh, Denise," Peter began. "I'm going to need lots of coffee today. It's going to be a hell of a day in the Oval!"

She turned around, walked over to the coffee bar, and started pouring a cup of coffee. Vicki, at the other end of the table, swallowed what she was eating and asked, "Why's that? What's going on today?"

"Well," Peter said as Denise sat the coffee down for him. "I'm meeting with Constance today about our reelection strategy."

"Reelection?" Gabby said. "Dad, you've only been in office for a little over a year. So why are you thinking about reelection?"

"Yes," Vicki said. "Shouldn't we discuss this as a family?"

"Well, what do you mean?" Peter asked. "I'm going to run for reelection. If I want to get reelected, I have to start thinking about it and set something up now so that I can begin campaigning next year and the year after."

"Oh, how I loved campaigning," Miranda sarcastically said before sipping her coffee.

"Peter," Vicki said. "Our family went through a lot the first time you ran. Do you think we can handle it now?"

"Why not?" Peter asked. "You all seemed to do fine the first time."

"But Ben and Delilah weren't having marital issues the first time. Peter, do we *really* want that to come out?"

"They'll be fine! They're grownups. They can handle their problems. We should just stay out of it."

"Peter," Vicki said, becoming more irritated. "Delilah ran out on their anniversary dinner last night. Imagine the country's reaction to it right now. Peter, imagine them going through it with you going through your reelection campaign."

Before Peter could get in another word, a cell phone started ringing. Miranda pulled her phone out of the pocket of her pajamas and looked at the screen. Jason was calling her.

Miranda gulped. "I need to take this." She got up, exited the dining room through the small archway on Gabby's side of the table, crossed the small hallway, and went into the sitting room. She sat down on one of the blue sofas and answered the call.

"Hey," Jason said. Miranda could tell that Jason was nervous. "How are you?"

"I am doing fine," she said. "You called just right at the right time. Mom and Dad were starting to get into an argument over his reelection."

"Oh, really," Jason responded. "I guess I have great timing." The two laughed. "So, what are you doing today?"

"Jason," Miranda said. "I can't do anything today." She paused for a moment. "In fact, I can't do anything with you for a little while."

"What's that supposed to mean?"

"I just need some time. I need to think some things over."

"So you're breaking up with me then?"

"No, no, no," Miranda said reassuringly. "I'm not breaking up with you. I just want more of a pause on this relationship."

"Oh."

"Just until I can think things out and process them. We have a lot going on right now."

"Yeah, I saw on the news this morning," Jason said. "I can't believe Delilah ran out like that."

Miranda sighed. "I was afraid of that."

"Yeah," Jason responded. "Well, if you need anything, you know how to get ahold of me."

"Thank you. Bye Jason."

"Bye. Love you."

* * *

The sun shined through the dark red curtains, allowing a beam of light to land right on Delilah's face. As she woke up, she began to move around, finding herself in a bed. She turned over to her right and noticed no one beside her. She let out a small sigh and carefully sat herself up in the bed.

Delilah looked around the bedroom and spotted a robe hanging on a nearby closet door. She made her way over to it and slipped into the robe before starting out of the bedroom.

She turned right, heading down the hallway and into a larger room, in which half of it served as the living room, and the other half served as a kitchen. Delilah heard bacon frying and soon spotted Clark cooking breakfast in the kitchen. Then she remembered the events of the night before. She remembered running out of her anniversary dinner and deciding to call Clark. She remembered how she came to his mobile home on the outskirts of DC and how she slept with him.

"Good morning," Clark said, interrupting her recollection of the night before. "I see you found the robe I left for you."

Delilah reexamined the robe. It was green with a few faint blue stripes forming a plaid design.

"Good morning, Clark," Delilah said back. She made her way into the kitchen portion of the room and took a seat at a small table that had four chairs around it. Clark began moving the bacon from the frying pan onto a plate.

"Last night was amazing," he said as he turned and set the plate of bacon on the table. "Don't you think?"

Delilah looked at Clark and flashed a small smile on her face. "To be honest, I don't remember a whole lot from last night."

"I would have been surprised if you had," Clark said as he set two more plates on the table for him and Delilah. "You were out of it right after we finished." He took a couple of pieces of bacon, placed all but one on his plate, and then took a bite out of the one he had left in his hand.

"Clark," Delilah stated as she took a couple of pieces of bacon for herself. "I hope you understand this . . ."

"If you're about to tell me that it's going to be longer before we can be together, I understand."

Delilah dropped a piece of bacon back onto her plate in disbelief. She stared back at Clark. "You mean to tell me that the same person who threatened to leave me if I didn't separate from my husband by the end of the week is now okay with me staying with him?"

"Yes," Clark replied before taking another bite from one of his pieces of bacon. "I understand now."

"What the hell is that supposed to mean?" Delilah exclaimed. "You had me worried all last night that it was over between us, and now everything is sunshine and rainbows?!"

"Delilah," Clark said as he moved around the table to Delilah's side. He knelt beside her, placing her right hand into both of his hands. "You had a difficult decision to make last night, and after pondering it through, you chose to come to me." Clark's eyes locked onto Delilah's, and a smile began to appear on her face. "I understand, Delilah. You just cannot leave Ben right now. You have a baby coming and so many things to think about. It's unreasonable for me to place any added stress on you."

Delilah continued to smile back at Clark. "Oh, Clark," she sighed. "I wish I had met you before I met Ben. It would have made things so much easier."

"Babe, sometimes it takes a few tries before you find the one you are meant to be with for the rest of your life." Clark leaned forward and kissed Delilah.

"It won't be forever. I'll leave Ben eventually . . . even if it means waiting until this baby is born."

"I understand."

"And Clark," Delilah added. "You best believe that we will get married when I do leave him."

* * *

The door to the entry hall of the Klimmings Mansion opened, and Ben crept in. He slowly latched the door behind him, standing in the hall alone. He didn't remember seeing any cars outside the house when he pulled in, so he knew no one was home. "Hello," he called out, double-checking. Ben took a step and listened carefully.

"Yes?"

Coming from the hallway to the right, Denise stepped out. "Hello, Mr. Benjamin. Is there anything I can get for you?"

"No, Denise," Ben replied. "I was just checking to see if anyone was here."

"I don't think there is anyone here, sir," she said. "Mr. Klimmings left for the White House right after breakfast. Miss Miranda went out shopping. Miss Gabriella is at school, of course. And Mrs. Klimmings went into the office just a little bit ago."

"Thank you, Denise," Ben smiled. "That's all I wanted to know."

"You're welcome, sir. I need to get back to cleaning. It's good seeing you again!"

"You too, Denise."

She went back down the side hall and turned into the first door on the right, heading into the kitchen. Ben took a couple of steps down the entry hall before stopping, turning to his left, and looking in the living room. He looked at the furniture which sat in the middle of the room, in front of the fireplace. Above the fireplace hung the large television. Then, he looked at the opposite wall with the portrait of the entire Klimmings family. Below it sat the bar.

As Ben stood there, he felt a sudden urge to pour himself a drink of the bourbon sitting on the top of the bar. With a deep breath, he made his way over to the bar, picked up a glass, opened the ice container, and dropped a few ice cubes into it. Then, he grabbed the bourbon, took the cap off the decanter, and filled his glass three-fourths of the way full. He examined the glass for a moment and then started drinking.

CHAPTER 5
CONSILIUM

A butler opened the door to the Oval Office, and in walked Peter, alongside Henry.

"What time is Constance supposed to be here?" Peter asked Henry as he moved toward the *Resolute* desk and took a seat in the chair behind it, adjusting his suit jacket and straightening his tie in the process.

He turned around to look out the window behind him. In front of the window sat a table lined with family photos of the Klimmingses. Navy blue drapes hung around the windows, and a dark blue oval rug lay on the floor in the center of the room. As is customary in the Oval Office, the presidential seal lay in the middle of the rug. Along the top and bottom of it were two quotes. Along the top, the quote read, "'The harder the conflict, the greater the triumph.' – George Washington." And along the bottom of the rug, the quote read, "'Action will delineate and define you.' – Thomas Jefferson." In addition, busts of prominent historical American figures such as Martin Luther King Jr., George Washington, and Abraham Lincoln sat on tables around the room.

"She is supposed to arrive around ten o'clock, sir," Henry responded. "Is there anything that you need? Coffee?"

"Yes," Peter responded, turning back to Henry. "I'm going to need more coffee. What I had this morning at home is not going to hold me over for this."

Henry gestured to a butler to get more coffee for the president. The butler headed off, closing the door behind him. Henry turned back, facing Peter. "So, what is the big deal about meeting Constance? Is there something between you two that I don't know about?"

Peter looked up from the desk. "No," he replied. "She and I are fine. I'm just not looking forward to this meeting." He paused for a moment. "Planning campaigns are so difficult."

"Mr. President," Henry began. "If you don't mind me asking, why are you running for reelection then?"

Peter sat silent for a moment. "It's not that I don't want to run for reelection." He stood up and turned to look back out the window on the White House lawn. "It's that I hate the constant bickering that goes on when you're running for office. So many people have to input their opinions, and I just want to do what I want to do, you know?" He turned back to Henry.

"Then do it," Henry said. "Mr. President, this is your campaign. You decide what you want, and you go for it."

The door opened to the Oval Office, and Martha stood in the doorway. "Mr. President," she said. "The vice president is here."

Henry took a seat on one of the cream sofas that sat in the middle of the room. "Send her in," Peter said. As Martha closed the door and went off to get the vice president, Peter took a seat behind the *Resolute* desk. As soon as he took a seat, the door opened, and a woman came into the room. She was dressed in a dark blue pantsuit, accentuating her straight, brown hair. She held a newspaper in her hand and approached the *Resolute* desk.

"Can you believe this?" she said as she slapped the newspaper down on the desk.

"Believe what?" Peter said as he took the newspaper.

The vice president, now with her hand on her hip, replied, "Speaker

59

White. She called us incapable of handling the current recession." She snatched the newspaper from Peter, opened it, and began reading. "House Speaker Rebecca White issued scathing remarks, criticizing the current administration's response to the ongoing recession ravaging the United States and the world. In her statements, the speaker called President Klimmings and Vice President Zeemer 'inapt' to handle the current crisis, saying, 'Mr. Klimmings needs to get out of his Silver Spring mansion and get himself to Washington.'"

The vice president threw the newspaper back onto the desk. "What the hell is wrong with that woman?"

"Constance." Peter rose from his desk. "Go ahead and take a seat."

Constance moved over to the sofa across from Henry. "That woman has been out to get us since we took office," Constance continued. "I just hope she loses the House in November."

"Unfortunately, that doesn't look to be the case," Henry interrupted. "Instead, if trends continue the way they are, it looks like Republicans are going to keep control of the House and potentially take the Senate from us in the midterms. That's why it is important that we have this meeting today."

"Well, what does that mean, Henry?" Constance asked. "Are you suggesting that we are going to lose in two years?"

"That is not what he is suggesting," Peter stated from his desk. "What he is saying is that if we don't start acting now, we have a potential to lose reelection in two years." Peter stood up from his desk and moved to the front of it. He took a chair and moved it over closer to Henry and Constance. "Constance, we did such a great job winning over the minority vote when we ran. I believe we can do it again."

"Peter," Constance began. "I'm a black woman. Every time I've ever run for office, I've always won the minority vote. Why? Because those people see themselves when they see me in this position. They see potential in themselves. They see potential in America."

"Do you think you would be okay with helping Democratic senators with their reelection campaigns?" Henry asked.

"I figured I'd already be doing that," Constance said. "What else am I going to be doing? That's my job. I support the president and his agenda, so I'm going to do what needs to be done to retain our power."

* * *

The elevator door opened, and Vicki stepped out. She walked down the short hallway and to the receptionist's desks. Ben's receptionist, Doris, sat at the first desk. "Good morning, Doris," Vicki said. "Is Benjamin here?"

"No, ma'am," Doris answered. "I haven't heard anything from Mr. Klimmings all morning. Is he doing okay?"

"I'm not sure," Vicki replied. "After what happened last night, I would be surprised if he even came in today. Would you let me know if he comes in?"

"Yes, ma'am."

Vicki headed over to Pam's desk, but before she could exchange pleasantries with her, the phone rang. Pam picked it up by saying, "Klimmings Incorporated, this is Pam." Vicki looked at her stack of mail on the desk and picked it up. Then Pam looked at Vicki, addressing her. "Mrs. Klimmings, President Wu of the People's Republic of China is on the phone."

"Go ahead and send it to my office," Vicki said. "I'll take it in there."

Vicki turned to her office, stepped inside, and closed the door behind her. She set her bag down and tossed the mail on a table. As she was heading to her desk, the phone started ringing. She took a seat at her desk and answered the phone, "Hello, President Wu, this is Vicki Klimmings, chief executive officer and board chair of Klimmings Incorporated. How are you today?"

"Good morning, Mrs. Klimmings," President Wu said over the phone. "I am doing fine. I'm calling about the deal I had set up with your husband. He says that you are interested in it."

"Well," Vicki started. "If I'm being honest about it, I'm not the biggest fan of it. I'm only doing it because Peter asked me to."

"Perfect," he responded. "He has you trained well then. Now, I plan to have . . ."

"Excuse me," Vicki interrupted. "What do you mean by 'he has you trained well?'"

"I mean that you listen to him. While you are in control of his company, you are still doing what you're told."

"Excuse me, President Wu. I don't *do* what I'm told. I'm a grown woman who makes her own decisions in life. Of course, I ask my husband for his advice from time to time, but I certainly don't allow him to dictate how I run this company. So anything that I decide is because I feel that it is the right thing for this company. Do you understand?"

There were a few seconds of awkward silence over the phone call. "We'll see," President Wu finally said. "Now, I need you to sign a couple of papers for this deal. I plan to send a few people over in a couple of days to get this done."

"No."

"Pardon me? What was that?"

"This is not a good time," Vicki said. "We have some things going on, and I need my CFO here to provide a signature as well. So you're going to have to wait."

President Wu sighed into the phone. "Vicki, I don't like to hear that."

"Well, you're just going to have to deal with it," Vicki said. "And that's Mrs. Klimmings to you."

Vicki hung up the phone before President Wu could get in another word. She pressed a button on the phone, paging Pam. "Yes, Mrs. Klimmings," Pam said over the phone speaker.

"If he calls back, don't put him through. I don't want to hear from him again today."

* * *

Miranda turned into the drive of the Klimmings Mansion. Her blue car sped down the property's driveway and came to a halt outside the front door of the mansion. She turned off her car, jumped out, and proceeded up the few steps to the door. She opened the door and entered the entry hall. Denise rounded the corner from the living room. "Miss Miranda," she frantically said as she led her into the living room. "I'm so glad you were able to get here so quickly."

Once inside the living room, Miranda saw why Denise had been so worried. Ben was passed out on the sofa, in front of the fireplace and television. On the floor in front of him laid an empty glass.

"He came in after you left this morning," Denise continued. "He asked where everyone had gone. I told him that everyone had left and that I needed to get back to cleaning."

Miranda examined the room more thoroughly as Denise continued to explain the situation. Finally, she noticed that the bourbon decanter was empty at the bar.

" . . . and that's when I called you," Denise finished. She looked at Miranda, who was now over by the bar, holding the empty decanter. Miranda took the top off and sniffed inside.

"Oh no," she said. "This is a lot worse than I thought it would be."

"I'm so sorry," Denise said, now with tears in her eyes. "I should have been with him. After what happened last night with Miss Delilah, I should have known that he needed someone to be with him."

"Don't be sorry." Miranda moved to Denise, taking her hands. "Nobody could have known that this would happen."

She turned toward Ben, still out cold on the sofa. He quietly moaned before emitting a belch, causing Miranda to smile slightly. She turned back to Denise, who still looked worried. "Don't stress too much about it. People get a little drunk all the time. Let's try to move him upstairs to his bedroom in case Mom comes home from the office early today."

She and Denise moved over to Ben and managed to pull him up from the sofa. As they lifted him into a standing position, his eyes opened a bit, but it was clear that he was still very drunk.

"Miranda?" Ben murmured. "Iz dah' chu?"

"Yes, Ben," Miranda said to him. "It is me."

"Chu're such a good sister!" Ben said to her, looking at her in the eyes. They moved through the archway to the bar's right and up the staircase.

"Watch your step, Mr. Benjamin," Denise warned him. "I don't want you to fall."

"*Denise?!*" Ben drunkenly exclaimed. "Well, I didn't know chu were here. How long have chu been here?"

Miranda and Denise looked at each other and smiled as they continued to help Ben up the staircase. Finally, they led Ben across the room at the top through a door opposite them on the left of the wall. They opened the door, moved Ben into the room, and sat him on the bed.

"Here, Ben," Miranda said. "You need to get some more rest."

"Well, what if I don't want to get more rest?" Ben asked, sitting up on the bed.

"You need to. Mom cannot see you like this." Miranda turned toward Denise, who was standing behind her. "Could you put on some coffee for him?"

"Yes, ma'am," Denise said before leaving the room and heading downstairs.

"Now," Miranda said to Ben. "I need to go. You make sure you get some rest and are sober before leaving this room. Okay?"

"*Okay . . .*" Ben said before laying back on the bed.

"Goodbye, Ben. Miranda turned and began to head out the door when she heard Ben speak.

"Miranda."

She turned around and saw tears in his eyes.

"Why did she leave me? Why did Delilah run out like dah'?"

Miranda paused for a second. Then, she headed over to the bed and took a seat at the end. "Oh, Ben," she sighed. "I don't think it was because of you. I think . . . maybe she has some things she's trying to sort out." Miranda smiled at Ben as he wiped some of the tears away from his eyes. "Don't blame yourself. I'm sure she will be back."

"Chu do?"

"Yes. I do." Miranda stood up from the end of the bed. "Now, you don't want to be drunk when she gets back, do you?"

Ben laid back down on the bed. "No."

"Then get yourself some rest. I'll be back soon."

She headed out of the bedroom and went back downstairs. "Denise," she called out. "I will be back soon. Keep an eye on Ben for me!"

Before Denise had the opportunity to respond, Miranda was out the mansion's front door. She opened the door to her blue car, started it, and circled the turnaround before heading out to the main road.

* * *

Henry closed the door to the Oval Office and turned to face Peter. "Well, Mr. President, I believe that that was a good meeting."

"I agree. We may not do the greatest in November this year, but dammit, we will win in two years."

"Here-ye!" Henry said as he took a seat on one of the sofas. The door opened to the office, and Martha stepped in.

"Mr. President," she said. "We've received a call from President Wu from China. He has requested to speak with you."

"That is fine," Peter said, somewhat confused. "I can take it in here."

"Sir," she added. "He has also requested that no translators or any other officials be on the line at the same time."

Henry rose from the sofa. "But the president always has officials on the line when speaking with foreign leaders."

"Mr. Gates," Peter said, calming Henry down. "It'll be okay." He looked back at Martha, still standing in the doorway. "I'll take the call."

Martha closed the door, and within mere seconds, the phone on the *Resolute* desk began to ring. Peter picked it up and answered, "Hello, President Wu. It's a pleasure getting to hear from you."

"Well, it is not a pleasure having to call you, Mr. President," President Wu scathingly responded. "Your woman does not know how to run a business, and she sure as hell doesn't know how to talk to another man."

Peter looked up at Henry, still standing in the room. He motioned for him to leave. Henry looked at Peter, wanting to say something, but turned instead and left the room.

"Excuse me, sir," Peter began. "I do not quite understand what you are talking about. What did she do?"

"Your woman does not know how to operate a deal. We had a call earlier today, and she decided that she would back out of the deal we had made."

"First off," Peter interrupted. "Stop calling her my woman. Her name is Vicki, and she is my wife. This morning, she was all for going through with the deal, but if you talked to her in the same way you've spoken to me about her, then I can't blame her for not wanting to go through the deal with you."

"Well, she needs to learn how to speak with a man then," President Wu added. "If she cannot, then she will . . ."

"Stop it. Stop it with the sexist remarks. That may work in your country, Wu, but it doesn't in mine."

There was silence over the phone. The few seconds that passed felt like minutes to Peter as he waited for President Wu to respond. "Well," he began. "Talk to your . . . wife. Maybe she will listen better to you than she will me."

"I can speak with her," Peter said. "But I will not tell her what to do. She runs my company now. She makes the decisions."

"I want this deal to work out for the both of us. Together, our two countries can achieve greatness."

"Yes," Peter said as he rolled his eyes. "Yes, they can."

"Goodbye, Mr. Klimmings," President Wu said. "Hopefully, we can come to some kind of final agreement soon."

"Thank you, and goodbye to you too."

The receiver on the other end clicked. Peter hung up the phone and sat at his desk in silence.

"MARTHA!!" Peter yelled out, breaking the silence. After a moment, the door to the Oval Office swung open, and Martha and Henry stepped into the room.

"Yes, Mr. President," she said. "Is there something I can help you with?"

"Get my wife on the phone. We need to talk."

* * *

Miranda's blue car pulled up outside Ben and Delilah's townhouse. She placed her car in park and turned off the ignition. She took a deep sigh before opening the door and stepping out. The cool April breeze hit her skin. She smiled as she felt the wind run through her hair. The tweeting of the birds filled her ears. Spring was always her favorite season.

She closed the door and proceeded to approach the front door. She paused for a moment, about to knock, but instead pulled out her keys, flipped through the various ones she had, and placed one into the doorknob, unlocking the door and stepping in.

The house looked like it always did. Miranda looked around at the living room, noticing some of the pictures of Ben and Delilah. Photos from their wedding day, trips, and family gatherings hung on the walls of the room. She looked at the pictures and thought about when the two moved into the house. It was all part of Peter's plan to get the American people to view the Klimmings family as one of them. The deal was that Ben and Delilah would live in a typical American home rather than stay at the Klimmings Mansion. Miranda remembered how Delilah's father, Jeremy, took the news that the two would be moving into the townhouse. He was furious.

It felt like a century ago. Now, the marital tensions between Ben and Delilah had grown, not that it wasn't evident that the two would have struggles in their future. Peter and Jeremy had constantly feuded when they were in business. However, things changed once Peter ran for president. Jeremy spent millions of dollars trying to get his Republican challenger into office. Once that failed, Jeremy took a different approach and decided to try to cut all ties to the Klimmings family, including destroying the marriage of his daughter and her husband.

Miranda had no doubt that Delilah's storming out of the restaurant during the anniversary dinner was due to family tension. She had just wished that something would change so that Ben and Delilah could be at peace.

Miranda heard the door open behind her, and she turned to see Delilah in the doorway, still in the black dress from the anniversary dinner the night before.

"What are you doing here?" she asked, puzzled that Miranda was standing in her living room.

"I was hoping I would find you here," Miranda said, moving to sit down on the couch. "What happened, Delilah?"

Delilah stood still for a moment, trying to think of some kind of lie to tell Miranda. She didn't want to tell Miranda about her affair with Clark, but she also knew she needed to explain why she ran out the other night.

"Is it because of the family?" Miranda asked. "Delilah, I understand that last night was a bit crazy, but that's no reason to run out."

Delilah paused, stepped inside, and closed the door behind her. "If I'm being honest, that is it. I just can't take the family drama anymore." She moved over to a chair that sat next to the couch. "Anytime we all get together, my dad and your dad just argue and bicker all the time. I just can't take it anymore."

Delilah hung her head low. She considered what she said and how much of it was the truth instead of a lie.

"Delilah," Miranda sighed. "Let that be a feud between our dads. You can't let it affect your marriage to Ben. You two love each other."

"I know." Delilah continued to hang her head, refusing to look up. "Miranda, I have something I need to tell you."

A puzzled look came across Miranda's face. "What is it?"

"Miranda . . . I'm pregnant."

Silence filled the room for a brief second. "That . . . That's amazing! Delilah, I'm so happy for you!"

Delilah now had tears in her eyes. "I don't know if I can do this with the family. I feel like this baby is going to start so much trouble, and no baby should have to go through that."

"Delilah," Miranda said. "Stop worrying about what the family thinks. If you love Ben, then screw everybody else! You do what makes you happy." Miranda stood from the couch and walked over to the door. She stopped, turned around, and looked Delilah in the eyes. "But Delilah, I think you should know that Ben's destroyed right now. Denise found him passed out on the sofa this morning . . . drunk."

Miranda moved a little closer to Delilah, kneeling beside her. "If you really love him, you will come over to the mansion and see him. I don't know how much longer I can keep him from doing anything he might regret."

* * *

Back in her office, Vicki sat going over some company records. She reviewed some of the documents that showed the impact of the recent economic recession when a buzz went off on her phone. Vicki pressed a button and said, "Yes?"

"Mrs. Klimmings," Pam said over the phone's speaker. "Your husband is on the phone."

"Send him through." Vicki set the papers down on her desk and adjusted herself in her chair. She had figured that Peter would call after her conversation with President Wu. The phone rang.

"Hello, Peter," Vicki said after picking up her phone.

"Vicki," Peter began. "What the hell did you say to Wu?"

"Now, Peter, you never mentioned to me how sexist that man is. He called me and went on about how I am inadequate to be running the company and stuff, and to be honest, I just didn't want to take his crap."

"Vicki, I understand that the man is a piece of shit. I get it, but you cannot mistreat him. Not now. We made a deal with him, and we gotta follow through with it. Who knows what else he will do before we follow through."

"Well, I'm not meeting him," Vicki said. "He is slime, and I will not put myself near him."

"You know you're going to have to now," Peter said. "There's no way he's going to want to sign anything unless you are there in person."

"Dammit. I don't want to meet him."

"Then have Ben do it. He's the CFO, after all. Wu only really needs one of you all to sign in person."

Vicki was silent on the phone. "What," Peter said again. "What is it?"

"Benjamin isn't here," Vicki said. "I still haven't seen him since the dinner last night."

"Shit," Peter sighed. "That damn Delilah. Does anyone know where she is?"

Vicki looked at her cellphone on her desk. She saw the text that Miranda sent previously about finding Delilah. "Miranda found her. She told her that she was so upset over the family drama that is going on."

"That's a load of bullshit. She and the rest of that damn Applegate family love stirring shit up."

Vicki sighed. "Miranda seems to think that she is upset about you and Jeremy feuding."

"Hmmm." Peter knew he wasn't going to win this argument. "Well, we need to work on finding Ben then. I'll see you tonight."

"See you tonight, honey. I love you."

"Love you, babe," Peter replied before hanging up. Vicki put the phone back on the receiver. She took a deep sigh, leaned back in her chair, and ran her hands through her hair.

* * *

The shower curtain opened, and Ben reached over and grabbed the towel hanging up. He started drying himself before stepping out of the tub. Then he slipped into his underwear before opening the bathroom door and heading back into the bedroom.

He looked around the room, remembering that this was his old bedroom when he lived in the Klimmings Mansion. The room had a darker theme, with all the furniture being black or dark brown, and everything was accented in red. Ben stepped into the closet and pulled out a shirt, putting it on without looking at what he had pulled out. Then, he walked over to a dresser and did the same with a pair of pants.

"Feeling better, Mr. Benjamin?" Denise asked, knocking on the bedroom door.

"Yes, Denise, I am," Ben replied. "You can come in, by the way."

The door opened, and Denise came into the room. She held a mug full of coffee. "I thought you may need another one," she said.

"Thank you, Denise," he said, coming over and taking the mug from her. "Thank you for taking care of me."

"You're welcome. Your family means a lot to me." Denise stopped as Ben took a sip of the coffee. "Is there anything else that you need,

Mr. Benjamin?"

"No. Thank you, though."

Denise turned and headed out of the bedroom and down the stairs. Ben sat down on the bed, taking another sip of coffee. "Mr. Benjamin!" he heard Denise call up from downstairs. "Miss Miranda is back!"

Ben sipped his coffee again, set it on the nightstand beside the bed, and headed downstairs. After reaching the bottom of the staircase, he rounded the corner to the left and went through the archway into the living room. He paused right in his tracks when he saw Delilah standing next to Miranda.

"Delilah?" he said in disbelief. "Are you back?"

She paused for a moment before saying, "Yes, Ben. I'm here."

"I found her back at the house," Miranda added. "She said that she ran out last night because she was overwhelmed with the family."

Delilah smiled at Ben before approaching him. When she reached him near the archway, she noticed that he had tears in his eyes. She held his hands and looked him in the eyes.

"I thought you were gone forever," Ben cried. "I thought I had lost you."

"No, Ben," Delilah said. "You're never going to lose me."

"Do you promise that?" Ben wiped away tears on his face with his hand.

"I do," Delilah said before hugging him. The two embraced for a moment before being interrupted by Miranda.

"Um . . . Delilah. Don't you have something you need to tell Ben?"

"Yes. Let's take a seat on the sofa." The two moved over to the sofa and sat down. Miranda sat in a chair adjacent to them.

"So, I have been feeling a little off lately," Delilah began. "So I got a test."

"Oh no," Ben said worriedly. "Are you okay? Do we need to go see someone?"

"No, no, no," Delilah interrupted, calming Ben down. "It's not bad. In fact, it's terrific news." She turned to look at Miranda, who was smiling back at her. This caused a smile to appear on Delilah's face. She turned to look back at Ben. "Ben, I'm pregnant."

Ben sat there, processing what she had just said. "Well . . . well . . ." He struggled to come up with words. "That's great!"

"I knew he'd love to hear it," Miranda added. "I'm so excited for you two. Congratulations!"

Ben leaned in toward Delilah, holding her hands. "Delilah, we're going to be parents!"

"Yes, we are!"

At this moment, the plan she and Clark had made all came back to her. She remembered that this moment wasn't supposed to be authentic. She wasn't supposed to be excited about getting back with Ben. She wasn't supposed to be excited about being a member of the Klimmings family. And she wasn't supposed to be excited about raising a child with Ben.

But she was.

CHAPTER 6
SEPTEMBER STRUGGLES

Spring turned into summer, and before anyone knew it, the cool, fall, September air had begun to settle in. It had been months since Delilah had told Ben about her pregnancy, and now she found herself lying in Clark's bed at his house. Her belly had grown significantly since April. While Ben continued to seem very invested in the pregnancy, he had drifted back into his old ways of constantly focusing on work.

Delilah turned over, looking at Clark, who lay beside her. Since Ben had been working more, she had grown more fond of Clark. She had been seeing him more and more, causing her to become very invested in his plan for her to leave her husband after the baby was born. As she kept thinking and looking at Clark, she caught herself saying aloud, "I love you."

Clark turned his head and looked at Delilah, their eyes meeting each other. "I love you too, babe," he said before kissing her. "What brings this on?"

"You're always here for me. Ben's been going back to work more and more, and I get so lonely at home." She paused to take a deep breath. "I'm just glad to have you here to help me through this."

"Delilah, you don't have to continue to put yourself through this. You can leave him now if you want. You don't have to wait until you have this baby to leave him."

"Yes, I do," Delilah said. "If I leave now, he will have more things to use against me to try to take my baby away from me."

"But we both know it's my baby, Delilah. You said it yourself."

"No, I didn't," Delilah said, sitting up in the bed. "I told you that it could be both of yours. I am being upfront with you, Clark. It probably is yours, but until I can be one hundred percent certain that it is yours, I can't do anything."

Clark sat up on the bed and put on his pants. He turned back to face Delilah. "Can't you just tell people that it's mine?"

"I mean, I could," Delilah replied. "But I don't think I can do that to Ben. If it's his, he has a right to know."

Clark displayed a look of displeasure on his face before taking his shirt and putting it on. "I just don't like the idea of you two being connected once you leave him."

"I understand that," Delilah said, sitting up on the bed now. "But Clark, we are always going to be connected. I am the daughter-in-law of the president of the United States. Anytime the media or anyone mentions Ben, somehow, I will be brought up. It isn't going to matter if it's a year after we break up or ten. I am always going to be known as Ben's wife to them."

Clark stood there for a moment, thinking things over. He looked at the floor, processing what Delilah had just said. Then, he looked her in the eyes and said, "I hadn't thought of it like that." He moved around the bed and sat down beside her. "Baby, you are going to go through so much for me. I feel like I'm being an absolute jerk right now. How can you ever forgive me?"

"Just give me time," she said. "Clark, I don't think you still fully grasp how big this is. You'll be found, and when they find out who you are, your face is going to be plastered all over the media."

"Oh my God," Clark whispered to Delilah. "I'm going to be painted as the bad guy, aren't I?"

Delilah nodded her head. "I'm sorry, Clark. That's just how it is. I love you, but honey, we have some tough times that we are going to have to get through, and it isn't going to be easy."

* * *

Peter sat at the head of the table in the dining room of the Klimmings Mansion, eating his breakfast of scrambled eggs with bacon. He looked up at Vicki, who was sitting at the opposite end of the table. She was sipping on some coffee and looking at some of the headlines on her tablet.

"Is today the day you go see President Wu?" Peter asked her.

She sat her coffee down on the table and looked at Peter. "Yes," she said disgustedly. "Can you tell that I am so excited to see him?"

Peter chuckled. "Well, I don't blame ya. If I could go with you, then I would, honey, but I can't."

"He just gives me the creeps."

"Why don't you take Ben with you?" Peter suggested. "He would do great over there, and it would get him away from here for a while and help clear his mind with things."

"I can't do that to him," Vicki said before taking a sip from her coffee. "Benjamin and Delilah have gone through so much and come so far this past summer. I don't think he's ready for an international trip just yet."

Peter took another bite from his scrambled eggs. "You know, I never did like the fact that he married that Applegate girl, but seeing how he reacted to her running out of that anniversary dinner made me realize just how much she means to him."

"She means so much to him," Vicki said before taking another sip from her coffee as Gabby came into the room.

"Good morning," she said to Peter and Vicki. She reached across the table, took a piece of bacon from the platter in the center, and bit into it.

"Well, good morning," Peter said to her. "You gonna eat breakfast with us?"

"I won't be down here for long," Gabby said. "Michelle is going to pick me up and take me to school."

Peter looked across the table at Vicki. "Gabriella," Vicki said. "Your eighteenth birthday is Thursday next week. Have you thought at all about what you would like to do?"

"Not really," Gabby said, sitting down in the chair next to Vicki. "Michelle, Dana, and I are going to do something that night, though. Is that okay?" Gabby looked at Vicki and noticed her looking at Peter. Then, she turned to Peter and saw him looking back at Vicki before turning to her.

"Gabriella," he started. "We wanted to do something together as a family for this. Whatever you want to do, but you have to tell us soon so that we can get the proper security stuff done beforehand."

Gabby shook her head. "It's always the Secret Service! Every single thing we do around here has to involve them. Why can't we just go back to the way things were?"

"Because your father is the president of the United States," Vicki chimed in. "He has to have that protection because there are so many crazy people out there."

"Well, *you* don't have that protection! Miranda doesn't. Ben doesn't. Why do I have to have it?"

"Gabby," Peter said. "Your mom has minimal protection because she requested so. Miranda and Ben declined protection, and for the most part, they don't need it because they try to stay out of the public eye."

"Then why the hell do I have to have it?"

"Language!" Vicki exclaimed. "You watch your mouth!"

Peter sighed. "You're still a child, Gabby. When you turn eighteen, then you can decide whether you want to keep the protection or not, but until then, you're going to have it."

"And your father will always have it," Vicki said. "Or at least he will while he's the president." She winked at Peter.

"Great," Gabby mumbled. She checked her phone and saw that Michelle had texted her that she was there to pick her up. "I've got to go." She got up and stormed out of the room. Peter and Vicki could hear the front door slam inside the dining room.

"What is her deal?" Peter asked. "She has been getting an attitude lately." He took some more bites of his breakfast.

"Can you blame her?" Vicki replied. "Her teenage years were filled with campaigning, and now this. That's a lot for a teenage girl to have to take in."

"Hmmm," Peter sighed. "I think that it is just teenage hormones and stuff. She'll get over it."

Vicki stared at Peter as he went back to eating his breakfast, and then she turned to look back at her tablet. She noticed some article about House Speaker Rebecca White blasting Peter in a news conference. "That Rebecca White lady really hates you, doesn't she?"

"You mean that bitch?" Peter wiped his mouth off with his napkin. "She's got nothing better to do in Congress, so she attacks me every day. Constance has had it with her."

"She and Constance seemed to get along so much when they were in the House together, though. What happened?"

"Apparently me. After I started running and rumors circulated that I would select Constance as my VP pick, Rebecca stopped working with her in the House. She wanted nothing to do with any of her success. Now she's turned the entire Republican Party into her playpen, and they all hate us."

Vicki took another sip from her coffee. "Well, it seems like she's moved on from them, and now she's working to turn the entire country against you."

"You're damn right she is," Peter said. "Right now, I need some miracle from God in November. Everyone knows that she is going to retain her power in the House, and the damn Republicans are set to take the Senate too."

Vicki paused for a moment. "Peter," she started. "Are you sure you want to run again? Wouldn't it just be simpler to just retire from politics, take the yearly pension, and come back to the company?"

"Hell no!" Peter exclaimed. "I am not letting that bitch win. We may not do so well in the elections this year, but believe me, a lot can happen in two years."

Vicki sighed and went to take another sip of her coffee but realized that her mug was empty. "Well, it just seems like a lot to me," Vicki said. "I couldn't do it." She stood up from her chair and adjusted her blazer. "I've got a plane to catch."

Peter stood up from his chair and rounded the table to kiss her good-bye. "Call me when you get to China. I love you."

"I love you too, Peter. I'll call when I get there."

* * *

The buzzer from his secretary rang on his desk, and Ben reluctantly pulled his attention away from his computer. He pressed the button on his telephone, saying, "Yes, Doris?"

"Mr. Klimmings," Doris said over the phone speaker. "Brad is here to see you."

"Send him in." Ben stood up from his desk and headed toward his office door. However, the door opened before he got there. The youngest man from the group that had met with Ben previously about the financial reports stood at the door. "Hello, Brad!" Ben welcomed him with his right hand extended.

"Mr. Klimmings!" Brad greeted Ben, shaking his hand. "It's so good to see you again!"

"Same goes for you," Ben replied, showing Brad to a chair in front of his desk. "Why don't you go ahead and take a seat?"

Brad sat down in one of the chairs, and Ben went around his desk and sat down in his chair. "So," he said. "What pleasure do I have seeing you today?"

"Well," Brad started. "I guess this is my way of apologizing to you for our previous meetings. I, along with the other guys, was tough on you, and in all honesty, really doubted how you would manage the financial crisis that had gone on. However, looking at some of the news reports that were sent down to us, it is evident that we were in the wrong, and with that, I apologize for doubting you."

Ben sat in his chair, nodding his head. He made a slight grunt before saying, "Where are the other two who usually meet with me for the financial reports?"

Brad took a deep sigh. "They were busy." He stopped to collect his thoughts. "Look, Ben. I am sorry for what's happened in the past, but I just can't seem to get them to share the same sentiment."

Ben nodded his head. "Well, it takes a real man to acknowledge his faults. I never thought much of the other two, you know."

Brad sat silent as Ben rose from his chair and made his way to the bar sitting beside the door. Ben opened a bourbon decanter and turned back to Brad, who had turned to face him. "Would you like one? I haven't had a glass of bourbon in a long time."

"Mr. Klimmings," Brad said. "Are you sure you need one?"

Ben slowly put the top back on the decanter. "What's that supposed to mean?"

"Well, it's no secret why you were gone from the company for that week back in the spring. They talked about it down in the financial department for the longest time."

"Go on," Ben said, slowly approaching Brad. "What were they saying?"

"We thought we were going to get a new CFO," Brad continued. "Believe me. I wasn't adding to the rumors. But someone had said that you were constantly drinking and stuff. Then, when we all heard about your wife running out of that dinner . . . some of the people down there thought that you needed to be gone."

"Well, she didn't run out, now did she?" Ben said. He was begin-ning to feel anger building inside him. "Was it them? Were those two old fools part of the discussion?"

Brad stood there, considering how he should respond. Finally, he said, "Yes. Yes, they were."

Ben turned around and took the top off the decanter again. Before pouring a glass, he stopped to say, "You know, if they didn't own a significant portion of company stock, I'd fire their old asses now."

He took the bourbon decanter and poured him a significant portion of bourbon before setting it back down and placing the top back on. Then, without turning to face him, Ben said, "That will be all Brad."

"Mr. Klimmings," Brad pleaded. "Don't let them do this to you. I know . . ."

"Thank you," Ben interrupted before turning back to face Brad. "I'll see you for the next report."

Brad hesitated for a moment. Then he sighed and walked past Ben out the door. As the door closed behind him, Ben turned back to the bar, glaring at the glass of bourbon. An indescribable urge grew within him to take the glass and down the whole thing. It was what he wanted. It was what he needed. He felt as if the bourbon was calling out to him, "*Ben . . . Ben . . .*"

He approached the bar, picking up the glass when he got there. Ben examined the glass for a brief moment before slowly lifting the glass to his lips, the edge of the glass lightly touching his smooth lips.

BEEEEP!!

Nearly dropping the glass out of shear startlement, Ben jolted around to his desk, forcing himself to jump back to reality.

BEEEEP!!

He was being paged on his telephone. He set the glass back down on the bar and made his way over to his desk. He pressed the button to his secretary answering the buzzer. "Yes, Doris."

"I just wanted to check on you, Mr. Klimmings," she said. "Brad left here in quite a hurry, and I wanted to make sure that everything was alright. Did he say anything to you?"

Ben took a deep breath for a moment, his eyes catching the glass of bourbon sitting on the bar. His thoughts rushed back to what occurred moments ago. He had never felt such an urge before, and it had been quite some time since his last taste of bourbon.

"No," he finally said. "Nothing happened in here. We just went over the financial records. That's all."

"Okay, then. Is there anything that you need from me?"

"No, thank you." As he was about to release his finger from the button, his eyes caught ahold of the bourbon sitting on the bar. His urge to drink had dissipated, but he knew that it could return, and the bar sitting in his office wouldn't allow for any decent outcomes.

"Actually," Ben said. "Can you get ahold of some of the other departments and see if they want any of the alcohol from the bar in my office?"

"I can do that, Mr. Klimmings," Doris answered. "Are you sure you want to have the bar removed?"

"Just the alcohol. I want to replace it with something else."

"Okay, sir. Will that be all?"

"Yes, it will be."

He released his finger from the button and made his way over to the bar, picking up the glass of bourbon he had poured earlier. He turned around and noticed one of his potted plants sitting in the corner of the room. He made his way over to the plant and dumped the glass into the pot.

"There you go," Ben said to the plant. "Have a drink!"

* * *

Miranda sat at a table at Finley's. She had a menu in her hand, looking it over, when Delilah took a seat across from her. "Sorry, I'm late. I got caught up in something."

"Oh, that's no problem," Miranda said, setting her menu down. "You're what, five months pregnant now?"

"Six next week," Delilah said, laughing slightly. "It seems like time is flying by!" She put her hands on her baby bump.

"And you and Ben aren't finding out whether it's a boy or a girl?"

"No, we prefer it to be a surprise. But, in all honesty, I'm fine either way."

"That's great!" Miranda said as the waitress came up to the table.

"Hello," the waitress greeted the two. "What can I get you two to drink today?"

"I'll have a water with a lemon," Miranda said to the waitress. Then, the waitress looked at Delilah, signaling her turn to order.

"I'll have the same."

"Alright, two waters with lemon," the waitress said. "I'll be back with those shortly."

As the waitress walked off, Miranda felt her phone buzz in her purse, which was hanging from the back of her chair. She turned, unzipped her bag, and pulled her phone out. She saw that it was a text from Jason and took a moment to read it.

Delilah, curious about what Miranda was reading, tried to get a glance at her phone. "What's wrong?"

"Oh nothing," Miranda replied, putting her phone back into her purse. "It was just a text from Jason."

"Really?" Delilah said, intrigued. "What did he have to say? You two haven't been together for a couple of months now, have you?"

"Well, it's complicated. We've been on a little break for the past couple of months. We just had some disagreements and stuff. Nothing too big, but he just texted and asked if I wanted to grab coffee sometime next week."

"Oh," Delilah said, leaning forward on the table as she began to get more invested in the conversation. "He wants you back, girl. Whatcha going to tell him?"

"I don't know. I've kinda liked being by myself for the past couple of months, but then again, I do want to see him."

"Then do it. It's not going to hurt anything to see him."

"You think?"

"Oh, yes. Just get coffee with him, and see what happens. There's no harm in that."

"Yeah, I guess there's not," Miranda said as the waitress sat their drinks down on the table.

"What are you all hungry for?" the waitress asked them.

Miranda signaled for Delilah to order first. "I'll have the Caesar salad," Delilah said. "Could I get some extra Caesar dressing on it, though?"

"You sure can," the waitress said. "And you, Ms. Klimmings?"

"Honey," Miranda stated. "You don't need to call me Ms. Klimmings. Miranda is just fine." She smiled at the waitress.

"Oh, I'm sorry," the waitress said. "Miranda, have you decided what you would like?"

"I'll have the watercress salad," Miranda said, handing the menu back to the waitress.

"I'll put those in for you two," the waitress responded, taking the menus.

As she walked off, Delilah looked at Miranda and said, "I can't see how you can eat that."

"Really?" Miranda said. "I think it tastes great."

"Blah," Delilah let out, disgusted at the thought of eating watercress salad. "It just sounds gross." She took a sip from her water. When she set the glass down, she noticed Miranda looking around the restaurant.

"Can you believe that the last time we were in this restaurant, it was for your and Ben's anniversary?" Miranda asked her.

"Haha!" Delilah laughed. "I don't think either of us figured that the night would have ended the way it did."

"No, we did not!" Miranda laughed with her. She took a drink from her water. "Do you feel that things have gotten any better between the two families?"

"Eh," Delilah shrugged. "Not really." She took another sip of her water.

Miranda shook her head. "I don't know why my dad and your dad disagree so much."

"It has something to do with some kind of business deal," Delilah said. "Something about Peter purchasing some software for his company and there was some kind of deal made with Dad, and he apparently broke it. There was a lawsuit, and Peter had to pay Dad a large sum of money. After that, the two have always been at each other's throats in the business world."

"Wow. Anytime I've asked Dad about it, he won't speak of it."

"I'm just sharing what my dad told me. Who knows if that's the whole truth or anything?"

The two laughed together. "I feel it best just to let them sort their own issues out," Miranda laughed. "It's better that way!"

"Yes, it is," Delilah agreed. She looked up and saw Clark in the back of the dining room. She smiled as she watched him work. Then she looked at Miranda and realized what would happen when she finally left Ben for Clark, and the smile fell away from her face.

* * *

"Mr. Klimmings," Pam said to Ben, who was standing by her desk. "Mrs. Klimmings had asked me to see if you could contact a couple of former employees of hers to see if they were interested in having their jobs back."

"Yeah," Ben began. "She mentioned that to me. How many does she want me to contact?"

"Three," she answered. "Starting with this James Smith guy. Apparently, he was very upset when she had to let him go."

"Alright," Ben said, picking up a paper with the contact information of the people. "And she's absolutely sure that there's enough money to rehire some of our laid-off people?"

"That's what she told me," Pam said.

Ben grunted and turned to head back into his office. When he reached his desk, he sat down and punched in James' phone number. He heard the phone ringing as he waited for someone to pick up the phone on the other side. "Hello?"

"Hello," Ben began. "Am I speaking with a Mr. James Smith?"

"This is him. Who might I ask is this?"

"I am Ben Klimmings, chief financial officer at Klimmings Incorporated. Our records indicate that a couple of months ago, Mrs. Klimmings had to lay you off due to some budget issues that we were facing here at the company. However, we have recently come into some additional funding, which would allow us to offer you your job back. Would you be interested in that?"

James hesitated to respond. "Well," he started, struggling to get words to come out. "Yes. Yes, I would!"

"Great!" Ben said. "How about you come in sometime next week, and we can get the paperwork together for you to sign and come back to work!"

"Oh, I can't thank you enough! We've been on unemployment the past few months, and it's just been so hard for my wife and three daughters."

"I understand," Ben said. "I'll see you next week!"

"Same goes for you!"

Ben smiled as he hung up the phone. He turned to look out the window behind his desk, taking in the view of the Capitol Building in the distance. As he gazed at the building, his smile only grew more prominent.

"Finally," he said to himself. "We're coming back."

* * *

Doors opened, and Vicki proceeded into a large red room decorated with Chinese flags and various dragons. President Wu sat at a table in the center of the room. The doors closed behind her, leaving only her and the Chinese president alone. "Mrs. Klimmings," he said to her extending his arm, offering a seat to her. "Welcome to China."

"Thank you," Vicki responded, forcing a smile onto her face. From the moment she stepped foot into the room, she felt uneasy about him. Vicki wasn't sure what it was, but something about him just made her feel so uncomfortable.

She took a seat in the chair offered to her. "So," she began. "Let's get this done, shall we?"

"Of course," President Wu said. "First, would you like any tea?"

"No, thank you. I just want to get this signing done."

"Are you sure? I would love to celebrate the start of this venture together."

Vicki hesitated, thinking it over. "Sure. Just one, though."

President Wu made his way over to another table, sitting against a wall. On it, he had a teapot and a couple of teacups. "Would you like sugar in yours?"

"No, thank you," Vicki said. She heard him pouring the tea and then stirring the tea with a spoon.

"I have to have sugar in mine," President Wu said, handing Vicki her teacup and then taking his seat next to her. "I've always liked things so . . . sweet." He winked at her as he took a sip of his tea.

Vicki nervously smiled back, drinking her tea to cover up her nervousness.

"So," she managed to get out. "Do you have the papers?"

"Yes." President Wu pulled out the contract from his jacket pocket.

"Here they are." He set them down on the table and pulled out a pen to sign them. "Would you like to go first?"

"No, you can go ahead," Vicki said, setting her tea down onto the table. "I need to get a pen." She started digging through her bag, trying to find a pen while President Wu went ahead and signed the contract.

"You can use mine if you want," he said, offering his pen to her.

"No," Vicki replied, holding up the pen she had just found. "I found one!"

She took the contract, looked it over, and signed it. "There ya go! The deal is done!"

She put her pen back into her bag and stood up from the chair. She turned to say goodbye to the president, but before she could say anything, she felt his lips meet hers. It all happened so fast. She didn't know what to do. Then, before she even processed what was happening, his tongue made its way into her mouth, and she felt his hand on her right breast.

Disgusted, Vicki pushed him off of her. "WHAT THE HELL?" she shouted, wiping her mouth off onto her arm. "What the hell is wrong with you?"

"I thought you wanted it," President Wu said. "All women want that, don't they?"

"No," Vicki disgustingly said as she grabbed her bags. "God, no!" She turned to leave the room, and the entire room moved with her. She closed her eyes, trying to recollect herself. Everything around her felt like it was spinning, and keeping her balance was becoming more and more difficult. Then, she tried to make her way to the door, stumbling over herself. She crashed to the floor, causing a thumping sound to echo in the room.

"Ah," President Wu sighed, approaching her. "It's working!"

"Whadid chu do?" Vicki asked, noticing her speech beginning to slur.

"Just be still," he responded. "Let it take effect."

Vicki, unable to fully concentrate now, began to panic. "Oh muh God," she managed to let out. "I need to get outta here."

She managed to pull herself up and make her way to the door, stumbling on the way and flinging it open. On the other side stood two men who had come with her on the trip.

"Help!" she called out. "I need help!"

CHAPTER 7
THE CHINA EFFECT

Jeremy sat in his chair watching the news on the TV. The news anchor was speaking on the recovering economy, presenting information supporting Peter Klimmings' policies enacted during his time in office.

"I don't want to listen to this crap," he muttered to himself. He searched around him for the remote to the TV and began flipping through the channels. "What was the name of that conservative channel again?"

As he flipped through the channels, his cell phone began ringing. Jeremy looked for it before finding it lying on the end table next to him. "Hello," he answered, irritated.

"Jeremy?" a voice said on the other line. "This is President Wu."

"Wu!" Jeremy exclaimed, sitting up in the chair. "Why are you calling me?! Don't you know Peter probably has the NSA listening in on everything I do?"

"Well, that may not be your only problem," the Chinese president said on the other end. "Vicki Klimmings met with me yesterday, and it didn't go as I had intended it to."

"Wu, if you didn't get those papers signed . . ."

"Oh, I got them signed . . ." President Wu grew silent on the other end. " . . . it's what happened afterward that I'm trying to tell you about."

"What happened?" Jeremy asked, growing more irritated as President Wu continued to draw out the conversation. "Tell me, Wu."

"Well, she wanted some tea, and so I gave her some. When I gave her the tea, I put in something to help relax her, and then I kissed her."

"Dammit, Wu! You drugged her?!"

"Who's drugging who?" Jeremy heard Cathie call out from the other end of the house. He quickly remembered that he wasn't alone and needed to quiet his voice before anyone else heard about his plan.

"No one, honey," he shouted back to her.

"I did not," President Wu defended himself. "She seemed very uneasy about the whole thing, and so I gave her something to help calm her nerves."

"That's called drugging her, you moron!" Jeremy whispered into the phone, frustrated. "Why'd you kiss her? What the hell was the point in doing that?"

"I thought she wanted it."

"Wu, just because someone is a woman, doesn't that she wants to have sex with you! You have jeopardized this entire thing!"

Silence filled the phone. "I did get the contract signed," President Wu said. "At least we have that."

"That could be our only saving grace."

* * *

Gabby approached her locker at school, spinning the lock to the appropriate numbers to unlock it. A blond girl with slightly curly hair came to her locker. "What's up, Gabs?" she said, leaning against the locker next to Gabby's.

Gabby gave her a slight glare before opening her locker. "Oh, just the same ole stuff, I guess," Gabby replied. "You?"

"Well," the girl said. "Other than counting down the days until graduation, not much."

"Michelle, we just started school a couple of weeks ago."

"So," Michelle smirked. "Aren't you ready to get out of high school hell?"

"Somedays . . ." Gabby said. "Somedays, I think to myself that I want to get out of here, but then on other days, I think to myself that maybe I'm not ready to leave just yet. After all, what's after this? College? Work?"

"Ummm . . . after this is college, but with parties, drinking . . . boys." Michelle leaned in, nudging Gabby, who continued to get things out of her locker.

"Speaking of parties," Michelle continued. "I have the perfect plan for your eighteenth birthday!"

"What is it?"

"Well, you know that club over on Maple? Well, we're going to hit it up!"

"Really?" Gabby said intriguingly. "That's the newest one in the city!"

"I know, and I got Dana a fake ID so she can come along. We're going to have a blast!"

Gabby sighed. "I forgot. Mom and Dad want to do something special for my birthday on Thursday."

Michelle shrugged her shoulders, brushing off what Gabby had just told her. "We'll just go afterward. That place doesn't close until three or four in the morning."

"Bet!" Gabby exclaimed. "Oh, we're going now!"

"Yes! That's what I'm talking about!" The bell rang in the background, signaling that the school day was about to begin, so the two began to head to their classes. Michelle turned around and shouted down the hallway. "I'll see you at lunch."

"Yes," Gabby called back. "See you later today!"

* * *

The door opened, and Vicki stepped into the entry hall of The Klimmings Mansion. The sound of pouring rain echoed down the hallway as she turned back to check on Denise, who was carrying her bags. As soon as Denise made it inside, Vicki closed the door, cutting off the sound of the rain.

"Oh, that's cold!" Denise stated as she shook off in the entryway. "Do you want your bags upstairs, Mrs. Klimmings?"

"No," Vicki said without making eye contact with her. "You can leave them down here for now so that they can dry."

"Well, would you like for me to put on a pot of tea?" Denise asked her. "Or coffee?"

"No, I think I'm just going to head upstairs to my bedroom for now." Vicki turned her head slightly to make eye contact with Denise. "I'm rather tired from my flight."

"I understand. I'll leave you be then." Denise turned and made her way into the kitchen to prepare the night's dinner. After she left, Vicki proceeded down the hallway, turning through the second archway on the left. Then, she proceeded up the stairs, entering her bedroom opposite the stairwell on the right.

Closing the door behind her, Vicki stood silent in her room, taking a deep sigh. Then she made her way over to the bathroom, turning on the lights and looking at herself in the mirror. Soon the flashback started, and everything that had happened during her encounter with President Wu played back in her mind.

Tears welled up in her eyes before they broke loose, streaming down her face. As she cried, she remembered opening the door and the two associates helping her escape. When asked about what had happened, she never told them about the incident but let them believe she had some kind of episode during her meeting.

She took a tissue from the tissue box sitting on the bathroom sink counter and wiped the tears from her face. Then she left the bathroom and took off her shoes before climbing into bed to take a nap.

* * *

Miranda opened the door to the George and Jefferson Coffee Shop in downtown D.C. As soon as she stepped into the shop, she spotted Jason sitting at a table, waiting on her. He stood up when she came over to him. "I'm so glad to see you," he said to her, pulling a chair out for her. "It's been so long."

Miranda took a seat, followed by Jason. For a moment, they just stared at each other, not knowing what to say.

"Jason," Miranda began. "I'm glad we were able to finally meet. I know it's been a couple of months since we last saw each other, but I do think that this has been what's best for our relationship."

"I agree," he said. "It's really shown me just how much I miss you."

Miranda smiled. A barista made her way to the table and placed two coffees on the table. After they walked away, Miranda examined the cup sitting in front of her. "Did you order for me?"

"Yes," Jason confessed. "I hope that's okay. I ordered your favorite."

"Raspberry mocha latte?"

"That's it. You didn't think that I had forgotten, did you?"

Miranda laughed before she took a sip of her coffee. She loved the raspberry taste. As she set the coffee back down on the table, she turned her attention back to Jason. "So, why did you want to have coffee today?"

"Well," he began. "In all honesty, I've missed you. When I look back at before, I realize just how much I screwed up."

"Yeah, you were a little apprehensive there at the end."

"And I realize that, and I just can't let myself be that way to you again. You mean so much to me." He reached out and took her hand. "Miranda, what do you think?"

Miranda contemplated her decision. Her eyes shifted from his face to her hand and then to her coffee while she considered what she would tell Jason. Then, finally, she said, "Jason, my family is having a little dinner tonight for Gabby's eighteenth birthday. I would love it if you could attend."

A smile crept across Jason's face. "Really?"

"Yes, I mean it. I would love for you to come over tonight."

"Count me in!"

* * *

"Mr. President, the speaker of the House is here to see you."

"Send her in," Peter said to Martha, who was standing in the doorway to the Oval Office. He was next to one of the sofas that sat in the room. Then, he looked over at Constance, sitting on the sofa next to him.

"God, help us," he whispered to her. Constance smirked before taking a sip of her tea and then placing it back on the coffee table. The door opened, and a woman stepped in. She was tall, slender, and had a head full of gorgeous red hair.

"President Klimmings," she said in a honeyed way. "I'm so glad to have this meeting with you on this gorgeous Thursday morning."

"Same goes for me," Peter lied, extending his hand to shake hers.

"Well, well, well," the lady said, ignoring Peter's offer. "I see I also have the company of the vice president today too. Lucky me!"

"Speaker White," Constance said, standing from the sofa. "Why don't you take a seat over here." She directed the speaker across from her.

"Oh, please!" she responded. "Call me Rebecca! I'm sure I've been called all sorts of things." Peter and Constance exchanged looks as Rebecca sat down on the sofa, tucking her yellow business dress behind her legs. "Peter, I hope you don't mind me addressing you by your first name, but I just hate official titles."

Peter laughed as he sat in a chair perpendicular to the two women. "Don't we all?"

"Well," Rebecca continued. "I wanted to speak with you today about our country's tax system. It has been a priority of the Republican Party for some time to overhaul the tax code in the United States. However, as we were looking through the current policies and agreements, we found something that could be a bit . . . troubling."

Rebecca stopped for a minute, glaring at Peter. "What is it, Rebecca?" he asked.

"Well," she continued before picking up Constance's teacup and taking a drink from it, causing Constance to turn toward Peter in disgust. "We looked at the tax codes with other countries, and when we looked at the United Kingdom's tax policies, we noticed something irregular with one of our nation's companies." She turned to look back at Peter. As she waited for an answer, she set the teacup back on the coffee table in front of Constance.

"Which company would that be?" asked Constance, breaking the tension between the two.

"Applegate Technology."

"Well, that's weird," Peter began. "That had to have been implemented before I took office."

"Except that it didn't. In fact, this particular deal didn't take effect until last year as part of an Executive Order." Rebecca continued to glare at Peter. "What was this for?"

Peter's mind raced as he tried to develop some kind of fib. He struggled to clear his thinking and get the words from Rebecca out of his mind. He just couldn't get past that fake tone of voice she spoke in.

"I'm sure there was some reason for it," Constance said. "Do you really expect him to remember every single thing he signed into law? Do *you* remember everything that you pass in the House?"

"No," Rebecca answered. "But I'm not the president, am I?"

"No, you certainly aren't," Peter replied. "And reasons for what I decide to pass and what I choose not to pass are entirely my own."

Rebecca looked at Peter, trying to see past what he was putting forward. "Well, I guess it is time for me to leave then." She stood up from the sofa and made her way to the door.

"Thank you for having me today, Peter," she turned to say before leaving. "It's such an honor to have been here today."

"That's Mr. President," Peter corrected her, standing from his chair and adjusting his suit jacket.

"Hmm," Rebecca smirked before opening the door and leaving the Oval Office.

"What the hell was all that about?" Constance asked as soon as the door latched behind Rebecca.

"That bitch is up to something."

"Well, I could tell. What was the deal with the tax code against Applegate Technology? Do you remember signing that Executive Order?"

"No," Peter lied. "I do not, but I am sure that I had sufficient reasoning for it, though. I would never do anything to hurt one of our country's own companies."

"The Peter Klimmings I know wouldn't do that. I'm just afraid of how she will paint this to the media. You know there's a whole crew out there that's waiting for her to speak with them."

"I know. We need to be more careful around her."

Constance turned her attention back to the coffee table, gazing at her cup of tea. "We also need to watch our drinks around her."

"We do?"

Constance reached down and picked up the teacup. "She took a drink out of my tea."

* * *

Vicki stepped into the kitchen and saw Denise working hard at cooking Gabby's birthday dinner. Denise had been preparing a large pot roast with corn, green beans, and mashed potatoes. A large birthday cake sat on the island for later that evening. After all she'd been through, Vicki had forgotten that Gabby's birthday dinner was that evening.

"Here," Vicki said, grabbing an apron and putting it on. "Let me help you with this." She went over and checked on the vegetables cooking on the stovetop.

"Mrs. Klimmings," Denise said. "You don't have to help. I've got this."

"Oh, no, no, no!" Vicki insisted. "I want to help. After all, it is my youngest daughter's eighteenth birthday." Vicki continued to help Denise when her phone began ringing. She quickly wiped her hands off on her apron and answered her phone.

"Vicki," Peter said on the other line. "I am running a little bit behind. It may be after six-thirty before I make it home."

"Okay," Vicki replied. "But you're going to need to be the one to explain it to Gabby."

"Oh, I know. She'll be okay, though."

"Yeah. You're her favorite anyway, so I wouldn't worry too much about it."

"Vicki, she doesn't have a favorite. She's just going through that usual teenage crap. Ben and Miranda did the same thing when they were her age."

"Yes, but they weren't as bad as she is."

Vicki turned around to make sure no one besides Denise was listening. "Do try to make it home soon. You know how Gabby gets."

"I will," Peter said. "Love you."

"I love you too. Bye."

Vicki ended the call and set it on the kitchen island. "Is Mr. Klimmings going to be late?" Denise asked as Vicki went to check on the food.

"Yes, but he shouldn't be too long. If you've got this, I am going to go ahead and go get changed for tonight."

"Oh, yes. I've got this."

"Alright, I'll be back in a bit."

Vicki took off the apron, placing it back where she had found it. She stepped out of the kitchen across the hall to the dining room, where she saw the eloquent setup for Gabby's dinner. She smiled and then stepped out into the entry hall, heading toward the staircase.

"Mom!"

Vicki stopped in her tracks and turned toward the front door. She saw Ben standing in the front entryway, closing up his umbrella.

"Will it ever stop raining?" Ben said as he shook off his umbrella and placed it in the umbrella holder.

"Benjamin!" Vicki exclaimed. "I'm so glad you made it!"

"Why wouldn't I? It's my baby sister's eighteenth birthday, after all."

"Well, I just hadn't heard anything. Come here and give me a hug." She leaned in, hugging him tightly. "Where's Delilah? Is she coming later?"

"Yes, she'll be by in a little bit."

"Good. I want to see her and check in on my grandchild."

"Her baby bump sure is growing."

"Good!" Vicki said. "I need to run upstairs to change. You just make yourself comfy down here until then!"

Vicki turned back down the entry hall and made a left to take the stairs. As she made her way upstairs, Miranda began her descent down the stairs. She took a left at the bottom and stepped into the living room, where Ben had taken a seat on the sofa. "Miranda!" he said, smiling. "I was just about to catch the news."

"Let me know what's interesting," Miranda said, making her way over to the bar. "Is there anything I could get you?"

"No, I'm good." The TV was consuming Ben's attention. The news anchor was discussing some story about Peter.

"So," Miranda began. "I saw Jason today."

"Oh, really?" Ben said. His focus was still fixated on the TV. "And how'd that go?"

"I would say that it was pretty well. In fact, he is coming over to have dinner with us tonight."

"Mmmh."

"Ben, did you not hear me?"

Ben took his attention off the TV and turned to Miranda. "I'm sorry. What did you say?"

"I said that Jason is going to join us for Gabby's dinner tonight."

"That's fantastic!" Ben said before pointing to the television. "That woman that Dad hates is on the news right now!"

Miranda, holding a glass of white wine in her hand, rolled her eyes and then turned her attention to the TV, where she saw Rebecca White standing outside the White House. She was at a podium with a plethora of microphones attached to it. A slew of reporters were behind the cameras, each wanting to as their questions.

"I would say that my meeting with the president was . . . counterproductive," Rebecca said on the TV. "In fact, every time I asked him something, he didn't seem to understand what was being asked."

"Speaker White!" one of the reporters called out. "Do you believe that the president has some kind of cognitive issue right now?"

"Oh, I wouldn't call it an issue just yet," she said. "But if I were him, I might go get checked out by the White House doctor." She winked at the camera before heading down the drive to the Capitol Police members standing by her car. The news anchor began talking about signs of dementia and other cognitive diseases. Then, the TV turned off.

"Now I understand why Dad hates her so much," Miranda said as she took a drink of her white wine. "How would he have dementia? He's only fifty-seven, fifty-eight?"

"He's fifty-eight," said Ben, grinning. He stood up and made his way over to the bar. After examining the drinks, he took seltzer water and poured it into a glass with some ice. Once done, he turned back to Miranda. "Have you ever thought that maybe Dad made a mistake running for office?"

Miranda looked back at him. "I hadn't ever thought about that. Why do you mention it now?"

"Well," Ben began, taking a seat back on the sofa with his seltzer water. "It just seems like so many things have gotten more complicated since he ran. The stock shares in the company are all jacked up, things with China aren't the best that they could be, and now he's got this woman on his back, making him seem like he is incompetent and that he doesn't know what he's doing."

"Ben," Miranda sighed. "People have been trying to make him look incompetent for years now. Heck, we did that all the time as kids."

"Yes, but that's different. Now he's got all kinds of people after him."

"But that's what he signed up for. He decided to run after the last president implemented all those new regulations, costing Klimmings Incorporated millions. He came home every day cussing and throwing a fit."

"Then he had enough and just said, 'To hell with this! I'm running for president.'"

"Exactly!" Miranda took another sip of her wine. "Has he made it any better?"

"You know, I don't know," said Ben. He laughed and took a drink of his seltzer water. "The recession and cutbacks haven't allowed anyone to see the positive effects of his policies."

"That's not good," Miranda said, shaking her head. "You know, I saw a poll last week on TV about the midterm elections coming up in November. They don't have Democrats fairing very well at all."

"No, they don't. I think Dad is going to be facing a Republican House and Senate in the next two years of his first term."

"Won't that make it a lot harder for him to get re-elected?"

"Yes. He won't be able to get anything done that he wants, and he'll have to convince the American people to give him another four years."

"Oh no," Miranda sighed. "I would hate to see him lose."

"Me too."

Miranda took another sip of her white wine as Vicki turned the corner by the stairs. "Well, I see you two have made yourselves comfortable!" she said. "What are we talking about in here?"

"Oh, just about Rebecca White," said Miranda before taking another sip of her wine.

"Don't talk about her around your dad," Vicki warned them. "He could go on about her for the entire night!"

* * *

"Do I look good in this?"

Delilah turned to face Clark, who still lay on the bed in his boxers. She was wearing a sparkling black dress that went to her knees.

"I think I would go with something other than black," he said. "This is just an eighteenth birthday party and not a funeral."

"I feel like this should be a funeral," Delilah muttered. "I don't know when the next family get-together will be my last."

Clark laughed from the bed as Delilah frantically changed into another dress. It was also sparkling, lined with sequin, but was silver and longer. "How about this one?"

"I like it," Clark said, sitting up on the bed. "How many maternity dresses do you have anyway?"

"Three. I figured that would be enough to get me through until the baby is born."

She turned back into the closet and found a purse that matched her dress. After she closed the closet door, Clark met her by the doorway to the bedroom. "I wish I could go with you."

"Yeah, and I wish I didn't have to go."

She leaned in and kissed him.

"But," she continued. "I'm running late, and I really have to go!"

"Text me when it's over," he said to her as she started down the hallway into the living room.

"I will. And you probably want to get some things together and head out yourself. I don't know if Ben is stopping by here or not."

"You just try to have some fun," Clark said back to her. "I'll be alright."

"Thanks, babe!"

The door closed behind Delilah as she left the house, leaving Clark alone in the bedroom. He took a deep sigh before he started scrounging around the room, collecting his clothes. He slipped on his pants and shirt before continuing his search for his socks. He promptly found one and put it on.

Scanning the room, Clark took a moment on the bed. *Where could it be? I had all my clothes in here.* He got down on his hands and knees and looked under the bed. Nothing. He looked under the bedside tables. Nothing. He even made his way over to the closet to see if it had managed to crawl over into the depths of Delilah's assortment of shoes. Nothing.

Frustrated, Clark stormed out of the room and down the hallway, closing the door behind him. He slipped on his shoes in the living room and exited the house, locking the door as he left. Then, he got into his car and started it. But, before leaving the townhouse, Clark pulled out his cellphone and sent Delilah a text saying: *Left a sock at the house. Couldn't find it.*

He sent the text, threw his phone in the passenger seat, and drove off quickly so that the neighbors didn't decide to start asking questions.

Back inside the house, a phone dinged and lit up, displaying Clark's text message. Delilah had accidentally left her phone at home.

* * *

Ben, Miranda, Vicki, and Gabby continued chatting in the living room. Gabby was explaining to her family about the plans she had later with her friends.

"Dana and Michelle are going to pick me up, and then we are going to go to that new club that's on Maple Street! I've heard it's like, the hottest place in town!"

"Wow!" Miranda said enthusiastically. "I haven't been to that one yet. You'll have to let me know if it's any good!"

Miranda looked over at Vicki, who didn't seem very approving of the entire plan.

"Well," Vicki began. "When I turned eighteen, *I* just had a big party with my friends, and we all stayed the night and watched a bunch of scary movies."

"That also sounds like fun!" Miranda said. "Maybe you could just have Michelle and . . . what's-her-name stay over tonight? I mean, you all do have school tomorrow, right?"

"No," Gabby insisted. "I want to be able to do the things that I want on my birthday."

"It was just a suggestion. Don't get all testy with me."

"I'm sorry. It's just, for once, I want to be able to do something that I want to do. I've already instructed the Secret Service to stop their constant following of me."

"You what?!" Vicki interrupted, setting her glass of white wine onto the coffee table. "You did what?!"

"I told you and Dad last week that I didn't want them around me anymore. And so, first thing this morning, I instructed them to stop following me and looking after me. I'm a grown woman now, and I can take care of myself."

Miranda quickly turned her attention to Ben, who, along with herself, tried diligently to mask their laughter at Gabby's statement. Finally, Vicki noticed the two and opened her mouth to say something, but the two chimes of the doorbell coming from the entry hall interrupted her.

"Who can that be?" asked Vicki.

Miranda stepped through the archway into the entry hall, taking a right to the front door. The rest of the family in the living room heard the door open, and Miranda call out, "I'm so glad you came!"

In a matter of seconds, Miranda appeared in the archway with Jason. "I'm not sure you all have met Jason yet," she addressed the family. "But, here he is!"

"Well, Jason," Vicki said, approaching him. "I've heard so much about you! I'm so glad to have finally met you!"

"It's also my pleasure, Mrs. Klimmings," said Jason. He could feel his hands quivering, and his cheeks reddened. He glanced over to Miranda, who gave him a nod of approval back.

"Oh, call me Vicki," Vicki corrected him. "Any friend of Miranda's is a part of the family! Jason, why don't you go on ahead and make yourself comfortable in the living room."

He looked at Miranda, who nodded slightly again, before making his way into the living room and conversing with Ben and Gabby. Vicki and Miranda stayed back in the entry hall.

"You landed yourself a real looker," Vicki whispered to Miranda.

"Thanks, Mom," Miranda blushed. "If I'm being honest, I can really see something happening between him and me."

"Well, he is the first man you've brought over in a while! Where'd you two meet again?"

"He worked for the city, and I ran into him when I had to drop off some documents for something."

Before Vicki could add anything, the door opened, and Peter slogged in with an inside-out umbrella. "Damn thing couldn't take the wind," he griped before tossing the umbrella down on the floor. "Now, I'm all soaked."

"You got that soaked from the walk to the house?" Miranda asked as Vicki tried to hold back laughter.

"Have you not seen how bad it's raining?" Peter said. "I half-expected to see Noah sailing down the Potomac on my way home."

By this point, Vicki could hold it in no longer. She chuckled aloud and moved into the living room before Peter could retaliate with some snarky remark.

"Is dinner ready?" Peter asked as he made his way into the living room, his shoes squeaking with every step he took.

"Well," Vicki said. "Everyone is here, except for Delilah. Ben, have you heard anything from her?"

"No," he answered. "But it is already seven, so let's just go ahead and eat. She won't be too upset that we started without her."

"If she's that upset," Peter said. "Maybe it'd teach her to get her ass in gear next time."

"Peter," Vicki sighed. "She's pregnant, you know."

"I don't give a damn. I'm the freaking president of the United States, and I got here when I said I would be."

"You were late, though."

"Yes, and I told you I was going to be late. I said that I was going to be home after six-thirty, and here it is . . . after six-thirty."

"Okay," Miranda said, breaking up the two. "I think someone is a little hangry. Let's just go ahead and sit down."

The family moved into the dining room and took their seats at the dining room table. Peter took his usual seat in front of the fireplace at the head of the long dining room table. To his left sat Miranda, with Jason sitting beside her. To his right sat Ben. Vicki sat at the other end of the table, and Gabby was to her left.

"Will this be all of you?" asked Denise after they all sat down.

"No," Peter answered her. "My slow daughter-in-law hasn't arrived yet, so leave a place for her."

Denise nodded and stepped out of the dining room, leaving the family to have their meal together. Jason looked over the pot roast, corn, green beans, and mashed potatoes lining the table. "Wow," he said. "This all looks so good."

"Yes, it does," Peter said. He looked at Jason and then back at the food before taking a double-take. "Who the hell are you anyway?"

"Dad," Miranda said. "This is Jason. He and I have been seeing each other for a while, and I thought that tonight would be a good time to introduce him to you all."

"What the crap?!"

Everyone seated at the table turned to the archway to the entry hall. Delilah stood there in her sparkling silver dress, accenting her baby bump. "You all couldn't wait on me?!"

She made her way over to the empty chair next to Ben and plopped down in it, taking her heels off and tossing them behind her.

"Why I decided to wear heels, I don't know," she said before she started helping herself to the mashed potatoes. Other family members began divvying out servings and passing the food around. Once everyone had food on their plates, they all began to eat.

"Oh my God," Jason said after taking a bite of the pot roast. "This tastes so good, and it's so juicy!"

"You can thank Denise for that," Vicki said. "She is our best cook in the house."

"We would be lost without her," Miranda chimed in. "She literally does everything that we need."

"She really does!" Ben said. "She is the best maid that we've ever had. I wish she'd come over to our house. What are you paying her, Dad?"

"Benjamin!" Vicki exclaimed. "You don't ask people that! You should know better!"

"He obviously didn't know better when he got me pregnant," Delilah muttered before plopping mashed potatoes into her mouth.

Gabby, who had hardly touched any of her food on her plate, snuck her phone out and checked it stealthily.

"Gabriella," Vicki said, noticing her daughter checking her phone. "You know the rules. No phones at the table."

"Sorry, Mom," she said. "It's just that Michelle and Dana are on their way over, so I need to leave soon."

"Gabby," Miranda said. "You haven't even touched your food yet. Denise and Mom have worked so hard for this."

"I know, but I want to be able to do what I want on my birthday."

"Just go," Peter chimed in. "If you want to leave with your friends, then go. We aren't going to hold you here if you'd rather be with them."

Gabby looked at her phone again before saying, "Thank you! They just texted and said that they are here!" She ran over and hugged Peter before running out of the dining room to the front door.

"She didn't even see her birthday cake," Vicki said as the sound of the door shut behind them.

"I'm sorry," Peter said. "She wouldn't have had a good time here if we made her stay any longer."

"But we had this scheduled! The least she could have done was stay here and pretend like she enjoyed it!"

Vicki rose from her seat and stormed out of the room, heading to the staircase and proceeding upstairs.

Peter sighed at the table as the rest of the family continued to eat awkwardly.

* * *

Vicki plopped down on the bed, taking off her heels and tossing them onto the floor. Tears flowed down her face as she sat alone in the bedroom. All she wanted was for Gabby to enjoy her birthday, but a knock at the door interrupted her self-loathing session.

"Mom," Miranda's voice called out from behind the door. "Are you in there?"

"Yes," Vicki said, trying to wipe all the tears off of her face. "Come on in."

The door opened, and Miranda stepped into the room. She instantly noticed the tears streaked down Vicki's face. "Mom," Miranda sighed. "Why are you letting this get to you so much?"

"It's not just that," Vicki said. "I mean . . . yeah, it's part of it, but there are other things too."

"Don't let Gabby get to you so much," Miranda said. "She's just being a spoiled little brat. So what?"

"But I feel like it's all my fault," Vicki cried. "I helped make her the way she is."

"No, you did not. Dad did."

"It's not his fault."

"Uh . . . yeah, it is. Have you not seen how he caters to her all the time? It's always the same with the youngest. They're always catered to. If you don't believe me, look at Delilah. Her parents catered to her when she was younger, and she still acts like the world owes her everything."

"Yeah. I guess you're right, but like I said, other things are bothering me."

"Like what?"

"I don't want to talk about it."

Vicki turned her attention away from Miranda.

"You never mentioned how your trip to China went," Miranda said, attempting to change the subject. "How was it? Did you get the deal finalized?"

Suddenly it all came back to Vicki. Her mind went back to her encounter with President Wu and how he had slipped something in her drink, how he kissed her, and how he had touched her breasts. Then, unable to control her emotions, her eyes were overrun with tears. "I don't want to talk about it."

"Mom," Miranda said, concerned. "What happened?"

She knelt in front of Vicki, trying to get an answer. "I don't want to talk about it," Vicki insisted.

"Something happened. What was it?"

Vicki looked at a picture on the nightstand and then back at Miranda. She tried her best to recollect herself. "President Wu," Vicki began, trying to speak between sobs. "President Wu . . . he . . . he . . ."

"Yes," Miranda interrupted. "What did he do?"

"He touched me."

"He touched you?!"

"He slipped something in my drink too, and then I got away. He couldn't do anything because I made it to the door."

"And what happened then?"

"My associates that were there got me help."

"And why haven't they said anything about it yet?"

"They thought I had some kind of medical emergency. I told them I was fine, and we left right afterward."

Vicki cried some more, and Miranda attempted to comfort her mother. She was shocked by what Vicki had just said.

"You've got to tell Dad," Miranda insisted.

"No," Vicki said. "I can't do that to him. He's got enough on his plate right now."

"You *have* to tell him. If you don't, then I will. This is too serious!"

"But what is he going to think of me? It's all my fault. I shouldn't have gone there alone."

"It is not your fault, Mom," Miranda stated. "You couldn't have known that he was going to do this. Just because he's a world leader doesn't give him the right to do whatever he wants. Dad will make sure that he receives some justice."

Vicki let a small smile show on her face.

"I'm going to go tell Dad that he needs to speak with you," Miranda said. "And then I'm going to mention to the rest of the family that it is time to go."

"Okay," Vicki said calmly, recollecting herself and figuring out how she would tell Peter about this.

"Mom, you can do this," Miranda said before heading to the door. She stopped and turned back to Vicki. "I love you, Mom."

"And I love you too, Miranda. Thank you."

Miranda exited the room and headed downstairs. She rounded the corner into the living room. Peter, Ben, Delilah, and Jason were all seated in the room, conversing and having drinks.

"Dad," Miranda said, interrupting them. "Mom needs to talk to you."

"If she's going to bitch to me about dinner . . ."

"Just shut up and get up there and talk to her!"

The entire room went silent. Miranda rarely raised her voice to her father, so Peter knew that this must be something serious. He rose from his chair and set his Scotch down on the coffee table.

"Well," he said. "I guess I'll go see what she needs then." He walked past her without making eye contact and proceeded to make his way up the stairs.

"Miranda!" Ben whispered. "Are you out of your mind? Nobody ever speaks to Dad like that!"

"No," Miranda said. "Trust me. I'm not."

"Then what happened up there?" asked Delilah with her ginger ale in her hand.

"I can't say," Miranda said. "But I do think that you all should leave now."

"Really?" Ben said. "This must be bad then. What did Mom do?"

"Just leave, Ben! C'mon, Jason. We need to go too."

"Alright," he said, rising from the sofa. "Where do you want me to put this?" He held up his glass of bourbon.

"Just put it on the table," Miranda said. "Denise'll take care of it."

Ben and Delilah left the room first, followed by Jason and Miranda. Ben opened the front door for them, allowing the cool September air to flood into the entry hall. The rain had ceased, but the clouds still covered the stars and the moon. They all made their way to their cars, and as Delilah and Ben took off, Miranda opened the door to Jason's black car.

"Well," he began. "I guess this is goodnight."

"Yes," Miranda said as Jason took a seat in his car. "I hate that this is how you got to meet my family."

"Oh, don't worry about it. It seems to me like your family is just like every other family in America."

"Really? I feel like sometimes we're a little bit extra."

"Okay, I wasn't going to say it, but now that you brought it up . . ."

The two chuckled together. "I had a really nice night," Miranda said.

"Me too."

"Goodnight, Jason."

"Goodnight, Miranda."

Jason closed the door and started up his car. He slowly pulled away and drove down the driveway, entering the small highway that ran in front of the Klimmings Mansion, and drove off.

Miranda looked up to the second floor of the mansion and saw the lights on in her parents' bedroom. She couldn't help but wonder how things were going up there. Goosebumps grew on her arms and legs as a cool breeze collided with her skin. She shivered and made her way back inside the mansion.

* * *

Peter stepped into his bedroom doorway, seeing Vicki seated on the bed. "What's wrong?" he asked her, but she remained silent. Peter took a step inside and closed the door behind him. "I'm sorry about letting Gabby leave early. I shouldn't have done that. I should have made her stay."

"Thank you," Vicki finally said. "But that's not what I needed to speak with you about."

"Then what is it?"

Peter took a seat next to Vicki on the bed, but she stood up and made her way to the fireplace located across from the foot of their bed. A TV hung on the wall above the fireplace, and Vicki could see Peter's reflection through its screen.

"It has to do with China," she said, feeling the heat of the fire press against her skin.

"China? Did something happen with the deal or something?"

"No . . . and yes."

Vicki turned to face Peter. "I should have listened to you when you suggested bringing Benjamin with me."

"Why do you say that?"

Vicki turned to face the fireplace. The heat pressed against her.

"Vicki," Peter said, standing up. "What happened?"

She turned to face Peter again. Tears streamed down her face. "President Wu . . . he . . . uh . . . he kissed me."

"He *what*?!"

"Then he touched my breasts. I . . . I . . . pushed him away . . . but he drugged me."

"Oh my God," Peter said, sitting back down on the bed. "That bastard!"

"I felt so disoriented, and I was slurring my words," Vicki continued. "I couldn't figure out what to do or how to tell you."

Rage boiled and grew inside Peter. He stood up from the bed and headed to the door.

"Where are you going?" Vicki cried. "Don't leave me, Peter. It wasn't my fault."

"No, it wasn't," he said, turning to her. "It was my fault. How dare I put you in that position. It's never going to happen again."

"Peter, it wasn't your fault."

"Yes, it was, and dammit, this is never going to happen again."

He stormed out of the room and began heading down the stairs.

"Where are you going?" Vicki cried out, trying to follow him.

"I'll be back," he hollered. "I've got a piece of shit to take care of."

CHAPTER 8

OPPROBRIUM

"President Klimmings made an unannounced trip to China yesterday," a news anchor said on the TV. "The White House says that the president decided to go on a tour of Asian countries in an attempt to strengthen relations between those countries and the United States. However, the governments of Japan, South Korea, and Thailand have stated that no plans have been made for the president to visit."

Ben turned off the TV and set the remote down on the couch. He ran his hands up his face and through his hair, trying to wake himself fully. He grabbed his cellphone and looked at the time. It was a little after ten in the morning.

He stood up from the couch and made his way into the kitchen. The fragrant smell of coffee filled the room. After grabbing a coffee mug from one of the cabinets, he poured himself a cup of rich, dark coffee. He took a sip and headed back into the living room.

Before he could sit back down on the couch, he heard a phone ding and, out of the corner of his eye, caught a small light. He shifted his attention over to the source, and his eyes fell on Delilah's phone. It was lodged between the cushions of a chair sitting to the left of the couch.

Ben turned around, peering down the hallway leading into his bedroom. Delilah was still asleep. Quietly, he pulled the phone out of the chair and looked at the screen. He noticed a text message from someone named Clark. Immediately, Ben's mind began racing with various thoughts, but before he could unlock the phone to look at the message, he heard a creak from the hallway behind him.

Startled, Ben jolted around, almost spilling his coffee in the process.

"Oh," Delilah said from the hallway. "Did I startle you?"

"Just about," Ben said, holding the phone out. "I found your phone."

"My phone!" Delilah took the phone from Ben. "I lost it before the dinner last night. Where was it?"

"It was between the cushions on this chair."

"Thank you so much, Ben!"

Delilah went into the kitchen to pour herself some coffee. While there, she continued talking to Ben, but he wasn't paying any attention to her. Instead, his mind was flooded with different scenarios and explanations for who Clark was.

* * *

"I just got off the phone with Dad," Miranda said, coming into the living room and sitting on the sofa next to Vicki. "He said that he still hasn't seen President Wu."

"How long is he going to keep putting him off?" Vicki asked. "He's been over there since yesterday."

"He said that he's going to meet with him whether President Wu likes it or not."

"Good luck with that."

Miranda sighed. "Mom, why did you wait so long before saying anything?"

"Miranda," Vicki said as she took the remote to the TV and flipped through some channels. "I don't want to talk about it."

She stopped on one of the news channels. The news anchors were talking about the Klimmings family when the camera cut to an interview with some guy.

"Mom," Miranda said. "Turn this up."

Vicki turned the volume up on the TV, and the two listened intently to what this man said.

" . . . and then afterward I took her to some house," the man said. "She said it was her friend's house, and that was it."

The camera cut back to the news anchors. "No word yet from the Klimmings family," said one of the anchors.

"Can you blame them?" the other anchor asked. "Their daughter just turned eighteen, and now they have this little scandal to go along with it."

"What are they talking about?" Vicki said to Miranda.

"I'm checking," Miranda responded as she scrolled through the news on her phone. "Oh no."

"What?"

"That guy is everywhere saying that he slept with Gabby on the night of her eighteenth birthday."

"You're kidding me!"

Vicki stood up from the sofa and made her way over to the stairs. "GABRIELLA!!" she shouted up the staircase. "GET YOUR ASS DOWN HERE RIGHT NOW!"

"Do you want me to leave the room?" Miranda asked, looking uneasy.

"No. I want you here as my witness."

Gabby turned the corner at the top of the stairs. Now in Vicki's line of sight, she said, "What do you want?"

"Did you know that you're all over the news right now? Some bum is on the news saying that you and him had sex."

"So what if we did? I'm eighteen now."

"Gabriella Marie Klimmings! You get down here now!"

"No."

"Don't make me come up there!"

"Go ahead. You don't scare me."

"That's it!" Vicki shouted. "Give me your phone, now! You're grounded for the rest of the month!"

"Why don't you come take it from me?"

Vicki huffed and started up the stairs. She made it about two steps up before Gabby turned and ran back to her room. The door slammed shut, and the sound reverberated down the staircase.

"That went well," Miranda said, turning the corner.

"Shut up," Vicki said as she came down the steps. "Or I'll take your phone too."

"You can if you can catch me."

Miranda turned and bolted through the living room, running elsewhere in the house. Still at the foot of the stairs, Vicki just shook her head.

"I don't know what I am going to do with you, Gabriella," she said to herself before looking back up the stairs. "I just don't know."

* * *

Peter walked down a hallway leading to double doors. Two Chinese men stood guard beside them. As Peter made it to the doors, the men opened them, allowing Peter to make his way into the big red room with the table in the center. He stood alone in the room, looked around, and turned back to the Chinese men at the doors.

"Where's President Wu?" he asked.

"He will be down soon," one of the men said.

"Tell him to hurry. He's left me waiting to see him for two damn days."

Peter took a seat in one of the chairs. As he waited for President Wu, he thought about what the president had done to Vicki. Inside, Peter was angry and disappointed at himself for letting Vicki travel to China alone. But that anger was very little compared to the pent-up rage he had for President Wu. *How dare he touch my wife!*

"President Klimmings! It's so good to see you again!"

Peter turned around and saw President Wu coming toward him,

hand raised, looking excited to see him back in China.

"I am so ready to finalize this deal," the Chinese president continued. "Then we can get this show rolling."

Confused, Peter rose from his seat. "What do you mean, finalize this deal? That's not why I am here."

"Oh. Well, I thought your woman had sent you here to finish what we had started."

"Finish what you started? Do you not remember what happened when she was here?"

President Wu had a confused look on his face. "Did I do something wrong, President Klimmings?"

"Yes, you did something wrong!" Peter shouted. "You assaulted my wife!"

"Oh," President Wu sighed before smiling. "It was just a little kiss."

"You touched her breasts!"

"Well, I'm sorry if your woman couldn't handle a decent business transaction. Maybe you should consider getting someone a little stronger for the job . . ."

Before President Wu could continue speaking, Peter felt his fist connect with the Chinese president's jaw. President Wu was on the ground, holding his face before Peter comprehended what he had just done.

"My face! My face!" President Wu cried out, flopping around on the ground.

"Don't you ever talk about my wife in a negative way again!" Peter yelled. "Do you understand?!"

"Yes, yes."

"Now, you can take your deal and shove it up your ass too!"

Peter turned and headed toward the door. His right hand was throbbing from punching President Wu in the jaw. Peter tried to shake out the pain, but it didn't work. He was almost to the door when he heard President Wu call out from behind him. "Wait!"

Peter turned around and saw President Wu pulling himself up from the floor with the help of a chair.

"This wasn't my idea," President Wu said. "It was never my idea."

"What are you saying?" Peter asked, approaching President Wu. "What do you mean?"

"Someone came to me with the idea to cripple Klimmings Incorporated. They wanted me to provoke you and make it appear that the only way we would stop would be if you started drilling for oil in the country. They had a piece of land that was worthless, and that was where they wanted the drilling to take place."

"Why? Why the hell would you do that?"

"Along with dramatically raising their prices, they threatened to pull all of their tech and software from China. We couldn't lose all that."

More furious than he was before meeting President Wu, Peter looked him straight in the eyes and asked, "Who was it?"

"Jeremy Applegate."

* * *

It was Monday morning as Vicki sat in her office. The TV in her office showed the morning news, which continued to cover the current scandal with Gabby. She took a sip of her coffee as she tried to get some work done but was interrupted by a knock at the door.

"Mom," Ben said in the doorway. "I have a question for you."

"Benjamin!" Vicki said as a smile lit up her face. "What is it? Take a seat!"

Ben came in and sat down in one of the chairs in front of Vicki's desk. "Well," he began. "It's about this authorization form for the fifteen million."

"Don't sign that just yet," Vicki interrupted him.

"Why?"

"Your father called last night. He said that something happened in China, and he needs to talk to me in person before we do anything."

"And he didn't say what happened?"

"No. He seemed furious, though."

"He's always mad," Ben said before standing up from the chair. "If you need me, I'll be in my office."

He turned and caught a glimpse of the news. They were showing pieces of the interview of the guy who claimed to have had sex with Gabby.

"Is there any truth to that?" Ben asked, turning toward Vicki.

"Yes, Benjamin," she said. "It's true."

"Oh, man. Does Dad know?"

"I haven't said anything to him yet. Benjamin, I just don't know what to do with your sister. She seems to be going wild."

"Wilder than Miranda and me?"

"You two didn't go wild," Vicki said. "The worst thing that happened would be you sneaking over to the Applegates' house at night to see Delilah."

"I couldn't help that they lived next door," Ben laughed. He stepped back over to the door. "I'm going to head back to my office in case you need me."

"Thanks," Vicki said before her cell phone started ringing. She picked it up and said, "Hello."

Ben hesitated to leave, trying to hear who Vicki was talking to.

"Yes, I can be there," she said. "Alright . . . See you then . . . Love you too."

She ended the call and put her phone in her purse.

"Who was that?" Ben asked as Vicki stood from her seat, rounded her desk, and headed to get her coat.

"That was your father," she said as she put on her coat. "He wants to meet me at the White House."

"Okay. I'll see you later then."

"You can come with if you want."

"I can't. I have a meeting with James Smith later today. He's one of the ones we're rehiring."

"Good," Vicki said as she walked out of the office with Ben. "I remember laying him off. I shouldn't be here when you rehire him."

"Won't he have to see you eventually? He will be working in the offices, won't he?"

"Yes, but the less he sees of me, for now, is what's best."

* * *

"This is a nightmare."

Miranda sat on the sofa in the sitting room of the Klimmings Mansion with her phone to her ear. "Jason, I can't even leave the house right now without the media hounding me for questions on Gabby."

"Really?" he said. "It's that bad?"

"Yes, and freaking Gabby thinks it's all a joke. I think she likes the attention." Miranda stood up from the sofa and stepped out of the room. She turned down the hall and made her way into the kitchen. "Today, when I took her to school, she expressed that she finally feels like she's getting some attention now."

"Well, she is eighteen. Weren't we all a little rebellious at eighteen?"

"I wasn't. I didn't even have my first boyfriend until college," Miranda said as she opened the fridge, taking out some fruit and putting some in a bowl. "Gabby slept with someone like twice her age!"

"Damn."

"Yeah. She's spoiled. Mom doesn't know what to do with her."

"And she's taking time away from us. I miss you so much."

"It's only been a couple of days, Jason," Miranda said, taking the bowl into the dining room. She sat down in her spot and began snacking on the bowl of fruit. "We'll get to see each other soon. Something else will happen, and the media will forget all about this."

"I hope they do," said Jason. "I have to run some errands later today. Want me to run by the mansion?"

"You can't. Dad has this place totally under lockdown. No one is allowed in except for family members."

"Wow!"

"I know. It's like I'm a prisoner because of my sister!"

"Well," Jason said. "I guess I should get going then. I'll call you later, okay?"

"Please," Miranda said. "I'm so lonely here."

"I love you, Miranda."

Jason hung up the phone and laid it on the bedside table. He was lying on his back in his bed, thinking about Miranda. *I hate it that she's locked up at home. She shouldn't have to face the consequences of her sister. She's so beautiful and perfect. She never does any wrong.*

As he continued to think about Miranda, his eyes drifted from the ceiling to the right wall parallel to his bed. A picture of Miranda from one of the Klimmings' family pictures was taped to the wall. Next to it was another photo of her. Next to that, another shot. Jason's eyes followed the row of pictures of Miranda. Over and over and over. Row after row after row. Photos ranged from formal events to family portraits to images caught by the media to photographs Jason had taken himself. The entire wall was covered with pictures of Miranda.

Jason let out a deep sigh as he took in all the images of Miranda and said to himself, "She's the most perfect person I've ever met."

* * *

The Oval Office door opened, and Vicki made her way into the room. Peter stood up from behind the *Resolute* desk and made his way to Vicki. They met in the middle of the room, and he kissed her on the cheek.

"I'm so glad you made it here," he said to her. "There's so much that I have to tell you."

"You mentioned on the phone that something happened," Vicki said as they both took a seat on one of the sofas in the room. "What was it?"

"First of all," Peter began. "You don't have to worry about messing with President Wu anymore."

"Why's that?"

"Apparently, Jeremy Applegate was behind the whole Chinese oil drilling deal. President Wu explained the entire scheme to me."

"Are you kidding me?"

"No, I am not."

"So Jeremy Applegate wanted President Wu to try to seduce me then?"

"No. I don't think he wanted that," Peter said. "I think President Wu just believes women are beneath him."

"Well, I could've told you that!" Vicki exclaimed. "What made you realize it now?"

"He said some awful things, Vicki, and I didn't like it, so I let him know."

Vicki paused for a second. "What did you do?"

Peter stood up from the sofa, turning his back toward Vicki. "I punched him," he said. "I punched that bastard right in the face."

"*Peter*," Vicki sighed. "Do you know how bad that's going to look if the international community finds out about this? You're the president of the United States! You can't go punching foreign dignitaries in the face, no matter how awful they are."

"I know! I just couldn't let that piece of shit continue to speak about you the way he was!" Peter turned back to Vicki and sat down beside her. "You're my wife. I love you, and I will do whatever it takes to support you."

Vicki smiled. "I love you so much, Peter." She leaned in and kissed him.

"I love you too, Vicki."

"Oh crap!" Vicki exclaimed before she began digging through her bag. "I forgot that Benjamin is meeting with people that we are hiring back at the company."

"And that's urgent how?"

"We were only going to bring these people back because of the deal with China. Since we aren't going through with that, I need to let him know that we can't hire them."

"Can't that wait unit you get back to the office?"

"No," Vicki said as she pulled her phone out. "One of them is this guy who flipped out when I laid him off a couple of months ago."

"Oh damn!"

"Yeah," she said as she put the phone to her ear. "I need to catch Benjamin before this guy shows up. I don't want him to have to go through that ordeal with this guy in the office."

* * *

"Thank you for coming in today, James," Ben said as he welcomed

James into his office.

"Thank you, Mr. Klimmings," James said as he took a seat in front of Ben's desk. "I cannot begin to express to you just how grateful I am for you all allowing me to return to my job."

"Well, the pleasure is ours."

Ben took a seat behind his desk and searched through some piled-up papers. "Now, I just need you to sign some papers."

Before Ben could find the papers he was looking for, the buzzer on his telephone rang. He clicked a button and said, "Yes."

"Mr. Klimmings," Doris said over the speaker. "Your mother is on the phone. She says it's urgent."

Ben glanced over at James, who was waiting patiently. "I gotta take this," Ben said to him.

"Oh," James said as he stood up from his seat. "I'll step out."

"Put her through," Ben said to Doris over the speaker. In just a couple of seconds, the phone started ringing. Ben took the phone and put it to his ear. "Hello, Mom."

"Benjamin!" Vicki said. "Do not sign that document on your desk."

"The one that's supposed to allocate the money? Why?"

"The Chinese deal is a sham! Do not sign that!"

Ben picked up the authorization forms. He studied them for a second before laying them back down on the desk. "So the deal with the Chinese is off then?"

"Yes," Vicki said. "And right now, until we can figure out what is going on, do not bring back those laid-off people."

Ben remained silent. "Mom," he quietly said. "James Smith is outside my office right now. I was just about to hire him back."

"Well, you can't. Without this deal, we don't have the money to bring those people back."

"Then what the hell do you suppose I tell him?"

"I don't know, Benjamin. You're the CFO! You can figure it out."

"And you're the CEO and board chair. You laid them off to start with, so why can't you bring him the bad news."

"Benjamin," Vicki sighed. "Just do it."

The phone clicked before Ben could say anything else. For a

moment, he stood helpless in his office. This would be his first real test since he stopped drinking months ago, and he had to tell someone that they would still be unemployed after all.

After taking a couple of deep breaths, he built up the courage to tell James. Ben straightened up his suit jacket, proceeded to his office door, opened it, and stepped out into the hallway. Doris and Pam sat at their desks, and James was seated beside Doris's desk.

"Is everything alright, Mr. Klimmings?" Doris asked Ben.

"No, Doris," Ben began. "It is not." He looked over at James, who slowly rose from his seat. "Unfortunately, Mr. Smith, we can not renew your employment here at Klimmings Incorporated today."

"What?! Why can't you?!"

"I'm sorry, James," Ben said. "After speaking with Mrs. Klimmings, I learned that the company has had some recent unexpected changes, which weren't expected. Because of that, we now don't have justification for allowing you and the others we laid off to return."

"Then why the hell did you call me back?!" James yelled. "Don't you know what this will do to my wife? My kids?"

"I'm sorry," Ben said quietly. "I really am."

"Don't lie to me. You Klimmingses are all the same! All of you all are so damn money-hungry!"

"Sir," Doris said to Ben. "Do you want me to call security?"

"No," Ben replied. "Don't." He looked James in the eye. "I'm sorry, James. I said it earlier. If we could've brought you back, I would. But, unfortunately, we can't."

"Whatever!" James shouted. He turned and stormed off down the hallway to the elevator at the end. James pressed the button, and the doors opened. He stepped inside and turned back to Ben and the secretaries before leaving. "You all will regret this!" he shouted back at them. "You'll all live to regret this!"

The elevator doors closed, cutting him off from further ranting. With his head down, Ben turned to head back into his office.

"Mr. Klimmings, are you okay?"

Doris was beside him now. Ben turned to look at her to say something, but the look on her face said it all. She looked scared and worried.

"I think I'm going to take the afternoon off," he said. "I'm going home."

He made his way into his office and began packing up his stuff.

"But Mr. Klimmings!" Doris exclaimed. "What do you want me to tell Mrs. Klimmings when she returns?"

"Just tell her I went home."

* * *

Jeremy switched off the TV and turned to Cathie, who gave him his ringing cell phone. "Thank you," he said to her. He waited until she left the room before answering the phone. "This better be good, Wu."

"I'm afraid it's not, Jeremy," President Wu said. "Peter knows."

"What?! How did he find out?"

"I told him."

"Why the hell did you do that? We had a deal, Wu!"

"I'm sorry, Jeremy. After he punched me, it just slipped out."

"Wait," Jeremy paused. "He *punched* you?"

"Yes. He punched me right in the mouth."

"And what did you do?"

"He was so upset," President Wu said. "I didn't know what I could do."

"How in God's name did you become the leader of China, Wu?" Jeremy asked, growing more frustrated with the president. "You control one of the biggest militaries in the world. Threaten him!"

"I can't do that," President Wu said. "Jeremy, I think it's best that this just blow over."

Jeremy laughed. "Think it over, Wu. If you don't retaliate somehow, there's going to be hell to pay. Remember that my company supplies the majority of China."

"What's that supposed to mean?"

"Retaliate, and you won't have to find out."

Jeremy hung up the phone before President Wu could get in another word. He set the phone down on the end table beside his chair and stood up. He turned to head into the kitchen when he saw Ryan standing in the living room with him.

"How long have you been there?" Jeremy nervously asked him.

"Long enough. Who was that?"

"It was nobody. It doesn't concern you."

"You were talking with the Chinese president, weren't you, Dad?"

Jeremy sighed. "It was just some things that happened between Peter Klimmings and President Wu."

"And you want China to retaliate?"

"Yes," Jeremy said. "Not to us, but to Peter."

Ryan stood still for a moment before a smile crept across his face. "I want to help."

* * *

Ben closed the door behind him. He took off his suit jacket and laid it down on a chair beside the door. Down the hallway, Ben heard the shower running. He made his way down the hall, into the bedroom, and to the connecting bathroom. "Delilah," he called out as he stepped into the bathroom.

"Geez!" Delilah jumped. "You scared me, Ben!"

"Sorry. I just wanted to let you know that I am home."

"Thank you for letting me know. I'm going to head over to see Mom after my shower. Do you want to come?"

"No," Ben said. "I'm not feeling up to it today."

"Well, if you change your mind, let me know."

Ben made his way back to the living room and plopped down on the couch. He ran his hands through his hair. Before he could do anything else, he noticed something light up on the coffee table in front of him. He leaned forward and realized it was Delilah's phone. Upon looking closer at the phone screen, he immediately recognized the name of the person who had just sent Delilah a text: Clark.

Ben peered down the hallway, checking whether Delilah was still in the shower. When he still heard the water running, he snatched the phone, unlocked it, and opened the message from Clark.

Are we still meeting tonight?

Ben's heart sank when he saw the message and every subsequent message that proceeded. Message after message, Ben's heart felt as if a hundred razor-sharp daggers had been slowly shoved into it. Over and over and over again, he read the secret messages between the two. He could feel the formation of tears along his bottom eyelids, pooling up, waiting to burst at any moment.

Left a sock at the house. Couldn't find it.

Ben sat motionless, listening for the shower. He heard it. Quickly, Ben locked the phone and set it back on the coffee table. He headed down the hallway and into the bedroom. Ben peeked into the bathroom to make sure Delilah was still in the shower before he began searching the room. He scanned every nook and crevasse. Then he came to the open door. Hesitating at first, Ben slowly swung the door over, almost latching it.

There it was. Behind the door lay a lonely white sock. Instantaneously, Ben realized that this sock must've belonged to Clark, and he was having an affair with his wife. The past few months had been fake. She had been cheating on him this entire time.

Ben made his way down the hallway, thoughts rushing in and out of his mind. Finally, unable to think clearly, Ben found himself in the kitchen, opening a cabinet, and pulling out a giant bottle of bourbon.

He placed the bottle against his lips and slowly took a drink. The warm liquid rushed through his body, instantly filling him, calming him, and making him feel better. Before he recognized what was happening, Ben had begun guzzling down the bourbon.

Gulp! Gulp! Gulp!

Pausing to catch his breath, Ben let out an "Aaah." He looked at the bottle. Almost one-fourth had been drunk. He turned, glanced back down the hallway, and took the bourbon bottle with him as he made his way out of the house.

* * *

Vicki stepped out of the bathroom, smoothing out her facial cream. Peter was lying on the bed watching the evening news, and Rebecca White was the guest on the program. Vicki glanced over to Peter and noticed the scowl on his face. She had never seen anyone elicit this type of response from Peter.

"Frankly, I feel that if Peter Klimmings can't handle his own family, then he can't handle the country," Rebecca said on the TV. Vicki slipped into bed and began tucking herself under the covers as Rebecca continued to speak. "Obviously, if he can't control his teenage daughter, then he can't handle the responsibilities of running the country."

Peter turned to Vicki, their eyes meeting. "I really hate that bitch."

"Peter," Vicki sighed. "You can't keep saying that all the time."

"Vicki, I don't know what else to call her. She's not human. Just look at her."

Vicki turned her attention back to the TV. Rebecca's entire persona appeared so superficial and over-the-top. "How'd she even get elected in the first place?" Vicki asked, turning back to Peter.

"I don't know. I just wish she hadn't been. My job would be a lot easier if she hadn't."

Vicki sat silent, not knowing how to respond. This moment was the first time she had ever seen Peter in such a vulnerable position, not knowing what to do or how to react.

"And when were you going to tell me about Gabby?" he asked.

"I'm sorry, Peter. I didn't know how to tell you. She has been so rude to me lately, and I didn't want to burden you with something so ridiculous."

"So our daughter is ridiculous now?"

"That's not what I'm saying, Peter."

Vicki took a deep sigh and looked back at the TV. Rebecca was still on, but they were discussing something other than the Klimmings family.

"Peter, she doesn't listen to me with anything," Vicki continued. "Anytime I ask her to do something, she retaliates and goes on the attack. When I asked her about this, she just snapped at me."

"Is it true then?"

"Yes."

"Dammit," Peter cursed. "I guess I need to talk to her then." He looked over at Vicki and noticed a tear running down her face.

"I feel like I'm just a terrible mom," she cried. "I never had this problem with Benjamin and Miranda. What did I do wrong this time that I didn't with the other two?"

"Vicki," Peter sighed, turning to comfort her. "You are not a bad mom. Every family has a rebel child."

"But I feel like I am."

"You are not. Dammit, Vicki, you are one helluva good mom. Look at how Ben and Miranda have turned out. If anything, blame Denise for the way Gabby turned out. After all, she spends more time around her than around us."

Vicki glared at Peter. "It's not Denise's fault," she scowled. "She is a good servant."

"Well, I can't argue with you there," Peter said, adjusting himself in bed. "We really don't deserve her."

Vicki and Peter sat silent, leaving the TV to be the only thing heard in the bedroom. "Turn that crap off," Peter said. "I'm tired of listening to them."

Vicki turned off the TV and began to lay back in bed. She switched off the lamp, leaving the two in the dark. "I'll talk with her this week, Vicki," Peter said. "I promise you that I will fix this."

* * *

Ding! Ding!

The elevator door opened, and Ben stumbled out of it, barely keeping his grip on the almost empty bottle of bourbon. Then, pausing for a minute to regain his balance, he began down the dark hallway leading to Doris and Pam's desks. The offices were empty, making Ben the only person there.

He paused outside his door and kicked it open. He took a swig of the bourbon and proceeded in.

Once behind his desk, he plopped into his chair, almost cracking the bourbon on the desk in the process. Ben set the bottle on his desk and began rummaging through the papers on it. One by one, he flipped through the employment papers for the people that Vicki had wanted Ben to rehire before the company pulled out of the deal with China. Then, in one swipe, Ben shoved all of them onto the floor.

"Don't need this anymore," he said before downing the remaining bourbon. "Aaaah."

He threw the bottle onto the ground, shattering it, and turned back to his desk. As he tried to examine everything in the room, on his desk, one document remained. He moved it closer to himself, looking it over very carefully.

"Authorization of fifteen million dollars," Ben whispered to himself. He continued to look over the page before noticing a signature line at the bottom of the document. He looked around his desk for a pen, knocking things off in the process. Finally, after opening one of the drawers, he found a black pen and scribbled his signature onto the document.

Smiling in approval, Ben stood up from his desk, stumbled out of his office, and tossed the paper onto Doris's desk before he continued to make his way down the hallway toward the elevator.

CHAPTER 9
A KLIMMINGS CRISIS

James Smith married his wife right after high school, which surprised no one as the two had been voted "Best Couple" in their high school yearbook. After a couple of years of marriage, they welcomed their first child, a daughter. James knew then that he needed to look for a job to provide for his new family.

After searching and searching, James was ready to give up. Nowhere would hire, and he had almost lost hope for finding a job when he noticed a "Help Wanted" ad in the local newspaper, piquing his interest. Klimmings Incorporated was looking for some help in its lower divisions. So, James applied for the position, interviewed, and got the job.

As the years went by, James and his wife welcomed two more daughters, and he found himself at the corporate level, working with Peter Klimmings. When Peter announced his candidacy for president of the United States, James remained and began working with Vicki Klimmings. James supported the Klimmings family, even campaigning for Peter by making phone calls when needed, placing signs around the area he lived, and knocking on doors. James valued and appreciated the Klimmings family for allowing him to make enough money to provide for his family.

However, after Peter was elected president and Vicki completely took over the reins of Klimmings Incorporated, things began to change. More and more, the company was visited by federal people. Every year the company was audited, and the overall mood at Klimmings Incorporated deteriorated.

Then the economy crashed, sending the company into chaos. People were being laid off left and right, each with the promise that they would get their jobs back once things were on the upswing. James and his colleagues never expected that cuts would occur in their department until they did. Vicki Klimmings called them into her office and laid them off with the same promise everyone else got. "Once things are on the upswing, you can bet that you'll have your job back. At Klimmings Incorporated, we value our employees."

It was the biggest joke told around the company. Nobody believed it, except James. He left the company, filled with anger at first, but then had high hopes of getting his job back. He even told his wife that he would eventually get his job back when he broke the news of his unemployment to her.

Six months had gone by before James had heard anything from Klimmings Incorporated. And then the phone call came. They wanted him back. His mood completely turned around. He was getting his job back. Finally, his life would go back to normal.

But then it didn't.

After losing his job yet again, James went into a downward spiral. His wife left him and took the kids because she was tired of waiting on this fantasy to happen. That night, as he sat alone in his house, looking at the notices of foreclosure laying on the coffee table in front of him, James' was drawn into the TV. The news anchors were discussing a recent scandal between Gabriella Klimmings and some man who had claimed to have slept with her.

So, James crafted a plan, staying up all night to do so. He watched as the sun came up that Tuesday morning, and hordes of teenagers filed into Theodore Roosevelt High School outside of Arlington. His eyes latched onto Gabby. She was walking into the building with her friends. No Secret Service agents were around her. Then James looked over to his passenger seat. His eyes ran up and down the two guns that lay in it. He took a deep breath as he prepared for his plan, which was about to be set into motion.

* * *

The elevator door opened, and Vicki proceeded to make her way down to her office, passing by Doris and Pam. She went into her office and took a seat at her desk. Before she could do anything, the buzzer on her phone went off.

"Yes?" Vicki answered.

"Mrs. Klimmings," Pam said over the phone. "There are some people from the financial department who want to speak with you."

"Why me? Benjamin is the head of finances. Let him take care of it?"

"Ma'am, he's not here."

"He's not? He's usually in before me."

"No. Nobody has seen him," Pam continued. "Doris came in this morning and found Mr. Klimmings' door open with an empty bottle on the floor."

"Oh no . . ." Vicki sighed and ran her right hand through her hair.

"That's not all. She also found a signed document on her desk."

"Well, what was it?"

"Mrs. Klimmings, it was the money authorization form."

"The one authorizing the fifteen million?!"

Pam hesitated before responding. "Yes."

Vicki hopped out of her seat and made her way to the doorway, speaking directly to Pam. "He signed the authorization form?!"

"Yes, Ma'am," Pam said. "And Doris had already filed it away before I came in. She didn't know."

Vicki turned her attention to Doris, who was seated quietly at her desk. "Where did you send it?" Vicki asked maniacally. Her breathing picked up in pace. "I need to stop this before anyone follows through with it!"

"I sent it where I sent all the financial documents," Doris explained. "Mrs. Klimmings, I didn't know that you didn't want him to sign it. If so, I wouldn't have filed it away."

"Oh my God, Benjamin," Vicki sighed, pressing her fingers against her temples and pacing back and forth in the office lobby. She felt the onset of a massive headache forming from the sides of her head and sprawling out around the front. "What have you done?"

* * *

"And now off to the stock market, where Klimmings Incorporated's stocks have taken a nosedive this morning after an insider at the company let it leak that the corporation is planning to move fifteen million dollars to another company in the Pacific Islands. This move is unexpected for the company as the rest of the country continues to recover from the recession. Along with Klimmings Incorporated's nosedive in stocks, the Dow Jones Industrial Average has also had a dramatic decline with experts saying that Klimmings Incorporated is to blame."

Cathie stepped away from the TV and into the kitchen. She had some scrambled eggs and sausage cooking on the stovetop. She turned off the stove and brought the food into the dining room, where two plates were set. "Ryan," she called out. "Breakfast is ready!"

She took a seat and dipped out some scrambled eggs for herself and Ryan. As she finished and was about to divvy out the sausage, Ryan came into the room. "Mom," he said. "This smells so good."

"Thank you!"

Ryan took a seat across from Cathie and helped her with the sausage. "You know," he said as he set some on her plate. "You don't have to make breakfast every day. We do have servants."

"I know. I just like cooking for my family."

"Mom, I'm literally the only one here right now. Dad left last night for China."

"I know," Cathie said. "I am assuming that you are aware of the news today then?"

"Yes." Ryan took a bite of his breakfast. "I saw that stocks are trash today."

"Do you think it'll hurt your father any?"

"Of course not. It's all the Klimmings family's fault that the stocks are that way anyway."

"Well, I guess that's good for your father then," Cathie said as she looked out the window. She could see the Klimmings Mansion across the field between their house. "I just worry about Delilah sometimes."

"Why do you say that?"

"She just doesn't seem to be herself anymore."

"Probably because of Ben Klimmings and that whole damn family."

Cathie opened her mouth to speak but was cut off by a sound effect from the television in the other room. Immediately, Cathie realized that the news was delivering a special report, so she stepped away from the table and went into the living room to catch what was happening.

"And we have breaking news right now," one of the news anchors explained. "Channel 8 News has learned that Theodore Roosevelt High School has been placed on a schoolwide lockdown. Law enforcement has been notified about the situation and is approaching the scene with caution at the moment. So far, no gunshots have been heard in the building, but unconfirmed sources say that a man with a gun has entered the building."

"Oh my God," Cathie said, turning to Ryan, who had joined her. "Are you seeing this?"

"And Jeff," the other news anchor chimed in. "If I'm not mistaken, Theodore Roosevelt High School is the high school that President Klimmings' daughter, Gabriella, attends, making this an even more dire situation."

* * *

Many people were crammed into the Oval Office. Members of the

Secret Service, FBI, and Capitol Police conversed with one another, planning their response to the situation unfolding at Theodore Roosevelt. Peter sat at the *Resolute* desk. Senior members of the Capitol Police, the Secret Service, and the FBI were seated before him. Henry was also among them.

"That's all we got right now, Mr. President," the chief of police said.

"Then what the hell are we doing then?" Peter shouted. "Why aren't we storming in there and shooting the bastard?"

"Mr. President," said one of the members of the Secret Service. "We don't know if he intends to harm your daughter right now. So, I don't think it's a good idea to storm in there at the moment."

"Well, dammit!" Peter shouted. "I'm not just going to stand by and let this son of a bitch attack my daughter!" He rose from his chair and quickly turned to the window. He gazed outside the window, examining the wind rustling through the trees on the White House lawn. "Mr. Gates, have you succeeded in reaching the FBI director?"

"No, Mr. President," Henry responded. "He's on vacation right now."

"Well, get ahold of him!" Peter demanded, finally turning around to face the people at his desk. "And Mr. Gates, issue an order to mobilize D.C. National Guard units to the school."

"Mr. President," Henry began. "Are you sure that's a good idea?"

"Yes. I want my daughter out of that situation!" Peter responded before turning to some of the members of the Secret Service. "And you all, get my family secured. Until we can figure out what is going on right now, I don't want them going anywhere."

* * *

Ben stepped off the elevator and was greeted by the bright fluorescent lights in the office lobby. His head ached as he made his way down toward Doris and Pam's desks. Both were busy answering the phones and rummaging through mounting paperwork on their desks. Before stepping into his office, Ben noticed members of the financial department entering and exiting Vicki's office. *Why are they meeting with Mom? Why didn't they set up a meeting with me instead?*

Doris glanced over toward Pam when she noticed Ben heading into his office. Pam glanced back and nodded. Doris stood from her chair and made her way into Vicki's office. Four men were seated in front of her desk in discussion with Vicki when Doris entered the room.

"Yes?" Vicki said, interrupting one of the men. Everyone turned to face Doris.

"Ma'am," Doris stuttered. "Mr. Klimmings is in his office."

"You're kidding?" Vicki said, standing up. "Gentlemen, I need to speak with my son."

The room fell silent as Vicki made her way out of her office and into Ben's. She immediately closed the door behind her when she stepped into his office. Ben sat at his desk, pouring himself some black coffee in an effort to relieve his massive headache.

"Mom," he said. "What is going on right now?"

Vicki remained silent for a few seconds, astonished that Ben hadn't heard what was going on. "You know, I figured you'd come in eventually, but today really is a shock."

"What do you mean? Why is everyone here?"

"You really don't know, do you?"

"Know what? What is going on, Mom?"

"Benjamin, you signed the authorization forms. You moved money into an account so that it could be untaxed."

"So what? I can just move it back. It's no big deal." He took a drink from his coffee and propped his feet up onto his desk.

"No big deal?!" Vicki exclaimed. "No big deal?! Benjamin, someone leaked it to the press! Our stocks tanked this morning. Klimmings Incorporated has been caught with its hand in the cookie jar, and it's all your fault, so get your damn feet off that desk right now and take this seriously!"

Ben quickly removed his feet from the desk and straightened up. He set his coffee down on the desk. "How bad is it?"

"Bad!" Vicki said. A tear pooled up along the bottom of her eyelid. "Benjamin, I have tried to give you the benefit of the doubt here. I have tried to help you out, but what you've done here crosses the line. I can't help you anymore. I cannot bail you out."

"I know. I know."

"Benjamin, I have to do it." Tears were beginning to stream down Vicki's face.

"What does that mean, Mom?"

"I need you to pack up your things, Benjamin. I cannot have you here."

Ben's heart sank as the words left Vicki's mouth. She couldn't even face him after saying the words. She turned away, sobbing.

"What?" he said. "I'm your own son. You can't fire me."

Vicki continued to face away from Ben. "I run this company, Benjamin. I can fire whomever I want." She turned to face him, exposing her tear-stained face. "And while I don't want to, you leave me no choice but to fire you." She turned toward the door and started to head out of the room, but she paused with the door open and said, "You have until the end of the day today to clean out your office." Then she closed the door before Ben could say anything, leaving him alone in his office to process what had just happened. He felt anger coupled with sadness. After all those times his mom had promised him that she wouldn't let him be removed from the company, she became the one to do it. She fired him.

Not knowing what to do, Ben headed for his office door, ready to plead with Vicki to allow him to stay on at Klimmings Incorporated in some sort of capacity. He flung open the door, preparing to beg to stay, but before he could say anything, he was pulled from his office. Men in suits filled the lobby. Vicki was over on one end with a group of them, and a new group surrounded Ben. Another group was escorting Pam and Doris out of the office, along with the guys from the financial department.

"What's going on?" Ben asked. "Why are there a bunch of Secret Service agents here?"

"Sir," one of the agents said. "We've been ordered to protect you."

"By whom?"

"By orders of the president of the United States. He's had reason to believe that there is a threat against the entire family."

By now, the Secret Service agents had moved Vicki over with Ben. "What's going on?" she asked.

"Have you not heard?" another agent said. "There's a hostage situation going on right now at your daughter's school."

Ben immediately looked over at Vicki, letting go of all the feelings of anger that he had toward her. He witnessed the rush of shock fill her face and took her in his arms, comforting her. "Oh my God!" she exclaimed. "My baby! Is she okay?"

"We don't know right now, ma'am."

"What do you mean, you don't know? Aren't you guys in that school getting rid of the perpetrator?"

"No one has stepped foot inside yet, ma'am. It's too dangerous right now."

"What?!" Ben exclaimed. "My sister is in there! What the hell are you all doing then?"

"I want to go," Vicki stated. "Take me there. I want to be there."

"Ma'am," the agent explained. "We can't take you there. It's too dangerous."

"I don't care how dangerous this is," she stated. "Take me there. I need to be there!"

* * *

The double doors flung open, and Jeremy stormed into the large red room. President Wu sat at the table in the center of the room. Before he could stand to welcome him to the country, Jeremy had already begun speaking. "Wu, what have you been doing? Why haven't you done anything yet?"

"Jeremy, I don't understand what you're getting at."

"Peter Klimmings came in here and punched you in the face. I would have thought that China would have done *something* by now so that he faces some consequences for his actions."

"Jeremy, I don't really think that's such a good idea. Peter has proven himself to be . . ."

"Reckless? Irresponsible? Anger-driven?" Jeremy interrupted. "Wu, this should show you just how dangerous Peter is when he is in power. You can't let him get away with this."

"Why can't I just leave it be? Wouldn't that be the best thing now? Your plan failed, Jeremy, and now my people are beginning to lose their trust in me."

"But you can change that, Wu. Play the victim here. Spin this your own way."

Jeremy took a seat in one of the chairs, glancing around the room, looking at the dragon art that hung on the walls and the Chinese flags periodically placed in the room. "You all still have state-run media, right?"

"Yes."

"Use it."

"How so?"

"Wu, do I have to spell it out for ya?" Jeremy stood up. "Call Peter. Try to reach out to him. I can guarantee you the conversation won't be good, and then spin it."

"Yes. That would be perfect. And then I can address my people and make it out that the president of the United States threatened me."

"If he doesn't threaten you over the phone, then I would be surprised, Wu. Together, you and I, we will get rid of Peter Klimmings once and for all."

* * *

"Do you know if Gabby is okay or not?"

"No, Miranda," Peter said over the phone. "I don't know yet. The National Guard is on its way to the school now. How are you, by the way?"

"I'm locked up in the house like a prisoner," Miranda said. "The Secret Service has shut down the entire road in front of the house. No one can get in."

"Good. I think this is just an isolated incident right now, but I don't want you all to be put in any danger."

"Who all is being protected right now?"

"Your mom, brother, you, and Delilah. Your mom and brother are at the office, and Delilah was taken to her parents' house. I did that so that Jeremy couldn't go anywhere." Peter giggled into the phone. When he didn't hear Miranda laughing back, the smile fell from his face. "Sorry, I just needed something to take my mind off of what's going on."

"Don't be, Dad. This is a scary situation."

"Yes, it is," Peter said. "Hey, I need to keep the lines open for updates, Miranda. I love you."

"Love you too, Dad."

Peter placed the phone on the receiver and looked up at Constance, sitting in the chair in front of his desk. A lot of the members of the Secret Service had left the office, leaving only a few military leaders who were talking amongst themselves.

"How is she?" Constance asked Peter.

"She's fine," Peter sighed. "I think she's just upset that Gabby is in this situation." Peter leaned over the desk, placing his hands on his temples. "God, why are they taking so long?!"

Constance stood up and made her way around the desk to console Peter. "It'll be okay, Peter," she said, placing her hand on his back. "She's going to make it through this. Nothing is going to happen to her."

Before Peter could respond to Constance, the door to the Oval Office opened, and Martha stepped into the room. "Mr. President," she called out. "The Chinese President is trying to phone you."

"Now is not a good time," Constance said. "President Klimmings has more important things to worry about right now than China."

Martha hurried out of the room, closing the door behind her. Constance turned back to face Peter.

"Thank you," Peter said. "I didn't want to talk to that bastard right now."

"I figured you didn't," Constance said as she took a seat in front of the desk. "You have too much on your plate right now. You don't need to worry about him."

The door to the Oval Office opened again, with Martha stepping in.

"I thought I told you that he didn't want to speak with President Wu," Constance shouted at her.

"Mr. President," Martha said, ignoring the statement made by Constance. "The first lady is on her way to the school."

"WHAT?!" Peter exclaimed. "Why the hell is she doing that? Why didn't the Secret Service stop her?!"

"Apparently, she insisted that she go."

"Dammit. I'm going to call her."

"Before you do that," Martha interrupted. "I have something else that I need to let you be aware of."

"Well, what is it?"

"I know that this may not be a good time, but the speaker of the House was on the news earlier. She announced that the House is creating a committee to investigate Klimmings Incorporated."

"WHAT?!" shouted Peter.

"Did she really?" Constance asked. "She couldn't have waited until after this crisis was over?"

"I guess not," Martha said. "I just thought I would let you know, sir."

"Thank you, Martha," Peter said. "I'm going to call Vicki."

"Are you sure?" Constance asked. "Why don't you take a few minutes to process all this first?"

"No, I can't. I have to fix this mess. After all, I am the president of the United States. If I can't handle this, how can I handle the country?"

* * *

"And so today," Rebecca White said. "I am announcing that the House of Representatives will be forming a committee in the next Congress to investigate Klimmings Incorporated and the president's connection to the company."

Reporters erupted with questions, trying to get Rebecca's attention. Then the screen went blank.

Cathie turned to Ryan and Delilah. "You would think that she would have the common decency to wait until tomorrow or later on this week to announce that."

"Yeah," Delilah said. "I feel for everyone right now. This is just not good."

"I don't," Ryan said. "After all the corruption, Peter is finally getting what he deserves."

"Ryan Dean!" Cathie exclaimed. "That is awful!"

"Yes, it is!" Delilah chimed in. "His daughter is in a hostage situation at school right now. Show some sympathy!"

"I wasn't meaning that," Ryan backtracked. "I meant he's getting what he deserves in Congress." He got up and poured himself a drink. "Jeez. I may hate him, but I don't want his daughter to die."

Cathie continued to scowl at Ryan before turning to Delilah. "Have you gotten ahold of Ben?"

"No," Delilah replied. "I've texted and called him all day, and so far, nothing."

"Have you tried the office then?"

"I would have thought that he'd be there, but when I tried calling, nobody answered."

"Strange. And you said that he didn't come home at all last night?"

"No, he came home. I was in the shower when he came in, and then when I got out, he was gone."

"Maybe he's out having an affair," Ryan suggested. "Those Klimmingses are corrupt in their business. It wouldn't surprise me if they were also corrupt in the bedroom too." He laughed to himself as guilt enveloped Delilah, and she looked to the floor, trying to hide her shame.

"That's not funny," Cathie said. "Can't you ever be nice when it comes to your sister's second family?"

"No."

"It's fine, Mom," Delilah said. "I'm sure he'll turn up somewhere."

* * *

Crowded together on the floor, Gabby and her classmates silently cried among themselves. Collectively, they feared for their lives. Gabby glanced over at Michelle, who was clinging onto her right arm with fear in her eyes. Then she looked back to the front of the classroom, where James Smith stood, two guns with him, one in his hands and another draped on his back. "Just stay here," he told them. "I'm not going to hurt any of you all."

Sniffs and whimpers among the teens in the room broke any silence that there could be. "It'll be okay, guys," James said again. "I'm not going to hurt any of you all. Once they see me, they'll all understand. Everything will be fine!"

"Why do you mean everything will be fine?" Gabby spoke up. "We're scared for our lives right now, and you're telling us that everything will be okay. Like that's supposed to make us feel better?"

"Gabby, no," whispered Michelle as she tightened her grip on Gabby's arm, trying to urge her to shut up.

"No, I want to hear his reasons!"

"You," James said. "You're the real reason I'm here. Your family fired me twice, for no reason! If I can prove that I'm willing to do anything, then I know that they'll have no choice but to hire me back!"

"Excuse me?" Gabby said, standing up. "Is that why you have us here?"

"Sit down, missy," James stated, pointing his gun at her. The class erupted with a collective scream.

"No! I'm not going to continue to let you hold us captive just so that you can get what you want." Gabby took a step toward James. "You know what that is? That's a douche move right there."

"Gabby," Michelle urged, motioning for her to sit back down. "Get back here. What are you doing?"

"Listen to your friend," James warned. "I'll use this if I have to."

"Shoot me, and say goodbye to ever being free again."

"I will if I have to. Like I said, I'm just showing them that I'm willing to do anything for my job."

"Do you really think anyone will hire you after this?" Gabby asked. "Instead of handling your problems like a grown man, you came here to hold a bunch of innocent teenagers hostage. You've committed a crime."

For a moment, the entire room fell silent. The teens looked at James and then back at Gabby, who had stopped making her way toward James. "Do you have anything else you'd like to add?"

Gabby shook her head.

"Good," James said.

BANG!

* * *

A black SUV pulled up to the scene of chaos outside Theodore Roosevelt High School. Without hesitation, the back passenger side door opened, and Vicki jumped out, adjusting her suit in the process. The captain of the National Guard squad approached her.

"Mrs. Klimmings," he said to her. "First off, it is an honor to meet you. I just wish it were under much better circumstances."

"How's my daughter doing?" she asked him, walking alongside him to the command center.

"To be honest, ma'am, we aren't entirely certain what is going on. A few minutes ago, we heard a shot inside the building. One of my men is setting up a visual on the gunman now."

"Shoot him if you get the chance. I want my daughter out of there."

Vicki felt her phone vibrating in her jacket pocket. It was too noisy with all the police officers, National Guard members, and media members to hear her ringer on her phone. She pulled her phone out and looked at the screen, seeing Peter calling her. She declined the call and put her phone back in her jacket.

"Ma'am," the captain said. "I promise you that you will get your daughter back safe and sound. We are doing the best we can."

"Well, if it was the best you can, why haven't you all entered into the building yet? Why are we waiting for more kids to die in there? Get them out!"

Tears streamed down Vicki's face. The captain put his hand on her shoulder, comforting her. "I promise you," he said. "We are going to get her out. Only one gunshot has been heard since this crisis began, and we're about to go in soon. Everything is going to be okay."

* * *

"AAAAHHH!!" Gabby screamed in pain. She clenched her left shoulder with her hand as she fell to the floor, writhing in excruciating pain. Blood was pouring out everywhere. She had never felt anything more painful than this.

The other teenagers had scattered away from her, scared that they would be shot next. Michelle moved over to Gabby, using her hand to apply pressure to help stop the bleeding.

"Dammit!" shouted James. "Look what you made me do, you bitch!"

"Don't call her that!" Michelle retaliated, taking her hand off Gabby and facing James. "You can't blame her for your mistakes." Blood dripped off Michelle's hand. "You've screwed up, now. You're going to jail for life! And it's nobody's fault but your own."

"Would you like to be next?!" He lifted his gun, pointing at her directly between the eyes eliciting a collective shriek from the teenagers in the room. "I mean it. I'll shoot!"

"Go ahead!"

Michelle stepped forward so that the gun was inches away from her. She closed her eyes and braced herself to hear the gunshot at any moment, but all that was heard was silence. Then, finally, as she could not withstand waiting any longer, Michelle opened her eyes and saw James clenching his heart. She looked at his hand and saw blood squirting out around it, spraying outward. Some even hit her in the face. Then, like a lead brick, James fell to the floor.

Michelle eyeballed the window on her right, and she noticed a large crack in it with a small hole in the middle. As she tried to process what had just happened, the classroom door burst open, and the National Guard and Capitol Police members stormed into the room. They promptly rounded up the teenagers and pulled Michelle away from James' dead body. One member of the National Guard radioed for the paramedics, mentioning the need for a stretcher.

* * *

Vicki watched as student after student was escorted out of the school. One by one, they passed by. She eyed each student in hopes that she would get some clue about Gabby. Then, the line ended. No more students came out of the building. Vicki watched as a group of police officers and National Guard members moved to help the students find their parents, and all Vicki could do was cry.

She planted her face into her palms, sobbing into them. Tears pooled into the cups of her hands as she began to accept that Gabby wasn't coming out of that building.

Finally, she felt a nudge against her arm and heard someone say, "Mrs. Klimmings, look!" She lifted her face from her hands, and paramedics brought out a stretcher. On that stretcher lay Gabby. As soon as Gabby's eyes met Vicki's, she smiled.

"Gabriella!" Vicki exclaimed before running toward her, embracing her tightly in her arms.

"Mom," Gabby managed to let out. "Mom, be careful with my shoulder."

"Oh, Gabriella. I love you so so much, honey."

She hugged her tightly, keeping careful not to mess with the wounded shoulder. As Vicki continued to embrace her daughter, she became unaware of the media cameras that had focused their attention on her, broadcasting this moment live across the news stations. Peter in the Oval Office. Miranda at the Klimmings Mansion. Cathie, Ryan, and Delilah at the Applegate Homestead. Ben from Klimmings Incorporated. Countless Americans watched as Vicki was reunited with her daughter. Nobody knew that this moment would later go down as one of the most famous moments of the Klimmings presidency.

* * *

"He never answered," President Wu said as he set the phone down, turning to Jeremy.

"You see," Jeremy said. "Peter Klimmings doesn't care about you. He doesn't care about China, and he sure as hell doesn't care about me or the rest of the American people. He only cares about himself. He only speaks to those that he needs something from, and in this moment, he feels that he doesn't need you anymore, Wu.

"But let me tell you this. One day, Peter will need you, just like he'll need me. And we'll remember this moment, right now. We won't give him the help he needs, Wu. And then, all of a sudden, Peter's world will come crashing down on him. Bit-by-bit at first, and then more and more, until he is left with nothing. Until he has lost everything. And then, that's when Peter will finally realize that he is, after all, just a man, like you and me."

President Wu sat down in one of the chairs beside him, processing what Jeremy had just said to him. "Jeremy, what do you suppose we do then?"

"Crush him."

PART 2

CHAPTER 10
SHE CARES SO MUCH

Gabby struggled to open her eyes, feeling groggy as she woke up. *Where am I? What happened?* She tried to move but was met with intense pain in her left shoulder. That's when she realized she was lying in a bed in a hospital room. As she looked around, her eyes caught someone sitting next to her. "Mom?"

Vicki was seated alongside Gabby, staying by her side since she was admitted to the hospital. She smiled at Gabby, allowing a tear to run down her face. "It's me, honey."

"What am I doing here?" Gabby asked. "Why am I so sleepy?"

"It's part of your medication, Gabriella. You were shot in the left shoulder, honey. The doctors did surgery and removed the bullet from you, so you've been in the hospital for a couple of days."

"*Shot?!* Am I going to die, Mom?"

"No," Vicki chuckled, wiping her cheeks with a tissue and realizing the medication given to her daughter had made her very loopy. "You aren't going to die from the bullet. You're going to be just fine."

"Where is everybody else?"

"Well, your dad, sister, and Delilah are in the waiting room. They didn't come in because you weren't awake yet. Would you like for me to bring them in?"

"Yes, please."

Vicki rose from her chair and made her way to the door. She opened it and spoke to one of the Secret Service agents. Soon after, Peter, Miranda, and Delilah came into the room.

"How are you feeling?" Miranda asked.

"Sleepy," Gabby responded.

"It's so good to see you," Delilah chimed in. "We were all so worried about you."

"It's good to see you too," said Gabby. She looked around the room, noticing that her brother wasn't present. "Where's Ben?"

"He's probably out drinking or something," Peter said as he crossed his arms and rolled his eyes. "Delilah, why don't you see what it is that's bothering him? After all, you two do live together." He chuckled a little to himself before he noticed Vicki scowling at him.

"Ben's drinking problem is no laughing matter," she said.

"Well, somebody has to mention it to him. How much longer are we going to let this go on?"

Delilah held up her hands, stopping the ensuing argument between the two. "I'll see if I can find him anywhere." She moved over to Gabby to say goodbye, placing her hand on top of Gabby's for a moment, and then left the hospital room.

"Mom," Miranda said after Delilah left. "Why *isn't* Ben here?"

"He's not that happy with me right now," Vicki said. "The last time I saw him, I fired him."

Miranda sighed. "Oh, Mom. You and I both know that's gonna destroy him."

"I had no other choice," Vicki said, turning away from Miranda and looking out the hospital room window. "He signed an authorization form allowing for an illegal transfer of money. In return, our stocks tanked."

"This is why I didn't give him the majority of my stocks," Peter chimed in. "I knew he couldn't handle the pressures of the job."

Vicki turned, glaring into Peter's eyes. "Well, perhaps if you hadn't decided to shove your business over to me, and chase your political dreams, then we wouldn't be in the situation we're in now."

"What's that supposed to mean?"

"You know exactly what that means."

Miranda placed herself between Peter and Vicki, attempting to diffuse the tension between the two. "Why don't you two have this conversation elsewhere?" She motioned to Gabby, who was lying on the hospital bed. Miranda couldn't distinguish whether she was coherent or in a daze. Still, she knew that it wasn't a good idea for her to hear her parents argue over family issues while she was coming to terms with being shot.

"Very well," Peter said. "I'm going to the White House." He turned and opened the door to the hospital room. "Call me if you hear any new updates."

"I will," Miranda said. Peter closed the door behind him, leaving Miranda and Vicki alone in the room with Gabby. Vicki plopped down in a chair beside Gabby's bed. She planted her face into her palms. It wasn't soon after that Miranda could hear her sobbing.

"What's wrong, Mom?"

"I feel like all this is my fault," Vicki sobbed.

"What do you mean?"

"That guy who shot Gabby was pissed at me, Miranda. He wanted to get back at me."

"How would you know that? He was crazy!"

"No, he wasn't, Miranda. I laid him off. He was mad at me because I had taken his job away. I destroyed his life!" Vicki plopped her face back into her palms, her sobs now filling the room. "It's all my fault!"

Miranda glanced over at Gabby, who had fallen back asleep. Then, she pulled a chair next to Vicki and sat next to her. Miranda put her arm around her mom, offering her some comfort. Vicki leaned into Miranda.

"None of this is your fault, Mom," Miranda said. "That guy decided to come into that school and hold all those kids hostage."

"I just can't keep the thought that I'm responsible out of my mind," Vicki said, continuing to sob. "My actions caused harm to my daughter,

Miranda, and I don't think I can ever forgive myself for that."

* * *

Ben packed his belongings into a cardboard box one by one. A single lamp dimly lit his office as he cleared off his desk. After tucking away the last item, he took a moment to look around the room. For the past two years, this office had become his second home.

He picked up the box and turned to leave. He took a step forward, keeping his attention focused on his belongings. Then, he finally turned his attention to the door and saw Delilah waiting for him. He jumped, startled, and dropped his box, causing a loud crashing sound. "Dammit, Delilah," he let out. "You scared me."

"I'm sorry, Ben," she said as she went over to help pick up what had fallen out of the box. "I just wanted to stop by to see how things were with you."

Ben glanced up at Delilah, and he remembered seeing the text messages from Clark. His mind came back to the moment he found the sock behind the bedroom door, and he glared at her with resentment. Then, as she put the last item back in the box, she looked up at Ben, noticing the look he was giving her. "What?"

He remained silent for a brief second. He wanted to say something to her, but he couldn't get the words to form from his mouth. "Nothing," he finally said. "Just thinking about something."

"Well, I can tell you what I'm thinking about . . . lunch! Eating is pretty much anything a seven-month pregnant lady thinks about."

"I'm not hungry," Ben said as he picked up the box and stood up. "In fact, I just want to go back home and unpack this box."

Delilah looked at Ben in bewilderment. "Ben," she said, struggling to stand up. "This isn't like you. Tell me what's wrong."

He looked at her as she put her right hand on his shoulder. As her eyes locked onto his, Ben couldn't understand how she could keep this secret from him. *How can she act like she cares so much?*

"You don't understand!" Ben snapped. "I just want to take this crap home, Delilah!"

He rushed past her and down the lobby to the elevator, leaving Delilah alone in the empty office.

* * *

The front door to the Applegate Homestead opened as Jeremy struggled to make his way in carrying all his bags. It was late at night as he tried to quietly make his way into the house. Finally, he maneuvered the last suitcase out of the door's path, and he was able to swing the door shut, leaving himself alone in the dark.

Struggling to tiptoe around his bags, he felt along the wall, trying to find the light switch so that he could see. Without any luck, he couldn't find it. Then just before giving up hope and deciding to proceed on in the dark, the light switched on. Jeremy swung around and saw Ryan standing in the doorway to the living room. "How was the trip?"

"It was eventful." Jeremy shoved his bags out of the way and made his way into the living room, sitting down in his favorite chair. Ryan sat down on the sofa beside him. "How were things while I was gone?"

"Oh . . . It was fine."

"Fine? While I was over in China, I saw that the Klimmings stock tanked. What the hell happened?"

"Something that Ben authorized. Word has it that his mom canned him for it."

Jeremy laughed. "I never would have thought that she would have the gall to do that. Has she done any press conference about it yet?"

"No. Don't you think she's probably a little bit more focused on Gabby?"

Jeremy leaned forward. "I'm confused. What does Gabby have to do with all of this?"

Ryan paused for a moment and cleared his throat. "You haven't heard? It's all over the news." He turned on the TV, changing the channel to the first news channel he could find. Immediately, an image of Vicki hugging Gabby on the stretcher outside the school popped up on the screen. The news anchors were discussing the nation's reaction to the hostage crisis at the school.

"Oh my God," Jeremy sighed. "When did this happen?"

"A few days ago. You seriously haven't heard about it?"

"No."

"Well, hell. You can't go anywhere over here without hearing about it on the TV, radio . . . you name it!"

Jeremy processed what he heard in his mind. He quickly realized that Peter must've been dealing with the crisis when he didn't answer President Wu's call. His face fell blank, and his heart sank within his chest as he understood what he had done and the implications that could follow.

"So tell me how China went," Ryan said, interrupting Jeremy's thoughts. "You said it was eventful. How?"

Jeremy turned, looking Ryan in the eye, gesturing toward the TV. "I think because of this little event, I finally turned President Wu against the Klimmingses."

* * *

Flinging the door open, Peter made his way into the Oval Office, plopping into the chair behind the *Resolute* desk. Henry, who was behind Peter, sat down in one of the chairs in front of the desk. "Mr. President, do you want to talk about what has happened these past couple of days?"

Peter looked up at Henry. "Not to you, Mr. Gates."

"Why?"

"Because I need to talk to Congress about it." Peter stood up and looked out the window, examining the White House grounds. "For far too many years, these tragedies have happened to so many people in our country, Mr. Gates. This time, it hit close to the heart of America. I cannot . . . I will not stand by and let these senseless tragedies continue to happen."

"What do you plan to do, Mr. President?"

Peter turned back toward Henry. "Mr. Gates, I need to speak to a joint session of Congress. We need better legislation on firearms in this country. We need background checks, a gun registry, and whatever it may be to further prevent these tragedies from happening again."

Henry sat silent for a moment. "Mr. President, are you sure you want to speak to a joint session now? After all, your State of the Union Address is in two months. Couldn't you bring it up then?"

"This cannot wait," Peter exclaimed as he fell back into his chair. "I cannot wait. America needs this legislation now!"

"Okay." Henry stood up. "I will contact Speaker White and make your request known to her." He proceeded to make his way to the door, and as he turned the knob to leave, he paused and looked back to Peter. "Mr. President," he added. "I know I work for you, but I consider you a close friend and someone that I can share anything with. If you ever need anything or anybody to speak with, you can count on me, sir."

Peter took a deep sigh. "Thank you, Mr. Gates." He even let a faint smile appear on his face. "I appreciate you and all you do for me. I couldn't have a better chief of staff."

* * *

The shower door opened, and Vicki stepped out wrapped in a towel. She proceeded to take another towel that was hanging beside the shower to dry her hair. She looked at the reflection of herself in the bathroom mirror while she worked on her hair. It had been a week since she had been home, spending each day in the hospital with Gabby. But Gabby was set to come home today, so Vicki wanted to clean herself up and look her best when her daughter returned home.

She exited the bathroom and opened the closet door, pulling out a casual pink top. Vicki was always conscious of how she looked anytime she went out into public. After all, she was still the first lady, even though she focused more on the work at Klimmings Incorporated rather than philanthropic opportunities. Not that she never participated in any philanthropy, but it just wasn't as important to her as the company.

After slipping on a pair of white pants, Vicki proceeded to fix her hair, fluffing it out to add in more volume. Then, she heard Denise call out from the bottom of the stairs. "Mrs. Klimmings, you have a visitor!"

"I'll be down in a minute, Denise."

Vicki fluffed her hair one final time before smiling at herself in the mirror. She left the bedroom, making her way down the stairs. She took a left at the bottom and stopped in the archway to the living room. A woman was standing at the bar, looking up at the family picture. She had long, thick, brown hair. Her skin was much tanner than Vicki's, and she was very elegant. "So this is the family, I see," she said, gazing up at the portrait.

"Yes," Vicki said. "What are you doing here?"

"Well, I came here to see my sister, of course." The woman turned around to face Vicki, and she immediately recognized her.

"Charlotte?"

CHAPTER 11

CHARLOTTE

Charlotte approached Vicki in the archway. "It has been too long," she said as she wrapped her arms around Vicki, embracing her tightly. "I'm so glad I finally convinced myself to make my way out here to visit you."

"*Charlotte?*" Vicki repeated herself in disbelief. "Is that really you?"

Charlotte let go of Vicki and put her hands on her shoulders, gazing into her eyes. "Of course it is! Who the hell did you think I was?" Then, she threw her arms around Vicki, hugging her again. "It's been too long, sister."

"Yes, it has! What made you decide to come out here?"

Vicki motioned for them to sit down on the sofa. "Well," Charlotte began as she sat down. "I saw you and your daughter on the news last week, and I thought that I needed to come visit you. How is she anyway?"

"She's doing fine. In fact, I was on my way over to the hospital to bring her home when Denise told me that you were here."

"Oh honey, go get your child. We can reminisce later!"

"Are you sure? I would feel horrible just leaving you here. Miranda is down at the hospital with her right now, so it's no big deal if I am a little bit late."

"Yes, I am," Charlotte said as she stood up from the sofa. "In fact, I have a better idea. Let's go get her together!"

Vicki hesitated before saying, "Okay. I can take us there."

"I wouldn't have it! You're going to ride with me!"

"Okay," Vicki responded. "Let me go get something real quick, and I'll meet you outside."

Vicki followed Charlotte out into the entry hall. After Charlotte walked out the door, Vicki turned to Denise, who was dusting off a buffet in the hall. "Is there something you need for me to get you, Mrs. Klimmings?" Denise asked as she set her dust rag down.

"Did she happen to say why she was here?"

"No, ma'am. Should I have asked?"

"No. Charlotte just doesn't show up for a visit. She wants something."

Before Denise could respond, Vicki proceeded out the door. Charlotte was standing by a bright red, top-of-the-line luxury car. "You like it?"

"Wow!" Vicki said as she made her way down the front steps. "How did you manage this?"

"George loves to spoil me." Charlotte laughed. "Honey, I figured you already knew that!"

"I just didn't think he would actually get you something that was this nice. After all, you don't have the greatest driving record." Vicki opened the passenger door and sat in the car. Charlotte followed, taking the driver's seat.

"What the hell is that supposed to mean?" Charlotte asked, closing the car door. "I'm a great driver."

Vicki chuckled. "How many of dad's cars did you total?"

Charlotte glared at Vicki. "Put your seat belt on then." She started up the car, placed it in drive, and began down the driveway toward the road. As they headed for the hospital, all Vicki could think about was why Charlotte had come. *What does she want?*

* * *

A football game was playing on the TV, but Ben's mind kept replaying the scene in his head. *Message after message, Ben's heart felt as if a hundred razor-sharp daggers had been slowly shoved into it. Over and over and over again, he read the secret messages between the two.*

"TOUCHDOWN!"

Ben snapped back to the TV where fans were celebrating in the stands. He got up and made his way into the kitchen, leaning over the sink and taking a deep sigh. Delilah had gone out for the day to run some errands, but all Ben could think about was whether or not she was visiting with this Clark guy.

Behind the door lay a lonely white sock. Instantaneously, Ben realized that this sock must've belonged to Clark. He made his way into the kitchen, pulled out a bottle of bourbon, and began drinking.

Bourbon.

Ben opened up the cabinet where the liquor was stored. He sorted through the bottles and couldn't find any bourbon. He looked over at the wine rack in the kitchen corner and then took his gaze back to the cabinet. He pulled out a bottle of vodka and looked it over. Quickly, he unscrewed the cap off the bottle and took a swig.

"This'll do," he said as he began looking for a glass. He opened another cabinet door, took one out, and set it on the counter. He examined it and then looked back at the bottle. He shrugged his shoulders and then took another drink from the bottle before heading back into the living room to finish the game.

* * *

"So why haven't I ever met her?" Gabby asked as Miranda pushed her in a wheelchair down the hospital corridor. Vicki walked alongside the two as they headed toward the front lobby, and Secret Service members followed from behind at a distance.

"She's just never made it around," Vicki said. "Your Aunt Charlotte has been very busy."

"Isn't she married to that guy who owns that team out in California?" Miranda asked.

"Yes, and your point?"

"You just mentioned she was busy."

The hospital's automatic doors slid open, and the three walked outside under the drop-off awning. In the parking lot, Charlotte stood waiting beside her bright red car. When she saw the trio heading toward her, she began waving hastily, trying to get their attention as if they hadn't already noticed her.

"As you can see," Vicki told Gabby, stopping in the middle of the parking lot. "Your Aunt Charlotte is very special."

"HEY!" Charlotte called out, still convinced that they hadn't noticed her. "Vicki, I'm over here!"

Vicki took a deep sigh before gesturing to Miranda to take Gabby to the car. "We're coming!"

The three made their way over to Charlotte, who continued hopping and flailing her arms as if they still hadn't noticed her standing there.

"I am so glad to meet you girls!" she exclaimed as Gabby tightened the brakes on the wheelchair. "I've seen you all so much on the TV. I just had to finally meet my nieces!"

"So you're Aunt Charlotte," Gabby said before struggling to stand from the wheelchair. Miranda and Vicki quickly rushed in to help her up. "How's come I haven't heard of you until today?"

Charlotte glanced over to Vicki, who had a look of guilt on her face. "You never spoke about me?"

"What was I supposed to say?" Vicki tried explaining. "Hey, guys. You have this aunt, who's married to this guy named Jim or Job, and he owns this baseball team."

Charlotte paused for a second. "His name is George, and he owns a football team." She turned to look back at Gabby. "So, how are you, honey?"

"I got shot," Gabby said. "How the hell do you think I am feeling?"

"Gabriella!" Vicki shouted. "Watch your language!"

Charlotte laughed to herself. "You think that's bad? Gabby, you should have heard some of the words your mom used when she was your age. She would make what you said sound like some kind of angel baby."

"*Angel baby?!*" Vicki snapped her head over to Charlotte.

"Yes. You know exactly what you used to say back in the day."

"But *they* don't know that! And I don't want them to know what I used to say."

The four fell silent for a moment, and only the sound of the wind rustling through the leaves of the trees surrounding the parking lot could be heard.

"I like her," Gabby said, interrupting the silence. "She needs to come around more often."

"I think we just need to go home," Miranda said. "Whose car would you like to go in, Gabby? Charlotte's or mine."

"I want to go in Aunt Charlotte's!" Gabby exclaimed. "She is cool!"

Vicki's and Miranda's eyes met. "I'll ride home with you," Vicki said. "Do you need help getting in Charlotte's car?"

"Honey!" Charlotte interjected. "I got this." She scooted in and helped Gabby into the car. "See you at the house?"

"Yes."

"Alright then!"

Charlotte closed the passenger door and then proceeded to sit down in the driver's seat. Miranda and Vicki began making their way over to Miranda's blue car when Vicki felt a vibration in her bag. She stopped to open it and pulled out her phone. "What is it?" Miranda asked as Vicki continued looking at the screen.

"Pam has been texting me. She needs me to come into the office."

"Why?"

"Major shareholders want to pull out. I have to go in, Miranda. Can you drop me off at Klimmings Tower?"

"Yes." Miranda and Vicki proceeded to the car. Once they got in, Miranda immediately turned the keys, starting the ignition. "How bad is it?"

"Bad. This could really hurt the company. They're calling together a meeting of the board."

* * *

Delilah opened the door to the house and immediately was smacked in the face with a strong alcohol fragrance. "Ugh," she said, closing the door behind her. "What is that smell?"

She scanned the living room and stopped when her eyes landed on an empty bottle of vodka lying on the floor. She knelt down, picked up the bottle, and examined it for a moment. Before she stood back up, she heard a noise from down the hallway. She set the bottle on the coffee table and then leaned against it, using it to help herself stand up.

She proceeded to go down the hallway, heading to her bedroom at the end. She opened the door and peered in. Ben was lying on the bed, passed out. On the floor next to him, she saw another liquor bottle. The smell of alcohol poured out of the bedroom, overwhelming her. She turned and went back into the living room, leaving the house through the front door. She pulled out her phone and called Ryan. The phone rang a few times before he finally answered.

"Ryan," Delilah said desperately. "I don't know what to do."

"What's the matter?" he asked.

"Ryan, it's Ben. He's been drinking. I think he's drank two bottles of vodka."

"Damn. What's he doing right now?"

"He's passed out in the bedroom. The whole house smells like alcohol."

"Leave him," Ryan said. "Come over to Mom and Dad's. Stay here for a couple days. You don't need to be around all that while you're pregnant with the baby."

"Are you sure that's a good idea?" Delilah asked, turning back to the house. "What if he needs help?"

"The only help he needs is what you can't give him. Get over here, and we can figure something out."

Reluctantly, Delilah took her attention off the house and made her way over to her purple car. She ended the call with Ryan and took a seat behind the wheel. After starting the car's ignition, she pondered for a moment, staring back at the house. Something kept telling her that she needed to let someone else know. She opened up her contacts and selected Miranda's contact information. At first, she started to send her a text message but deleted everything she had typed out and decided to call instead.

"Hello?" Miranda said when she answered the phone.

"Miranda," Delilah began. "If you get a chance, could you check on Ben? I think he has been drinking again, and I'm concerned about him."

"Oh no. I'll swing by your house and see how he's doing. Is everything okay with the baby?"

"Yes. I just feel tired all the time now. My ankles are always swollen too." Delilah said, allowing a brief smile to flash across her face. "I'm ready to pop this kid out."

"Before you know it, you will," Miranda said. "Hey, I'm going to drop Mom off at Klimmings Tower, and then I am going to stop by and check on Ben. I'll talk to you later and let you know how he is doing."

"Okay. Thank you, Miranda. Bye."

Delilah ended the call, put her car in reverse, and pulled out of the driveway, heading toward the Applegate Homestead.

* * *

"I guess that was Delilah," Vicki said as Miranda pulled the car in front of the main entrance to Klimmings Tower.

"Yes, that was her," Miranda said as she placed the car in park and turned to look Vicki in the eyes. "He's not doing so well, Mom. I think we need to really think about doing something to help."

"Good luck getting your father to do anything. He seems to think that Benjamin needs to man up. I disagree, though. He just needs some help."

"Then why don't you talk to him about it? Ben needs our help right now."

"I have. Right now, all your father seems to care about is his reelection in two years. He knew he would lose the Senate in the midterms, and now that the Republicans control all of Congress, he feels that he needs to be there for everything now. He needs to be involved in everything, and he needs to be planning for the next election."

Vicki turned to look at the entrance to Klimmings Tower. She looked up at the reflective bluish-gray windows that coated the outside of the tower. She admired the building's height, the second tallest structure in D.C., next to the Washington Monument. Her mind went back to when Peter had the building commissioned. He promised many politicians campaign donations if they amended the Height of Buildings Act of 1910. This allowed him to build Klimmings Tower higher than any other building in Washington, except the Washington Monument.

"Mom." Miranda broke her concentration on the building. "Is something going on between you and Dad?"

Vicki turned her attention back to Miranda and let out a faint smile. "Nothing that hasn't been going on before. Your father is just being your father."

"Are you sure?"

"Yes, I am." Vicki unbuckled her seatbelt and opened the door. "Now, I've got to go in and see what these stockholders want from me."

"Mom," Miranda said before Vicki closed the door. "I love you."

"I love you too, Miranda." Vicki closed the door and proceeded to head into the building. She made her way through the lobby, greeted the security guard on duty, and entered the elevator. Once she reached the 30th floor, she stepped out of the elevator. Then, she headed down the hallway to the lobby of Klimmings Incorporated. Pam quickly bolted around her desk and met Vicki before she could step into her office.

"Mrs. Klimmings," she said. "The board members have already begun their meeting."

"What?!" Vicki exclaimed. "Without me?"

"Yes, ma'am."

"I'm the freaking board chair. Why the hell would they start it without me?"

Before Pam could add any more, Vicki had already started down the hall to the boardroom. As soon as she got to the double oak doors, she flung them open and stepped into the room. All twelve board members fell silent. Then, after pausing for a moment to make eye contact with each member, she began to head over to the big chair at the head of the conference table that each member was seated around.

"I see you opted not to wait for me."

"Mrs. Klimmings," one of the board members said. "We were under the impression that you were not coming to this meeting. In fact, we were told that you haven't been in the office at all for the past couple of weeks."

"That's because my daughter was shot!" Vicki exclaimed. "What the hell? Do you people not watch any of the news?"

"We understand that," another board member spoke up. "But we just weren't certain that you would be here today."

"Well, I am now," she said. "So please, go ahead and pick up where you all were. I'll catch up."

"Well, Mrs. Klimmings," the board member said. "Before you came in here, we were discussing the stockholders and their displeasure with the company's decisions at the current time."

"What decisions would this be specifically?"

"Ma'am, the decision to allocate a large sum of money into a foreign account."

"I never signed off on that," Vicki stated, standing from her chair, "And I fired Benjamin for it, and then I stopped that authorization in its tracks."

"We also don't approve of the cancellation of the deal with China," said another board member.

"That deal needed to be canceled. It was not going to be good for the company."

"And public opinion of Klimmings Incorporated is at an all-time low," another board member spoke up. "Shareholders are preparing for a massive sell-off. If something is not done, we are going to have to take matters into our own hands."

Vicki leaned forward, glaring the board member in the eyes as if she were looking deep into his soul. "And what is that supposed to mean?"

"I think you know very well what that means, Mrs. Klimmings. Every leader can be replaced, and that includes you too." The board member took his focus off of Vicki and looked at the other board members in the room. "I think this meeting can be adjured."

As the board members concluded the meeting and filed out of the room, Vicki fell silent. She plummeted back into the chair at the head of the table, enveloped in her thoughts. After the last person left, the room fell completely silent, except for the chatting of the board members amongst themselves in the lobby, before they finally made it to the elevator to leave.

* * *

Denise opened the front door to the Klimmings Mansion, and Gabby stepped foot into the entry hall. "Welcome back, Miss Gabriella!" Delilah said. "It's so good to have you back!"

"Thank you, Denise," Gabby said. "I missed you."

She leaned in and hugged Denise, who was very careful with how she hugged her so that she didn't irritate her wounds. Charlotte came in behind them, scanning the walls and ceiling of the entry hall.

"Your parents could really do something different with this hall," she said. "It needs more pop."

"What do you mean?" asked Gabby, turning to Charlotte.

Charlotte leaned in closer to Gabby. "It means your parents are bland," she whispered.

Gabby let out a laugh before she noticed the disapproval on Denise's face. Charlotte proceeded to make her way down the hall toward the sliding glass doors at the end of the hall. She slid the door opened and stepped out onto the back deck, looking out over the large swimming pool and the marble light posts beginning to illuminate the patio around the pool. Then, she turned back toward Gabby and Denise. "I guess this place isn't all that bad. They have an exquisite back garden."

"*Garden*?" Gabby repeated. "Mom's garden is down that hallway." She pointed down the hallway between the dining room and kitchen.

"Do you not call that the back garden?" Charlotte asked, approaching Gabby and Denise. "What do you call it then?"

"The back patio and pool."

"Oh my God. They've middle-classed you!" Charlotte grabbed ahold of Gabby's hands in desperation. "Don't worry, honey. I can fix you. I can make you into the symbol of wealth that you deserve to be."

Denise rolled her eyes at the dramatized scene that Charlotte was displaying. "I'm even more glad that I opted to take you out to my favorite stores before coming here," Charlotte continued. "We've really added a lot of variety to your wardrobe now, haven't we?"

"I guess so," Gabby said before yawning. "If you don't mind, Aunt Charlotte, I am going to go lay down before Mom and Dad come home."

"That's perfectly okay, honey. You get some shut-eye before your parents come home."

Gabby gave Charlotte a quick hug and then proceeded down the entry hall, taking a left to head to the stairs. After Gabby disappeared, Charlotte turned to Denise, who was still standing there. "And what do you do around here again?"

"I'm the family's housekeeper," Denise responded. "I help to manage the house for the family throughout the day."

"And you're the only one?"

"The only one in the mansion. There are a few others that will run the grounds. Mow the lawn. Clean the pool. Things like that."

"Well," Charlotte said as she made her way into the living room. "Get me a coffee. Decaf."

Denise cocked her head in disgust. No member of the Klimmings family had ever spoken to her with such disrespect. "I'll be right back, Miss Charlotte," Denise said as she turned to head to the kitchen.

"Excuse me. That's Mrs. Lee to you. No servant has ever spoken to me by my first name. And you will not be the exception. Do you understand?"

It became almost impossible for Denise to hide the look of disgust on her face, but somehow, she managed to do it. "I am so very sorry, Mrs. Lee," she said sarcastically before turning back toward the kitchen.

"When you finish with my coffee," Charlotte continued. "You can unload my car out front. We bought lots of clothes."

With her back turned to Charlotte, Denise rolled her eyes and proceeded to head into the kitchen.

Charlotte sat down on the sofa in the living room, looking at the decorations on the wall. Contrary to the entry hall, she really liked how the living room was decorated. The light yellow walls with the white trim, the plants in the corners of the room, and the furniture strategically placed throughout the room complemented one another.

Her thoughts were soon interrupted by the front door opening. Charlotte jumped up from the sofa to greet Vicki but stopped in her tracks when she realized that a man had come in, instead of her sister.

"And you are you?" Peter asked Charlotte, standing in the entry hall.

"I am Charlotte Lee," she said. "And you are?"

"I'm Peter Klimmings. Ma'am, don't you recognize who I am? And what are you doing here?"

"I've never taken a liking to being called 'ma'am.' It makes me sound so old and rigid."

"That's not what I asked. What are you doing here?"

"Well, honey. I am Vicki's sister. I presume that you're her husband?"

"Yes. Yes, I am." Peter motioned for them to move into the living room. They both took a seat on the sofa. "Vicki never told me about you, Charlotte. I hope you can understand my amazement right now."

"I wouldn't be surprised that she hasn't spoken of me. In fact, it's been years since she and I have spoken to one another."

"That is strange," Peter said. "Why the hell did you two go so long without speaking?"

"We got into it over some dumb stuff. I think the divorce from her first husband pushed us to the breaking point. Harsh words were said, and then we went our separate ways." Charlotte stood up and walked over to the bar, looking at the large family portrait hanging above it. "We spoke some since, but not regularly. She always sent a Christmas card, but I can't lie and say that I sent one back."

"I'm sorry that happened," Peter said to her as Denise came back into the living room. "Denise, would you mind pouring me a bourbon, please?"

"Yes, Mr. Klimmings," she said as she handed Charlotte the coffee. "It would be my pleasure!"

Denise stepped over to the bar, placing some ice into a glass and then pouring the bourbon for Peter. Then she turned around with the glass of bourbon and began her way over to Peter. Unfortunately, she accidentally collided with Charlotte, who had just taken a sip of her coffee. A substantial amount of coffee spilled over the edge of the mug and onto Charlotte's hand, arm, and down her dress. Even though the coffee's temperature had cooled some, Charlotte was stunned by the spillage and dropped her coffee mug, shattering as it hit the floor.

"YOU DUMBASS!" Charlotte yelled. "YOU'VE RUINED MY DRESS!"

Peter vaulted from the sofa to intervene in the situation. He took the bourbon from Denise and separated the two. "Charlotte," he said. "It was just an accident. She didn't mean to do it."

By now, Charlotte was crying, mourning the loss of her dress. Denise backed away and hung her head, fearing the repercussions of what just happened.

"I'm so sorry, Mr. Klimmings," Denise apologized. "I'll go get something to clean it up!"

As Denise left the living room, she made sure to lock eyes with Charlotte and displayed a faint smirk on her face. Charlotte's emotions shifted from being upset to angry. However, she was still rational enough to realize that she couldn't do anything without Peter thinking that she was some kind of lunatic.

Denise ran into the kitchen, and the front door swung open. "Help!"

Peter ran into the entry hall and saw Miranda dragging in Ben, who was slumped over her shoulders. "Help me!" she called out.

Peter took Ben's other arm and helped lead him into the living room, where the two plopped him onto the sofa. He fell over and went to sleep.

"What the hell happened to him?" Peter asked.

"Delilah called me today," Miranda said as she took a seat in the chair closest to the entry hall. "She was worried about him and asked that I go over to the house to check on him."

"And she couldn't?"

"Dad, she's seven months pregnant. Her ankles are swollen, and she doesn't need this added stress on her before her baby is born." Miranda looked over at Charlotte, who was wiping away the remaining tears from her eyes. "Are you crying?"

"Don't ask," Peter said before taking a swig from his bourbon. "It's been eventful around here."

"Wow. And the whole family isn't even gathered together." Miranda turned and looked around the room. "Where is Mom anyways?"

"She texted me earlier. She won't be in until later tonight. I guess something happened at the office today. Do you know anything about it?"

Denise came in with lots of towels, made her way across the room, and began cleaning up the spilled coffee. Charlotte glared down at Denise as she wiped the floor.

"Since she won't be here soon," Charlotte said after taking her attention off Denise. "Would you mind showing me to the room that I would be staying in?"

Peter looked over at Miranda. "Did your mom say anything about her staying here?"

"No, she didn't."

"Well," Peter said, confused. He walked past Charlotte through the archway leading to the room with the staircase. He passed the stairs and opened both doors on the wall parallel to them. "How about one of these? One is a green theme, and the other is more of a brown theme."

"I'll take the green," said Charlotte.

"Great!" Peter said. "I hope you enjoy your stay with us, Charlotte. Now, I am going to go change before dinner."

"Same here," Miranda added before jumping up to follow Peter up the stairs leaving Charlotte and Denise alone in the living room.

"Bags are in the trunk of my car," Charlotte reminded Denise. "Don't break anything."

Denise looked up at Charlotte and stopped cleaning up the floor. She stood up, glared at her, and then proceeded through the entry hall and out the front door. Charlotte walked over to the green bedroom by the staircase. She looked in and saw the queen-size bed and adjoining bathroom, shared with the brown bedroom.

"I really do hope I enjoy my stay here," Charlotte said to herself as she stepped into the room. "Because I don't plan to leave anytime soon."

CHAPTER 12
JUST ANOTHER KLIMMINGS THANKSGIVING

Vicki opened her bedroom door to find Peter reclined in bed, watching the eleven o'clock news on the TV that hung above the fireplace. "You're home!" he said to her, pausing the channel so that the only thing heard in the bedroom was the crackling of the fire.

"Yes, and I ran into Charlotte when I came in," she said, closing the door behind her. "Why would you let her stay here?"

"I just assumed that she would be staying here."

"Well, you thought wrong." She stepped over to the walk-in closet and started changing.

Peter sat in the bed, puzzled. "What the hell was that supposed to mean?" He got out of bed and walked over to the closet. "You've never told me about Charlotte. How was I supposed to know that she wasn't staying with us?"

Vicki turned to Peter. "Charlotte never comes just to visit. She always wants something, Peter. This time isn't any different."

"Then why is she here?"

"I'm not entirely sure yet. But I can guarantee you that she's here for something."

Vicki took her attention away from Peter and pulled out some silk pajamas from a drawer. At the same time, Peter went back to bed and watched the news. They began reporting on the sharp decline in Klimmings Incorporated stocks, and almost immediately, Vicki stepped out of the closet, glanced at the TV, and then back at Peter. "Oh no. We're not watching this now."

"What the hell happened today? Miranda told me that you had to go into the office."

"I don't want to talk about it," said Vicki. She was finally fully dressed in her pajamas and climbed into bed. She fluffed her pillow and planted her head into it. "The board wanted to meet today. They're making threats. At this point, Peter. I don't know what to do."

Peter turned off the TV and set the remote on the bedside table. "If it matters at all, I think you're handling everything perfectly."

Vicki turned over, facing Peter. "Thank you, dear. I know my problems may seem minute to what you have to deal with, but I really appreciate it that you listen to me."

"I'll always listen to you, Vicki. I love you."

"I love you too," Vicki said before sighing and changing the subject. "You've not mentioned anything about Rebecca White recently. Have you two finally mended wounds?"

Peter squinted his eyes at Vicki and grumbled, "No."

Vicki fell silent, not knowing what to say. She looked down toward the fireplace, watching the flames flicker up and down while listening to the cracking sound of the fire. Finally, she turned to Peter and asked, "So did Denise really intentionally knock Charlotte's coffee all over her?"

Peter let out a small laugh. "I think so," he said, continuing to laugh. "But I don't blame her. She kind of had it coming to her."

"She probably did. She's never taken kindly to any house staff. Her husband, George, apparently has to hire new people all the time."

"Damn. She's just that much of a bitch, then?"

"To be frank, yes. I don't know how else to put it."

The two laughed together before finally saying their goodnights and shutting off the lights. Peter quickly fell asleep, but Vicki tossed and turned all night. Anytime she would close her eyes, she kept dreaming of the board meeting from earlier in the day.

* * *

More and more of the fall leaves fell to the ground, and the air got cold and crisp. Thanksgiving was right around the corner, and the Applegate family didn't have any plans for the holiday. For the moment, all Cathie could think about was planning dinner for Jeremy and Ryan. She stood in the pantry, examining the assortment of foods lining the walls. So many choices, yet Cathie remained unable to make a decision.

As she stood there, Jeremy stepped in with the mail in his hands. "More bills," he grumbled as he sorted through the envelopes, stopping at a cream-colored envelope and pulling it from the stack. "What's this?"

"What's what?" Cathie asked, coming out of the pantry. Her eyes landed on the envelope that Jeremy was proceeding to open. "Oh . . . I think I know what that is."

Jeremy pulled out a card and tossed the envelope onto the counter-top, along with the other pieces of mail. He then began reading over the card. "What the hell?"

"Is it what I think it is?"

"It's an invitation from Vicki Klimmings to attend the Klimmings Thanksgiving Dinner this year!"

"Yep," Cathie said. "That's what I figured it was going to be."

Jeremy looked up at Cathie and held out the invitation. "How did you know this was going to be sent here?"

"Because we get one every year." Cathie pulled out a bar stool from under the counter on the kitchen island and took a seat. "Every year, Vicki invites us, and every year, I throw it in the trash because I know you don't want to deal with that family other than when we go over there for Christmas."

Jeremy set the invitation on the counter in the pile with the rest of the mail. "Now they probably think we're a couple of rude people, Cathie. Why didn't you ever ask me?"

"I just figured I would know the answer. You hate them, Jeremy."

"I don't *hate* them," Jeremy said as he took a seat next to Cathie. "They just piss me off sometimes."

"That's why I haven't ever asked you."

Cathie got off the barstool and went into the living room, sitting on the sofa. Jeremy followed her in shortly after.

"We should go this year," he said.

"You're kidding, right?" Cathie turned her gaze to Jeremy, looking dumbfounded. "You're going to sit at the same table as Peter Klimmings on Thanksgiving and be thankful for everything you have in front of you?"

"It's just one day, Cathie. I can get through one meal with the man."

"*Really?* Do you not remember the anniversary dinner at Finley's?"

"What I remember from that night was Delilah getting scared and running out of that restaurant. Then a couple of days later, we found out she was pregnant." Jeremy took a seat in his chair. "Hell, I'd be scared too if I found out I was carrying an heir to the Klimmings fortune."

"This is what I was meaning," Cathie pointed out. "You can't keep these comments to yourself. What'll happen is that I'll accept this invitation, and then you're going to say something stupid and get us all in trouble."

"Cathie, I promise that I won't let that happen," Jeremy said, leaning in closer to his wife. "I will be on my best behavior there."

"Are you sure? I've wanted us to mend fences with the Klimmings family since our kids got married." Cathie stood from the sofa and took a few steps across the room before turning to Jeremy. "I feel like sitting down for Thanksgiving dinner is the best way to start the healing process between the two families."

Jeremy stood up and approached Cathie, taking her hands. "Darling, I couldn't agree more. Go call Vicki, and tell her that we'll be joining them for Thanksgiving."

Cathie smiled, let go of Jeremy's hands, and headed into the kitchen to call Vicki, leaving Jeremy alone. He turned to the front door and stepped outside on the front porch, turning toward the Klimmings Mansion. He gazed across the field, staring at the colossal white manor. He thought back to all the times he and Peter fought over business in the past. *This won't work. I can never forgive Peter for what he has done to me.*

* * *

Clark sat on the couch in his apartment as Delilah came out of the bathroom. "The best part about having this baby is that I won't have to go pee all the time," said Delilah as she plopped down beside Clark. Her due date was a little over a month away, and her pregnancy was really showing now. She let out a deep sigh as she tried to recline back on the couch.

"I'm so glad you're here right now," Clark said to her. "We haven't been able to see each other as much lately. I was beginning to think you were dumping me."

"No. I just haven't felt like going anywhere." Delilah tried to adjust herself on the couch but failed to get comfortable. "In fact, the only reason why I'm here is that I can't be around Ben right now."

"What has he been doing?'

"He's been drinking a lot lately. I don't know what to do about it, Clark."

Clark sat there for a moment. "It's funny," he said. "We've been waiting for the opportune moment for you to leave him, and yet, here he is presenting you with such a reason to do so."

"You think that now is the best time? I may not be in love with him anymore, but I don't want to destroy him."

"I think it is the perfect time. It will give you so much leverage in the courts. You'll get to keep our baby and take a large sum of money from Ben." He took Delilah's left hand in both of his. "Delilah, we could start a new life together."

Delilah fell silent, gazing at the opposite wall and engulfed in many thoughts.

"Delilah," Clark interrupted. "What's wrong?"

She turned to face Clark, looking him directly in the eyes. "Honey," she began. "It scares me. It scares me about the divorce. It scares me about having the baby." Tears filled her eyes and started falling down her face. "It scares me thinking about who the father is, and it scares me that you are so certain that it is yours."

Clark leaned in and hugged Delilah as she cried harder into his shoulder. "Baby," he said, consoling her. "It's fine. You're going to be fine."

"But what if I'm not," Delilah cried. "What if we find out that the baby is Ben's? I don't want to disappoint you."

"You will never disappoint me. I love you so much." He pulled Delilah off him, leaving saliva and tears all over his shoulder. Then, he looked her directly in the eyes. "And even if the baby is Ben's, he will never know it. That baby is ours, and together, we are going to raise it."

Delilah looked back into Clark's eyes, and a small smile appeared on her face. "What did I do to deserve you? You are so perfect."

"No, you are," Clark said and hugged her again.

* * *

Denise came into the kitchen, passing Vicki, who was checking on the turkey as it was baking in one of the ovens. She went to the stove and checked on the mashed potatoes and corn. "Are you excited about the Applegates coming, Mrs. Klimmings?" Denise asked as she stirred the corn.

"Yes and no," Vicki responded as she closed the oven door to the turkey. "I've wanted them to join us for Thanksgiving for a few years now, but every time I've sent an invitation, they have always declined. Now that they've finally accepted, and it's Thanksgiving Day, I'm beginning to have second thoughts."

"Don't they always join us for Christmas? How would this be any different?"

Vicki joined Denise at the stove, looking at the mashed potatoes. "Because there are presents at Christmas. Who knows how they are when it comes to being thankful."

The two laughed together before Vicki stepped out and crossed the entry hall, heading into the living room where Gabby was sitting, watching TV.

"Gabriella," Vicki said. "What are you doing? The Applegates are going to be here soon, and you're not even ready yet!"

"Yeah, yeah," Gabby said without taking her eyes from the TV. "I'll get ready soon."

"No. You'll get ready now."

"I'm watching the Macy's Thanksgiving Day Parade! I'll get ready in a little bit!"

"Excuse me?"

"I don't even want to eat turkey!"

"I don't care. We have company coming over, Gabriella. You need to go get ready."

"Fine," Gabby said, standing from the sofa and heading through the archway to the stairs. She passed Charlotte before heading up the stairs and slamming her door. Charlotte winced as the sound echoed down the stairs and then proceeded to make her way into the living room, where Vicki turned off the TV.

"Somebody made her mad," Charlotte said. "What happened?"

"Just normal Gabriella stuff," Vicki replied before sitting down on the sofa. "She was like this a lot before the incident at school. Since then, she's settled down some, but lately, it's been resurging. I don't know what her deal is."

"Probably just some teenage rebelliousness. Every teenager goes through some kind of rebellion. That's what they do."

"I understand that, but Miranda and Benjamin were never like that."

"Every family has a rebel. After all, weren't you quite the rebellious one?"

"I was not the rebel! You were!"

"Not as much as you were."

Vicki glared at Charlotte, refraining from saying anything that she would regret. Instead, she decided to stand up and head back toward the kitchen.

"Do you need any help in the kitchen?" Charlotte asked before

Vicki got to the kitchen door. "It's bad enough that your servant can't do it all."

Vicki stopped in her tracks, turned, and headed back to Charlotte. "For your information, she can handle it. I just want to help out because I like to cook. And it's Thanksgiving, so I like to add my personal touch to the special meal."

Vicki turned to leave the room but stopped again and spun back around to Charlotte.

"Also, I am tired of hearing about how Denise isn't up to your satisfaction. She is part of our house staff, and we treat her like she is part of our family. If you don't appreciate that, then you should consider leaving!"

Charlotte fell silent, not knowing what to say. "Now," Vicki added. "I'm heading back into the kitchen."

She turned and headed back into the kitchen, leaving Charlotte all alone. After waiting for a moment, Charlotte started to head back through the archway as Miranda was coming down the stairs. "What is going on down here?"

"Your mother doesn't handle stress very well," Charlotte said to her. "You need to keep an eye on that."

Charlotte continued across the entry hall and went to the family room in the back wing of the house. Miranda started to follow her but stopped in the entry hall, figuring it would be best not to, instead turning to the dining room. Denise was in there adding decorations to the large table and fireplace mantle. A fire had been started, which added extra warmth to the room.

"Tell me this isn't going to be a huge cluster, Denise," Miranda said to Denise as she added some extra fluff to the garland of fall leaves lining the table.

"If you don't mind me saying," Denise said, taking her eyes off the table decorations and looking at Miranda. "When isn't it?"

Miranda chuckled and looked down at the dining table, tweaking a decoration. "I just don't have a very good feeling about this today."

"I think it will be fine, Miss Miranda."

"Yeah. I think you're right." Miranda took her attention from the table and looked back at Denise. "I'm going to go call Jason. He should be here by now."

Miranda stepped out of the dining room into the entry hall. She took out her cellphone and called Jason. It rang a couple of times before he answered.

"Jason," Miranda started. "Are you on your way?"

"Not yet," Jason said, standing shirtless in his living room. He was wearing dress pants and socks, but some dress shirts were lying out on his couch. "I'm about to leave the apartment soon."

"Please hurry. Things are already interesting around here today. I need you here."

"Babe, you don't know how much I love to hear you say that."

"I know," Miranda said. "Just please hurry. See you soon!"

"I lo . . ."

The call ended. Miranda had hung up. Jason put his phone in his back pocket and took one of the white shirts from the couch, putting it on as he walked back to his bedroom. He flicked on the light and stopped just past the doorway, examining the wall adjacent to his bed that was covered with pictures of Miranda. He smiled as he looked over each different image.

He proceeded to walk over to the wall and placed his hand on one of his favorite pictures of Miranda. "I'll always be there for you," he said to himself. "You're my everything, baby. I'm never going to let you go."

* * *

Denise opened the front door and greeted the Applegates. Jeremy and Cathie smiled and gave their pleasantries to Denise as they came in. On the other hand, Ryan did his best not to acknowledge her. He did not want to be inside the Klimmings Mansion. Moreover, he despised the Klimmings family so much that he intentionally chose not to wear his best suit to the meal.

Denise led the Applegates into the living room, where Delilah was reclined on the sofa. "Hey!" she said, trying to sit up. "You made it!"

"Yes, we did," Cathie said, sitting in the only open space left on the sofa. "Your brother didn't want to come."

"Yet, here I am," Ryan chimed in.

"Anyways. How are you doing? How's our grandbaby doing?"

"Oh, they're doing just fine," Delilah said as she put her hand on her baby bump. "I'm just ready to have this kid."

"I bet you are. I'm just so excited to meet the baby. Aren't you Jeremy?"

Cathie turned to Jeremy, who was examining the living room. He caught Cathie staring at him and said, "What?"

"What are you doing?" Cathie asked him. "Are you looking over their house?"

"I'm looking for termites. I need to know if we need to have our house sprayed again."

"I can assure you," someone said from across the room. "This house doesn't have any termites."

Cathie and Jeremy whipped their heads around and saw Peter standing in the archway on the other side of the living room. "Peter," Cathie said, heading over to him to hug him. "Thank you for letting us share this Thanksgiving Day with you and your family."

"Thank my wife," he said as he made his way over to the bar. "It was her idea."

"Well, we'll be sure to thank her then," Jeremy said.

"Would any of you want a drink?" Peter asked, heading to the bar. "Ryan, you want anything?"

"No, thank you," Ryan said. "I don't drink this early."

"Really? Hell, I figured you'd have to drink all the time living with your father."

"*Peter*," Delilah sighed. "Do we need to do this right now?"

Peter turned around, holding two glasses of Kentucky bourbon. "I'm sorry," he said before taking one of the glasses to Jeremy. "Here ya go, Jeremy. Have a drink!"

"Thank you," Jeremy said, confused. "I didn't ask for one, though,"

"I know, but I figured you needed one. You see, I know about your little deal with President Wu."

"His what?" Cathie interjected.

"He didn't tell you guys?" Peter said as he sat down in the chair beside Delilah. "He made this deal with President Wu over in China to sink Klimmings Incorporated. It almost worked too, so I give you kudos on that!" He held up his glass of bourbon to toast Jeremy's failed attempt at bankrupting the company.

"When were you going to tell me about this?" Cathie asked Jeremy.

"Honey, it's not as bad as it sounds."

"Really? You wanted to come over here knowing that you had this little deal all lined out. Was it so that you could figure out what the Klimmingses are up to?"

"Mom," Delilah interrupted. "Talk about it later. I'm sure it's not that big of a deal, just like Dad says."

"You wonder why Ben was fired from Klimmings Incorporated?" Peter asked Delilah. "It's because of this damn deal. I guess one night, after some fight between you and him, he came in drunk and signed the authorization papers for the deal. Why do you think the company is in such disarray right now, Delilah? It's because of him falling for this asinine deal."

Delilah sat still, looking over Peter's shoulder. He turned toward where she was looking and saw Ben standing in the archway, dressed in a suit with a purple tie.

"Thanks for the support, Dad," Ben said before heading over to the bar to pour himself a Scotch.

"Are you sure you should be drinking right now?" Peter asked him as he rose from the chair and made his way toward Ben.

"I'm going to need something to get me through this day."

"Ben," Peter whispered to him at the bar. "Put the drink down. You do not need anything to drink."

"And you know what I need?" Ben took a sip of the freshly poured glass of Scotch. "Maybe Mom should hire you as chief financial officer, or whatever the hell I was. I'm just some disappointment right now."

The room fell silent as Ben looked over at Delilah. She remained expressionless on the sofa. She wanted to cry but held in her tears so that her husband wouldn't notice how upset seeing him drink made her.

Finally, Ryan decided to break the silence in the room. "Isn't this going to be so much fun?!" He turned and headed down the entry hall to use the bathroom at the end of the hall, next to the sliding glass door.

Before anyone else could say anything, the doorbell rang. Denise, who was still in the living room, made her way through the people and out into the entry hall. She opened the front door to greet Jason. "Hello, Mr. Jason."

"Well, hello, Denise," he said as he stepped inside. "Where is Miranda at?"

Without missing a beat, Miranda came around the corner into the entry hall, followed by Vicki. "Right here," Miranda said, hugging Jason.

"Is the turkey done yet?" Peter asked Vicki.

"Yes. It's all done, and we can go ahead and get seated."

Denise made her way to the kitchen to help bring the food out to the dining room. As she and Vicki moved the food into the dining room, everyone else took their seats. Peter sat in his customary seat at the head of the table in front of the fireplace. To his left sat Miranda, followed by Jason, Ryan, and Charlotte. Vicki sat opposite Peter, followed by Gabby, Cathie, Jeremy, Delilah, and Ben.

After they all were seated, Vicki looked up at Peter and said, "Peter, on this Thanksgiving Day, why don't you say a prayer over our meal?"

Peter hesitated as everyone at the table turned their attention to him. "Uh . . ." he let out. "Go ahead and bow your heads."

Everyone at the table bowed their heads, and Peter began the Thanksgiving prayer.

"Our Father, thank you for this meal that you have blessed us with. Thank you to the wonderful cooks who helped prepare it: our beloved Denise and my lovely wife, Vicki. Both of which are two damn good cooks."

Cathie opened her eyes, giving Peter a look, but he continued.

"Thank you for the past few years, Father. You have blessed my family in a variety of ways. Thank you for allowing me to be elected as our country's forty-ninth president. You have continued to bless me and this country, and I know that you will give me another four years in office."

"Or maybe He won't," Jeremy muttered.

"What the hell is that supposed to mean?" Peter asked, turning to Jeremy, halting the prayer,

"Gentlemen," Vicki chimed in, trying to diffuse the tension.

"It just means that maybe He doesn't want you to continue your presidency," Jeremy continued. "You know, maybe it isn't His will anymore."

"Oh my God," Delilah whispered to herself, placing her head into the hands on the table.

"Peter . . ." Vicki said, continuing to calm the tension.

"Excuse me?" Peter started, standing from his seat. "I am a good president, thank you very much! I am in the process of bringing this country out of its worst recession since the COVID Pandemic. I have negotiated new trade deals for this country, and I have a decent approval rating by the people of this nation. So why wouldn't God want me to continue my duties to this country?"

"Maybe He wants someone who actually acts godly."

"And who would that be? *You?* Hell, you deceived my company, Jeremy. You negotiated with a man who tried to sexually assault my wife. How the hell does that make you any more godly than me?"

"PETER!" Vicki shouted. "Just finish the damn prayer!"

Collectively, the table fell silent. Peter looked Vicki in the eyes and saw how irritated she was. She had spent all morning in the kitchen helping Denise prepare this grand meal to celebrate Thanksgiving, and in just a matter of minutes, he and Jeremy were ruining the entire meal. Peter retook his seat, bowed his head, and finished the prayer. "And with all that, Lord, we thank you for all that you have given us. Amen."

"Amen," they all said.

But before anyone could say anything else, Charlotte turned to Vicki and said, "Are all of your Thanksgiving prayers like that?"

"No," Vicki grumbled back as Peter began to carve the turkey. Charlotte turned over to Ryan, noticing him for the first time.

"Hey, handsome," she said, flirty. "Who are you again?"

"Ryan," he said. "And you are?"

"Oh, I'm Charlotte. But let's talk about you for a moment. How did you get that beautiful hair of yours?"

"From one of my parents, I guess."

Ryan smiled at Charlotte, and she winked back at him. Then she turned back to Vicki, who was glaring at her. Before Charlotte could say anything to her, both of their attention was brought to Ben, who called out, "Let me carve the turkey for once!"

"Ben, no!" Peter said sternly. "You've been drinking too much. You aren't going to butcher this turkey!"

"You don't think I'm good enough, do you?"

"That's not what I said." Peter set the carving utensils down.

"Ben," Cathie chimed in. "Maybe you could do it at Christmas?"

"Like he'll let me cut it then. I've never been good enough for anything."

"You want to carve the turkey?!" Peter shouted as he grew more irritated. "Fine. Carve the damn turkey, then!" He shoved the turkey and carving utensils over to Ben.

"Are you sure you got this, honey?" Delilah said as he picked up the carving utensils.

"Yes," he said before taking a sip of his Kentucky bourbon that was sitting on the table. "I've got this, Delilah."

"Hey Ben," Ryan interrupted. "Try not to mess this up like you did your family's company."

Immediately, Ryan realized he should not have said that, especially since Ben had been drinking and had a knife and carving fork in his hands.

"You don't think I can do this?" Ben asked as he stood up from his seat and grabbed hold of the turkey platter. "Then you cut the turkey then!" He shoved the turkey platter across the table toward Ryan. As the turkey zoomed across the dining room table, the mashed potatoes were pushed into the green beans, causing the gravy to spill over onto Gabby's plate and staining the elegant white table cloth that lay underneath it all. Candles were knocked over into the pies and corn before finally, the turkey slid off the table, landing between Ryan and Charlotte.

"Oh my God!" Charlotte exclaimed as the turkey grazed her dress. "My dress! You crazy dumbass! You ruined my dress!"

Chaos ensued at the table with Peter, Ryan, and Jeremy yelling at Ben. Miranda hung her head and repeatedly apologized to Jason, and Gabby whipped out her phone to video the entire scene. All Vicki could do was plant her face into her hands.

With tears running down her face, Charlotte jumped up from her seat and tried to run out of the room. She took two steps before she stepped on the turkey. She slipped and collided with the floor with a loud thud!

Shocked by everything happening, Denise ran over to Charlotte, checking if she was okay.

"Get away from me," Charlotte wailed. "I don't need your help!"

"Are you okay?" Cathie asked after making her way over to Charlotte.

"Do I look okay?! My dress is ruined!" Charlotte continued to lay all sprawled out on the floor, bawling.

As she cried and the rest of the family members held Ryan back from punching Ben, Vicki lifted her head from her hands. She whispered to herself, "Just another Klimmings Thanksgiving."

* * *

Laying on her bed, Gabby replayed the Thanksgiving dinner video, laughing each time her aunt slipped on the turkey and fell, flinging it under the table in the process. As she started to replay the video again, she heard a knock on her door.

"Gabriella?"

She recognized the voice to be Vicki's.

"Yes, Mom?"

"May I come in?"

"Sure."

Gabby quickly locked her phone so that Vicki couldn't see that she had videoed the incident earlier in the day. Then the door opened, and Vicki came in.

"What a day it was," she said, closing the door behind her.

"Yes, it was."

"I didn't think we were ever going to get the Applegates to leave. I don't blame Ryan for wanting to punch out Benjamin. In fact, between you and me, he kinda deserved it."

Gabby laughed a little. "Yeah, he really did. In fact, we all should've punched him. He ruined your delicious turkey."

Vicki sat down at the foot of Gabby's bed and smiled. "Ha! It's such a good thing we have Denise, though. She came through with volunteering to get us that takeout from her favorite Chinese place."

"Yes! It was surprisingly good!"

"Too bad Aunt Charlotte didn't eat any of it. I think we've finally got her calmed down now. I would've thought she was upset about falling on the turkey, but nope! She was upset over the dress."

Gabby laughed out loud, and Vicki joined with her. The two continued laughing when the door to the bedroom opened.

"What are you two laughing about?" Miranda asked, standing in the doorway.

"Oh, just laughing about Aunt Charlotte," Gabby said in between laughs. "If you could have seen her slip and fall on that turkey . . ." Gabby continued laughing, unable to finish the sentence.

Miranda smiled, stepped into the room, and closed the door behind her. "Well, I was too busy apologizing to Jason," she said. "I'll be surprised if he keeps talking to me after Ben's little stunt today."

"I think he will," Vick said. "He's a good man, Miranda. You really did pick out a winner."

"You think so?"

"I agree," Gabby said. "He is very sweet, and I feel like he fits in so well!"

"Yes, he does," Vicki added. "And, one day, both of you will have the man of your dreams. We'll have our family holidays, and us Klimmings women will get to laugh together, just like we are now."

Miranda smiled and said, "That will be so nice."

She turned to look at Gabby, who was smiling. Immediately, Miranda recognized that Gabby was portraying the fakest smile she had

189

presented in a long time. She knew her sister and could tell whenever she was uncomfortable like she was during this moment. After all, why would she be? She was only eighteen anyways. She had plenty of years to worry about marriage and such.

"Well," Vicki said. "I'm going to go to bed now and put this day behind me."

"Goodnight, Mom," Miranda said.

Gabby hesitated for a moment, breaking herself out of deep thought. "Goodnight!"

"I love you girls," Vicki said as she opened the door.

"Love you too," Gabby and Miranda responded.

Vicki closed the door behind her, leaving Gabby and Miranda alone. Miranda looked at Gabby and was preparing to say something when Gabby said, "Do you want to see the video of Aunt Charlotte slipping on the turkey?"

"Of course!"

Gabby scooted over in the bed, leaving room for Miranda to join beside her. Gabby unlocked her phone and started the video, giving the two one more reason to laugh after an interesting Thanksgiving Day.

CHAPTER 13
THE CHINESE DRAGON

Delilah flung open the door to the townhouse, barging in. "I can't believe you behaved that way!" she shouted as she stomped through the living room. Behind her came Ben, who looked carefree at the moment.

"I wasn't going to let them talk to me that way," he explained, closing the door behind him.

Delilah whipped around toward Ben. "You single-handedly ruined Thanksgiving, Ben! And with that, any hope of my family ever liking you has gone down the drain! They will never forgive you!"

"I don't give a damn if they will ever forgive me!" Ben stepped closer toward Delilah. "And I don't think you care either."

"What's that supposed to mean?"

"Oh, Delilah! Don't give me that crap!" Ben plopped down on the couch. "I've seen the text messages. I've found the socks. Admit it, Delilah. You don't care about me anymore. Instead, you spend all your free time around this Clark guy, don't you?"

Delilah remained silent, shocked at Ben's revelation. *He knows.*

She moved over to the recliner and sat down. "How long have you known?"

"Since before Gabby's accident."

"That explains so much."

"And when were you going to tell me about him, Delilah? Or were you ever? Were you just going to let me keep moping around while you slept with every young, single boy in the D.C. metropolitan?"

"I . . . I . . . don't know."

Ben lept from the couch and went into the kitchen, pulling a beer from the refrigerator. "C'mon, Delilah," he said as he used the bottle opener to take the top off. "When were you going to decide that our marriage was finally over?" He came back into the living room, sitting back down on the couch where he was earlier. "Were you going to wait before or after the baby was born? Or better yet, is that baby even mine, Delilah?"

Delilah sat quietly in the chair, filled with guilt and unable to speak.

"Answer me, Delilah. Is the baby mine?"

"I . . . don't know."

"What? You don't know?"

"I said that I don't know!" she said, standing up. "I'm leaving." She made her way over to the door, grabbing her keys on the way out.

"That's right," Ben said as she went out the front door. "You just run away from this, just like you run away from every problem you've ever had!" He got up and opened the front door, standing in the doorway as Delilah backed her purple car out of the driveway and drove away.

* * *

"I hope my family didn't scare you away," Miranda said, talking on the phone with Jason. "They aren't normally this crazy."

"Ha!" Jason laughed. "That was nothing. Before my parents divorced, they fought with each other all the time."

"I still can't apologize enough for the way they acted."

"Miranda," Jason started. "It's been a week and a half since Thanksgiving. It's okay. If I were bothered by it, I would have stopped talking to you by now."

They both laughed together on the phone. "Well, I'm glad you continue to put up with me and my family."

"You know I always will, babe."

"That's so sweet of you, Jason. I'll text you later, okay?"

"Okay, babe. I love you."

Miranda ended the phone call, setting her phone down on the coffee table, leaning back on the sofa, and running her hands through her hair as she took a deep sigh. Before she could process her thoughts, Vicki rounded the corner of the stairs, storming into the living room.

"Have you looked at the news?!" she exclaimed.

"No."

"Get a load of this!" Vicki snatched the remote and turned on the TV. Immediately, the video of the Thanksgiving fiasco appeared on the screen. It showed Jeremy restraining Ryan, keeping him from attacking Ben, and Peter yelling at Ben. Suddenly, the camera shifted over to show Charlotte slip and fall on the floor. Then, the video cut back to the talk show hosts who were laughing at Charlotte's ungraceful fall. "This is obviously Gabriella's! Did she post this online?"

"I don't know," Miranda said as she took out her phone and began scrolling through her social media accounts. "Uh . . ."

"What? She posted it, didn't she?"

"Yeah. It's right here on her Instagram."

"Let me see." Vicki snatched the phone out of Miranda's hand. "She has over two hundred thousand likes!"

"Yeah. She doesn't have her account set on private either, so that number is just going to go up."

"Your father is going to flip when he finds out about this," Vicki said as she handed the phone back to Miranda. "He's already worried about reelection. How am I going to spin this?"

"She could take it down," Miranda suggested. "Have her take it down when she comes home from school today."

"That's a good idea! What if I had someone pick her up from school and bring her home early to do that?"

Vicki turned to head back upstairs to grab her phone but stopped after hearing a terrible shriek come from the back wing of the house. She jolted around to Miranda, and they both ran back to the family room, where Charlotte was seated on the sofa, watching the TV in horror. It wasn't long before Vicki and Miranda realized what she was shrieking about.

The Thanksgiving video that Gabby had taken was playing on the TV. However, on this channel, the program had edited the video to add cartoon sound effects when Charlotte slipped on the turkey and again when she hit the floor. Charlotte turned to Vicki, crying, and said, "Why did she let this out? I look like such a fool!"

"I don't know why she let it out, Charlotte, but we are going to be sure that she takes it down."

"What's the point?! I'm ruined!" Charlotte fell over on the sofa, burying her face in a pillow, and sobbed. Vicki motioned to Miranda to leave the room, and they both backed out slowly, heading back into the entry hall.

"This is ridiculous," Vicki said as they stopped in front of the archway leading to the two guest bedrooms and stairs.

"Is she always this dramatic?"

"Yes. She always has been."

"Wow. I can see why you never reached out to her."

"Well, there were some other things that happened as well."

"What was that?"

"When I divorced my first husband, she sided against me during our divorce hearings. She thought I was making a mistake divorcing him, and she told the judge that. He almost didn't grant the divorce because of it."

Miranda paused, figuring out what to say. "I'm sorry that happened, Mom."

"It's okay. In actuality, I'm glad it happened. It taught me not to trust her as much as I had before. Charlotte can be quite manipulative. Watch her."

Miranda processed what Vicki was saying. She hadn't heard her mom speak so ill of her aunt before. "Mom, Charlotte didn't have anything to do with the end of your first marriage, did she?"

"No! Bill and I just fell out of love. Our marriage lasted only two years, and in the end, we both decided to end it together."

"Then why did Charlotte testify at the divorce hearing?"

"Well, she felt that we were rushing the decision. Between you and me, I think she wanted me to stay married to him because of the money he had."

"That doesn't make any sense. Does she not know that Dad has money?"

"He didn't when we first got together. He had just started Klimmings Incorporated, and only after we were married did he make it into the great company it is today." Vicki looked down at her watch. "I need to find Denise and have her send someone to pick up Gabriella. We're going to have to have her take that post down."

Vicki took off down the entry hall, taking a left toward the kitchen, leaving Miranda alone. Miranda turned to look back toward the family room but decided not to bother Charlotte. Instead, she stepped into the adjacent room, going up the stairs and to her bedroom.

* * *

Rebecca White stood outside the Oval Office, waiting for Peter to be ready for her. Without realizing it, she was tapping her foot, making a slight thumping sound each time her foot hit the floor.

"Would you like to sit down?" a visibly irritated Martha asked.

"No," Rebecca responded. "I do not want to sit down. I want to see the president."

"As I said earlier, he told me that he will send out one of the butlers to let you in when he is ready."

"I hope he is soon. I don't have all day."

Rebecca turned her attention back to the door. Without her realizing, Martha made a visible look of disgust. Never had anyone been so disrespectful to the president while in her office. So badly, she wanted to say something but held her tongue for the sake of Peter's, not her own. She didn't want to do something that would make things harder for the president.

The door opened within a few seconds, and a butler stepped out. "The president is ready for you, Madam Speaker."

"Thank you," Rebecca responded before she passed by the butler. Her eyes immediately noticed the navy blue drapes hanging around the large windows behind the Resolute desk as she stepped in. Then she turned her attention over to the cream-colored walls, the oak trim, the hardwood floor, and finally, the dark blue rug with the quotes by George Washington and Thomas Jefferson embroidered along the top and bottom of it.

"Rebecca!" Peter exclaimed, bringing her attention from the room's décor to himself. "It's so good to meet with you again!"

Peter met Rebecca in front of the *Resolute* desk, offering a chair for her to sit in. Once she was seated, he sat behind the desk.

"Mr. President," she began. "I doubt that you will be sharing the same feelings about this meeting after you hear what I have to say." She took a moment to adjust herself in the chair and crossed her legs. "I have to deny your request to address a joint session of Congress, Mr. President."

"May I ask why?"

"Because we felt that with January coming next month, you will have that opportunity to address a joint session during your State of the Union address. Plus, we also think that with the new Congress expected to be sworn in next month, you won't have any time to push through any new legislation before then."

"So you're just going to sit in the Capitol Building and do nothing until then?"

Rebecca stood from her seat, adjusting her blazer. "No, Mr. President. What we are going to do is listen to the American people. They want you out, Peter."

"What the hell do you mean by that?"

"They voted out the Dems, Peter." Rebecca leaned onto the *Resolute* desk making direct eye contact with Peter. "They voted them out, and they wanted us instead. And in two years, they're going to vote you out, Peter. As the leader of the Republican party, I can guarantee that I will support what the American people want."

Peter rose from his seat, continuing to keep eye contact with Rebecca. "Go to hell, Rebecca."

She laughed out loud. "With you as our commander-in-chief, we're already there." Rebecca turned and proceeded to make her way out of the Oval Office, leaving Peter speechless. She was led down halls by two Secret Service agents, who stopped by the entrance to the West Wing so that she could put on her red coat. Then, two butlers opened the doors so that she could leave.

She proceeded to step out under the awning and turned to the right, heading down to the press, who immediately started snapping pictures as she approached them. Hearing the continuous clicks of the cameras, Rebecca smiled and put her hands in her coat pockets to keep them warm.

"Speaker White!" one of the press members shouted. "Can you describe your conversation with the president?"

Rebecca approached the plethora of microphones set up for her to speak. "We had a very enlightening conversation. Unfortunately, it appears that President Klimmings is living in a fantasy and is continuing to refuse to listen to the desires of the American people."

"How is the president living in a fantasy?" another reporter called out.

Rebecca smiled and chuckled. "You'll see. You'll all soon see."

* * *

"You delete that right now, Gabriella!" Vicki said to Gabby, who was sprawled out on her bed.

"I don't see why it's such a big deal," Gabby responded. "It's already spread to the media, and people are loving it." She sat up on her bed. "It's exactly what this family needs to help build up their public image."

"Your aunt is devastated right now! If you could have seen how she was wailing earlier today, you would have felt so guilty!"

"I didn't think about that . . . Aunt Charlotte will be okay though. She's a grown woman!"

"Have you met Charlotte? Have you not seen how she reacts to things?"

Gabby let out a laugh. "You're right, Mom. She won't be able to handle it."

Vicki sat down on the bed beside Gabby. "So, are you going to delete the video then?"

"I guess," Gabby sighed. "But just because the video is taken down doesn't mean that it's going to be erased off of everything else. That video will never away. Everyone has already seen it."

"That's exactly why you will be writing your aunt an apology letter."

"Really?!"

"Yes, ma'am. And if you still want Michelle to stay the night tonight, then you best get to writing soon." Vicki slid off the bed and left the room, closing the door behind her. Gabby sat alone on her bed before she sighed, pulled a notebook out from her backpack, and began writing.

* * *

Across the field, the Klimmings Mansion looked so beautiful in contrast to the setting sun. Delilah looked out the window, admiring the view. She thought about the Klimmings family and what they might be doing right now.

"Missing them already?"

Delilah jolted around. Ryan was sitting at the island in the kitchen. "Ryan!" she exclaimed. "You scared the crap out of me."

"Sorry. I just came in here to grab a quick snack and found you looking out the window. You don't miss them already, do you?"

"No," Delilah said as she took a seat across from Ryan. "I don't miss them already. It was a lovely view, and I was taking it all in. The mansion doesn't look as beautiful up close as it does from here."

"Tell that to Dad. He wishes that he could build something to block it all out."

Delilah laughed. "He never did like them, even before I married

Ben. Where is he anyway?"

"On some trip for work. He's been on a lot of business trips lately."

"Really?"

"Yes. Applegate Technology has been keeping him busy." Ryan hopped from the barstool and made his way over to the refrigerator. He opened it and began looking for something to snack on. "So, other than admiring the view, why were you looking over at the Klimmings Mansion?"

Delilah sighed. "I just keep thinking about Ben. Anytime I try to think of something else, Ben's face somehow makes its way back in. I can't get rid of him."

"Why is that? You two haven't seen each other or spoken in over a week."

"Well, we *have* spoken," Delilah confessed. "Kinda. I mean, he's texted me a few times, but I haven't responded most of the time."

Ryan closed the refrigerator and turned toward Delilah. "And what did he say?"

"He's apologized a few times. A couple of other times, he's questioned whether he's the father. I just can't deal with him right now."

"Why would he question if he's the father?"

Delilah fell silent, keeping her gaze toward the counter and refusing to look Ryan in the eyes.

"Delilah," Ryan said. "Why would he be questioning if he's the father?"

She brought her attention back to Ryan. "I'm getting pretty tired. I think I'm going to go lay down." She stood up and left the room without saying anything else. For a moment, Ryan just sat silent as he pieced the puzzle together in his mind.

"Oh, Delilah," he whispered to himself. "What have you done?"

* * *

The family remained quiet as they ate their dinner. Vicki looked up from her salad, making eye contact with Peter. Beside her, Charlotte nudged her lettuce around on her plate. Jason and Miranda, who were next to her, quietly finished their salads. No one was sitting on the opposite side of the table, making the whole table look very unbalanced.

Finally, Vicki couldn't bear the silence any longer. "How was work, honey?"

Peter glared at Vicki. "Do you really want me to talk about it?"

"Please do! We need something to disrupt this weird silence."

"Amen to that," Jason chimed in as he finished the last piece of his salad.

Peter turned his head toward him and took another bite of his salad. "Rebecca White came to visit me today," he began, turning back to Vicki. "She denied my request to address a joint session of Congress. She feels that since we lost the midterms, the next Congress should decide how we go from here."

"What?!" Vicki exclaimed. "How can she do that? They're supposed to be America's representatives!"

"She's got the upper hand right now. She holds all the cards, Vicki. These next two years are going to be hell." Peter took another bite of his salad, finishing it off. "That's why we *all* need to watch how we behave in public." He turned toward Charlotte, who was very quiet. "It also came to my attention that there was a video that was leaked . . ."

"It was not leaked!" Charlotte interrupted, slamming her fork down on the table. "That little turd posted it online for everyone to see!"

The dining room fell silent once again, only to be interrupted by the side door opening and Denise rolling in the cart with the Wagyu steaks, along with the other sides of the meal. "Dinner is served!" Denise announced as the door closed behind her.

"Denise, just leave that over there," Peter said, pointing toward a wall. "We've got to deal with something first."

She parked the cart against the wall and headed out of the room.

"Charlotte," Vicki said. "I already told you, Gabriella deleted the video. It's not posted anymore."

"But the damage has already been done! My life has been ruined!" Charlotte jumped up and ran out of the room, crying. The rest of the family glanced at each other in the wake of what had just happened.

"I thought you told me that it wasn't always like this," Jason whispered to Miranda.

"It usually isn't," she said. "Charlotte isn't usually here to make it this way."

Peter brought his attention back to Vicki. "Where is Gabby, anyways?"

"She's upstairs with Michelle. They ordered pizza and are just hanging out. Do you want me to get her?"

"No. I think it would be a good idea for those two to stay away from each other for a while."

"I'll talk to Charlotte later," Vicki said. "She's got to cut this out."

"I agree," Peter added before getting up from the table and making his way over to the steaks on the cart. "Now, who's ready for some steaks? These things cost me a whole helluva lot of money, so you all better eat up!"

"I'll have some!" Jason said, jumping up from his chair, holding his plate out.

Peter glanced back at Jason and smiled. He picked up one of the Wagyu steaks with the pair of tongs and placed it onto Jason's plate. "Bet you haven't ever had a steak as good as these?"

"I bet not!"

"Hell, he's gonna go back home and tell his friends that not only did he eat a damn good steak, but the president of the United States served him." He pointed the tongs at Jason. "Not many people can say that!"

Jason chuckled and headed back to his seat. Miranda let a smile flash across her face when Jason's eyes made contact with hers.

"Don't ya just sit there! Come on and eat!" Peter said, motioning with the tongs for everyone to come up. Miranda took her plate and made her way up to Peter, followed by Vicki. As they were getting their food, Denise came back into the room carrying five servings of crème brûlée.

"Oh my goodness!" she exclaimed. "Mr. Klimmings, I can serve that for you!"

"It's alright, Denise. I got it."

"Are you sure, Mr. Klimmings?" she sat the crème brûlée on the table and came over to Peter.

"I'm sure, Denise. It's fine!" Peter said as he plopped a steak on his plate. "If you want to move these sides to the table, then that would be great, though."

Denise jumped in, grabbed a couple of the sides, and moved them over to the table. As she set the last one down, Peter added, "You may want to make a plate for Charlotte. One of us can take it to her, but she won't be dining with us."

* * *

Laughter filled Gabby's room. Gabby and Michelle were sitting on the bed in their pajamas, rewatching the video of Charlotte from Thanksgiving.

"I still can't believe you caught that," Michelle said as the video ended.

"Neither can I!" Gabby laughed. "When I'm having a bad day, I just rewatch it."

"It's literally one of the best things I've ever seen!" Michelle opened the box of pizza that sat on the bed with them and took out a piece. "But why did you take it down? You were gaining so many new followers, and it had so many likes?"

"Mom asked me to. Aunt Charlotte apparently had a meltdown over it?"

"Damn. Is she okay now?"

"I don't know. I haven't seen her in the past couple of days."

"Gabby," Michelle said before taking a bite out of her pizza. "You have to apologize to her. Tell her you didn't mean to upset her when you posted it."

"I did. Mom forced me to write an apology letter to her."

"Okay, but you should still tell her that you're sorry. Anybody can write a letter."

Gabby fell silent, looking down at the bed. Michelle tried to grab her attention again but had no luck.

"Gabby," Michelle said. "Gabby, what's wrong?"

She looked up at Michelle with tears in her eyes. "I can't get that day out of my mind, Michelle. Every time I close my eyes, I see him."

Michelle took a deep sigh, set her slice of pizza back on the pizza box, and took Gabby by the shoulders.

"Gabby," she said. "You have to talk to someone about this. Tell your mom. Tell your dad. Tell somebody. It's understandable to be haunted by this, Gabby, but this was over a month ago. You need to talk to someone."

"But I talk to you? Why can't I just talk to you?"

"Because I'm eighteen years old with no experience to help you cope and deal with the trauma of going through that. Dammit, Gabby, you were shot by this guy who held us hostage to get back at your mom. That's some messed up shit right there!"

"I know. I know."

"Promise me you'll talk to someone."

Gabby took a deep sigh. "I promise," she said before wiping away the tears from her eyes.

"Good." Michelle leaned in and hugged Gabby, who let a small smile appear on her face. The two embraced for a bit before letting go, returning to looking at each other. As their gaze met, Gabby felt something inside her. Something she hadn't felt before.

In this moment, nothing else mattered to Gabby. It was just her and Michelle. Two good friends. Two best friends enjoying the evening together. Yet, at that moment, Gabby began to do something she had never felt the urge to do before as she closed her eyes and leaned in toward Michelle, who did the same. Finally, their lips met, and they kissed for the first time.

Gabby's stomach erupted with butterflies. Her lips connected to Michelle's, and within a second, the kiss was over. Michelle had pulled back, looking embarrassed. "I'm so sorry."

"Don't be," Gabby said. "I'm not."

"I shouldn't have done that." Michelle began to fidget with her hair. "I . . . I . . . Don't tell anyone about that."

"I won't." Gabby grabbed hold of Michelle's hands. She felt how much she was trembling. "Michelle, it'll be okay. You'll be fine."

Michelle took a deep gulp and closed her eyes for a second before opening them again. "I think I need to go to bed now."

"Alright then," Gabby said as she began to move things off the bed. "Let me just clear this off then." Gabby took the pizza box and set it on her bedside table next to the lamp. Then she looked back over to Michelle, who was making herself comfortable under the covers, facing away from her.

"Goodnight, Michelle."

"Goodnight."

Gabby pulled back the covers and climbed into bed, facing away from Michelle. She turned off the lamp and let the dark fill the room. The butterflies that had once made themselves home in her stomach were gone now. Instead, Gabby just laid in bed, pondering to herself about what had just occurred.

* * *

Charlotte heard two knocks on the door before it opened. She looked over at the door and saw Vicki step into the room with a tray of food. "I thought you might like this," she said, placing the tray on the bedside table.

"Thank you," Charlotte responded drearily.

"What's wrong?" Vicki sat down at the end of Charlotte's bed. "Why are you still upset over all of this?"

"It's not just that. Other things are playing into it."

"Like what? Tell me."

Charlotte sighed. "He's left me for someone else, Vicki."

Vicki's heart sank deep into her stomach. She wasn't expecting this to come from Charlotte.

"That is why I came down here," Charlotte confessed. "I didn't know what else to do, so I packed my things and left."

"How did you find out?"

"I looked through George's phone. I saw the messages between him and one of the cheerleaders from his football team."

"Oh my God," Vicki sighed. "I'm so sorry, Charlotte."

"You didn't know." She wiped tears from her eyes. "But that's it. That's why I came back here."

"Do you know what you're going to do next?"

"I don't know," Charlotte sighed. "I guess, at some point, I'll have to go back to California to figure things out."

"Are you going to stay with him?"

"Hell no! He can stay with his harlot cheerleader!"

Vicki chuckled. "Good," she said. "I was going to have to smack you if you weren't going to leave him."

Charlotte smiled. "Thank you for bringing me some food. I think I'm going to stay in here tonight, though."

"That's fine," Vicki said as she stood from the bed. "If you need anything, just holler for me, okay?"

"Okay."

Vicki opened the bedroom door, turned back to Charlotte, and said, "Goodnight, Charlotte."

"Goodnight."

She closed the door behind her and began to make her way upstairs when she heard the doorbell. She paused a moment before deciding to answer the door.

"I got it, Denise," she called out as she made her way through the living room and out to the entry hall. Vicki unlocked and opened the front door. A police officer met her on the other side. "Can I help you?"

"Mrs. Klimmings," the police officer said. "We have your son with us. He's very drunk, and we weren't sure whether you would want us to take him to the tank or here."

Vicki peered over the officer's shoulder and saw a very disoriented Ben held up by two other police officers. She sighed, "Bring him in. His bedroom is upstairs. The door on the left."

The officers proceeded to lead Ben into the house. Vicki turned to help them find Ben's bedroom when she saw Denise. "Denise," she said. "Can you show them where Benjamin's bedroom is?"

"Yes, ma'am," she said before directing her attention to the officers. "Follow me, please."

Vicki followed them to the stairs, staying behind as the officers took Ben up to his room. "What's going on?" she heard Charlotte ask from behind.

Vicki turned around, seeing Charlotte standing in the doorway to her bedroom. "Benjamin," she said. "He's going to need all the help we can give him."

* * *

The double doors flung open, and Jeremy stepped into the large red room. In the center of the room sat President Wu. He stood from his chair as Jeremy approached and offered him a seat. "Take a seat, Jeremy."

"This isn't a social call, Wu," Jeremy said as he sat down. "I'm here because you have yet to offer any retaliation on Peter Klimmings."

President Wu sat back in his chair and laughed. "You Americans are all the same. So impatient."

"It's almost been two months!"

"Patience, Jeremy. Have patience." President Wu stood from his chair and turned to face the dragon statue behind him. He looked over the golden statue, admiring how it had been sculpted and formed. "Aren't dragons just fascinating?"

"What the hell does that have to do with anything?"

President Wu turned back to Jeremy. "Power, strength, and good fortune. All of which the Chinese dragon symbolizes. He who harnesses the power of the Chinese dragon controls everything." He sat back down in his seat and crossed his legs. "Jeremy Applegate, you do not hold the power of the Chinese dragon. I do. Peter Klimmings does not hold the power of the Chinese dragon. I do."

Jeremy gulped. "Then what do you plan to do with that power."

"When Peter Klimmings is least expecting it, I will unleash that power upon him. I will get my revenge on him for humiliating me like he did. And when he's finally had enough, then and only then, will I finally crush him and destroy him for good."

Jeremy could not believe what he was hearing. He was surprised at what the Chinese president was saying. Never would he have thought those words would be coming from his mouth.

"And Jeremy," President Wu said, interrupting Jeremy's thoughts.

"Yes?"

"Don't you ever think about crossing me the way he did."

"And why would I ever do that?" Jeremy asked nervously.

"I just know how you are," President Wu said, standing from his chair and turning back to the dragon statue. "Because if you do so, Jeremy, your company . . . your fortune . . . everything will be gone. Do you understand?"

Jeremy's eyes widened. "Yes, sir. I understand what you mean."

CHAPTER 14

A VERY KLIMMINGS CHRISTMAS

S lowly and with great ease, Ben began to open his eyes. The light making its way through the slit in his eyelids caused him to close his eyes tightly. For a moment, he pondered whether to keep them shut and attempt to fall back asleep or try to open them again. Ultimately, he decided to wake up and fight through the blinding light to open his eyes.

The first thing he noticed was the ceiling. *This is not my house.* He turned his head and immediately discovered that it was the sun shining in from the window across the room that offered the blinding light when he woke up.

Ben sat up in the bed and rubbed his eyes. He noticed the dark walls and quickly realized that he was in his bedroom at the Klimmings Mansion. Then he saw Peter sitting in a chair in the bedroom corner.

"Why am I here?" Ben asked, rubbing his eyes again.

"Why are you here?" Peter repeated the question. "Do you not remember last night at all?"

"No."

"Ben, you were brought here last night by the police. You were drunk. Your mother was horrified. What the hell happened?"

Ben thought about what had happened before it finally hit him. He remembered telling Delilah that he knew about the affair. The sound of her car speeding off down the road played back in his mind again.

"I don't remember," he lied. "It's all a blur."

"Ben, that's not good. You're drinking so much that you can't remember what the hell went on. So what is going on?"

"I told you. I don't remember."

"That's a load of shit, son."

"It's the truth!" Ben scooted over in the bed, trying to get out when an intense pain spread throughout his head. "Oh my God. What is that?"

"Hangover," Peter said. "I was surprised you hadn't felt the headache any sooner."

He stood up and walked past Ben's bed and into the bathroom. "Do you remember if you have any pain medicine in here?"

"No," Ben said, rubbing his head, trying to alleviate the pain. "I haven't slept here in a while."

"That's a lie. You slept here a couple months ago when you were drunk, and Miranda had to take care of you." Peter came back into the bedroom and sat down on the bed. "Ben, I'm worried about you."

"Well, don't be. I'm a twenty-six-year-old adult. I know what I am doing!"

Peter sighed. "Do you still want the pain medication?"

"Yes."

"I've got some in my room. Let me go get you some." He stood up and left the room, leaving Ben alone. He sighed and ran his hands through his hair as he thought about Delilah and the baby. *Is it even mine? Am I actually going to be the father?*

* * *

"What do you mean they won't see me?!" Vicki shouted from behind her desk. Pam was standing on the other side of her desk, looking rather startled from Vicki's outburst.

209

"When I told the members of the board that you requested a meeting with them, they quickly shot it down," Pam said. "Mrs. Klimmings, they won't meet with you unless you are submitting your resignation."

"What?!" Vicki lept from her seat. "After all my family and I have done to build this company, they're pulling this crap?!"

"I'm sorry, ma'am."

"Why should you be sorry?" Vicki said as she came around her desk. "You did nothing wrong, Pam. It's those entitled board members' fault."

Pam flashed a smile across her face. "Is there anything else you need, Mrs. Klimmings?"

"No. If the board isn't going to meet with me, then I guess there is no point in me being here." She walked over to the coat tree and put her coat on. "I probably won't be in until the new year, Pam. We'll see how they like that!"

"But Mrs. Klimmings, what would happen if I needed you for something?"

"Call the house. You know the number, Pam. And besides, it'll be fine while I'm out. Nothing ever happens during this time of year anyway." She squeezed past Pam, opened the door, and stepped out into the lobby before turning around to say one last thing before leaving. "Oh, and Pam, if I don't hear from you before then, Merry Christmas!"

* * *

Gabby sat on the sofa in the living room, admiring the Christmas tree between the fireplace and the archway leading to the room with the staircase. The twinkling white lights hanging on the tree caught her attention early on. As one light flashed on, it caused the glittery silver and gold ornaments to shimmer.

She continued to admire the tree, along with the other Christmas decorations placed around the room. As her eyes ran across the greenery above the fireplace, her mind began to drift back to the last time she spoke to Michelle. She remembered both of them leaning in, letting their lips touch each other. Feeling something she had never felt before.

"Admiring the Christmas décor?"

Gabby snapped back to reality. She looked to the entry hall archway and saw Charlotte standing with a cup of coffee. "Yeah," Gabby managed to say. "It's so pretty."

"Absolutely gorgeous!" Charlotte said as she came into the room and sat next to Gabby. "I guess you're out of school for Christmas then?"

"Yeah. Yesterday was our last day."

"And Christmas is next Monday! They don't give you very much time off, do they?"

"No, they don't," Gabby chuckled. "But at least we don't go back until after the start of the new year."

"That's a plus!" Charlotte took a sip of her coffee. "Gabby, I've been meaning to talk to you."

"If it's about that video, I'm so so sorry, Aunt Charlotte." Gabby's eyes began to flood with tears before bursting and running down her face.

"Oh, my dear child," Charlotte said, quickly setting her coffee on the end table and comforting Gabby. "It's alright, honey. It's okay."

She was surprised at Gabby's reaction. She came into the conversation prepared to explain how and why it was wrong to post what she did.

"I'm . . . just . . . so . . . sorry," Gabby managed to say between sobs.

"Like I said, honey. It's okay. I'm fine right now."

Gabby sat up and wiped her eyes and nose on her arm. "I've just got a lot going on right now."

"Like what, honey? You can tell me anything."

Gabby processed what Charlotte had just said to her. *Should I tell her? Can I trust her with my secret?*

"It's . . ." Gabby stuttered, trying to decide whether she could trust her aunt to keep such a sensitive secret. After all, how would her parents react to it? Michelle didn't respond to her kiss the way she had hoped, and what if her family reacted similarly?

"It's nothing. Just school stuff."

"School stuff?" Charlotte repeated. "Forget about it, Gabby! You're on holiday break, honey! Enjoy yourself!" She took her coffee and took another sip. Then she realized that Gabby didn't have any. "Would you like for me to get you a cup? I can make it special, just like I made mine!"

"How is that?"

"I add some eggnog in it," Charlotte whispered. "Some eggnog that's made special." She winked at Gabby.

"How special?"

"Oh, my little friend, brandy, helps out."

Gabby laughed. "Sure," she said. "I'll try it."

"That's my girl!" Charlotte set her coffee back on the end table and made her way through the entry hall and into the kitchen, leaving Gabby alone in the living room. Her smile on her face faded as she returned to her thoughts about Michelle. She pulled out her phone and looked over her text messages. One after another were texts she had sent to Michelle since the sleepover, yet no response was received.

"What did I do?" Gabby whispered to herself. "Why did I have to kiss her like that?"

* * *

"Vicki Klimmings!" Cathie said, surprised. "You were one of the last people I thought would be here."

"Yet, here I am," Vicki said as she hugged Cathie.

"Come in. Come in." Cathie stepped out of the way so Vicki could enter the house. Immediately, Vicki noticed the Christmas garland lining the tops of bookcases and the large fluffy Christmas tree standing in the living room.

"I love your tree!" Vicki said as she went over to it, feeling the tips of the branches with her hands. "The choice of colored lights is fascinating, though."

Cathie stood beside her. "Well, we've always loved the way the trees look with all the different color lights on it." She sighed and felt the tree branches too. "Christmas is such a magical time of year, isn't it?"

Vicki turned to Cathie and smiled. "Isn't it?"

"So Vicki, why have you decided to pay us a visit today?" She directed Vicki into the kitchen. Cathie had just made a nice warm batch of hot apple cider. "Would you like some?"

"Sure!" Vicki said, taking a seat at the island. Cathie poured two mugs of cider and handed one to Vicki before taking a seat across from her. Vicki took a slight sip before setting the cider down on the countertop to cool. "I decided to stop by today because I wanted to confirm your attendance for Christmas."

"You mean you still want us over for Christmas?" Cathie laughed. "Don't you remember the train wreck at Thanksgiving?"

Vicki chuckled and took a sip of her cider. "Well, yes. But things are different now, Cathie. Ben and Delilah are going through a rough patch, and I genuinely feel that Christmas will help boost their spirits. After all, Delilah should be having a baby anytime now."

Cathie took a deep sigh. "You're right, Vicki. They need to work this out." She took a sip of her cider and leaned into Vicki. "Between you and me, Delilah needs to get out of here. She's driving me crazy!"

Vicki laughed. "Is it because of the pregnancy?"

"It must be!"

"And it won't just be the Klimmingses and the Applegates like it usually is for Christmas. Peter decided to invite the Zeemers over as well."

"The vice president and her husband?"

"Yes, Cathie. I need someone to talk to who's not in politics."

The two laughed together for a bit. As they went on, Delilah had managed to make her way into the kitchen without being noticed.

"Vicki," she said, surprised. "Why are you here?"

Vicki turned, and the smile fell from her face when she saw Delilah, whose shirt barely covered her baby bump. Her ankles were also more than twice their usual size. Vicki opened her mouth but failed to figure out whether to answer Delilah's question or ask her how she was doing.

"Delilah," Cathie interrupted. "Vicki came by to extend her invitation for us to join them at Christmas."

"Why?"

"Well, we always go over there for Christmas, so I don't see why this year would be any different."

"Doesn't anyone remember Thanksgiving?" Delilah opened the fridge and pulled out a dill pickle from the pickle jar. She took a large bite out of it. "Ben and I separated after Thanksgiving because of how bad it was."

"I know," Vicki sympathized. "But maybe bringing everyone back together for Christmas will help mend things."

"Whatever," Delilah said. "I'm going to go watch some TV."

She made her way out of the kitchen, taking another bite of her pickle. Her chewing could be heard as she left the room.

Cathie turned to Vicki. "You see what I mean," she whispered. "She's very grumpy when she's pregnant."

Vicki chuckled. "You don't think it's a bad idea for all of us to get together again?"

"Absolutely not. The only ones I could see an issue out of would be Ryan and Ben. Maybe Jeremy and Peter too, but I'll just tell my guys that they need to be on their best behavior!"

"I'll have a discussion with mine too."

"So that's it then! We'll be there!"

* * *

Peter straightened his tie in the mirror, looking at his reflection. He noticed the number of gray hairs mixed in with the blond. The wrinkles on his forehead had replicated over the past two years, and no matter what anti-aging creams he had chosen to use, nothing stopped the wear and tear that the presidency had taken on him.

His attention drifted behind him where his eyes caught the Christmas tree that stood beside the bed. He admired the flocked tree with the shimmering white Christmas lights embedded within the snow-covered branches. He smiled as his eyes made their way over each ornament before he noticed Vicki standing next to the tree, watching him. "Admiring the tree?"

Peter chuckled. "How long have you been standing there?"

"Oh, not too long." She approached Peter and placed her hands on his shoulders, locking her eyes into his. "Have I ever told you how much I love the Christmas season?"

"Every year."

"It's so joyous and happy. It's almost like nothing else matters during this time."

"But it does. Vicki, you know that the company's problems will still be there when you return after the new year."

"Of course I understand that," Vicki said, pulling away from Peter and turning to look back at the tree. "I just need this time to take a break from it all."

Peter sighed. "Yes. It's shitty what they're doing to you, darling."

"Can you blame me for leaving for the break?" Vicki turned back toward Peter.

Peter stepped forward, this time placing his hands on Vicki's shoulders. "No. I probably would have done a lot worse."

He leaned in and kissed Vicki, embracing her in his arms. No sooner than they kissed, Gabby opened the door. "Oh God!" she swore.

Peter turned to Gabby. "That'll teach ya to not open our door without asking."

Vicki laughed as Gabby gagged. "I came up here to tell you two that Denise has the dinner ready. The Applegates and Zeemers are already here too."

"That's fantastic," Vicki said. "How are they doing downstairs?"

"Well, Jeremy is discussing the world events with Mrs. Zeemer, Charlotte cannot stay away from Ryan, and Delilah looks so uncomfortable."

"You invited Delilah?!" Peter jerked his head back to Vicki.

"Yes. Is there a problem?"

"Have you not been paying any attention to what has been going on between her and Ben?"

"I have noticed," Vicki said, making her way to the door. "But Benjamin is strong. He'll be fine. Plus, Cathie and I think that this would be a good way for them to overcome their differences."

Peter sighed. "Whatever. I'm not going to let this ruin my Christmas. Are you ready to head downstairs?"

"Yes," Vicki said, extending out her arm. "Would you like to guide me down to the party?"

"It would be my pleasure." Peter took Vicki by her arm, and they both began to head downstairs, preparing themselves for what could occur.

* * *

Ben sat in the family room, trapped in his thoughts. It had been a few days since his last taste of alcohol, and all he could think of was how the liquor sitting on the bar in the room was calling out his name.

"Benjamin . . ."

He turned on the TV and flipped it over to the Channel 8 news, trying to escape from the voices within his head, constantly calling out to him.

"Benjamin . . ."

He stood from the sofa and proceeded to make his way over to the bar, placing the palms of his hands on the bar and leaning over to look at all the drinks. Bourbon. Vodka. Brandy. It was all there.

"Dad will be so pissed," he said to himself as he observed all the drinks.

"Benjamin . . ."

He closed his eyes, trying to fight the urge to pour himself a drink. "I have been good the past few days. One can't hurt, can it?"

Ben picked up the bottle of vodka and poured himself a glass. He set the bottle back on the bar and opened the ice bucket so that he could plop some ice cubes into the glass. Then he picked up the glass and held it in front of him. He studied the glass of vodka before taking a drink of it. He held the glass back in front of him, studying it again. Then he downed the rest of the drink until all that was left were the two ice cubes in the glass.

"Aaaah," he let out as he placed the glass back on the cart. He smiled as he felt a warm sensation fill his body. He turned to head out of the family room but stopped when he saw Delilah standing at the entrance to the room. Tears were pooling in her eyes.

In an instant, guilt overcame Ben. He knew he was backtracking. He shouldn't have had that drink. *I should have just gone into the living room with everyone else when I had that urge.*

"What have I done?" Delilah said, just loud enough for Ben to hear. "This is all my fault."

Ben opened his mouth to say something, but Delilah had already turned and made her way down the entry hall before he could come up with some kind of explanation for her.

"No, Delilah," he whispered to himself. "It's not your fault. It's both of ours."

* * *

The table was packed full of people for Christmas dinner. Peter, sitting at the head of the table, looked over to his left. "James," he said. "I feel it is only appropriate for you to lead us in prayer tonight."

James nodded to Peter before asking the table to bow their heads. James was a big, tall black man and Constance's husband. He had been the head pastor of the Washington Pentecostal Church of God for the past fifteen years. James had increased attendance dramatically during his tenure at the church, and his messages were broadcast across the nation on various channels every Sunday morning.

As James led the group in prayer, Peter opened his eyes and observed everyone at the table. Across from James, and to Peter's right, sat Ben, who had his eyes closed and head bowed. To James' left sat Miranda, followed by Jason, Ryan, and Charlotte. Vicki sat opposite Peter, and to her left sat Constance, Gabby, Cathie, Jeremy, and Delilah. All had their heads bowed and eyes closed out of respect, except for Delilah, who made eye contact with Peter when his attention came to her. Their eyes locked onto each other's, and Peter could immediately feel the tension grow in the room.

"Why did you sit me next to Ben?" Delilah mouthed to Peter as James continued to pray.

Peter shrugged his shoulders. "It wasn't me," he mouthed back. "Vicki and your mom helped create the table placement."

"I want to be moved."

"You're going to have to take that up with them."

As the silent conversation between the two continued throughout the prayer, Vicki sensed that something was going on, so she opened an eye. She noticed Peter and Delilah and immediately glared at Peter. His attention snapped over to her.

"Sorry," he mouthed to her, and he closed his eyes and bowed his head.

"Amen," James said. Everyone lifted their heads and opened their eyes. Denise, who was waiting off to the side with the food, began to make her way around the table to serve everybody.

"I see you have your house servant serving us this time," Jeremy piped up. "Is it because of the actions of a few at Thanksgiving?"

"Jeremy!" Cathie kicked him, causing him to jolt downward. "Don't you dare start anything."

"That's okay, Cathie," Peter said. "Ben here has learned from what happened." Then he directed his attention over to Ryan. "Have *you*, Ryan?"

"Sure," Ryan responded, rolling his eyes.

Charlotte put her hands on Ryan's left arm, gazing at him. "Has anyone told you that you have the most beautiful eyes?"

"Charlotte," Vicki mumbled at her. "He is company, and you are sitting across from the vice president!"

"So?" Charlotte said. "She's not blind." Charlotte turned to Constance, who was across from her. "Aren't his eyes just gorgeous?"

Constance chuckled. "They do look very nice."

"Thank you," Ryan said to her. He turned over to Charlotte. "Tell me if I'm wrong, but I feel like someone has a little crush on me."

Charlotte laughed. "You're not wrong."

Jason turned to Miranda, displaying a very uncomfortable look on his face. "What is going on?" he whispered to her.

"I don't know," she whispered back. "Just stay quiet and hope nothing happens."

Denise finally made her way all around the table, serving everyone. She pushed the cart against the wall and headed out of the dining room to the kitchen. No sooner than the door closed behind her in the kitchen did Jeremy decide to pipe up again.

"So, Peter. How are you preparing for that investigation?"

The table fell silent. The only sound heard was silverware clinking on the china. Cathie put her elbow on the table and planted her face into her hand, trying to hide the embarrassment that came from her husband's question.

Peter smiled before answering Jeremy's question. "Why would I need to prepare? I haven't done anything wrong. After all, *I* don't conspire with foreign entities."

Jeremy's smirk fell from his face, and Cathie turned toward him, glaring. "Are you happy, now?"

He turned to Cathie, meeting her glare. "So, Mr. Zeemer," Jeremy said, trying to change the subject. "How are things going at the church?"

"Reverend Zeemer," James corrected him. "It's Reverend Zeemer, not Mr. Zeemer."

Jeremy looked over at Miranda, seated next to James, and saw her holding in her laughter. He shook his head. "Sorry," he said to James. "I forgot that you are Reverend Zeemer."

"It's fine," James laughed, appearing to joke with Jeremy. "The church is doing great. We actually broke our record for attendance at last night's Christmas Eve service, so when we come back after the Christmas holiday, I am fully expecting to receive that raise that I have been asking for."

Cathie glanced over at Jeremy, who exchanged looks with her. The rest of the table opted not to talk about James' comments, except for Gabby, who set her silverware down. "You're what?"

"I'm asking for that raise," James reiterated. "I've been working hard lately leading the Washington Pentecostal Church of God, so I feel that this is something I deserve."

"But you're already one of America's highest-paid preachers. Why do you need more money?"

"Honey," Constance said, leaning toward Gabby. "My husband is at the church all the time. He has devoted himself to serving the Lord and spreading His word."

"If he's going to be doing that, then why does he need more money? He has deals with all kinds of companies, and his messages are broadcasted everywhere!"

"Gabriella," Vicki intervened. "That's enough!"

"But I want to know the answer. Why does he need more money? What good will it do, Mr. Zeemer?"

James opened his mouth to respond but was cut off by Vicki. "Gabriella, let's go talk in the family room."

Gabby stood up from her seat and stormed out of the dining room. Instead of turning right to head to the family room, she went ahead into the room across the entry hall and ran up the stairs. Vicki stood up and set her napkin on the table to follow her but was stopped by Miranda.

"Wait!" Miranda said. Vicki turned back toward her. "Let me go up and talk with her. I don't think it'll help any if you went up there."

Vicki sighed and sat back down. "Go ahead."

"I'll be right back."

Miranda headed out of the room and up the stairs as the rest of the table continued eating.

"You two have been very quiet," Jason said to Delilah and Ben. "Is there something wrong?"

"No," Delilah smiled. "There's nothing wrong at all, is there, babe?"

Ben looked up at everyone sitting at the table. This was his opportunity to make a scene and expose Delilah for the cheater that she was. He opened his mouth, preparing to say something but stopped himself before anything came out. Instead, he just sighed. "No."

* * *

Miranda opened the door to see Gabby sitting on her bed with her face buried in her hands. She was crying.

"Honey," Miranda said, coming into the room and sitting next to her. "What is the matter?"

"They don't like me," Gabby sobbed. "Nobody likes me. I'm just worthless."

"That's not true! Everyone likes you!"

Gabby turned to Miranda. "No, they don't! You see how Mom treats me all the time. She's always acting like I'm just a waste of space."

"She does not think you are a waste of space!" Miranda put her hand on Gabby's back, trying to console her. "That's just how she is. She's always been a big rule follower."

"That's because she doesn't like me!"

Miranda sighed and rolled her eyes. "Why doesn't she like you?"

"Mom doesn't like me because I'm . . ." Gabby stopped speaking and turned away from Miranda. She buried her face in her pillow, hoping that Miranda would go away.

"Mom doesn't like you because you're what?" Miranda asked, but Gabby wasn't offering any answer. "Gabby, what is going on?"

"Just go away."

"I'm not leaving until you tell me what's going on!"

Finally, Gabby lifted her head and faced her sister. Tears were still in her eyes. "Do you promise not to tell anyone?"

"I swear."

"And you promise that you'll still love me after I tell you?"

"Gabby, I will always love you no matter what. You're my favorite sister!"

She smiled and then took a deep breath. "Miranda, I think that I'm bisexual."

Before Miranda responded, a huge weight felt like it had been lifted from Gabby's shoulder. Her stomach loosened up, and she finally felt free. Then, Miranda leaned in and hugged her. "Oh, Gabby. Why would you think that would change how I think about you? I will always love you, no matter what."

Gabby looked at Miranda and smiled again. "Don't tell anyone, though! I'm not ready for people to know yet."

"I promise you that this is safe with me. When you are ready to come out, you will be able to come out to whomever you want."

Miranda hugged her again. "I'm so proud of you, though. I'm sure that took a lot of courage."

"It did."

Miranda smiled at Gabby. "Do you feel better?"

"I feel so much better," Gabby said. "It feels like a weight has been lifted from my chest."

"Good." Miranda stood up from the bed. "Are you ready to head back downstairs? It might be time to open presents."

"Sure."

"Let's go, then!"

* * *

The families gathered in the family room to open presents. As wrapping paper gradually covered the floor, Vicki noticed that Charlotte kept getting more comfortable with Ryan on the sofa, who wasn't pushing back. In some ways, it appeared that he wanted her to keep going. As they kept getting closer, it became more difficult for Vicki to hide her distaste for Charlotte's actions, especially with the vice president and her husband seated alongside them.

Finally, just as Charlotte practically laid herself across Ryan, Vicki decided to do something about it. "Charlotte," she said, standing up. "I need to speak with you for a moment."

"Right now?"

"Yes. Just out here in the entry hall."

Charlotte kissed Ryan on the cheek before leaping up and heading out to the entry hall with Vicki. "What do you want to speak with me about?"

"What the hell are you doing?!" Vicki asked sternly. "You are still a married woman, Charlotte! Why are you throwing yourself out there to Ryan?"

Charlotte looked toward the floor out of shame. "I'm not just throwing myself out there, Vicki. Ryan is a very nice person, and George is cheating on me anyways. We are as good as divorced right now."

"But you're not, Charlotte. What are the courts going to say if it comes out that you are already shacking up with another man?"

"It's not going to come out!" Charlotte turned back toward the family room, ensuring that no one's attention was directed toward them. "It's just a little fun."

"Charlotte, you forgot that you are the first lady's sister. You're going to be followed by the press!"

"Just let me have some fun, Vicki. God, are you that much of a prude now that you don't understand when anyone else wants to have some fun?"

Charlotte turned to head back into the family room, but Vicki grabbed her by the arm, stopping her in her tracks.

"Dammit, Charlotte," she said. "I understand when someone has fun, but the court doesn't. Who makes all the money in your marriage right now, Charlotte? You or George? If he finds out that you're out here whoring around, do you really think that the court is going to let you take a substantial portion of his fortune?"

Charlotte's eyes widened. "They can do that?"

"Yes, so you need to watch yourself, Charlotte." Vicki let go of Charlotte, who stood there for a moment, looking back at Vicki and processing what she had just told her. Then she turned back around and headed into the family room, leaving Vicki alone in the entry hall. She stood, watching as Charlotte, once again, made her way over to Ryan.

She sighed and headed back into the room as Gabby began opening the gift Miranda had given her. "What is this?" Gabby said as she pulled an envelope out of the box that she unwrapped.

"Open it," Miranda said.

Gabby opened the envelope and pulled out a card. She began reading it out loud.

"It says, 'Gabby, you have grown up during a time where Dad's company has gone through many changes. It's gone public and grown exponentially. When he decided to run for president, he gifted me all of the stocks he owned in the company, which totaled fifty-one percent. He recommended that Mom become the chief executive officer to the board, who overwhelmingly approved her confirmation and appointed

223

her board chair. Later, your brother, Ben, became the chief financial officer based on a similar recommendation.'"

Miranda glanced over the Ben, who was sitting in the far corner of the room near the basement stairwell. He had no interest in the matter and displayed a look on his face like he wanted to be anywhere but in the family room at that time.

"'Since you've turned eighteen,'" Gabby continued reading. "'I feel it is time to gift you your portion of the Klimmings fortune. After the Christmas holiday, we will be meeting with my attorney to transfer to you the sum of fifteen percent of my portion of stock in Klimmings Incorporated.'" Gabby dropped the card before she finished reading it. She turned to Miranda, who had a big smile on her face. "Is this for real?"

"Yes," Miranda said. "You're eighteen now, Gabby. It's time for your fair share of the company."

Gabby smiled and jumped up to hug Miranda.

"What the hell?" Peter exclaimed from across the room. "I gave you that stock for a reason, Miranda! You were to continue to maintain control of the company!"

Miranda let go of Gabby. "And I will, Dad. I'll still have thirty-six percent of the company's stock. It's still the majority of the stock."

"At least she *has* stock," Ben chimed in. "You gave me nothing when you left the company."

"That's not true!" Peter snapped. "I recommended you to be CFO of the company, and you blew it. You drank yourself into signing a disastrous deal for the company and left your mother to pick up the pieces of the mess you left behind!"

"I didn't leave anything behind!" Ben shouted, jumping up from his chair. "She fired me!"

"She didn't have a choice! She had to fire you!"

The room fell silent. No one spoke a word as the tension between Peter and Ben grew. Finally, Peter made his way over to the bar to pour himself a drink. He grabbed the bottle of Scotch and a glass when something caught his attention. "Whose is this?" Peter asked, holding up a glass containing a tiny bit of water.

"I wish it had been mine," Jeremy piped up. Immediately, Cathie punched him in the arm, signaling that right now was not the best time to be himself.

"Seriously," Peter said again. "Whose is this?"

No one spoke a word, and Peter held the glass up to his nose, smelling the inside of it. "Vodka."

He looked over to Ben, who had his attention fixed to the floor. Peter stepped over to him. "Was this yours, Ben? Have you been drinking tonight?"

Ben continued to stare at the floor, ignoring Peter.

"Peter," Vicki chimed in. "Don't do this right now?"

"No, Vicki. If Ben's been drinking, he needs to admit it right now in front of everyone." Peter turned his attention back to Ben. "Is this yours?"

Ben smacked the glass out of Peter's hand and ran out of the room. The glass shattered on the floor near Charlotte, causing a shriek from her. Peter began to storm out of the room after Ben but stopped when he heard the front door slam shut.

He turned around and looked at the room. Everyone sat motionless, trying to process what had just happened. He scanned everyone: Gabby, Miranda, Jason, Jeremy, Cathie, Delilah, Ryan, Charlotte, Constance, James, and Vicki. Then his attention flew back to Delilah, who was crying on the sofa.

"What did you do to my son?" Peter asked her.

"Peter!" Vicki interjected.

"No, Vicki! This needs to come out now! What the hell happened between you two?"

More tears began to fall from Delilah's eyes. Finally, Jeremy stood from the sofa. "I think it's time for us to go."

"So you're just going to avoid the question then?"

"She owes you no explanation, Peter," Jeremy stated. "Whatever happened is between her and Ben. C'mon, guys. We're leaving."

Cathie helped Delilah stand from the sofa, and the two began to make their way out of the room and down the entry hall. They only stopped once for Cathie to wish Vicki a "Merry Christmas." Jeremy followed behind, making direct eye contact with Peter as he passed by.

"Text me," Charlotte whispered to Ryan as he stood up and caught up with his family.

As the front door closed behind them, the remainder of the people in the family room sat silent. "Way to go, Peter," Vicki said. "Once again, another holiday has been ruined." She had tears pooling in her eyes. She turned to Constance and James. "I'm so sorry!" she apologized before running out of the room and heading upstairs.

Peter sighed and passed by everyone else in the family room, heading down the small hallway leading to the library in the back of the room. He turned left and opened a door halfway down the hallway, closing it behind him.

"Where'd he go?" Constance asked Miranda.

"That's his office," Miranda responded. "It's modeled after the Oval Office, but a lot smaller."

"Dude," Jason chimed in. "That's actually kinda cool!"

Constance laughed. "Tell your mom not to be sorry. I work with your father, so this isn't anything new for me."

Miranda smiled. "I think she will appreciate that."

"It was nice getting to meet you all, though!"

"Yes," James said. "It was good to meet you all."

"Safe travels home," Miranda said, standing up from her chair. She guided Constance and James down the entry hall and bid them farewell at the front door.

She made her way back into the family room. Denise had already begun to clean up the wrapping paper. "Well, that was something," Gabby said to the small group.

"Are you sure you have normal family gatherings?" Jason asked Miranda, laughing.

She smiled and shrugged her shoulders. "We always have before. I guess everyone is just on edge right now."

"Oh my God!" Charlotte exclaimed. "I totally forgot!"

"What did you forget?" Miranda asked.

"I was going to announce something tonight, but Vicki caused me to forget when she lectured me out in the hall."

Gabby moved over to the sofa next to Charlotte. "What is it?"

"I was going to tell the family tonight that I have decided to move here permanently."

"Inside the mansion?" Miranda asked nervously.

"No! I'm planning to move to the D.C. area! I've been looking in Bethesda and Great Falls, and they have some pretty nice houses for sale." She leaned in toward Gabby. "Your aunt is going to be here to stay!"

CHAPTER 15

NEXT STEPS

Gabby closed her locker, holding her math book close to her. She started to make her way down the hallway, trying not to draw any attention to herself. She kept her head down as she meandered through the small clusters of students gathered in the hallway, conversing with each other during their passing period. Only once did she look up to double-check where she was going and stopped when she saw Michelle at the end of the hallway.

She felt the butterflies stirring up within her stomach as she set her eyes on Michelle. She hadn't spoken to her since the sleepover when the two kissed, and she wasn't sure they were even still considered friends.

Finally, she took a deep breath and headed down the hallway toward Michelle. As she got closer, she noticed that Michelle was talking to Dana.

"Gabby!" Dana called out. "Over here!"

Gabby felt a smile grow on her face. *Good! She hasn't told her about our kiss.* Gabby felt a rush of relief run through her as she joined Michelle and Dana in the hallway.

"How was your Christmas?" Gabby asked the two.

"Oh, mine absolutely sucked," Dana began. "I wanted that new phone for Christmas, and my dad, of course, bought me last year's release and not this year's. I was so pissed off about it."

"That's awful," Michelle said.

"Did you tell him that it wasn't the one you wanted?" Gabby asked.

"Yes," Dana said. "Then he went on about how I need to be grateful for what I have and that it's a privilege for me even to have a phone." She scoffed. "What do our parents even know anyways?"

Michelle quickly agreed with Dana while Gabby just laughed to herself. Then, the three girls began down the hall, conversing with one another until Dana had to step into a classroom for her class, leaving Gabby and Michelle.

The two girls remained silent after Dana left, glancing at each other here-and-there. Finally, Gabby had enough.

"Michelle," she began. "I didn't mean anything by it, you know. It didn't mean anything. It was just a small kiss."

Michelle stopped. "I know, Gabby. I just don't know how to process all of this."

"I understand. I shouldn't have kissed you."

"It's not even that," Michelle added. "It's just . . ."

"What?"

"You."

"*Me?*"

Michelle sighed. "Gabby, it's just a surprise that you're gay. All those times we spent together . . . all those nights we stayed together."

"What are you meaning by this?" Gabby asked as she felt her heart plunge into her gut. She couldn't believe the words coming out of Michelle's mouth.

"It's just . . ." Michelle continued. "I think we shouldn't talk for a bit. I've got to process all this."

Unable to form words, Gabby just stood there, tears in her eyes. Finally, Michelle turned around and made her way down the hallway, leaving Gabby alone as the bell rang.

* * *

Delilah looked through her phone. Over and over were texts from Ben. As she scanned over the texts from Ben, she saw the hateful messages from him. She laid back on the sofa and took a deep breath, placing her hand on her baby bump. Sitting there, Delilah thought about all the memories she and Ben had.

"If I hadn't had that stupid affair . . ." Delilah spoke to her bump. "Everything would be fine right now."

She sighed and then rolled over to her side. She laid there for a moment before hearing a notification sound on her phone, and then unlocked her phone and read the message.

"Oh my God!" Delilah said aloud.

"Baby! The baby is coming!" Cathie came running into the living room in a frenzy. "Are you alright? Let me get you in the car!"

Delilah sat up as quickly as she could. "Mom! Mom! The baby is not coming. It's all fine."

Cathie's arms fell to her sides. "Well, shoot." She plopped down in an armchair beside the sofa. "I thought I was going to be a grandma today."

Delilah smiled. "Soon."

"So if it wasn't time for the baby, what was it?"

"I got a text from Miranda. She told me that Peter decided to move Ben into the Klimmings Mansion. Apparently, after storming out at Christmas, he's been constantly drinking."

"Oh dear," Cathie said. "Are you okay? You taking this well?"

"I guess." Delilah laid back on the sofa, trying to get more comfortable. "I think the hardest part about all of this is that I feel like it's all my fault. Ever since I became pregnant . . ."

"Honey, don't talk like that! You did nothing wrong! Yours and Ben's marriage had its tough parts before you became pregnant."

"Yet, I still feel as if it is my fault." Delilah turned on her side as much as her baby bump allowed her to. Her mind wandered off to the first time she met Clark, remembering her desperation as Ben worked long hours at Klimmings Incorporated. She remembered how she felt so lonely and unwanted as he would come home from work and relax on the couch, watching TV, only talking with her very seldom. It didn't take long for her to find Clark and meet him.

As Delilah continued her thoughts, Cathie rose from the chair, watching Delilah on the sofa. She sighed before turning out of the room, leaving her daughter to deal with her thoughts on her own.

* * *

Ben sat up, looking around the room, trying to figure out where he was. Finally, he recognized the dark walls as his bedroom at the Klimmings Mansion. Ben tried to get out of bed but felt a large thumping against his head, prompting him to remain seated.

He heard a vacuum starting up outside his bedroom as he sat there. He slid off the bed and made his way over to the door, feeling the pounding inside his head with every step he took. He opened the door and saw Denise vacuuming in the room at the top of the stairs. She was startled when she saw him standing in the doorway and turned off the vacuum. "Good morning, Mr. Benjamin! Did I wake you?"

"No, you didn't," Ben replied, pressing against his temples. "Could you go get me a double vodka from the bar, though?"

Denise sighed. "I can't do that, Mr. Benjamin."

"Why not?"

"Mr. Klimmings ordered me last night to lock up all the alcohol. The only things on the bar right now are water and some sodas."

"Are you kidding me?" Ben stepped out of his bedroom. "Why am I here anyway? I don't remember being brought here."

"Mr. Klimmings had you brought here last night. He said that you would be staying here permanently."

Ben took a deep sigh, feeling more annoyed inside. "Thank you, Denise." He passed by her and began to make his way down the stairs, one step at a time. His headache worsened with each step he took.

Finally, at the bottom, he made his way into the living room to check out the bar. Like Denise had said, all the alcohol had been removed from the bar and locked up.

Ben turned around, not knowing what to do. He wanted a drink so badly but couldn't find anything to satisfy his urge. Instead, he plopped down on the sofa, defeated, and laid his head on one of the pillows, immersing himself in his thoughts.

* * *

"Do you even know when the next board meeting is?" Vicki asked Pam. The two were in Vicki's office. Vicki was seated behind her desk, and Pam was standing on the other side.

"No, ma'am," Pam replied. "They won't tell me. The only thing that I've been informed of is that the board is still not confident in your leadership."

"Well, what the hell is that supposed to mean?" Vicki rose from her chair. "Are they still wanting me to resign?"

Pam sighed. "Not exactly."

"Well, then what do they want?"

"Go ahead and sit down, ma'am." Pam motioned for Vicki to sit down, and she did. Pam took a seat across from Vicki. "The board is meeting next Thursday to vote on removing you from the position of CEO and board chair of Klimmings Incorporated, Mrs. Klimmings."

Vicki's eyes widened, and she felt her heart drop into the pit of her stomach. "They *what*?"

"They want you out, Mrs. Klimmings. They didn't want you knowing, but one of my friends who is friends with a board member told me about what they are planning."

Vicki sat silent for a moment, trying to process what she heard. It had almost been three years since she began her tenure as the company's head. All this time, yet one mistake has warranted her ousting from it.

"Thank you, Pam," she said quietly. "That'll be all."

Pam rose from her chair and exited Vicki's office, leaving Vicki all alone. Tears began running down her face as she openly sobbed. The sounds of her crying echoed off the walls of her office. Not knowing what else to do, Vicki pulled out her cellphone and called Peter. As she heard the dialing sound, Vicki tried to stifle her sobs so that she could make out a coherent message for Peter when he picked up the phone.

"Hello."

"Peter," Vicki cried. "Peter, I don't know what to do."

"Whoa. Whoa. Whoa," Peter said, trying to calm Vicki. "What the hell is going on?"

"The board . . . they're trying to get rid of me, Peter."

"Oh my God," Peter sighed. "Why the hell are they trying to do that?"

"Over Benjamin. They won't let all that go, and now I'm going to be gone and lose your company!" Vicki bawled into the phone as more tears fell from her face. "I'm so sorry, Peter!"

"Vicki," Peter said, trying to calm her down. "Get ahold of Miranda. See if she has finalized her transfer of stock to Gabby. If she hasn't, she will be your saving grace, Vicki."

"Why do you say that?"

"Because she still owns fifty-one percent of the company. She is your crutch, Vicki. Now call her!"

Vicki hung up the phone and set it on her desk. She took a tissue and wiped the tears from her eyes, recollecting herself before she took the phone and dialed Miranda's number.

* * *

Miranda looked down at her phone as it vibrated in her hand. She saw that her mother was calling, but she didn't feel like now was the best time to speak with her, so she ignored the call and put her phone in her purse. She looked up and saw Jason in the kitchen, pouring her a glass of soda. He came into the living room, handed Miranda one of the glasses, and sat down on the couch next to her.

"I saw you looking at your phone earlier," he said before taking a sip of his drink. "Was someone calling you?"

"Yes," Miranda said. "It was my mom." She smiled and then took a drink of her soda. "If it's important, she would leave a voicemail."

Jason laughed before looking deep into Miranda's brown eyes. For a moment, he felt lost in her eyes. "Jason." He snapped out of it and noticed Miranda was looking at him with an uncomfortable look. "What are you looking at?"

"You," he replied.

"Me?" Miranda didn't believe him. "You seemed like you were really engrossed in something."

"I was," he admitted, smiling as he looked back into her eyes. "You have the prettiest eyes."

Miranda chuckled nervously and sat her glass on the coffee table. "Thank you."

"Miranda," Jason started as he set his drink on the coffee table as well. He took ahold of Miranda's hands. "Have we ever discussed where we plan to go?"

"What do you mean?"

"Like where we want our relationship to go."

"What's next?" Miranda was confused. She didn't understand what Jason was meaning. "Jason, we've only been dating for about three months."

"We've been together since October," he said. "But we were together for a while before that. I think it's been plenty of time for us to take the next step."

Miranda pulled back. "Next step?! Jason, before October, we had been separated for six months. It's too soon to begin talking about a next step."

Jason smiled. "I don't think so."

Inside, Miranda felt more and more uncomfortable. This was not sounding like the guy she thought she knew. With each word that came out of his mouth, Miranda felt the urge to leave Jason's apartment and rush home. She stood up from the couch and took her purse. "I need to get going, Jason."

"Hold on," he said, leaping up. "I have something to show you." He took her hand and began to lead her away from the couch. Miranda hesitated but took a small step and then followed Jason's guidance. He took her out of the living room and down the hall toward his bedroom. He opened the door and led her in.

Miranda's eyes made contact with the left wall as soon as she stepped foot in Jason's bedroom. Photo after photo lined the wall from the top down to the bottom. Every single image was of her, and as she continued to look over every picture, Miranda's stomach turned. She felt sick. She felt scared. *What kind of person has a wall covered in pictures of their girlfriend?*

"Jason . . ." Miranda whispered. "What is this?"

"It's you," he said as he stepped behind her and planted himself to her right. "It's all you." He turned to her, taking her hands. "Miranda, you are all that I care about. You are my everything. I love you so much, baby. And I think it's time for us to take a step toward marriage."

Miranda's eyes widened. "Jason, no. It's too soon. This is not normal." She motioned to the wall. "You need to get some help, Jason."

"Maybe you just need some time," he suggested. "Go ahead home, and think about it." Jason stepped over to the wall, running his finger down Miranda's cheek on one of the pictures. "You're my everything, Miranda. My only purpose in life is to serve you."

Slowly, Miranda trembled as she backed out of the bedroom. Once she made it through the threshold, she turned and bolted down the hallway, into the living room, and through the apartment door. As the door slamming echoed throughout the apartment, Jason stepped out back into the living room.

"Oh, Miranda," he said to himself. "You'll see that we're meant to be together. One way, or another . . . you'll see."

CHAPTER 16

POWER MOVE

Vicki flung open the door to Miranda's bedroom. She saw her daughter lying on her bed as she barged in, casting the door shut behind her. "Why didn't you answer your phone when I called you?"

"When did you call me?" Miranda asked as she sat up. "I don't remember . . ." She stopped and remembered the phone call. She was sitting on the couch in Jason's apartment as he brought in two sodas: one for him and one for her. It was only right before he took her back to his bedroom for the first time to show her the distressing display that covered the entire wall beside his bed.

"Miranda," Vicki said. "I needed you earlier. I need your help!"

Miranda brought her attention back to Vicki. "What is it? What do you need, Mom?"

Vicki stepped across the room and sat in a chair at the desk across from Miranda's bed. "Miranda, have you finalized the transfer of Gabriella's portion of Klimmings Incorporated stock?"

"No, I have not." Miranda stood up from the bed and took a step closer to Vicki. "And to save you some words, no, I am not going to change my mind. That was Gabby's Christmas present from me . . ."

"Miranda . . . I'm not wanting you to change your decision."

"You're not?"

"No."

Miranda plopped down on the bed, bewildered. Vicki moved over to sit beside her. "Miranda, I need your help."

"What's wrong? What's going on with the company?" Miranda looked very concerned. She had never felt this sense of desperation from her mom before.

"The board is trying to fire me from the head of the company. Miranda, next Thursday, they are meeting to finalize the votes. I need you to be there. You still hold fifty-one percent of the stock. You can change the course of the vote."

Miranda took a deep breath. She stood up and made her way across the room. "Mom, I've never been a part of the company. How is it going to look if I just show up now?"

"It'll look like you've decided to take an active role in the business."

"And what do you think Ben is going to think about this? You fired him, remember? He's out, and now, your daughter is suddenly on the board of directors."

"Benjamin has more important things to worry about than the company: his marriage to Delilah, his unborn child, his compulsive drinking problem."

"But you don't think this will make it worse, Mom?"

"No," Vicki said, standing up from the bed. "I don't think it will." She proceeded to move up next to Miranda. "Miranda, you don't have to do this if you don't want to. I don't have to remain on as head of Klimmings Incorporated."

Vicki opened the bedroom door and stopped in the doorway on her way out, turning back to Miranda. "But could you ever live with yourself knowing that you could have kept the company under Klimmings family control?"

She closed the door behind her, leaving Miranda alone in her bedroom, who let out a deep sigh. She moved over to her bed and laid out on it. She took her phone out and unlocked it. The first notification on the screen was from Jason. *What's up?*

Miranda locked her phone and tossed it beside her on the bed. She turned over to her side, facing away from her phone, trying to process everything going on.

* * *

Peter entered the Situation Room, making his way over to the seat at the head of the large conference table. Military generals all stood along each side of the table, waiting for Peter to sit. Once he was seated, he motioned to the generals that it was okay to sit down. Then he looked over to his left at the secretary of defense. "Eric," he said. "Whatcha got for us?"

"Mr. President," the secretary of defense said. "We have learned about some new military drills conducted by the Chinese government near the Basa Air Base in the Philippines. While we believe that as of right now, the Chinese government poses no harm in our troops stationed at the base, we feel that the increasing rate at which China is conducting these drills is becoming more and more alarming."

Peter looked puzzled. "Eric," he began. "What do you mean by this? Are they just flying around, or are they sailing close by? What the hell are they doing?"

"Mr. President," Eric continued. "We don't really know. They've just been flying by. It was seldom at first, but over the past two weeks, the fly-bys have really picked up."

"How the hell do you not know? We're the United States of America. We're supposed to know all this crap."

Eric sat, unable to answer Peter's question. Instead, he turned to his left toward the general sitting beside him, giving him a look that pleaded for help explaining the situation to the president.

"Mr. President," the general said as he leaned forward to get a more direct look at Peter. "What Secretary Bird is trying to say is that the Chinese government will not return any of our inquiries into the situation. Their generals and military leaders will not respond to our calls. Our request to meet with their commanders was met with a refusal to meet. Hell, even the Chinese ambassador to the U.S. has declined a video conference with the U.S. ambassador."

Peter looked even more puzzled as Eric and the rest of the generals continued. He let them continue to spew information onto him before he broke in, "Do I need to call President Wu?"

"Mr. President," Eric responded. "Do you think he'll even answer one of your calls?"

"Probably not," Peter said as he picked up the phone and held it to his ear. "But it's worth a shot." He directed his attention to the operator on the other end of the phone. "I need to speak with President Wu from China."

The operator worked to get connected to the line with China. Peter heard the phone dial and dial and dial. It felt like an eternity as he continued to listen to the dialing sound, waiting for President Wu to answer so that the two could discuss what was going on, but no one ever answered.

Peter placed the phone on the receiver and turned his attention back to his generals. He tried his best to maintain a decent composure, but on the inside, his blood was boiling. Peter hated it anytime he was snubbed by another world leader. He stood up from the conference table and turned, leaving the Situation Room as the rest of the people in the room scrambled to stand up.

As the door shut behind him, Henry Gates caught up with him. "Mr. President," he called out to Peter. "What happened on the phone with President Wu?"

"Nothing happened," Peter stopped in the corridor and turned to Henry. "Mr. Gates, something is going on with China, and we have no clue what the hell it is and why they're doing it."

* * *

Charlotte looked up across the table at Ryan. He was dressed in a suit and purple tie. Charlotte could have sworn that he knew that purple was her favorite color.

"Who told you?" she said, smiling at him.

"Who told me what?"

"That purple is my favorite color . . . Who told you?"

Ryan looked down at his tie and shrugged. "Honestly, I didn't even know that it was your favorite color."

The two laughed and then stared into each other's eyes.

"Charlotte," Ryan asked. "How does someone like you come from the Klimmings family?"

Charlotte chuckled before taking a sip of her white wine. "It's simple. I'm not a part of the Klimmings family. I'm just Vicki's half-sister."

"Half-sister?"

"Yes," Charlotte began. "We have the same mom, but different dads. I wish it were some juicy story, but unfortunately, it's not. Vicki's dad died, and our mom decided to shack up with some guy. Then, along came me, and he disappeared."

"Damn," Ryan said. "I'm so sorry about that."

"Don't be!" Charlotte took another sip of her wine. "I'm not. Look at where I wound up at." She took her wine glass and held it up. "Eating dinner here with you!"

"You're right about that!" Ryan also held his glass of wine up, clanking it with hers. "So, what brought you here?"

"Well, some things happened out in California, and I decided that I wanted to come out here to D.C. to see what intrigued my sister so much about this place."

"Shouldn't the answer to that be simple? Her husband is the president of the United States."

"But he wasn't always," Charlotte said. "He founded Klimmings Incorporated here many years before he ever entertained the idea of running for president."

"Yeah, I guess he did."

Charlotte looked around the restaurant. She hadn't been to this one before. "What was the name of this place again?" she asked Ryan.

He looked up at her and said, "Finley's."

"This place is so nice. Where did you find this place?"

Ryan sighed. "Well, let's just say that this place has some good memories for me."

* * *

Sitting at the breakfast table, Peter scrolled through his tablet, looking at the Thursday morning news. In front of him sat his breakfast which consisted of scrambled eggs and bacon. He took a bite of his scrambled eggs as he began reading an article about Klimmings Incorporated. As he continued through, Vicki came into the dining room, made her way over to the breakfast bar, and began serving herself.

"Would you like for me to get Denise in here?" Peter asked her.

"No, I can handle this myself," Vick said as she turned and headed back to the dining room table to set her plate down at her spot. She had a variety of fruit on her plate. Before sitting down, Vicki headed back over to the breakfast bar and poured herself a cup of coffee.

"Have you seen this?" Peter asked as he turned the tablet around to face Vicki. "Apparently, some insider from the company has come forward and said that the board is planning to oust you today."

Vicki took a sip of her coffee. "Yep. That's what their plan is."

"Hasn't Miranda come in and fixed it all? She still has controlling stock in the company, doesn't she?"

"Yes, she does," Vicki said. "But she is concerned with how it will look with her coming in and using her shares to keep me in charge."

"Why the hell would that matter? We own the company. We should be able to do whatever it is we want with it."

Vicki took another sip of her coffee. "Well, we did own the company before we decided that we should go public with it."

"We had to do that so that I could run for president," Peter stated. "And doing that was one of the best things for the company. It's grown exponentially since then and is now one of the largest clean energy corporations in the United States."

"Peter, I understand that, but that still won't help me to retain control of Klimmings Incorporated. We are going to lose our company unless Miranda steps in." Vicki picked up her coffee to take a drink but stopped before the mug met her lips. "Right now, we are at her mercy."

* * *

Miranda opened the door to Ben's bedroom. He was lying on his bed with a pillow over the top of his head. "What do you want," Ben asked from under it.

"Are you alright?" Miranda asked as she sat at the foot of Ben's bed.

"I'm fine. I just have this terrible headache."

"How many days has it been since you've last had a drink?"

Ben sat up, taking the pillow off his head. "It's been two days. I managed to find something in the kitchen, which helped. Now, I'm back to where I was."

Miranda sighed. "Well, it's a process." She tried to encourage Ben without sounding like she was preaching to him. "You just have to be vigilant and keep up the work. It's hard."

"What do you want, anyway?" Ben was beginning to become agitated.

"Well," Miranda began. "I came in here because I wanted to talk to you about the company."

Ben gave her a look of disgust. "And why the hell would I care about what happens to that place?" He laid back on the bed. "Mom already fired me from it anyways."

"Well, I'm in a tricky predicament right now. Mom needs my help in keeping control of the company."

"I guess the board wants her out now?"

"Because of you," Miranda said. "But since I haven't officially transferred the portion of stock over to Gabby, I still have the ability to block whatever it is the board is wanting to do."

"So you're going to be Mom's saving grace, then," Ben said. "You saved her, but you let poor me get thrown to the wolves." Ben took the pillow and put it back over his head.

Miranda stood up and moved to the other side of the bed, sitting beside Ben. "I have a plan in mind," she said to him. "A plan that could get you a spot back in the company."

He took the pillow off his head, looking Miranda in the eyes. "And what would that be?"

"I have to speak with my lawyers first," Miranda said, standing up. "But if it works, you won't have to worry about trying to get back in the company anymore."

She made her way over to the door and opened it to leave. Before she left the room, she stopped and turned back toward Ben. "But first, Ben," she said. "I need you to sober up. I cannot let you back into this company if you are a drunk. We cannot have that looming over this family."

* * *

"Wu, you've got to be kidding me right now!"

Jeremy sat in his chair on the phone. He had been in a tense phone call with the Chinese president for a while, urging him to step up his revenge tactics against Peter.

"You're just flying by an air force base, Wu," Jeremy continued. "I need you to attack Peter at the heart. Make him suffer."

"Jeremy," President Wu responded. "It takes time, you see. First, we must build up our threats. If we want to make him look like the bad guy, we must paint him like the bad guy."

"What does that mean, Wu? What are you trying to tell me?!"

"Patience, Jeremy. That's what I'm trying to tell you."

"Wu, I'm not playing games now. Something needs to happen . . . and soon."

Jeremy hung up on President Wu and tossed his phone on the end table, and pressed his fingers against the pressure points on his face. Then, he looked up and saw Delilah grabbing her bag and preparing to leave the house.

"Where are you going?" he asked.

"Out," said Delilah. "Why do you ask?"

"Delilah, you're nine months pregnant and due any day now. You

243

can't just be heading out and doing whatever you want right now."

Delilah glared at Jeremy. "Dad, I will be fine. I have my phone if anything happens."

She headed to the front door, opened it, and left the room, leaving Jeremy alone. He took a deep sigh, stood up, and headed out of the living room and into the kitchen. Cathie was standing at the stove frying bacon. Jeremy approached her and took in a deep breath, inhaling the smell of the bacon. "Smells good."

"Goodness!" Cathie exclaimed as she jumped from being startled. "How long have you been there?"

"I just came in," Jeremy said, taking a seat at one of the bar stools at the island.

"Well, the bacon will be ready in a minute," Cathie said. "What was the deal going on in the living room between you and Delilah?"

Jeremy sighed. "She decided to head out."

"This late in the pregnancy?!"

"Exactly."

"Is she crazy?! Her water could break at any moment! What would she do if she was out and went into labor?"

"She told me that she had her phone, and she would be okay."

Cathie smiled. "She gets that arrogance from you, you know."

"Yeah, I know."

Cathie put the bacon on a plate and placed it down on the counter. "So, what was the deal with this Wu guy?"

"What do you mean?" Jeremy asked as he took a piece of bacon.

"I heard you yelling at some guy you called Wu earlier."

Jeremy thought about his call with President Wu, concocting a lie as he reflected on the conversation.

"Oh!" he said. "Wu is one of my financial people at the company. We've been trying to consolidate some of our assets, and he's just not listening to what I want him to do."

Cathie nodded her head. "Okay . . . so why don't you just fire him if he's not following your directions?"

"Well," Jeremy lied. "He's been with us for a while, so I'm just treating this as something minor."

"It didn't sound so minor earlier."

Jeremy took a bite out of his bacon and then changed the subject. "This is some pretty good bacon!"

"Don't change the subject, Jeremy," Cathie said. "You're up to something, aren't you?"

Jeremy set his piece of bacon back on the plate. "Am I ever not up to something? I run a business. I'm always doing something."

"You best not be getting involved between Delilah and Ben, Jeremy. Those two need to work things out on their own."

"I promise you, Cathie. I am not getting between those two. That's too much of a mess, even for me."

* * *

Vicki closed the door to her office, holding her laptop snugly against her. She looked over at Pam, who was sitting at her desk. Without saying anything, Vicki flashed a tiny smile on her face, which Pam reciprocated, showing her support to her boss.

She continued down the hallway, leading to the board meeting room. She stopped in front of the oak double doors and took a deep sigh, trying to process what the meeting would entail. Her fate and future at Klimmings Incorporated would be decided during this meeting.

Vicki pulled open one of the doors and made her way into the room, stopping at the head of the conference table. She looked over all the board members who were seated at the table. Some of them she had known since she came on as head of the company, and others she had only known for a year or less.

Before sitting down, Vicki adjusted her lavender pantsuit, straightening it up. "So," she addressed the board members. "Is there any reason why I wasn't notified of this meeting until today?"

The board members fell silent, but Vicki continued. "In fact, had my secretary not been told by someone close to you all, it wouldn't have been until my husband read an article this morning in the Washington Post saying that the board of directors at Klimmings Incorporated were planning to fire me as the chair of the company. How do you explain yourselves here? Planning to fire the head of a multi-billion dollar company without giving them a chance to explain themselves . . ."

The room remained silent for what felt like many minutes. Finally, one of the board members spoke up. "Mrs. Klimmings, apparently, we have an insider issue."

The rest of the room erupted in laughter, leaving Vicki looking helpless. Nothing that she had said resonated within any of the men in the room.

"So," said another member. "Since she already knows why we are here, why don't we just go ahead with our vote then?"

"Wait! Wait! Wait!" Vicki called out. "You're in such a hurry to oust me. Who would you even have replace me?"

"That's a good question, Mrs. Klimmings. We already have a candidate in mind, actually." The board member pressed a button on the phone, which sat on the conference table. "Send him in."

Vicki turned her attention to the oak doors as they opened, and a woman led in Ryan Applegate.

"*You?*" Vicki let out. "You chose him?!"

"Mrs. Klimmings," the board member said. "Meet your replacement, Ryan Applegate. I'm sure you two have met before."

"Ryan," Vicki said, standing up. "Does your mother know about this? What would she say to you?"

"Well," Ryan began. "Lucky enough for me, she doesn't know anything about it yet. And she won't know anything about it until after this is all finalized and released to the press." He stepped in closer to Vicki. "Plus, my dad will handle her."

"Jeremy!" Vicki shouted. "This is his plan, isn't it?"

"Well, Mrs. Klimmings," said the board member. "I guess it's only fair for you to know the truth before we terminate you. Before Thanksgiving, Jeremy Applegate approached us with a deal that we just could not resist. He would allow for Klimmings Incorporated to be fitted with all the newest tech and software from Applegate Technology. Then in return, he would push for Klimmings Incorporated clean energy units to be brought into municipalities with which Applegate Technology works with. It was too good of a deal to pass up."

"Then why the hell wasn't I ever notified of this?" Vicki asked.

"Because you were the problem," the board member said. "In order for this deal to be official, we had to get rid of you. And so now, here we are!"

"Quit screwing around!" another board member called out. "Let's get on with the vote!"

The rest of the board members agreed and prepared to vote out Vicki, who was left bewildered at the head of the conference table. She looked over at Ryan, who had the smuggest look on his face, ready to become the next chair of the board.

"We'll make this simple," the board member said. "All in favor of terminating Vicki Klimmings as board chair and CEO of Klimmings Incorporated, say, 'I.'"

The board members began to cast their vote to affirm Vicki's ousting when the double oak doors flung open. Vicki jerked her attention to the doors and saw Miranda storm into the room dressed in a business suit. "And all that oppose, say 'I.'"

"Mrs. Klimmings," one of the board members said, baffled. "We weren't expecting you to be here today. Unfortunately, we don't have a seat at the table for you."

"That's fine," she said. "This'll only be quick." She turned to look at Vicki, who had tears pooled in her eyes. "I am using my fifty-one percent share of stock and voting rights to allow Vicki Klimmings to remain in the role of CEO of Klimmings Incorporated."

The board members in the room let out a gasp. Miranda turned toward Ryan, recognizing that he was in the room. "Oh, hello, Ryan!"

He glared at her, refusing to greet her back.

"What about the position of board chair?" one of the board members asked. "What is your vote on that?"

Miranda sighed. "It has become evident that one person holding the title of CEO and chair of the board is too much for them to efficiently manage. So, because of that, I hereby use my fifty-one percent share of stock to instate myself, Miranda Klimmings, as chair of the board of Klimmings Incorporated."

"What?!" one of the board members yelled out.

Another one shouted, "You can't do that!"

"I just did," said Miranda as she moved over to the seat Vicki was in. She looked at her mom, who had an astonished look on her face, as she took the chair. "I believe that this chair is now mine."

Ryan turned and stormed out of the room, letting the double doors slam behind him and causing Vicki to jump. Then she looked back at Miranda and smiled as chaos erupted throughout the boardroom.

* * *

Delilah sighed as she lay on her bed in her townhouse. She turned over to her left and saw Clark lying beside her. "One last time in this place," she said to him and smiled.

"I can't believe you two are finally going through with all this," Clark said to her. "It just seems like a couple of months ago that you weren't wanting to divorce, and now, here you are preparing to sell the house."

Delilah laughed. "Well, I wouldn't say we're getting divorced just yet. Neither of us has officially filed, nor have we mentioned it to each other."

"Yeah, but it's coming."

"It definitely is," Delilah said before letting out a chuckle. She smiled, looked around the room, and heard a popping sound. "What was that?"

"I don't know," Clark said as he sat up, looking down the hallway into the living room. "I don't see anything."

Delilah tried to sit herself up but couldn't. Then, she felt a warm liquid run down her leg as she moved around. Her eyes widened as she realized what had happened.

"Oh my God, Clark," Delilah gasped. "My water just broke."

CHAPTER 17

BE STILL MY HEART

Clark jumped up from the bed, looking at Delilah, perplexed. "Just now?" he asked as he ran his hands through his hair, not knowing what to do. "Your water just now broke?"

"Yes!" Delilah said. "It's leaked out everywhere on the bed." She tried to look down at the mess before looking Clark in the eyes. "Clark, I need you to take me to the hospital."

* * *

Rebecca White sat in her office at the Capitol Building sorting through some papers covering her desk. She took a deep sigh and then set them aside in an already growing stack. As she grabbed another stack to begin looking through them, her secretary entered her office, carrying more papers.

"You've got to be kidding me?" Rebecca said. "More papers?"

Her secretary sat the stack on Rebecca's desk and said, "This is the last of the records you asked for me to pull, Madam Speaker."

"These are all useless," Rebecca said, throwing her hands in the air. "We've initiated the committee investigating the president and his company, and I don't have anything to give them. What am I going to do?"

Rebecca spun around in her chair, looking out the window over the National Mall. Snow was sprinkled throughout the grass where a light dusting had occurred earlier in the day.

"Madam Speaker," her secretary said. "I would suggest that you look through those papers."

Rebecca turned around, intrigued. "Why? What's in there?"

"You'll just have to see." The secretary left Rebecca's office as she took the new stack of papers and began to look through them.

"*Oh*," Rebecca said, intrigued. She flipped through more of the papers and laughed. "Oh, Peter. What have you gotten yourself into?"

* * *

"Cheers!"

Miranda and Vicki clanked their glasses of white wine together. They were both seated in front of a window at Finley's, celebrating their victory from the board meeting. Then the two took a sip of their drinks and set them back down on the table.

"I can't believe that you made yourself board chair?" Vicki asked.

Miranda smiled back at her mom and said, "Well, I decided that you needed some extra help in the company. You don't need to be worried about the board so much all the time."

"Well, thank you, Miranda." Vicki held up her glass of wine, toasting Miranda and her actions.

Miranda smiled back at her mom and took a sip of her wine.

"So," Vicki began. "You haven't mentioned Jason in a while. How have you two been? Is everything okay?"

Miranda's smile fell from her face as her mind jumped back to the last time she saw Jason. All the pictures covered his wall like a shrine in a creep's basement. She shuddered at the thought of it.

"Are you alright, Miranda?"

Miranda snapped out of it, redirecting her attention to Vicki, who looked at her with a concerned look.

"Did something happen?" Vicki asked. "Miranda, did something happen?"

Miranda took a deep breath before answering Vicki's question. "I texted him yesterday and told him that we needed to take a break for a couple days."

"What?! I thought you two were doing fine!"

"I thought so too. Apparently, I was wrong." Miranda paused for a moment, considering whether she should tell Vicki about the wall of pictures. "Just some things came up that I hadn't known about."

Vicki sighed. "Oh, Miranda . . . I'm so sorry."

"I guess it just wasn't meant to be."

Vicki leaned forward and took Miranda's hands. "Miranda, you'll find someone. Someday, the right man will come into your life."

"Yeah," Miranda said. "I'm sure that someone special will come one day."

"Listen up! You're only twenty-nine, Miranda. You still have plenty of time to find someone who will treat you extra special."

"I know." Miranda let go of Vicki's hands and took a drink of her wine. She set the wine on the table and prepared herself to tell Vicki about the wall of photos in Jason's bedroom when her phone started ringing. She took her purse off the back of her chair and pulled out her phone, looking at the screen and then back at Vicki. "It's Delilah."

Miranda swiped the screen and held the phone to her ear. "Delilah, what's going on?"

"Miranda!" Delilah shouted over the phone. "Miranda! I need you to get ahold of Ben!"

"Why? What's going on?"

Miranda looked at Vicki with a worried look. Vicki leaned across the table and asked, "Is the baby coming?"

"The baby is coming!" Delilah shouted. "I'm heading to the hospital now! Get Ben!"

Before Miranda could respond to Delilah, she hung up. Miranda looked back up at Vicki, who had pulled her phone out of her bag. "She hung up," Miranda said. "We need to get ahold of Ben."

"I'm already on it," Vicki said as she held her phone to her ear, waiting for Ben to answer. "Let's go ahead and head over to the hospital."

Miranda and Vicki jumped up from the table. They headed out of Finley's and stood under the awning, waiting for the valet to bring Miranda's blue car around. Vicki found no success in reaching Ben, so she decided to try Gabby. While the two waited, they were unaware that Jason sat watching in a parking lot across the street adjacent to the restaurant.

* * *

Gabby sat on the sofa in the living room at the Klimmings Mansion. The TV was on, but Gabby wasn't paying any attention to what was playing. Instead, she had her phone out with Michelle's Instagram page pulled up. She just looked through Michelle's following list and noticed that she was no longer following her on the platform. When she realized that, Gabby's heart dropped and her stomach churned. She had an increasing urge to cry but managed to keep every tear held inside her.

She looked back down at her phone and saw that her mom was calling her. "Yes, Mom," Gabby said as she answered it.

"Gabriella," Vicki began. "Miranda and I are on the way to the hospital right now. I need you to find Benjamin and tell him that Delilah is having the baby."

"Okay," Gabby said dryly. "Anything else?"

"I figured you'd be excited. Why no enthusiasm? You're going to be an aunt."

"I'm sorry. Next time, I'll scream and holler."

Vicki looked over at Miranda, who was driving. Miranda glanced back at Vicki and mouthed, "What's wrong?"

Vicki shrugged before saying into the phone, "Just tell your brother so that he can meet us at the hospital, okay?"

"Okay," Gabby said before hanging up. She tossed her phone down onto the sofa and began heading upstairs. "Ben! Get your stuff ready!

You're going to be a dad!"

As Gabby made it to the top of the stairs, she made her way over to Ben's bedroom door and knocked. "Ben, are you in there?"

She opened the door and found Ben lying on his bed with a pillow laying over his forehead. He opened his eyes and looked over at Gabby. "What is it, Gabby?"

"Ben, you need to get ready. Your wife is at the hospital."

"Really?" He sat up in his bed, letting the pillow fall to the side. "She's really having the baby, now?"

"Yes. Hurry up and get yourself ready. We gotta go to the hospital." Gabby turned and stepped out of his bedroom but stopped before going down the stairs. She turned and faced Ben again. "Do I need to drive you there?"

Ben rubbed his forehead. "I think so. This damn headache won't go away."

Gabby sighed. "Well, hurry up, then." She turned and went back down the stairs and plopped back down on the sofa. She took her phone and looked back at Michelle's Instagram page. She clicked the "unfollow" button. Then she sat still for a moment as a message popped up, asking if she was sure she wanted to unfollow Michelle. Finally, Gabby approved the message.

As she continued messing around on her phone, Ben stood up from the bed. He took a couple steps over to his dresser, opened a drawer, and pulled out a grey t-shirt. He pulled off the shirt he had on and applied some deodorant before wearing the grey t-shirt.

He made his way out of the bedroom and stopped at the top of the stairs. His head continued to pound as he took a deep breath before heading down the stairs. With each step, his head throbbed even harder, feeling like someone was swinging a hammer into his temples. His vision began to blur from the outside inward. He took another step, and his vision swirled around, causing him to lose his balance.

Tumbling down the steps, one after another. As he continued down the stairs, Ben lost consciousness making him unable to brace himself as he fell to the bottom and whacked his head on the wall by the archway to the living room.

Gabby leaped from the sofa, running to Ben's side. "Oh my God! Oh my God!" she screamed. "DENISE! Help! Ben's hurt!"

Denise came running along the side of the staircase and fell to her knees beside Ben. "What happened?" she asked.

"He fell down the stairs! Denise . . . what do we do?!"

"Call for an ambulance, Miss Gabby! Now!"

Gabby scrambled over to her phone and struggled to dial 9-1-1 as her hands were shaking. "Hello," she said when the operator picked up. "This is Gabby Klimmings. We need an ambulance over here at the Klimmings Mansion now!"

* * *

Clark slowed the car to a stop.

"Why are we stopping?" Delilah cried out in pain. "I'm going to have this baby soon!"

"Traffic is at a stop," Clark explained. "I guess there was an accident because of the snow."

"It's just a dusting! Why can't people figure out how to drive in the snow!"

"In their defense, it is DC. Traffic always sucks here." Clark chuckled and then looked over at Delilah, who wasn't very amused. "Sorry."

"Just get me to the hospital, now!"

Clark looked in the mirrors. "There's an exit over here. Lemme see if I can get off here." He whipped the car across lanes of traffic, trying not to cause another accident with any oncoming vehicles, and made it to the exit. As they drove off, Delilah could hear cars honking at them in the distance.

"I shouldn't have left Ben," she said. "I wouldn't be in this situation if I hadn't."

Clark continued driving, not knowing how to respond to Delilah's revelation. Finally, the map navigator app redirected him, giving him new directions to get to the hospital.

* * *

Charlotte lay in bed, looking over at Ryan. He turned to look her in the eyes and smiled. She smiled back at him and kissed him. "I haven't had a night like that in a long time," she said.

"I couldn't agree more," Ryan said. "You were amazing."

The two kissed again as Charlotte's phone began ringing. "Who can this be?" she said, irritated as she turned to pick up her phone off the bedside table.

"Who is it?" Ryan asked as Charlotte's facial expression changed when she saw who was calling.

"It's Gabby. Why is she calling me?" Charlotte put the phone to her ear. "Hello."

"Aunt Charlotte," Gabby said frantically. She was in the back of the ambulance with Ben and some other paramedics. "I need you right now. Ben is on his way to the hospital. He fell down the stairs and hit his head pretty bad."

"Oh my God," Charlotte gasped. She glanced over at Ryan, who had sat up on the bed. "Which hospital are you going to?"

"They're taking us to Walter Reed. Dad has an order in place for all of us to get medical attention from there."

"Gabby, have you called your mom?"

"Not yet. Charlotte, I need you with me. Please come!"

"I'll be over soon! Don't panic."

Charlotte ended the call and flung the covers off her, getting dressed. "I gotta go," she said to Ryan.

"What happened?" he asked her.

"Ben fell down the stairs. He hit his head, and Gabby is really shaken up about it all."

"Hell," Ryan said in disbelief. "I wonder if Delilah knows yet."

"She didn't say anything about it. She was panicking."

As Charlotte continued dressing, Ryan lept out of bed and threw on his clothes. "I'll walk you out to your car," he said as Charlotte grabbed her bag.

He opened the door and led her down the stairs and through a hall-way that led to the living room. In the living room, Jeremy was helping Cathie put her coat on. "Dad . . . Mom . . ." Ryan said to them. "Where are you guys going?"

"Vicki called us," Cathie said, noticing Charlotte behind Ryan. She glanced over to Ryan and gave him a disapproving look. "She said that Delilah is on her way to the hospital."

"So she knows about Ben, then?" Ryan asked.

"Why the hell would she be going there for Ben?" Jeremy exclaimed. "She's having her baby."

"Oh no," Charlotte gasped. "Not right now."

Cathie stepped closer to Charlotte, looking concerned. "Charlotte, what's wrong?"

"My niece, Gabby, called earlier. Ben is on his way to the hospital, as well," she said. "He fell down the stairs and hit his head pretty hard."

* * *

Peter sat at the *Resolute* desk in the Oval Office, listening to Henry speak about states that the president and vice president needed to visit the most in the upcoming reelection campaign. He looked over at Constance, who seemed very intrigued by the entire speech. Peter rolled his eyes.

"So, Mr. Gates," he spoke up. "Which of these states has the closest possibility of swinging blue?"

"In all honesty, Mr. President," Henry responded. "Florida and Ohio are the two closest. They're only favoring Republicans by five points, right now."

"Are you kidding me? They voted for us during the last election. Why are they swinging back?"

"Sir, most Americans aren't as happy about our economic recovery as you would think they are."

"But we're out of the recession now, aren't we?"

"Technically, yes, but I don't think most Americans are feeling the benefits of that just yet."

Before Peter could get in another word, Constance spoke up. "Mr. President, I think what Henry is trying to say is that we just need to stop by those states more than what we did during the first campaign. It should be fine because you'll have me throughout the whole thing."

"That's if the president chooses to continue to have you as his vice president," Henry said. He turned to Peter for an answer, but Peter glared at him.

Constance turned to Peter. She looked perturbed at Henry's comment.

"Peter," she said. "Are you planning to remove me from your administration? If so, I'd like to know now."

Peter slowly turned his head back to Constance, pausing for a minute before he responded. "Of course not, Constance. I don't know why Mr. Gates would suggest such an asinine thing."

"I just wanted you to know of your options, Mr. President," Henry said, shrugging his shoulders.

Peter opened his mouth to respond but heard a knock on the door to the Oval Office. He turned his attention to the door and saw Martha step in. "Mr. President," she said quietly. "Your daughter, Gabby, is on the phone right now. She says that it is extremely urgent."

"I'll take it," Peter said as he took his phone off the receiver. "Gabby?"

"Dad!" Gabby exclaimed on the phone. "Dad, you need to come here!"

"Gabby, slow down! Where are you at? Why do I need to come?"

"Dad, Ben fell down the stairs and hit his head. We're at the hospital right now."

"Where? Walter Reed?"

"Yes. Dad, please come quick!"

"I'll be there soon, honey. Did you tell anyone else?"

"I haven't been able to. Mom called originally to tell me that Delilah was in labor, and Ben and I were getting ready to go to the hospital when he fell."

"Oh, dammit! I'll be right over, Gabby. Hold on!"

Peter placed the phone back on the receiver. "Is everything

alright?" Constance asked, standing up, concerned.

"No. Ben is hurt. I gotta go to the hospital." Peter jogged over to the door and opened it, startling Martha at her desk. "Martha, I need to head to Walter Reed, now!"

* * *

Vicki and Miranda came into the waiting room where Gabby was sitting. "Gabriella," Vicki said. "How fast were you driving? There's no way you could have gotten here before us."

"Mom," Gabby began. "I've got something to tell you." She swallowed hard, trying to calm herself. "Ben . . . he's in trouble."

Vicki fell silent. "What kind of trouble?"

"He fell down the stairs and hit his head." Tears began to pool in Gabby's eyes. "Mom, he went unconscious. He hasn't woken up since the fall." Gabby started crying, and Miranda immediately moved in to hug and console Gabby.

"Oh no," Vicki finally let out. "This can't be happening right now." She turned and ran her hands through her hair and began pacing. Charlotte and the Applegate family arrived in the waiting room as Vicki walked back and forth. Cathie stepped in, hugging her.

"How are they?" she asked.

"Gabby just told us about Ben," said Miranda. "I don't think she's heard anything from the doctor yet."

"What about Delilah?"

Miranda turned to Gabby. "Have you heard about Delilah yet?"

"I don't think she's shown up yet."

"Where could she be?" Charlotte chimed in. "It took us an hour to get here after Gabby called us."

Vicki turned to Charlotte, just now realizing that her sister was in the waiting room. She gazed at Charlotte and then over to Ryan, putting two-and-two together. "Charlotte," Vicki said. "Can I speak to you outside the waiting room?"

Charlotte nodded and stepped out with Vicki. "What do you want to talk about?" Charlotte asked her.

"What did I tell you about seeing Ryan?" Vicki asked. "I told you to stay away from him."

"Okay."

"Then why were you with the Applegates, then?"

Charlotte remained quiet, not answering Vicki's question, so she leaned closer to Charlotte. "Answer me."

"We went on a date," Charlotte began. "It was an innocent date, at first."

"At first?"

"Yes. It was innocent at first, but then things grew, and the next thing I knew, I was in his bed."

"So you two slept together?"

"Yes."

"Charlotte," Vicki sighed. "Why can't you just listen to people?"

"I'm sorry! I screwed up once again, Vicki! I can never live up to your standard of perfection."

Charlotte turned to leave but ran into Peter, who had just arrived. "Where are you going?" Peter asked her.

"I was getting ready to leave," Charlotte grumbled. "Nothing I do is ever good enough for your wife!" She glared back at Vicki.

"Don't leave just yet," Peter said. "You're going to be a great-aunt soon!"

"*Great?!*" Charlotte let out in disgust.

"Peter," Vicki chimed in. "Delilah hasn't arrived yet."

"Yes, she has," Peter said. "She was being taken in when I arrived. Some guy was with her too, but the hospital wouldn't let him in."

"That's great news!" Vicki turned to Charlotte, who had ended her pouting fit. "Charlotte, could you tell everyone in the waiting room that Delilah has arrived?"

Charlotte stepped away, heading into the waiting room to share the news that Delilah finally made it to the hospital with everyone who was in there. Vicki waited until Charlotte was out of earshot before she spoke. "Have you heard about Ben?"

"Yes," Peter said. "Gabby called me earlier and told me. Do you know how he fell down the stairs? Was he drinking again?"

"I don't know. I hadn't asked Gabby about it yet."

Peter sighed. "I can't believe this is happening. I had hoped that he would have powered through his urges before the baby was born."

"I guess this is just much worse than any of us thought," Vicki said, hugging Peter.

"Yes, it is," Peter said, sighing again. "You know, as I think about this, I can't help but think about how things are going to change when this baby is born."

"What do you mean by that?"

"We're going to have to start getting along with the Applegates. We're going to share a grandchild."

Vicki let go of Peter. "Are you being serious?"

"I . . . I think it would be for the best." Peter looked at Vicki, who had a smile growing on her face. "I feel that we need to learn to set our differences aside. I mean, just look at what's happened with Ben and Delilah.

Vicki hugged Peter again. "Peter, I think this is a great idea. It's time to let the past bury itself."

* * *

Jeremy handed Cathie a coffee, who smiled in return. She was sitting next to Ryan as they continued waiting for news on Delilah and Ben. Cathie took a sip of the coffee and then set it on the table next to her. She turned to Ryan and quietly asked, "So when did you two become a thing?" She motioned to Charlotte, sitting across the room next to Gabby.

"We're not a thing, Mom," Ryan replied. He shifted around in the chair, trying to get more comfortable.

"If you two aren't a thing, then why was she in your bedroom before we came to the hospital?"

"It was just a one-time thing."

"Does she know this?" Cathie raised her eyebrows as she looked at Ryan. "You do know she's married, right?"

Ryan jerked his attention toward his mom, looking her in the eyes.

"She's married?!"

"Yes," Cathie said. "She's married to some guy who owns a football team out in California."

Ryan sighed. "She never even mentioned that to me."

"Well, now you know."

Cathie reached over and grabbed her coffee, taking a sip from it while Ryan processed what he had just been told. He considered speaking with Charlotte but stayed in his seat when he saw Peter, Vicki, and a doctor step into the room.

"Is this everyone?" the doctor asked Peter.

"Yes," Peter said as he and Vicki took a seat. "This should be everyone."

"Let me first begin with congratulations," the doctor announced. "Mrs. Klimmings just gave birth to a baby girl weighing six pounds and ten ounces about ten minutes ago."

"That's wonderful!" Vicki exclaimed as Jeremy and Cathie hugged each other.

"Yes, it is," Peter said to Vicki.

"I can't believe it," Ryan said, turning to his mom. "I'm an uncle."

"Yes, you are," Cathie responded to Ryan. "And we're finally grandparents!"

"So are we!" Vicki said with a giant smile displayed across her face.

"But that's not all the news I have to share," the doctor added as he interrupted the celebration. "We need to talk about Mr. Klimmings."

"What's wrong with him?" Vicki asked. "Is he going to be okay?"

The doctor took off his glasses and sighed. "There's no easy way to answer that question other than by saying that only time will tell. Mr. Klimmings suffered a severe hit to the head when he fell down the stairs. His brain has massive swelling right now as a result of it. These next few days will be critical."

"What does this mean?" Peter asked, raising from his char.

"Mr. President," the doctor sighed. "Unfortunately, your son is in a coma, and we don't know how long it'll be before . . . or *if* he ever wakes up."

CHAPTER 18

DELILAH'S BABY

"Mrs. Klimmings, are you ready to meet your daughter?" a nurse asked Delilah, who was lying in her hospital bed. Her hair was disheveled, and she wasn't wearing any of the designer makeup that she usually donned.

"Yes," Delilah said, trying to sit up in the hospital bed. "I can't wait to finally meet her."

The nurse stepped out of the room to get the baby, leaving Delilah alone. She thought back to the birth and the doctors rushing out of the room with the baby because of an abnormality, which later turned out to be nothing. Once again, Delilah tried to get comfortable but was too sore to move very much.

Within a couple of minutes, the door opened, and the nurse came back into the room carrying a baby. "Mrs. Klimmings," the nurse said. "Meet your baby girl."

She gently laid the baby into Delilah's arms and on her chest, allowing Delilah to have her daughter close to her. Delilah looked into her daughter's big blue eyes. She felt a warming sensation in her heart and couldn't help but smile.

"Hello, Katherine," she said to the baby. "I'm your momma."

Katherine kept looking at Delilah, taking in the sight of her mother. Delilah continued to smile as she and her daughter just stared at one another, taking in the beauty of each other.

"It's a shame her father couldn't be here," the nurse said as she witnessed the moment. "I've been praying for Mr. Klimmings."

Suddenly, Delilah was brought back to reality. She recalled how Clark had reacted after learning about the pregnancy.

Clark took a deep breath and calmed himself. He looked Delilah in the eyes. "Delilah, I don't care if it's Ben's or not. If it's his, he doesn't have to know it. We could just as easily raise yours and Ben's baby as we could yours and mine."

It became evident to her that taking the baby and running away with Clark wasn't going to be as simple as she had thought it would be. Delilah held out Katherine for the nurse to take back to the nursery.

"Miss," Delilah said to the nurse as she took the baby. "By any chance, could I get a paternity test on her?"

"Sure," said the nurse. "Why would you want one though . . . just outta curiosity?"

"Oh, Ben asked for one," Delilah lied. "I guess he doesn't trust me. You know we are separated, right?"

"Oh, yes. I've seen all kinds of stuff in the tabloids about it."

Delilah chuckled to herself as the nurse started out of the room, but as she was about to close the door behind her, Delilah stopped her for one more question.

"Nurse," she said. "You mentioned that you were praying for Ben. Why? Did you see something in the tabloids about him?"

"No, ma'am," the nurse said, stepping back into the room. "Have you not heard about him?"

"I guess not."

"Well, it happened earlier today. I guess you must've not heard about it because you were here."

"What happened to him?" Delilah was beginning to get worried.

"Mr. Klimmings is in a coma right now. He fell and did a number on his head. We won't know how bad things are until the swelling goes down on his brain."

Delilah felt her stomach drop, feeling more helpless than ever. Guilt overcame her as she thought about leaving Ben and the implications that it caused. Ben's excessive drinking increased from the moment she left, and Delilah felt at this moment that everything was her fault.

The nurse finally left the room, closing the door behind her, just as a tear fell from Delilah's eyes.

* * *

"Ben Klimmings remains in a coma almost a week after reportedly falling down the stairs and hitting his head. His estranged wife? Well, she was discharged from the hospital early yesterday."

"Yet, things aren't looking so good over at Klimmings Incorporated either. A week after the president's eldest child made herself the chair of the board, more and more stockholders have been engaging in a massive sell-off of Klimmings Incorporated stock, sending the future of the company into the unknown."

Constance turned away from the TV, dropping a sugar cube in her hot tea. She took a sip of it as she continued watching the morning news show.

"And it's interesting that you point all that out because the president has been too caught up in dealings with China and his own upcoming reelection campaign that his whole family is practically falling apart around him."

"Yes, if Peter Klimmings is the glue that holds his family together, then they are in need of something a whole lot tougher."

Constance turned off the TV, taking another sip of her tea as James stepped into the room. "Why'd you turn off the news, honey?" asked James as he looked in a mirror on the wall, straightening up his tie.

"I got tired of listening to them talk about the president and his family," she said as she took another sip of her tea. "Everything that happens with his family always turns into how it'll affect his reelection. I'm just tired of it."

"Oh, try not to get too upset about it. I'm sure it'll all be fine at the end of next year when it comes time for the election."

Constance stood up and moved over to James, helping him with his tie. "Truth be told," she said. "I don't think he will get reelected."

"You don't?"

"No."

"Why?"

"What has he done? Fixed the economy? The average American hasn't benefitted from his policies at all."

James looked back in the mirror after Constance helped with his tie. "But how have his policies affected the rich and powerful?"

Constance paused, thinking it over. "I mean, they've benefitted from it all."

"That's all he needs then. It's what we do at the church. Nobody cares about what the average Joes of America want. It only matters what the people who hold the power want."

Constance stepped back over to her tea and picked it up, leading James to the door. "I guess you have a point, then," she said. "History has always worked out for the rich."

"Well, it didn't work out very well for Marie Antoinette." The two laughed as James opened the front door. He turned back to Constance. "But you learn from the mistakes of others. As long as you give the ordinary people an idea that what is happening is what they want, you will be just fine. Constance, you're going to be just fine."

James began to step out the door, heading to the steps to descend from the front porch of Number One Observatory Circle. He stopped, turned around, and said one more thing to Constance. "And Constance, if you think that Peter's chances are sucky, you can always run against him and take the Democratic nomination. A lot of people still support you."

He proceeded down the stairs to his motorcade, which would take him to the Washington Pentecostal Church of God. Constance remained on the porch as James left, pondering how his suggestion would remain a viable option.

* * *

Cathie stood in the kitchen mixing a large salad bowl with tongs. Classical music played in the background as Cathie worked in the kitchen, keeping her mind concentrated on the task at hand.

As she continued putting the salad together, Jeremy stepped into the kitchen. "Lunch almost ready?" he asked, sitting down on a barstool and placing his arms on the island.

"Almost," said Cathie. "I just have to mix in the dressing, and then we'll be able to eat." She stepped over to the refrigerator and took out a bottle of balsamic vinaigrette dressing, proceeding to pour it over the salad. "Vicki called me today."

"She did?"

"Earlier." Cathie set the dressing bottle on the countertop and took the salad tongs to toss the salad. "She mentioned to me that Peter had spoken to her about moving on from this ridiculous family feud."

Jeremy looked at Cathie, intrigued. "He did?"

"Apparently so."

Jeremy let the statement process for a second. "And how do we know that he's just not saying this to stab me in the back later?"

Cathie turned to Jeremy, slamming the salad tongs on the island countertop. Balsamic vinaigrette dressing flung all over the countertop. "Dammit, Jeremy! Do you always have to question the motives of that family?!" She turned back toward the salad. "After all, you set them up with that China deal. That was all you!"

Jeremy remained silent as Cathie turned to face him again, looking him dead in the eyes.

"I congratulated Vicki on remaining on as CEO of Klimmings Incorporated, and you know what she told me? She told me about your plan to take over Klimmings Incorporated," Cathie continued. "She told me how you had Ryan set to take over the company. I can't believe you, Jeremy!"

Jeremy sighed. "I will never be able to forgive Peter for screwing me over."

"Oh my goodness, Jeremy! That was fifteen years ago! Drop it!"

Cathie tossed the salad tongs on the counter. "Because if you can't drop it, and you can't cooperate with the Klimmingses, I don't know if I can stay married to you."

Jeremy's eyes widened. "You're joking, right?"

"Does it look like I'm joking, Jeremy? I can't keep doing this. Look at our daughter right now. Look at her husband. What's happened to them is both our fault and the Klimmings' fault." Cathie sighed. "If we just got along with each other, none of this would have happened!"

She stormed out of the kitchen, leaving Jeremy sitting alone at the island.

* * *

Dana opened her locker, tossing two textbooks in, before slamming the door shut and spinning the lock. She turned to her right and ran into Michelle, who was waiting.

"Michelle!" Dana said, surprised. "What the hell do you want?"

"I need to talk to you," Michelle said as she began to walk Dana down the hallway, meandering in and out of clusters of students. "Gabby kissed me."

Dana stopped in the middle of the hallway, causing a kid behind her to run into her, resulting in a few exchanged choice words. "What?!"

"She did!" Michelle continued. "It was early last month, right after Thanksgiving."

"Why didn't you tell me?!" The two started down the hallway again. "That's why Gabby's been acting so weird."

"When we came back from Christmas, I told Gabby that I needed some time to process all this," Michelle added. "I don't know what to do, though."

"Well, I can tell you this," Dana said, leaning into Michelle. "There's room for only one lesbian in this friend group, and we both know that's me. I'm not going to fight her over you."

"I never said I was gay," Michelle said. "I only said that I was interested in trying some things. You know . . . experiment."

Dana laughed and sarcastically said, "Oh, yeah."

She leaned in and kissed Michelle. "When I said that I was going to experiment, I learned something about myself."

"And what was that?" Michelle asked.

"That I only liked girls," Dana said, smiling great big. Michelle smiled back before turning to head into the classroom they were beside. As she made her way in, she made eye contact with Gabby, who had witnessed the entire conversation.

* * *

"Mr. President," Martha said, standing in the doorway of the Oval Office. "President Wu from China is on the phone."

"Thank you, Martha," Peter said, turning in his chair to look at Henry, who was sitting on the opposite side of the *Resolute* desk. "I'll take it in here."

Martha closed the door to the Oval Office as Peter picked up the phone and put it to his ear. Henry took another phone and put it to his ear, listening in.

"President Wu," Peter said, answering the phone. "It's nice to finally get to speak with you."

"Don't waste your time with pleasantries, President Klimmings," President Wu said. "We both know that our relationship is very strained."

"Indeed, it is." Peter glanced over at Henry. "I guess I'll just come out and ask you why you are continuing to act out military fly-bys near one of my Pacific bases."

"I believe that what we are doing isn't against any international laws, Peter."

"Well, we would like for you to stop."

"And what if we don't?"

Henry jerked his attention to Peter, shocked by the sudden aggression brought by the Chinese president.

"Are you asking me what we're going to do if you opt not to stand down?"

Silence fell on the phone. Peter looked back at Henry, who wasn't hiding his surprise very well.

"I think you know what I mean," President Wu finally said before hanging up.

"That son of a bitch hung up on me!" Peter exclaimed as he set the phone back on the receiver.

"I heard," said Henry as he put his phone back on the receiver. "What are you going to do about this? He sounded like he's up to something."

Peter sighed. "I need to speak with Secretary Bird. I am going to give the order for the Basa Air Base to begin conducting military drills more regularly, patrolling the air space around them. We must show them that we aren't going to let them do whatever the hell it is they want."

Peter stood up from his seat and turned, looking out the window behind him. "They need to know that you just can't screw around with me."

* * *

Clark closed the townhouse door behind Delilah as she set a car seat holding Katherine down on the floor, bending over to unbuckle her newborn. She took Katherine down the hallway and laid her in the crib in her bedroom.

When she came back to the living room, she paused to see Clark sitting on the couch, searching through the TV channels to find something to watch. She then looked into the kitchen at the cardboard boxes packed tight with some of her belongings. She was preparing to sell the townhouse and permanently move back into the Applegate Homestead. Delilah sighed and then went over to the couch and sat next to Clark, resting her head on his shoulders. He stopped what he was doing and looked over at her.

"You don't know how long I've waited for all this," he said to her. "I'm just finally glad that all this waiting has finally paid off."

"Me too," Delilah said. "I just wish Ben wasn't in that coma." She lifted her head from Clark's shoulder. "I know it's not my fault, but I keep having this feeling inside that it's all because of me."

"Babe, it's not your fault. You didn't cause him to fall down those stairs."

"I know. I know." Delilah sighed, running her hands through her hair. She was about to say something else when she was interrupted by her phone ringing.

She looked at Clark and then over at the car seat where her phone was before she got up and snatched it, answering it. "Hello?"

"Hi. Is this Mrs. Delilah Applegate Klimmings?" a woman said on the other line.

"Yes, this is her," Delilah said.

"Mrs. Klimmings," the woman said. "We are calling to give you the results of the paternity test you had requested on your newborn a week ago."

Delilah turned to Clark, who was scrolling through some social media feed, not paying any attention to Delilah at the time. "What are the results?" she asked.

"Well, Mrs. Klimmings," the woman started. "We took the saliva swab from you and your husband, and after testing it thoroughly, we concluded that your husband, Benjamin Klimmings, is indeed the father of baby Katherine."

Delilah fell silent as her eyes widened and her mouth dropped open. Clark had just caught a glimpse of her and responded by saying, "What? What's going on?"

Delilah took the phone from her ear, looked at Clark, and told him the truth. "Clark, Katherine is Ben's."

Clark was speechless. Delilah might have well just shattered his dream with the news she just delivered to him. At this moment, the two just stared at each other, processing this news through each other's glassy eyes coated with tears.

"Mrs. Klimmings?"

Delilah broke eye contact with Clark, looking down at her phone in her hand. Then, she put the phone to her ear and responded. "I'm still here."

"Congratulations, Mrs. Klimmings. I'm sure you can't wait to share the news with Mr. Klimmings whenever he pulls through this. Our thoughts and prayers are definitely with him and you during this time."

Delilah looked back at Clark, who was wiping his eyes with his shirt. "Thank you," Delilah said. "We really do need them right now."

* * *

The elevator door opened, and Vicki and Miranda began down the hallway to the lobby of Klimmings Incorporated. They passed by Doris' empty desk and Pam, who tried to grab their attention but failed to. The two Klimmings women went into Vicki's office, closing the door behind them. Vicki proceeded to take off her scarf, gloves, and coat, hanging it on the coat tree in her office. As Miranda did the same, Vicki took a seat behind her desk.

"Miranda," she began. "We gotta do something with the current stock situation."

"It's getting worse, isn't it," Miranda said as she took a seat in front of Vicki's desk. "Maybe I shouldn't have made myself the board chair."

"That wouldn't have mattered," Vicki said. "They were planning to have a mass sell-off anyways."

"When I checked this morning, our stock price has dropped by about twenty-five percent."

A knock was heard at the door, and Vicki called out for whoever it was to come in. The door opened, and Pam stepped into the room, politely saying, "Mrs. Klimmings . . ."

"Yes, Pam," Vicki said. "What's going on?"

"We've just had our first board member resign," Pam said. "And apparently, there are more to come."

Vicki sighed and leaned back in her chair. "You've got to be kidding me."

"Mom," Miranda said. "What's this mean?"

"They're trying to sink us, Miranda!" Vicki exclaimed. She ran her hands through her hair, not knowing what to do. Then she noticed Pam waiting in her office. "Thank you, Pam. I'll let you know if I need anything."

"Yes, ma'am," Pam said before leaving the room.

As Pam closed the door behind her, Vicki sat her elbows on her desk. She used her fingers to press against the pressure points on her forehead, trying to alleviate an oncoming headache brought on by this situation.

"Things were so much easier when we owned the company," Vicki said as she continued to apply pressure.

Miranda perked up in her seat, intrigued by what her mother had just said. "What did you just say?"

"It was easier when we owned the company."

"Mom . . . do you hear what you're saying?" Miranda leaned in toward Vicki. "Why can't we just own the company again?"

Vicki lifted her head from her fingertips, looking at Miranda. "What?"

"Together, Gabby and I will own fifty-one percent. If you pitch in and purchase a bulk of the stock, we could own the company again."

"That's not a bad idea," Vicki said, sitting up in her seat. "If we own a majority of the stock, we could vote to privatize the company. Then we wouldn't have to worry about stockholders or prices per share."

"We can do that?"

"We can." Vicki stood up from her seat. "Would this be something you'd be interested in? I would need your help purchasing the stock."

Miranda thought it over for a second before agreeing.

"Great!" Vicki said as she made her way over to the coat tree.

"Where are you going?" Miranda asked as she stood from her seat.

"We need to head to see our accountant," Vicki said, putting on her coat. "We need to move fast on this if this is something we want to do."

Miranda grabbed her coat and followed Vicki out the door. They passed by Pam's desk, where Vicki informed her that they would be back. Then, they headed down the hallway to the elevators. Vicki pressed the button, and the elevator to the left opened. They both stepped onto the elevator and pressed the button that would take them to the ground floor of Klimmings Tower.

After the door closed, the other elevator's door opened, and a man stepped out and approached Pam's desk.

"How can I help you?" Pam asked, looking up from her desk. The man was holding a bouquet of flowers in a vase. Pam looked him over, feeling that she had recognized him from somewhere.

"I have these flowers for Mrs. Klimmings," the man said to Pam.

Pam squinted her eyes. "For Vicki Klimmings? Are these from the president?"

"No. This is for Miranda."

"And just who is this from?" Pam asked, standing from her chair.

"These are from Jason," the man said. "I'm her boyfriend."

Pam laughed. "That's where I recognized you from!" She stepped around her desk. "Let's set these in the empty office next to Vicki. It used to be her bother's office before he left."

Pam opened the door and led Jason in. He placed the flowers on the desk and turned to Pam. "You think she'll like them?" he asked her.

"I think she'll love them."

"Great!" Jason stepped out into the lobby. "I'm going to head out now before she gets here. I want this to be a surprise for her."

Pam sat back down at her desk. "Oh, I think she'll definitely be surprised. She's had a lot on her plate lately."

"I know," Jason agreed. "I'll see ya around!"

He turned and headed toward the elevators. As he pressed the button for the elevator, a smile grew across his face.

* * *

Delilah sat down beside Ben's bed. This was the first time she had seen him in a state of comatose. The only thing she could hear in the room was the consistent beeping of the heart monitor attached to Ben. She looked at her husband, seeing how helpless he looked.

"Ben," she said to him. "I've got something to tell you."

Her response was met with the sound of the heart monitor, but Delilah continued.

"I had our baby last week, Ben. You heard me . . . our baby. Her name is Katherine. She's named after my mom."

Delilah stopped to wipe a tear from her eye. She looked at Ben. His eyes closed, and the sound of the heart monitor echoed off the walls in the room.

"Ben," Delilah struggled to continue. "I'm so sorry for what I have done. This is all my fault."

She bent over, sobbing into her hands. "I don't think you'll ever forgive me, but I am so sorry for all of this."

Delilah used her sleeve to wipe her eyes. She stood up and made her way over to the door, turning around to look at Ben once more before leaving.

"I love you, Ben."

She kissed her hand and blew a kiss toward him before opening the door. As she stepped out, she heard something from behind her, causing her to turn around. Ben still was lying in the bed. Delilah turned around to head out once again but heard the sound again. She turned back to Ben and saw him slightly move and groan.

"Oh my God!" Delilah exclaimed as she ran over to his bed, falling to her knees. "Ben! I'm here, Ben!"

He continued to shift slowly, groaning more and more. Delilah pressed the button to call in a nurse, and not soon after, someone came over a speaker in the room asking what the issue was.

"He's waking up!" Delilah called out. "Someone come quick!"

She leaned over to Ben as he groaned some more. His eyes were slowly trying to lift open.

"Come on, Ben! You can do it! Come on, babe!"

* * *

Charlotte slammed the sliding glass door shut as she entered the Klimmings Mansion through the back. Vicki stepped out of the living room, looking down the entry hall at Charlotte, who looked distraught.

"Watch the door," Vicki called out. "You can break that by slamming it shut like that."

Charlotte glared at her sister before taking a right to head toward her bedroom. Vicki followed her into her bedroom. "What's wrong,

Charlotte?"

"He stood me up!" Charlotte flung around to Vicki. "I waited in that restaurant for hours, and he never showed."

Vicki looked confused. "Who stood you up?"

"Ryan!" Charlotte said, plopping down onto her bed. "I waited for him for so long, and he never did show."

Vicki sighed before sitting next to her sister. "Did you call or text him to see why he never came?"

"I did. He took forever to respond, but when he did, he told me that he thought it best if we spent time apart."

"I think that it's honestly best for both of you two to spend time apart."

Charlotte stared at her sister in disgust. "Can you ever be supportive of me, Vicki? Every single time, you're always telling me what to do and criticizing me!"

Vicki jumped up from the bed. "Charlotte, you're married! You can't be dating right now!"

"You're forgetting something! George cheated on me! I have every right to pay him back."

"I'm not arguing with you," Vicki said, heading to the door. "I've got other things to do."

She stepped out of the room, closing the door behind her. After taking a deep sigh, Vicki proceeded to head through the archway into the living room where Peter, Miranda, and Gabby were gathered. She went over to the bar, where the alcohol had been brought back out, and poured herself a double vodka. Then she turned around to the rest of the family and took a sip.

"Charlotte," Vicki said, holding up her drink, explaining to the rest of the family why she was drinking.

Peter nodded his head, acknowledging the reason.

"So," Miranda began. "I got a call from Delilah earlier. Ben woke up today."

"Did he?" Vicki said. "That is such great news!"

"Yes, it is!" Peter said. "Finally, this family can be back together again." He leaned over and hugged Gabby. "And we are so happy for you too, Gabby."

"Yes, we are," Vicki said. "If it weren't for you, Ben may not have made it."

Gabby let a small smile appear on her face, catching Miranda's attention. She remembered what Gabby had shared with her on Christmas and noticed how it was affecting her mood. Since the hostage crisis at her school, Gabby had not been acting her usual self, and it was becoming more evident to Miranda that things were not getting any better for her.

"So, Miranda," Vicki said, interrupting Miranda's thoughts. She turned over to Vicki, trying to give her attention to her. "Would you like to share our plan with the rest of the family?"

"What?"

"Our plan. You know . . . the one we discussed today in the office?"

Miranda remembered and recalled their plan to privatize the company.

"So," Miranda began. "Mom and I were at the office today, and we learned that a board member had resigned from his position on the board of directors. Pam also shared with us that more were expected to begin resigning within the next few days."

"I heard about this today during one of my meetings," Peter said before turning to Vicki. "What the hell is going on in the company? Why are we losing so my shareholders?"

"It's all a domino effect from that Chinese deal setup that Jeremy put us through," Vicki tried to explain. "But listen to what Miranda has to say. We have a solution."

Peter turned to Miranda. "I'm intrigued now."

Miranda smiled before continuing. "Technically, Mom put the idea in my head, but we were talking, and I realized that between Gabby's shares and my own, we own fifty-one percent of the company. With so many shareholders selling off right now, it wouldn't be a bad idea to begin purchasing those shares and build up our interest in the company."

"And then," Vicki said. "Once we own a significant portion of stock, we could call together a vote and move to privatize the company, bringing its ownership back into the hands of the Klimmings family."

"Once we do that," Miranda said. "We can divvy up voting rights amongst ourselves so that we can decide what's best for the company, together as a family."

Peter smiled as Miranda finished explaining their plan. "I love it," he said as he took his glass of Kentucky bourbon and took a sip. "Just leave my name out of all of it, and this will work great! I can't have that bitch, Rebecca White, on my ass anymore than she already is."

"Is it getting worse?" Vicki asked, sitting in a chair.

"It is. She's really into this investigation with the new Congress. The Republicans are having a heyday with it all."

"That's terrible!"

As the adults continued to talk, Gabby took out her phone and saw a message from Michelle. She stepped out of the living room into the entry hall to look at the text. It told her that she needed to check social media.

Curious about why she needed to check her social media, Gabby opened up one of her social media accounts. No sooner than opening it up did Gabby find out why Michelle had told her to look at it. Her heart plunged into her stomach, which was churning. Resisting the urge to throw up, Gabby stared at what was posted.

Dana had made a post saying: *Gabby Klimmings is a lesbian. Don't believe me? She kissed my girlfriend, Michelle.*

Gabby gagged and ran down the entry hall to the bathroom beside the back sliding door. She made it to the toilet in time to hurl. She wiped her mouth and fell to the floor, trembling. Her body shook, and her heart pounded faster and faster, making it more difficult for her to breathe.

Gabby's biggest secret had been leaked, and there was nothing she could do about it.

CHAPTER 19
RISE OF THE KLIMMINGS FAMILY EMPIRE

Gabby heard a knock at her bedroom door as she laid back on her bed, staring at the ceiling. She had never felt more helpless than how she did at this moment. Inside, she felt a sense of relief in knowing that her big secret was finally out there. Still, that sense of relief was also met with the amplifying terror of having to face her parents with this revelation.

The knock was heard at the door again, but a voice came along with it this time. "Gabby, are you in there?"

Gabby recognized Miranda's voice, turning her head toward her door. "Come in."

The door slowly opened, and Miranda stepped into the room. "What's going on? You disappeared tonight and never returned," Miranda said as she closed the door behind her and sat at the foot of the bed.

Gabby turned her attention back to the ceiling. "Dana posted it," Gabby told her. "See." She tossed her phone down to the end of the bed beside Miranda.

Miranda took the phone and looked at the social media post. "Oh no," she sighed. "Why would she do that?"

"Because when she stayed the night, I kissed Michelle." Gabby turned over to her side, facing the wall behind Miranda.

"Why would she post that you're a lesbian," Miranda asked. "I thought you were bisexual."

"I am," Gabby said. "I never told Dana or Michelle that I was. I guess they just assumed that I was gay."

"Have you spoken to any of them?"

"Hell no! I don't even want to look at either of them."

"I think that's a good idea," Miranda said as she stood from the bed and headed to the door. She turned back toward Gabby. "You do know that you're going to have to tell Mom and Dad now, right? The media will find this and take off with it."

"I know," Gabby said with tears running down her cheek. "I wasn't ready for this, Miranda."

Miranda came over to Gabby, who had sat up on the bed, and hugged her.

"I'm so sorry, Gabby," Miranda said. "I wish this hadn't happened."

Gabby cried on Miranda's shoulders, her sobs filling the room.

"I'll be here when you tell them, Gabby," Miranda said. "I promise you." She let go of Gabby and looked her in the eyes. "I will not let you go through this alone."

* * *

Ben lay in his bed, watching the news on the TV that hung on the wall.

"Several Chinese warships have been spotted in the South China Sea as tensions between Washington and Beijing continue to grow," a news anchor said on the TV. "This comes after President Klimmings reportedly spoke with China's President Wu earlier this week and urged him to stop the military fly-bys of the Basa Air Base in the Philippines. While the base is run mostly by the Philippine Air Force, many U.S. airmen are stationed at the base, as the United States Air Force still operates out of there. President Klimmings is expected to provide a news conference later today where he will discuss the United States' strategy on dealing with the Chinese government."

Ben heard a knock at the door, and before he could say anything, it opened, and Vicki stepped in and said, "Hey!"

"Hi," Ben said as he tried to sit up some in the hospital bed.

"How are you feeling?" Vicki said as she closed the door behind her and sat in a chair beside Ben.

"Better," Ben said as he turned off the TV. "I was just catching up on what I missed while I was out for a week. What the hell is going on with China?"

"Oh, nothing. Just your dad and that creep over there have been getting into it with each other." She crossed her legs. "I'm sure the news will find something else to talk about later."

Ben smiled. "I have no doubt that they will."

"So, are you sure that you're alright?"

"Yes, I am. The last thing I remember before my episode was changing my shirt. Do you know what all happened?"

"Yes," Vicki said. "You fell down the stairs and hit your head."

"I figured that," Ben laughed. "The doctors only told me that I had hit my head, but they didn't mention anything about what happened leading up to it."

"You had us scared there for a minute, Benjamin."

"But I'm all better now. The doctors told me that if nothing changes, I may be able to come home tonight."

"Well, I sure hope nothing changes. We miss you." Vicki placed her hand on top of Ben's, giving it a slight squeeze.

"You seem like you're in a bit of trouble, though," Ben said.

"What do you mean?"

Ben motioned to the TV. "When I was watching the news, they talked about the company and the stocks. It seems pretty bad."

"It is," Vicki said, nodding her head. "Last night, Miranda and I spoke with your dad and sister about purchasing the majority of stock and privatizing the company."

"When do you plan to do that?"

"Soon. Probably later today."

"You think you can wait until I get out of here?"

Vicki turned to look Ben in the eyes. "Why?"

"I want back in, Mom," Ben said. "Ever since you fired me from the company, I feel like I've had no purpose. You left me with nothing."

Vicki hung her head in shame. "I won't be able to give you a permanent role, Benjamin."

"Why not?"

"Once we privatize the company, we plan to hand out a portion of voting rights to members of the family. We can each have a role within the company and its leadership changes."

Ben sat up further in the bed. "I want to be a part of this, though. Give me something with purpose."

"Okay, Benjamin," Vicki said. "I can have our financial advisor meet you today. Then you can purchase the shares through him today." She stood up from her seat. "And Benjamin . . ."

"Yes?"

"You *have* something purposeful. You have a daughter now." Vicki walked over to the door and opened it, turning back to Ben one more time. "Maybe you should call Delilah so that you can meet her."

Ben remained silent as Vicki left the room and closed the door. He took the remote to turn the TV back on but stopped before pressing the button. He sighed and turned to his cell phone, sitting on the table beside the bed. Then, he set the remote down beside him and grabbed his phone, unlocking it, clicking on the contacts app, and scrolled down to Delilah's name. He studied her contact info, preparing to call her, but decided not to. Instead, he locked his phone and tossed it to the side.

* * *

Miranda stepped off the elevator and headed to Pam's desk. "Good morning, Pam!" she said, greeting her. "Anything for me today?"

"No, Mrs. Klimmings," Pam said. "Nothing today, except that you were almost wrong about it being morning."

"Oh, was I?"

"Made it by three minutes." The two women laughed. "You do have that meeting with your financial advisor later today about purchasing more stocks."

"Has my mom been in to discuss the portion she'll purchase?"

"Not yet. Her meeting is also this afternoon."

"Well," Miranda said. "I'll be in the empty office, working on some things, if you need me for anything."

"Actually," Pam said, stopping Miranda before she went into the office. "Jason dropped off some flowers for you yesterday. They should still be in there."

Miranda's heart dropped as she heard Pam tell her about Jason dropping off the flowers. Suddenly, her mind flashed back to seeing that wall covered with pictures of her.

"Throw those out," she said.

"What?"

"Get rid of them, please. And don't ever let him back in here again."

"I thought . . ."

"Just please do what I ask," Miranda snapped. "He and I are no longer together. Just get rid of them."

"Yes, Mrs. Klimmings," Pam said as she made her way around the desk and into the empty office. Miranda tried to control her breathing before heading back down the hallway to the elevators. She stepped onto it and made her way back down to the ground floor, heading through the lobby to the valet.

"Please bring my car around quickly," she told the valet, handing him her keys.

"Yes, ma'am." He headed away to fetch her car, leaving her standing outside the lobby in the cold. As she waited for her car to be brought to her, Jason watched from across the street.

* * *

Cameras snapped pictures, and reporters erupted with questions as Peter walked into the Press Briefing Room and approached the podium. "Thank you all for coming in today," Peter spoke. "I am gonna speak for a little bit, and then I'll open up the floor for some questions."

He surveyed the crowd as reporters started recording on their phones and preparing their pens and notepads to take notes when he began speaking.

"As most of you know," Peter began. "The Chinese government has initiated multiple military drills near the Basa Air Base in the Philippines. While the Philippine Air Force manages the air base, the United States Air Force operates out of there with some servicemen and women stationed at the air base. Since my conversation with President Wu a few days ago, the Chinese have been gathering some of their naval warships in the South China Sea.

"While U.S. Intelligence believes that the threat is very minimal, my administration is taking this very seriously. In the coming weeks, we will be deploying more troops to the Philippines in an effort to double our presence in Southeast Asia. We cannot allow China to believe that they can do as they please, and any aggression shown by President Wu will be met with, quickly and swiftly."

Sounds of camera shutters clicking and reporters calling out "Mr. President" filled the room as everyone tried to get their questions answered. Peter surveyed the crowd before choosing a reporter to ask a question.

"Mr. President," the reporter began. "What would the next steps be if China continues to ramp up pressure against your administration? What will happen then?"

"That's a good question," Peter said. "At this time, we cannot divulge any new information as to what we will be doing. But I can assure you that we will be taking the steps necessary to protect America and her interests."

"Aren't you afraid of a potential conflict with China?"

Peter paused and took a deep breath, carefully choosing his words wisely. "I don't foresee this becoming an issue where this escalates into anything more than what is going on right now."

Once again, reporters erupted with questions. Peter scanned the crowd before heading back to the microphone on the podium and said, "Thank you."

He turned to head out of the Press Briefing Room as cameras snapped photos, and the press continued to push for more questions to be answered.

* * *

"Are you sure you want to authorize the purchase, Mr. Klimmings?"

Ben had a laptop sitting on his lap in a video call with the Klimmings family financial advisor.

"Yes, I do," he said. "Buy the shares."

"Okay," the advisor said. "I will get that done quickly. Is there anything else you need for me to do?"

"That'll be all. Thank you." Ben closed his laptop, ending the video call with the financial advisor. He looked up at the TV on the wall of the hospital room. It was on the same news channel that he was watching earlier.

"The DOW Jones dipped three hundred points following President Klimmings' comments on China today in the Press Briefing Room," said one of the news anchors. "This comes after China's continued aggression shown in the South China Sea. Japan's prime minister, Akio Yamashita, condemned China's actions today, calling them 'reckless' and 'irresponsible.' So far, President Wu of China has yet to react to any of President Klimmings' remarks."

Ben turned off the TV before he heard a knock at his door. He turned toward the door just as it opened and saw Delilah holding a baby in her arms. For a moment, the two looked each other in the eyes, not saying a word. Finally, Ben broke the silence. "What are you doing here?"

Delilah stepped into the room, holding the baby tight. "I thought it was time for you to meet your daughter."

Ben scowled. "Are you certain she's mine?"

"Yes. We had a test done." She moved closer to Ben. "Just ask the nurses. They can give you the results."

Ben glared at Delilah as she remained standing beside him, holding Katherine. "Let me see her," he said to Delilah, holding out his arms to take the baby.

Delilah stepped closer and placed Katherine in his arms. He took her close to him, looking into her big blue eyes. "What's her name?"

"Katherine," Delilah said. "I named her after my mom . . . I hope that's okay."

Ben continued to have his gaze trapped by Katherine's eyes. "Why wouldn't I be okay with it? She's not mine, anyway."

Delilah looked at Ben, feeling a lump growing in her throat. "You don't really believe that, do you?"

He focused his attention back on Katherine. She looked back at him and smiled. He smiled back at her as tears filled his eyes. He said, "I love you," and kissed her forehead.

He lifted her, handing her back to Delilah. "I'll be in touch with you," Delilah said.

Ben remained quiet, wiping the tears away from his eyes as Delilah headed to the door, opened it, and left him alone in the room.

* * *

Miranda stepped out of the George and Jefferson Coffee Shop with her large, hot caramel macchiato coffee. The cold January air hit her face as she made her way down the sidewalk. Steam rose from the hot coffee, keeping her hands warm.

She couldn't help but think about the flowers at the office. *Why won't he leave me alone? Why does he feel the need to keep trying?* She continued down the sidewalk, surrounded by people. As she walked, she looked at the passing cars and stopped when she noticed a black car pass by. *That looks really familiar.* She tried to examine the car some more but couldn't get a good look at it as it continued driving on.

"Move, lady!" A man called out as he walked past Miranda.

"Sorry!" she apologized. "Sorry!" She continued walking and stopped in a group of people waiting for the traffic light to change so they could cross the road. She took a sip of her coffee, feeling the warmth enter her mouth and travel down her body. As she continued waiting, she looked around at some of the buildings, the people, and the vehicles driving past. And then that's when her attention caught the black car passing by again.

Miranda's eyes widened when she finally recognized the car. "Oh no," she said to herself before turning left and continuing down the sidewalk. She picked up her speed, trying to get away from the black car before it circled back.

By now, she was running. Her white coat caught air, causing the bottom half to glide in the wind behind her. Finally, Miranda saw an alleyway to her left, quickly bolting down it, and turned around to watch the street, waiting for the black car to drive by at any moment.

She stepped backward, waiting for it to pass by, but it never did. Then, after a few minutes, Miranda let out a sigh of relief and went to leave the alley. But as she stepped forward, she felt something grab her left arm. She tried to turn to see who it was, but an arm came around her right side and pressed a white, soaked rag into her face, clasping over her mouth and nose. Miranda dropped her coffee and tried to resist, but she was overwhelmed with a sweet odor, and the world around her began to fade.

Within a minute, Miranda fell unconscious. The person put their arms under her armpits and drug her further down the alley, leaving only the spilled coffee and empty cup on the ground.

* * *

"He's home!" Vicki called out as she opened the door for Ben to step into the Klimmings Mansion. She closed the door behind them and helped him take off his jacket, hanging it on the rack in the entry hall. Gabby and Charlotte turned the corner from the living room, smiling when they saw Ben. Gabby threw her arms around him, hugging him tightly.

"I'm so happy to see you," Gabby said, still hugging him. "You scared me so much, Ben."

"I heard," he said before releasing from the hug and looking Gabby in the eyes. "But I promise you this . . . I will never be drinking so much that something like that happens again."

"Well," Charlotte began. "I wouldn't say *all* alcohol is bad."

Ben laughed. "For me, it is. I'm not touching that stuff anymore." He turned to glance at Vicki and then back to Charlotte and Gabby. "Before I left the hospital, I met with a couple of doctors. They taught me ways to help deal with cravings for alcohol. They also gave me some contact info for some accountability groups to join."

"That's wonderful!"

Ben looked up the entry hall and saw Peter, who had just stepped out of the archway that led to the staircase. For a second, he didn't know how to react. His dad had always been so judgmental of him, holding high expectations for his only son.

"Come give me a hug, son," Peter said, extending his arms and smiling great big. Ben made his way over to Peter and hugged his dad. "I'm so glad to see you home."

"I'm so glad to be here, Dad."

Vicki motioned for the rest of the family to move into the living room. At the same time, Peter and Ben had their moment, but it wasn't long before the two made their way into the living room as well. Ben sat down on the sofa, next to Gabby and Charlotte. Peter made his way over to the bar to make himself a drink. He asked if anyone else wanted anything, and Vicki requested a club soda, trying to support Ben and his vow to stay away from the liquor in the household.

Peter poured himself a glass of Kentucky bourbon and a glass of club soda for Vicki. He turned and handed his wife her drink and then made his way across the room to sit in the chair next to Ben.

"So," Vicki started. "I spoke with our financial advisor today, and I heard that you purchased a large portion of stock, Benjamin."

"I did," he said. "I'm glad to finally have a role in the company again."

"Well, you sure did throw our plan into motion." The entire group laughed. "I met with him later today and purchased a large portion, as well." Vicki took a sip of her club soda. "I'm sure that we'll be in the news again tomorrow."

"Where's Miranda?" Gabby asked, trying to change the subject.

"You know," Vicki said. "I haven't heard from her all day today.

She was supposed to meet with the financial advisor today, but she missed that meeting. Pam told me that she saw her at the office, but she wasn't seen since this morning."

"Do you know where she could be?"

"I'm guessing she went to see Jason to talk things through," Vicki said. "She mentioned to me that they had some issues, but she didn't even purchase any stocks today, either, which is peculiar." Vicki took another sip of her club soda. "Another thing that is strange is who I was told purchased some of the Klimmings Incorporated stock today." She turned her head over to Charlotte, who wasn't making eye contact with Vicki. "Charlotte, why did you buy stock in our company?"

She gulped. "I wanted to help out," Charlotte said. "I felt that since I am making the D.C. metropolitan my new home, I might as well do something to help out the family."

"Wait," Peter said. "You're making this your home?"

"Yes, dear," Charlotte said. "I mentioned something at Christmas, but that was after the big blow-up fiasco." Peter and Vicki exchanged looks. "Anyway, I'm purchasing a home in Bethesda."

"What?!" Vicki exclaimed. "Why didn't you think to mention this again?"

"I don't know. I was just busy with things, and then the stuff with Ben happened. It just slipped my mind."

Vicki sighed. "I wish this wasn't a club soda. I could use something strong right now."

Ben chuckled. "I think it'll be okay, Mom. Aunt Charlotte hasn't been any trouble. In fact, I think she's been quite enjoyable."

Charlotte turned to Ben and smiled. "Thank you, Ben."

"You're welcome." Ben stood up from the sofa. "Now, if you all will excuse me, I'm gonna go lie down upstairs. Sleeping in the hospital bed hasn't given me the greatest rest."

"Missing those silk sheets, are ya?" Peter called out before laughing.

"Pretty much," said Ben. "Goodnight!"

"Goodnight," the family called out as Ben left the living room through the archway to the stairs.

"I best head to bed too," Charlotte said, looking at the time on her phone.

"Really," Vicki said. "It's not that late."

"I know, but sometimes I just need to get my beauty sleep."

"Well, goodnight then."

Charlotte left the same way Ben did and headed to her bedroom. Vicki took a sip of her club soda and noticed Gabby looking at her phone with a troubled look on her face.

"Gabriella," Vicki said. "What's wrong?"

"Oh, nothing," Gabby said as she continued looking at her phone. She had the social media post that Dana had made pulled up.

"Don't lie, Gabriella," Vicki said. "I can tell when you're lying."

"Yes," Peter chimed in. "And by the look on your face, we can tell that there is something really bothering you."

Gabby looked up from her phone, showing that she had tears in her eyes. Her lips quivered.

"Do you think Miranda will be home soon?" she asked.

"Honey," Vicki said. "If she's not home right now, then she's probably staying the night at Jason's."

Gabby let out a deep sigh. "Well, then . . . I have something to tell you."

"What is it, honey?" Peter asked, sitting his bourbon on the table beside him.

"A couple months ago, after that crazy guy held me hostage at school," Gabby started. "I began to feel different about things. I began to see things differently." She gulped. "One of those things was my friend, Michelle."

She looked at Vicki and Peter, who were listening intently. "And I felt something that I had never felt toward her . . . or anybody else . . . before."

"Gabby," Vicki broke in. "Are you trying to tell us . . ."

"That I like girls?" Gabby interrupted. "Yes."

She looked down at the floor, avoiding eye contact with her parents. Then, she began sobbing, filling the living room with her crying. Vicki quietly moved from her chair over to the sofa beside Gabby, wrapping her arms around her.

"Oh, Gabriella," she said to her. "Oh, honey, we don't think anything different of you. We still love you just the way we did before."

"I still like boys, though," Gabby managed to say between sobs. "I just think I'm bisexual."

"Bisexual, gay, straight," Peter said. "It doesn't matter, Gabby. Whatever you find yourself to be, we are going to love you, no matter what."

Gabby looked up at her father for the first time, and he was smiling at her. "I'm proud of you," he said. "My baby girl is growing up."

Gabby let a small smile appear on her face. "So you don't think anything of it?"

"Only that you are our daughter," Vicki said. "And we will always love you, Gabriella."

Gabby smiled and hugged her mom. The enormous weight on her chest had finally been lifted, and she was finally free from the constant burden of worrying about being outed or outing herself.

"There's just one thing," Peter said, interrupting the moment of peace Gabby was experiencing. "How many people have you told?"

"I've only told you two and Miranda," Gabby said. "I guess Michelle knows too because I kissed her back in November."

"So not many people know then?"

"Well, Dana did make a social media post outing me as a lesbian, but that's not entirely true." Gabby turned to Vicki. "And luckily, not many people have seen it."

"Peter," Vicki said. "Why do you want to know all this?"

"Well, hear me out," Peter said. "Could you possibly wait until next year before you publicly come out as bisexual?"

"Next year?!" Vicki exclaimed. "Do you know how much courage it took her to tell us just now?"

"I know. I know," Peter said. "I am asking for a lot, but I really need this favor."

Gabby's happiness had left her face. "How is me being bisexual a favor for you?"

Peter leaned forward in his chair. "You see, I am running for reelection next year, and right now, I am not on track to do very well. However, let's say you were to wait closer to the Democratic National Convention to come out publicly. In that case, I believe that we would have a much better shot at winning the presidency for a second term."

Gabby remained speechless. She couldn't form the words to respond to her dad's request.

"What the hell is wrong with you, Peter?" Vicki asked. "How dare you ask your daughter to continue to remain in the closet just so that it benefits you."

"I'm not asking her to remain in the closet," Peter backtracked. "I'm just asking her not to go public with this until the convention next year. She can tell all the people she wants to right now at school. What I am asking for is that the big social media post comes next year."

Gabby scowled at her father. "It never fails," she said. "Every time I begin to believe that the people in this family actually love me, something like this happens." She jumped from the sofa and ran out of the room, heading through the archway and up the stairs.

Vicki glared at Peter, disgusted, as the sound of Gabby's door slamming shut reverberated down the stairwell. Denise turned the corner from the entry hall and stepped into the living room. "Mr. and Mrs. Klimmings," she said. "Is everything alright?"

"No," Vicki said as she stood up from the sofa, taking her attention from Peter to Denise. "Everything is just the way it's always been." She made her way over to the archway by the stairs, paused, and turned back to Peter and Denise. "Goodnight."

She stormed up the steps, leaving Peter and Denise alone. Peter stood up and swallowed the remainder of his bourbon before handing his empty glass to Denise. "Would you mind taking this for me?"

"Sure, Mr. Klimmings," Denise said. "Anything else I can help you with tonight?"

"I'm going to sleep in the guest bedroom next to Charlotte's. Would you mind preparing that for me while I take a shower?"

"Certainly. Will that be all?"

Peter ignored Denise's question and made his way out of the living room, leaving her standing alone, bewildered after yet another

Klimmings family squabble.

CHAPTER 20
AN EVENING AT THE KLIMMINGS MANSION

"Good morning on this first day of February. In today's top news, the Klimmings family has reclaimed control of the family empire. In a stunning move by Vicki Klimmings, the family moved to purchase a large portion of the company's stock. With Miranda Klimmings' fifty-one percent controlling interest in the company, the family now owns more than eighty-three percent of the energy company. Vicki Klimmings said in a prepared statement this morning that the family was moving to privatize Klimmings Incorporated to keep it in the family's best interest.

"The move by the Klimmings family has not been met well by everyone. Speaker of the House Rebecca White called out the family this morning, saying that the Klimmings family has created a 'huge conflict of interest for the president.' Speaker White later mentioned that the special investigation of President Klimmings' dealings with Klimmings Incorporated will look into the recent developments."

Peter turned off the TV. He turned to Henry, who was sitting in a chair beside the *Resolute* desk. "It's not that bad, is it, Mr. Gates?"

"Not as long as you don't show preferential treatment to the company," Henry responded. "However, I'd be cautious, Mr. President. You don't want the American people to think that you are using this office to benefit your family."

Peter nodded his head in agreement, thinking back to what happened the previous night when Gabby came out to Vicki and him. He remembered how upset Gabby was when he asked her to wait before coming out publicly.

"If nothing else were to happen that boosted my popularity, what do you think would happen?"

Henry took a deep breath. "Mr. President," he said. "If you have no legislative or popularity victories between now and Election Day next year, I honestly don't see you getting reelected."

Peter sighed. "That's what I was afraid of. Thank you, Mr. Gates."

"There's still plenty of time, Mr. President," Henry said, leaning a little closer to Peter and placing his hand on the desk. "Plus, we don't even know who the Republican nominee will be."

"I think I have an idea of who it may be, though."

Before Henry could respond, the two heard a knock at the door. It opened, and Martha stood on the other side. "Mr. President," she said. "The speaker of the house is here to see you."

Peter glanced over to Henry. "Go ahead and send her in." He stood from his chair and went around the desk to greet Rebecca White. She was wearing a yellow business dress and held a file of papers in her left hand.

"Madam Speaker," Peter said, extending his right hand to shake hers. "It's so good to see you."

"Thank you for letting me meet with you, Mr. President," she said, shaking Peter's hand. "I know we didn't have a meeting scheduled, but I wouldn't have come over had I not thought that this was of utmost importance."

Peter gestured toward the two sofas in the center of the room. "Please, let's have a seat."

The two moved over to the sofas, each sitting on their own. "Mr. Gates," Peter said. "May I speak with Speaker White alone?"

"Certainly." Henry made his way out through one of the side doors out of the Oval Office.

"So," Peter began. "What was so important that you needed to speak with me?"

"First off," Rebecca said, crossing her legs. "You must calm down the rhetoric on China."

"What do you mean calm down the rhetoric? Do you not see what they are doing?"

"I do, Mr. President, but we don't want to be seen as aggressive."

"How are we being aggressive, Rebecca? Tell me."

"You're sending more troops over to the Basa Air Base, Peter. You're speaking with the media, issuing threats against China. What you are doing is reckless and, frankly, threatening our democracy."

Peter was flabbergasted. "What the hell?! How in the hell am I threatening democracy?! Do you not see what they're doing over there?"

"I do," Rebecca said. "But Mr. President, I suggest you send some members of your administration over to speak with the Chinese . . ."

"We tried that!" Peter interrupted. "They refused to speak to me." He stood up from the sofa. "So if you don't have anything else to say to me, then I suggest you leave. This meeting is over."

"Oh, but I do have something else." Peter turned to face Rebecca, who was standing, holding out the file of papers. "As you know, we've been investigating you, Peter. And for the longest time, we kept coming up with nothing on you."

"That's because I haven't done anything wrong."

"Let me finish," Rebecca said, raising her eyebrows at Peter. "We couldn't find anything, that is, until recently." She gently shook the file, urging Peter to take a look at it. He reluctantly took it and opened it. As he looked through the pages, Rebecca continued. "I know about the little deal you have with the United Kingdom. Forcing Applegate Technology to pay higher taxes for importing to the country screams quid pro quo."

"It's not quid pro quo," Peter said, glaring at Rebecca. "It's done in the best interest of the United States. They tax them, and we receive some of that money back."

"Then it's abuse of power," Rebecca said. "Either one won't look very good when it comes time for reelection, Peter."

"Is that a threat, Rebecca?"

She took a step closer to Peter. "Look at it as a promise." She snatched the file away from Peter and smiled. "I look forward to a quick diplomatic solution to China." She turned and headed back over to the door through which she came in. Before leaving, she turned to Peter. "Hell, include me in the team that negotiates with China, if you will. I'd be happy to help come up with a swift solution to this disaster that's ensuing in the South China Sea."

Rebecca opened the door. "After all," she said again. "Impeachment wouldn't look good on you heading into reelection."

She stepped out of the room and closed the door behind her. Peter headed behind the *Resolute* desk and took the phone, paging Martha.

"Yes, Mr. President," she said.

"Martha," Peter began. "Get me Secretary Bird, now. I need to discuss sending more troops over to the Basa Air Base."

* * *

Students moved past Gabby during the passing period at school while she surveyed the crowd, looking for Dana. She looked and looked before she finally spotted Dana down by her locker. Dana's brown hair was pinned up in a bun, which she only ever wore when she was having a good day.

Gabby started down the hall, determined to get to Dana. She squeezed between the high schoolers, bumping into a few of them occasionally, which was generally followed by a few expletives thrown out behind her, but she continued on. Dana had just closed her locker and turned around when Gabby reached her. Dana's eyes widened when she saw her and said, "Gabby . . ."

Gabby shoved Dana against the lockers, causing a resounding clanking of the metal doors down the hall. The students in the hallway stopped to watch what was about to go down.

"Why the hell would you post that?" Gabby asked her quite loudly.

"How dare you do that!"

"I'm sorry, Gabby," Dana said. "I know I shouldn't have done that, but you were really coming onto Michelle, and I just wanted to show her some support."

"Support? The hell it is! You just wanted to get back at me because you have a thing for Michelle. You always have!"

"Gabby," Dana said, trying to quiet her. She had noticed the growing crowd surrounding them. "We need to talk about this elsewhere."

"Why?!" Gabby shouted. "Everybody already thinks that I'm a lesbian! Why shouldn't they know just how much of a bitch you are?!"

Gabby pulled her arm back and slugged Dana in the face. The students all gasped, and chatter immediately broke out as they anticipated a fight between the two girls. Dana placed her hand on her left cheek, trying to assess the area Gabby had just punched. She glared at Gabby and started to say, "You mother . . ."

"Alright! Alright!"

A teacher had approached the scene and pulled Gabby away from Dana. "There will be no fighting today, ladies," he said. "Dana, you get to class."

She huffed before taking off down the hallway. The teacher looked at the crowd of students who were waiting to see what would happen. "Don't you all have class to get to?" he asked, causing the group to scatter. Finally, he let go of Gabby. "Are you alright?"

"Yes."

"Look, Gabby. Between you and I, she deserved that punch."

The statement caused Gabby to jolt her attention to the teacher.

"Some of the students in my AP class this morning showed me the post. Are you sure you are okay?"

"I am," Gabby said. "I guess everybody knows now."

"If you need anyone to speak with, you can always talk with me," the teacher said. "My sister is a lesbian. She's been married for about four years now. If you want, I can always try to get you two in contact."

"Thanks," Gabby sighed. The last thing she wanted right now was to talk to someone else about her sexuality.

"Anyways," the teacher continued. "I'm going to pretend that I didn't see anything, okay?"

"Okay."

"Alright, now get to class."

Gabby walked away, heading down the hallway, smiling as she thought about how good it felt to punch Dana in the face.

* * *

Ben stepped into his mom's office, greeting her with a smile. Vicki looked up from the computer at her desk and smiled back at Ben.

"Benjamin!" she said. "It's such a surprise to see you here!"

"I thought I'd stop by," he said as he took a seat in front of Vicki's desk. "I have to be downtown anyway."

"What for?"

"Delilah called me this morning. She said that she wanted us to meet for lunch to discuss some things."

Vicki's smile melted off her face. "Be honest with me. Do you see yourself having a future with her?"

Ben focused down on the floor, keeping eye contact broken from Vicki. "When I found out about the affair, I was ready to end everything. I was determined to file for divorce from her, but then, I saw Katherine." He sighed. "From the moment I held her in my arms, I fell in love with her."

"Benjamin," Vicki said. "That's the same feeling I had when I first held you and your sisters. Every parent feels that."

He smiled. "But I don't know what to do now, Mom. Seeing Katherine made me think about what matters. Hearing Delilah apologize for what she's done really made me think about things."

Vicki sighed and took off the glasses she was wearing while working on the computer. "Do you really believe her?"

Ben remained silent. He looked Vicki in the eyes and swallowed. "I think so . . . I don't know."

Vicki stood up and made her way around the desk, sitting in the chair next to Ben. "Look, Ben. I'm not going to tell you what to do. I'm just going to give you this piece of advice. Do whatever it is that you feel is the best for you. Don't do it because it'll benefit everybody else. Do it because it helps you and makes you happy."

Ben smiled. "Thanks, Mom."

"You're welcome, honey."

Ben hugged his mother before getting up to leave. When he made it to the door, he stopped and turned back to Vicki. "Have you heard anything from Miranda yet?"

"No," Vicki said, standing from her chair. "It's odd. Normally she would tell me if she was staying the night at Jason's, but this time, nothing."

"Have you texted or called her?"

"I have texted, called, and left a voicemail. So far, no response."

* * *

Her eyes slowly opened, letting the orange hue of the room fill her vision. Miranda groaned as her vision adjusted to the room's lighting. She tried to move her arms but couldn't. Then she looked down at her hands and noticed that they were tied to the chair she was sitting in. She tried to open her mouth but felt something rough. She couldn't speak and realized that she had a rope tied around her, holding a gag inside her mouth. She fidgeted some, beginning to panic, and tried to figure out where she was.

As she looked around, she began to recognize the place as Jason's apartment. She took in as much as she could but could not see everything because of her restraints. That's when she saw it—the wall covered with images of herself. Picture after picture coated that wall. The same wall had appeared in her thoughts, dreams, and nightmares since Jason first showed it to her. She made a noise in her mouth, trying to scream in panic.

"I see you've woken up."

Miranda jerked her head to the door. She saw Jason standing in the doorway holding a mug of coffee. Steam rose from it as he stood watching her.

"How are you, baby?" he asked before he set his coffee on the dresser beside the doorway. He approached Miranda, looking more menacing as he came closer. Inside, the panic grew larger and larger. Finally, when he made it to Miranda, he knelt on his knees beside her. "What's wrong, baby? You've never been this way before?"

She squirmed in the chair, trying to get away but remained unsuccessful.

"You know," Jason said. "I've always thought you were the prettiest girl I've ever seen. All those years I spent watching you . . . taking pictures of you . . ." He took his right hand and placed it on the side of her face, using his thumb to caress her cheek. "Now, I've finally got everything I've always wanted."

He leaned in and kissed her on the cheek, tasting the saltiness of her tears on his lips. "Tastes so good," he said before kissing her gagged mouth. Miranda began crying profusely. Tears fell down her face, and snot ran out her nose. Jason continued kissing her face before moving down to her neck, slowly unbuttoning her blouse one at a time. Miranda wanted to get away from him. She wanted to run but couldn't do anything. All she could do was sit there and let Jason do as he pleased.

* * *

Delilah sat at the table at Finley's, looking over the menu. She was torn between ordering the classic Greek salad or the Caesar salad. The Caesar salad was her favorite, but she wanted to try something different for a change.

As Delilah contemplated her order, Ben stepped into the restaurant and set his eyes on her. He stopped just long enough for her to look up at him. She smiled when she saw him and motioned for him to join her. Ben took a deep sigh and then approached the table, sitting across from her.

"I'm so glad you agreed to join me for lunch," Delilah said. "Do you want to go ahead and order? I can flag down the waiter and get your drink placed."

"No," Ben said. "That's not necessary."

"Oh." Delilah's smile fell from her face. She took her glass of water and took a sip from it. "Do you know why I wanted to have lunch with you, Ben?"

"I have an idea," he said as the waiter came to the table and set a glass of water down in front of him.

"Sir," the waiter said. "Would you like anything to drink?"

"No," Ben said. "The water is fine."

"I'll be back in a bit for the rest of your order," the waiter said and then went off elsewhere in the restaurant.

"Ben," Delilah began. "In the last three years, I have failed to be the wife you deserved. Especially in this last year, I have lied, cheated, and done things behind your back. Throughout the entire pregnancy, I left myself . . . and I left you wondering who the father of our dear Katherine was." Delilah reached out and took Ben's hands. "Ben, I cannot even begin to make this up to you. All I ask is that you give me another chance. Give *us* another chance."

Ben remained quiet, processing the mini-speech Delilah had just delivered. As he thought things through, Delilah said one more thing, "Ben, if you don't do it for us, then please, do it for Katherine."

He looked up from the table and shook his head. "I can't do that."

"What?"

"Delilah," he began. "It's over. We cannot continue this just to benefit our daughter. Our marriage began to die from the moment you started the affair with that guy. What was his name, again?"

"Clark."

"Clark. Our marriage started dying the moment you and him started having sex. No matter what either of us does now, our marriage is dead. Our relationship is dead."

He stood from his seat, looking at Delilah, noticing the tears streaming down her face. "Delilah," he said. "I will always love you. You are the mother of my child . . . our child. Together, we will be great parents for Baby Katherine, but we aren't going to stay married."

Delilah nodded her head as she pulled her bag off the back of her chair and dug through it for a tissue. Deep down, she understood everything Ben had just said but also wanted none of this to happen.

"You'll hear from my lawyers in a week or two," Ben said. "I don't want anything of yours. All I want is a clean, easy divorce."

"I understand," Delilah let out between sniffles. "I want us to remain friends."

Ben leaned down, closer to Delilah. "We have to be. After all, we have a daughter to raise."

He turned and made his way out of Finley's. For the first time since he could remember, Ben had finally made a decision not based on the outcome for others but rather, the outcome in his best interest. He had never felt prouder of himself.

* * *

Charlotte stepped out of her car, closing the door behind her. She looked up at a large brick house. On the outside, it was easily three stories. Black shutters flanked each window. She looked up at the majestic home as a man approached her.

"Here you go, Mrs. Lee," he said to her, holding out a set of keys. "Here are the keys to your new home."

"Thank you," she said as she took them. She went up the walkway to the front awning. As she took the two steps to the front door, she turned around and took in the immaculate yard. Every blade of grass appeared to be cut precisely the same height.

Charlotte turned back to the door and unlocked it. She opened the door and stepped into the grand foyer of the house. A large spiral staircase ran up the middle of the room, leading to the second and third-floor mezzanines. She made her way up the stairs, taking it all in.

As she reached the third floor, she looked at the view from the top. "It's all mine," she said to herself. "Finally, something to call my own!"

* * *

Night had fallen before Ben made it home to the Klimmings Mansion. He came in through the front door of the entry hall and turned the corner into the living room.

"There he is!" Vicki called out. She stood up and went over to him to hug him.

"How did things go with Delilah?" she whispered while they hugged.

Ben let go of Vicki. "I told her that I wanted a divorce. I believe that's what's best for the both of us."

"Especially for you?"

"Yes."

Ben looked into the living room and saw Peter standing by the bar. He grinned back at Ben.

"Son," he said. "I think that was a wise choice!"

Peter turned around and poured a glass of Scotch. "Now," Peter continued, taking a sip of his drink and turning back to Vicki and Ben. "Where the hell is Miranda?"

"I still haven't heard anything from her," Vicki said. "I'm starting to get a little worried."

"That's it," Peter said as he set his drink down and pulled out his phone. "This isn't going on much longer."

"What are you doing?" Ben asked.

"I'm calling people. They're gonna search everywhere for her. She's out there somewhere."

"Don't you think that's being a little excessive?" Vicki asked. "After all, she's only been gone for a day."

"Vicki, she normally texts you every single day. There is something wrong."

Peter put his phone to his ear and stepped out of the living room. Vicki turned to Ben with a worried look on her face. "What if there actually is something wrong, and I've been over here thinking it's been nothing this whole time?"

"Mom," Ben said. "You can't blame yourself for this. You didn't know."

"But I should have noticed something was wrong when I hadn't heard from her for the day." Vicki moved over to the bar and poured herself a glass of white wine. "Benjamin, I've had my attention so focused on you this past week that I've neglected everyone else."

Ben hung his head in shame. Vicki noticed and quickly tried to backtrack her statement.

"But, Benjamin," she said. "This isn't your fault. It's mine."

"I know it's not my fault, Mom," he said. "But you've got to stop blaming yourself. Dad will get ahold of the right people, and they will find Miranda."

Ben leaned in and hugged Vicki. Peter stepped back into the living room, saying, "I got a couple police departments looking for her." Vicki let go of Ben and came over to Peter, hugging him. "They're going to find her."

"Thank you, Peter," Vicki said, clinging to him.

As the two hugged, Denise came into the living room, telling them that dinner was ready.

"Benjamin," Vicki said after she stopped hugging Peter. "Could you go get Gabriella from upstairs? She's been in her room an awfully long time."

"Sure, Mom," Ben said before heading out through the archway to the stairs. He made his way up the steps and turned to the right when he reached the top. Gabby's door was closed, so he stopped outside and politely knocked.

"Gabby," he said. "It's dinner time."

He waited for a response but heard nothing from inside her room. Ben took a deep breath and knocked again, this time a little harder than he had initially, and the door shifted slightly open.

"Gabby," Ben said as he tried to peer in through the tiny slit the door created. "Are you in there?"

He pushed the door open to get a good look in the room, and he saw Gabby lying on her back on the bed.

She must be sleeping. Ben thought as he came a little closer to the bed. "Gabby. Wake up."

He examined Gabby, and his heart plunged into his stomach when he discovered the gunshot wound in her chest.

"Gabby . . ."

He put his right hand on her right arm, shaking her. "Oh my God. Oh my God. Oh my God!" Ben began to panic as his mind raced through what he was witnessing. "MOM! DAD! COME HERE QUICKLY!"

Ben continued trying to wake Gabby when Vicki and Peter made it to the doorway to Gabby's room.

"What's wrong, Ben . . ." Vicki fell silent when she saw Gabby's lifeless body. "Oh my God!"

She came into the room and fell to her knees beside Gabby's bed. "No. No. No. No. No. This can't be happening," Vicki cried. "Peter, this can't be happening! She's our baby girl!"

Vicki began bawling and wailing in Gabby's room as the initial shock began to subside and the realization of Gabby's death sank in. Ben looked over at Peter, standing in the doorway, motionless and silent.

"What's wrong?" Ben heard Denise call out as she began to come up the stairs. Before she could get a glimpse into the bedroom, Peter stepped outside the room and closed the door.

"Denise," he said quietly. "I need you to head downstairs to the basement for a moment."

"What? Why?"

"Just do as I ask."

Denise looked at Peter, concerned, but turned and headed down the stairs. Peter pulled out his phone from his suit jacket pocket and called someone. "I need you up here now, and I need all the rest of the Secret Service agents to move all the house servants down to the basement."

He ended the call and then came back into the room. Vicki was lying over Gabby, crying, and Ben was now by the door.

"Dad," he said. "There's no gun in here."

"Not now, Ben," Peter said. "We must act quickly."

"What do you mean by that?"

Before Peter said anything, something that Henry Gates had told him earlier that day came back to him. *"If you have no legislative or popularity victories between now and Election Day next year, I don't see you getting reelected."*

Suddenly Peter thought about how the American people would view him if the news came out about the death of his daughter. How would it affect their perception of him? Would they begin to see him as weak while he and his family publicly mourned the death of his daughter? Would other countries try to take advantage of the situation? And ultimately, would he be reelected?

"Oh my God."

Peter turned around and saw the head of the Presidential Protective Division for the Secret Service. "Don," he said as he approached him. "We need your help with something."

"Mr. President," Don said. "Do I need to have a car pulled around front? Let me get some of my men."

"No," Peter said sternly. "Do not get anymore of your men involved."

"What?"

"Don, I need you to get your agents away from the house so that they can't see anything, you hear?"

"Sir, some are already in the basement with the servants."

"Leave them there. Dammit, Don. We need your help badly."

Peter looked over at Vicki, who was running her hand through Gabby's hair.

"My baby," she said. "My baby is dead." She started crying more. Tears continued to pour down her face.

Peter turned back to Don and said, "I need you to go down to the family plot by the large tree, near the first lady's garden. When you get there, I need you to dig a hole." Peter looked over to Ben, who was astonished to be hearing this. "Ben, maybe you could go down and help Don?"

Ben's mouth fell open. "You aren't serious, are you, Dad?"

"I am. Ben, this family has so much riding on the next year and a half. We cannot let anything divert us from the path we must take."

Don looked over at Ben. "Mr. Klimmings, would you show me where the family plot is?"

Ben hesitated but finally made his way out of the room, leading Don downstairs and leaving Peter alone with Vicki and Gabby's body. He looked over at Vicki and let out a deep sigh.

"Vicki," Peter said as he approached her. "I need you to step away from her. We're going to take care of everything."

"Where are we sending her?" she asked Peter.

"Nowhere," Peter said with some tears in his eyes. "I have some people preparing her final resting spot now."

Vicki's eyes widened. "We're burying her tonight?!"

"Yes, Vicki. It has to be this way."

* * *

Delilah opened the door to the nursery at the Applegate Homestead, approaching the crib to see Katherine sleeping. She reached down and adjusted Katherine's onesie.

"Oh, Katherine," Delilah said with tears in her eyes. "You're not even a month old, and yet I already feel as if I have failed you."

She placed her hands on the side of the crib, watching her daughter peacefully sleep.

"Because of me, you won't be able to grow up with your parents together. Because of me, you will always have to go back and forth from visiting me and your dad." Delilah wiped her eyes with her hand. "And I'm so sorry, honey."

"It's not your fault."

Delilah jerked around. Cathie stood in the doorway. "Come here, Delilah," she said with her arms stretched out.

Delilah ran over to her mom, hugging her tightly. "He wants a divorce, Mom," Delilah cried. "It's all my fault. I screwed everything up!"

"No, you didn't," Cathie said. She held Delilah in her arms as she cried. "You two just weren't meant to stay married. So many marriages end up not working out. It'll all be okay, Delilah."

* * *

The cold air of the winter's night was felt by the three members of the Klimmings family as they watched Don shovel dirt back into Gabby's grave. They were out by the family cemetery, a small area set off to the back right side of the Klimmings Mansion, behind Vicki's flower garden with a large oak tree in the middle.

As Don scooped the last bit of dirt back onto Gabby's plot, Vicki held on tightly to Peter's arm, laying her head against him as tears fell from her eyes. Ben, who couldn't believe the events taking place in front of him, looked up at the stars, barely seeing any through the leaves of the oak tree.

"So we are the only ones who know?" he asked.

"Yes," Peter said. "And we will remain the only people who ever know about what's happened tonight."

"So, what does that mean?"

"That means that we will speak nothing about this . . . to anyone. Nobody must ever know what happened tonight."

Vicki let go of Peter's arm, crossing hers as she tried to stay warm out in the cold February night. She remained silent, only allowing her tears and sniffles to be heard. Peter put his hand on her back, trying to console her.

"I know it will be hard," Peter went on. "But we must act as if nothing happened. Because if our family's influence is to survive, then we must remain strong. These desperate measures taken tonight will save us from so much speculation, so many questions, and so much backlash from the people around us."

Ben looked at his father, trying to hide his disapproval of the whole situation. He wanted to say something, but he knew that nothing beneficial would come of it if he did.

Then he looked over at Vicki. She remained silent, standing so still, fending off any shiver that went through her body. It was as if her spirit had left her. Ben stepped over and hugged his mom.

"I love you," he said to her, but she gave no response back. Instead, she just stood completely still with a few tears trickling down her cheek.

"This is the way things must be," Peter finally said. "Our family is still in power." He looked at Don and then over to Ben and Vicki. "We are in control."

Then, Peter swallowed the lump that had grown in his throat, recollecting himself in all the ways he could. He knew he had to be strong. For his family would never be the same again.

SAMUEL VOYLES first envisioned *Desperate Measures Volume 1* during his first year of high school in 2011. He began writing short stories of about seven to ten pages each for his friends and family to read. After graduating from high school in 2015, he began crafting the first draft of the book over the summer prior to starting his first year of college. However, it wasn't until 2020 before Voyles began to revise the four chapters he had already written. Then, in February 2021, he started spending more time working on the book before finishing it a year later in 2022.

Voyles lives in Southern Indiana, where he teaches middle and high school English full-time.

www.ingramcontent.com/pod-product-compliance
Lightning Source LLC
Chambersburg PA
CBHW032149190626
46814CB00005BA/1909